Jason Side
Identity

Ibrahim Shabazz

How does one define the medium in which one perceives and ponders in the sense of outer?

ISBN-13: 979-8-218-18157-4

First Edition

Cover Illustration Copyright © 2023 by Ibrahim Shabazz

jasonsideis.com

Ponder and ponder, questioning the entity of embodying the personification of definition.

How does one think and breakdown this plight
which is not contingent on one's own experiences?
What are the questions at hand?

There will be more, will there not?

Is that more or less a matter of perception?

Identity

What Is The Essence
Of An Identity?

"So...who's he?"

"The hell's up with him?"

Shut up for a second and let me just exist...I feel like it's hard to exist, at least for me—

"It's gotta be dyed!" Someone roared with exaggerated laughter, seemingly staring straight at me. I had my face, eyes and all, turned towards the window. Still, I could feel the stares, almost worse than piercing knives pricking my skin. Wait, that's a lie. It's worse than that. They may be pricking my skin; although, they are aiming for my essence.

What is the essence of an identity? This is something I question myself about more frequently than just daily. It is a thought that goes through my head every second since the day I could cultivate thought and contain a memory. I've been trying to find an answer since that cultivation. I do so even now, as I sit on this bus going towards some high school, as voices of school kids around my age alternate in volume. The ages range from fourteen to eighteen; their conversations do not. I already know they're mostly about me—

"And those gotta be contacts.

"I still think they're contacts."

"How old do you think he is?"

Seventeen—

"They don't look like contacts, they look real…and his hair too…"

They—

"There's no way it's real," someone cackled.

Hold on, that's another lie. Not the is or isn't real part, I mean the finding of the answer part without more conclusive evidence. Well not a lie technically, just a wrong use of words—

"Bruh, where is he from!? HaHHa!"

Gah, my head was and is scrambled. What I meant was that I already knew the answer. It is only the daily existence of accepting who I am, the life I am living, the playing cards I have been dealt, as if this is some sort of twisted game. Identity is something that defines oneself based on how one fits parameters. And I most certainly have figured that much out. Admittance and acceptance.

The bus turned left nearly as if it jerked for joy to bring torture. I slid left towards the black aisle in my gray fake leather seat. My fingernails gripped the seat, accidently ripping more fake gray leather into pieces. Based on the ruckus, the other people had to grip their seats as well. Some collided with each other and laughed like a comedic sentence just hit its punchline. There was no one to collide within my area. I sat alone.

The bus screeched to a halt in front of the school. Its double front doors opened as the stop sign on the side flipped out into view of any cars that thought that now would be their time to pass. It wouldn't be the best time to pass, especially within eyesight of on-campus security sitting ten feet away in their parked car.

Instantly, kids stood up ready to pile off the loud transportation. Loud laughter. Endless chatter. Feet fell against the aisle, creating more sound than small splatters. My head was still turned towards the window as I looked at the school. Through the window, kids in a range of voices and clothing could be seen grouped together as they walked towards the school. Although, their conversations couldn't be heard since the window and noise from the bus blocked out all words. I'll stay in my seat and wait for everyone to completely pile off. Then, that's when I'll get off.

All routine.

The bus gradually became quiet in terms of voices and movement, signaling a clear coast. For the first time today, I turned my head left to the interior of the bus. The walls a dark white, the seats all gray. The entirety of it all was empty of people, although one could tell there were people just there. Papers were almost seemingly thrown purposefully on the floor. Trash paralleled. Candy wrappers and the emptiness of chip bags were in sight. Crumbs of food were lying about. Now that I think about it, I haven't eaten yet.

Well, that's normal.

Without looking, I gingerly gripped my bookbag to my right. It was an old, faded grayish color. The material was so thin I expected it to rip any second.

Anyway, I picked it up and stood nearly absentmindedly as if I had practiced this action an endless number of times. My bones softly cracked as I slowly stood up, mainly from my legs and lower back. I slowly slid left out of my seat, staring straight down at the floor. Dodging the trash was always expected. Step over a wrapper and an empty bag. I now stood in the center of the aisle. Having my head facing forward, I took my time walking straight down. I pulled my bag along not by any of its straps or loops. Simply, I held my

3

grasp on the side of its top. I passed the bus driver and took an even slower time going down each of the three steps. Through the open double doors, I kept the same pace towards the high school. The bus sped off, leaving me alone. No one in sight.

That's usual.

My shoes scuffed the ground the whole walk to the slightly light-smudged blue double doors. The doors each had a small window one nearly had to stick their face into to essentially use it the way it was intended. It was easier to see inside today since it was partly cloudy this early morning. The other side showed the beginning or the end of a hallway full of activity. Only the chests of some people showed through the spotted glass. Some kids walked slowly down the hall next to someone. Others rushed and ran, apparently in a hurry or high on joy. They all wore various styles and colors.

I slid my bookbag strap over my right shoulder as I stood an inch from the door. My head lowered as I looked at the black door handle, my right fingertips grazing it. My tips barely gripped it. I grabbed the handle and slowly pulled.

A blast of uproar hit my ears and the air outside. Now the full scene was shown instead of only parts of the bodies. It seemed even more chaotic, loud and electric with energy which adults would simply describe as youth. Kids zipped and zagged aimlessly it seemed. The explosion of sound was endless. Typical high school, I presume.

Before the door was even halfway open, I let it go and slightly slid myself inside. I shuffled a few inches forward and the door closed behind me, not exactly softly, but not exactly loudly. I put both my hands in my front pants pockets and started down the hallway. My eyes looked forward, yet they made no contact with any other. They didn't even glance at other eyes.

All routine.

I turned right into a less heavy traffic hallway and kept

straight. The hallway was a bit dark. Old lights were used in this hallway. They all could have been eternally stuck on dimmed. It is slightly an old school building after all, here since the 1950s or 1960s if I'm correct. Regardless, it was kind of hard to see anything in the hallway, except myself to an extent. My brown skin wasn't exactly dark and wasn't exactly light. It was right in the middle. It tried to blend in with the surroundings, ultimately seemingly making it juxtapose even more with it and everything else. Of course, with my other features, blending in was nearly impossible. Juxtaposing was simply the only possibility. All usual.

Admittance and acceptance.

I turned left into a third hall, and the floor lightened to a color that was once white that darkened with age. There was somewhat more activity in this than the last, but not as much as the first hall I entered. This hallway was slightly brighter compared to the last. Classroom doors were tanned brown and more visible. It was a short hallway. At the end of the hall, it gave way to a river of kids accompanied by a river of noise, just like the first hallway. I could either go left or right into this new hall and drown in the river. Thankfully, my class wasn't far.

I shouldered left and crept into the crowded hall. It barely took more than three steps, and to my immediate left was my classroom. I stood in front of the door and slid my left hand out of my pocket. I grasped the door handle and rotated it downward. A river of kids passed around behind me, bringing noise with it. I pulled open the door and began trying to slip through the crack without bumping the river. The door cracked open more and more and skimmed part of my body as I went further inside the classroom. At last, I pulled my foot inside, and the door closed thereafter.

The classroom itself was an assortment of warm brown, brass colors with beige walls. The wall in front had a chalkboard that obviously hadn't been cleaned. All the walls of the room were decorated with arts, writing, history, and more. Some of the arts were pictures of statues with a lack of worldly historical context. African and ancient-looking statues could be seen in the pictures. There were also actual physical statues of this accord sitting around. Other arts displayed were pictures and references to literature of all types. Some I haven't heard of, while a bit of it I vaguely think I've been introduced to before. Some of it was simply art with no references to literature or history whatsoever.

It wasn't the smallest or biggest classroom. There was a good number of tan-colored desks and navy blue metal chairs behind each desk to hold about thirty people. The desks were shaped like a stadium, curved facing the direction of the chalkboard, but not curved enough to where people would instantly notice this curvature. The one difference was that the very back desks on the right side of the room were turned more than just slightly; they were turned a complete ninety degrees so they were facing the class instead of the front. Two desks connected to these desks, and instead of facing the class they faced the front. This set of desks together made what looked to be a small letter L. The letter L desks were certainly full of clutter, except for one where the two directions of desk met to create the letter itself. This L desk formation was kind of near the teacher's desk, which, of course, was the largest desk in the entire room.

The teacher's desk was the tidiest part of the entire classroom. Blank white line paper had a small stack on the desk's center. A pen stayed on top of the stack. One side of the desk had a stack of papers with words and pen marks all over it. It was next to the classroom phone, which was on the farther corner from that side. The other side had stacks of books from corner to corner. The desk itself was mahogany, specially being a dark forest brown in color, and was placed towards the right back corner of the room.

Behind the desk was a very nice-looking black rolling chair.

Behind that was a window with its beige blinds closed and a potted plant to the left below it. To the right of the desk was a small mahogany bookcase that rested against the room's corner.

There was also a bookcase on the left side of the room. It was against the wall, but this time not in the corner. It was decorated with statues of African and ancient-looking figures. The shelf itself was glossy with no dust, just like the entire room itself, including the white, long, tile ceiling. The lights were off, allowing a little light through the blinds to barely illuminate the room.

The left and right side of the room were only considered as such from standing in the doorway. Once seated, since the desks faced the front of the room where the doorway was, left and right would flip to the opposite.

Normal.

I took both my hands out of my pockets and waded through the room. My fingertips grazed a desk here, the back of my hand grazed a desk there. I went directly to where the desks were shaped like an L. I grabbed a seat at the only desk with no stuff on top of it, which was where the desks connected to make that L. This desk was facing into the room, making the sitter's back face against the wall. To the right, some space away, was the teacher's desk. There was enough space for isolation. I slid my bag off, leaning it on a nearby desk as I slid myself into the empty seat.

—Bell went off, signaling people to go to class. Noise further filled the hall outside– Rang again to let them know to hurry. From across the room, the sound of the doorknob turning pierced through the atmosphere yet merging with it in a seemingly orthodox way as if it was nothing but normalcy. Footsteps followed with conversation. The footsteps became louder as more kids came. Predictably, the lights were turned on. More footsteps followed gradually. Seats screeched as they moved and were sat on. Flaps of clothes came along with chatter. Looking at it, I don't even need to—

"Awh man he's here again! Ha!"

The room was beaming with activity; yet was still—

"It's gotta be dyyyye!"

Not warming up even slightly. Certainly always—

"What's this dude's name anyway?"

Should I even say—

"Shoot, I don't know. I don't really care."

The same voice said that right on cue. Or was it different? Not sure, could be any—

"Here she comes!"

"Already?"

"Hurry up!"

"Did we have homework?"

"Yo."

"SShhhhh."

"Don't 'SShhhhh' me!"

"Aight aight aight aight."

Seats scooted. Rushed sounds filled half the room. The door made a small sound when it closed from the last kid entering, and the room receded to a hush. Then, the door opened, stayed open as if in some dramatics, and closed as if the dramatics suddenly died like the before classroom chatter. The sound of shoes walked into the room and became closer to me.

"All quiet." A voice noted.

Steps continued. Patiently taking their time.

"Everyone in their seats," the same voice noted. The voice was a woman's. Stern, yet not in a rude way. Professional, yet not in some way that was impersonal. Was, yet wasn't, soft-spoken. Her voice filled the room with soul, culture, and knowledge. Articulate. Calm. It took command effortlessly without suffocating any opposition and the world around.

"Seems everyone is ready for class," the same voice continued in a way that gave the effect that it was talking to itself. The steps towards the teacher's desk stopped.

"Who read the book?" The voice questioned. Silence followed. The steps continued their pause. "August has just begun." One light step. "School has been in session since last week." The steps halted again. "No one?" Silence.

"This, simply put without an elaboration, is a history slash literature class." The voice raised the volume a bit to show the magnitude of what she was talking about. Two steps sounded from the direction of the middle of the room. "In this class, you will learn history, literature, connections of two, cultures all intertwined." The shoes creating the step sounds slid to a halt. "There is *even. More*…than that to it. Locations. Dates. Art. All connected. Society, and when going in deeper, how it changes past to fit the now."

The steps began walking towards the teacher's desk. They walked past in front of me and the sound of a rolling chair rolling backwards lightly went through the air. A plush noise squished as someone sat in the chair and the chair itself rolled forward. The voice's owner just sat down at the teacher's desk.

"Attendance is important to history," the voice continued seamlessly from the desk. "Which is why I shall take it now."

Groans went off through the people in the room.

Attendance. Now I have to—

"Clara Blon."

My—

"Here."

I don't—

"Marcus Graceland."

Some things I'd—

"Here."

Name. My name. That's something I'd rather keep to myself. It doesn't mean anything. More importantly—

"Here."

It'll bring attention to me. I'll have to speak…Looking at it this is—

"Courtney Mathis"

All routine.

"Here."

Silence in my mind. Used to this by now. The real question, is anything different?

Admittance and acceptance.

"Jason Side."

Pause. I never do anything the first time. Sometimes, whoever takes attendance skips over my name.

"Jason Side?"

"Oh, it's this dude," someone softly pointed out to their friends. Whispers and a few giggles followed. More hushed commotion went through the class. My eyes may be aimed at the ground, yet I could feel all heads and eyes turned in my direction. I raised my head slightly to straighten it in the direction of the teacher. I wasn't looking at her or her desk in particular. I looked in the general area. I stared as my mind was invariably stagnant.

Who am I?

I slightly raised my arm and slid it back into my pocket, showing I was here.

That is true. I am here.

"This dude." A whisper. Some chatter, quiet and hushed. Some about my hair, others about my eyes. Me in the sense of generalities.

Here

Admittance and Acceptance.

All routine.

From there the rest of the class passed like a blur like everything else. Past or present? Future? Seems the same. I am sure for class I had to open books and read something. I am pretty sure I had to write. I am certain. I didn't pay attention; however, it always is the same. The other classes blurred together, math, science, and what not. People blurred. During lunch, I sit at some long table somewhat towards the right side of the lunchroom; it's the only empty table. Another class here and there, a bus ride off the premises included. It was exactly as the bus ride up, with the exception of walking through a bunch of stares and silent conversations to get off my stop. I stepped off the bus, knowing I was the only one for this stop, and paused for the bus to drive off, which it quickly did.

The wind rustled my clothes as I stood on the sidewalk. There was a bit of a chill at past three in the afternoon. No sun was in the sky. It was only cloudy. The sky now had a dark tint to it, a grayish blue. It kind of looked like winter, even though it wasn't near. The atmosphere almost looked foggy, but that too it was not.

Sidewalk across the street, street to my left, and sidewalk I stood on. I slid my hands into my pockets and began walking forward. My shoes scraped the ground as I went. No cars drove past. No crickets. Slightly silent.

The house I took residence in was ahead to the right. I did not have to look. In fact, I was looking down as I walked, staring at my feet taking turns going forward. I just knew. The scraping of the sidewalk seemed to get louder. The house is—

Scrape.

Getting closer.

Scrape.

I stopped in the midst of a driveway and looked to my right. The color was gray, a standard looking driveway. The front lawn was recently cut and was intersected with this driveway. The front yard to the right of the house was bigger compared to the small sliver on the left. There wasn't much yard at all when looking at it. The house itself was made out of bricks and was an assortment of dark browns. The triangular roof was the darkest of the browns. The front door, the porch awning, the beams of any windows, and the garage were all the same shade. The house itself, such as the front and sides, was a slightly darker tan color. There were three windows, the longest one on the lower half of the house, and two small ones on the upper. There was a little bit of shrubbery under the lower one. The interior was blocked by white curtains as usual.

This was a house. Just a house. In a normal neighborhood of everyday life. Exactly the same as any house.

Admittance and Acceptance.

All routine.

Scrape.

I walked to the front door, stepping onto the porch. The awning cast a shadow over me and around the ground where I stood. The door is always unlocked around this time. I do not have a key. My hand gripped the circular bronze-colored door handle. Cold to touch. I twisted the handle. Still cold to touch. I twisted it further. A quiet click broke through the air. I pushed the door forward. I stepped inside the house. The door closed behind me.

The floor I stood on was a light brown hardwood. The walls were whitish beige and close to my right and left at the entrance. My shoes clicked on the floor as I walked for—

"Oh, here's the boy."

To my right, there was a circular opening entrance to another room. In this room, sitting on a leather couch, was an older penny brown skin man. He was in his forties and had a deep voice. Bald head, dark eyes, kind of not skinny nor not fat—

"Ruins the atmosphere." He said to someone in an entirely different room—

"Oh, he might hear us," He responded to whatever was said. "Good, it doesn't matter."

I kept going down the hall. The man's voice was more distant—

"My point. Doesn't that tell you something?"

The circular wall opening started to disappear from the corner of my eye—

His laughter rose.

I gripped my hand on the door handle to the room where I take residence in—

"Yeah."

I turned the doorknob and pushed the door to my left —

"Trade it in."

I stepped into the room and pushed the door to close—

"Close it all the way," his voice rose after me.

The door clasped shut. An old worn out dark brown door with a fake gold and hardly shiny circular handle. The room itself was small, comparable to a closet to a certain extent. The walls were an off tint whitish beige that looked like it wasn't tended to. Bare, no art or life to it. No closet or anything like that. One small window opposite to the door had an off-white curtain that was always closed. The carpet should have been in between a light and dark gray, but age made it closer to black. The light in the room was dim since it could barely shine past the closed curtain. The bed, about the size of a twin, had no sheets and pillows, but did have a thin dark blue blanket. The frame was silver stainless steel, which had practically no use. It had no headboard and barely worked as a frame. The whole thing was pushed to the back left corner of the room near the window. In the back right corner of the room was a small dark brown drawer with not very much to it. There was a small lamp on top of it.

As small as the room was, most of it was empty. From door to bed there was nothing except space. A total disconnection between. Silence.

All routine.

Admittance and Acceptance.

I slid my bag off my shoulder and gripped it in my right hand. From here, I walked over to the drawer and set the bag against it.

I looked down and gripped my shirt. It was dark blueish gray and looked knitted. Certainly, it was not. If anything, it almost looked like a thermal shirt, yet it didn't look and feel hot. Strings hung out; it was nowhere near new. Decrepit, hanging on to life. There was a small hole in the left sleeve's elbow. The shirt was much too big for me. Loose, shapeless. I began taking it off with my head popping out from the bottom. I gripped the rest of the formless shirt and pulled it off my arms.

My shoes were old, a hole almost forming in each that wasn't too noticeable. There were scratches everywhere. The shoes weren't anything special. They were just normal dark gray shoes. I untied the laces and took them off. My black socks were taken off next.

The pants I wore were dark, grayish. They too were very loose, being too big for me. I deal with whatever I have. I undid my shedding black belt and slid the pants off. I grabbed everything I took off, shirt, belt, pants, socks, shoes, then folded them on top of each other, putting them next to the bag. I stepped away from that pile and slid into the bed. The blanket was pulled over me except the upper half of my face.

The bus goes to school. Everyone gets off. Then me. Classes. Lunch. Classes. Bus. Home. Bed. Wakeup, bus, classes, lunch, classes, bus, home, bed.

All routine.

Admittance and acceptance.

Identity. What is the essence of such a thing? Couldn't an identity be anything thought up in the heads of people? Is it something agreed upon or just the one? A one? What is the definition of such?

My hair stuck out in front of my eye. I slid my hand from underneath the covers and grabbed it. 4c hair. Afro-textured. Yet…

White.

Not some sort of blond. Not silver. Not gray. Natural. Not dyed. Nothing manufactured. White exactly. A bright white.

One that looked like it shined. One that glowed in light. One that popped out regardless of convenience or circumstance.

White.

My hair was not picked out in the shape of an afro. It wasn't particularly long or short, the front barely stopping at my chin when it was pulled down. The white hair was kind of spiked up, like the shape of frozen fire. All over the place.

White.

I pulled a strand down in front of my eye and stared at it. Stared. Eyes…

Orange.

My eyes were a different color entirely. It was not similar to brown or yellow. It wasn't in between two different colors in the color scheme.

Orange.

They were bright orange. An orange exactly. Nothing else but orange. Irrefutably orange. The color was just that. Natural. No contacts. Not manufactured. They were normal in shape. Normal in every possible way. They were just that bright pop out of nowhere and everywhere color.

Orange.

White hair. Orange eyes.

I let go of the strand of white hair and slid my hand back underneath the blanket.

All routine.

Admittance and acceptance.

How does someone define oneself? Or does someone else have to do it? Is it based on hair and looks? Is it the eye color or the body? Is it the clothes they wear? Or it is what transpires in their life, what happens around them? How do people interact with them? Do they interact at all? Is it the characteristics?

All routine.

Admittance and acceptance.

But what defines characteristics is identity. The same as

cultivating an answer on a bus or laying in a small bed.
Routine
Admittance.
Acceptance.
Silence…
Identity.
White hair.
Orange eyes.
Characteristics.
Silence…
The answer is that this all ties together. Together, this creates an identity. Defines it.
Who am I?
What is identity?
All connected. All routine. Admit. Accept.
All the above.

Can Life Be Epitomized As Change, Stagnation, Or Simply Seeing A Distant Perception?

"You better remain quiet."

The same man from yesterday, deep voice and bald as ever. He was aiming at only me. No one else around for him to talk to. He opened the front door rushing me out.

"This is life. What can be different?" He slammed the door behind me. I walked left to the bus stop and stood in the sunless early morning. The bus showed itself, screeching to a quiet halt and opening its doors at its stop. I stepped inside. I looked straight down the aisle past all people's eyes—

"Here he is." Someone brought attention to...

I used the corner of my eyes to find an empty seat. There was one in the middle section to the left. I stepped towards it. Bags shuffled. Voices and conversations copied—

"Same shoes…"

"What do you call those?"

I slid into an empty seat—

"Bruh."

The bus drove off. Then the day goes on.

"Aw, you stole the good seat," said in some joking manner. It was to my left, not particularly close but certainly not far.

"I like the emergency window seat. It's cool!" The same voice, in the same tone.

I was in fact sitting next to the emergency window. "Emergency Exit" was written in black across the glass. A red lever with a red metal cover on top of it was under the words.

"I'll sit here then." Same voice, volume decreasing, meaning the person is going somewhere else.

The bus kept driving, finally stopping in front of the school. Everyone off, then me. Walk down the halls, pass people's eyes. To the classroom door and inside. Sit in the usual empty seat. African and other art surrounded me. Bell rings and footsteps came—

"Still here, again."

Seats filled as the room filled with noise. A sudden quiet and footsteps followed. The teacher for history and literature class. Class blurred. Then another two, math or science or both. Lunch. Another class. Bus.

"The emergency seat again?"

Looking to my right, I saw that I actually was sitting next to it.

"It's all good. I'll sit over here."

Bus stop. I get off. Walk to the front door of the house I take residence in. Turn the doorknob and step in—

"He's here earlier than usual." A voice traveled down the hall, as the door shut behind me. It sounded like it came from the bald man. Nothing different.

I stepped down the hall and made it to the door of the room I take residence in as chatter cluttered through the house—

"I'll push him out early tomorrow like I did this morning."

I grabbed the doorknob and turned it, pushing the door open. I stepped inside—

"Oh really? Ah Ha."

The door—

"I want more time without him too."

—closed behind me. I took my clothes off. They were extremely big on me, exactly like the clothes yesterday and every day. They were just a different color but still faded and worn-looking. I went to bed and woke up the next day.

"Maaaaan, you're always taking the emergency exit seat."

I looked to my right and saw the red lever. I did take the emergency seat again; I just wasn't trying to. I heard shuffling to my left. It sounded like someone was taking a different seat somewhere across the aisle.

I shouldn't sit here anymore. Whoever that person is. Or people. What is the difference? The bus stopped, everyone got off. I got off after everyone departed and went to literature and history class. Two other classes follow.

Then lunch.

The lunchroom was any other type of lunchroom, just as the school was any other type of school. The room was mainly an off-white color with no windows, just a room that was almost a box. There was a hallway intersecting at the back. Each lunch table was long with black trim on the sides. They had an off-white surface that was more off than the off-white that made the room. There was space between each table to walk between. The chairs accompanying the tables were dark navy blue and made of metal. There were about six chairs per side, with none on the shorter ends.

I sat on the right side of the table, towards the edge but not exactly on it. The lunchroom was filled with noise. Conversations. Shrills. Shuffling. Clicking. Liquids moving. A crowd, a sea of sound. This was all around me. Not in close proximity.

My table was empty except for me. No one was close to it. The sources of the crowd of sound were blurred. It could not be fully seen like a picture too close to one's eyes. It was practically like a camera unfocused with the only focus being on the immediate empty table and seats.

All cold.

The room did have a chill to it. A chill pervaded everywhere, as if a small wind was whooshing back and forth past me and the empty table and seats. It was a great contrast to the noise around. How long does lunch last? About twenty minutes if I'm correct. Could be less, or more. Doesn't make a difference.

Time.

Noises around swelling.

Passes.

Right on cue the bell rang, ending lunch for this period. The sound swelled like an explosion. Chairs rubbed, screeched, and scraped against the hard tiled white floor. Movements, slow and rushed, were leaving chairs. The room itself was emptying out. It was all distant.

I slightly moved my head left and right and focused to see the room practically empty. I slid my seat back, grabbed my bag, stood up, and headed for whatever class I was about to go to. After that, another bus ride. This time, I made sure not to sit by the emergency exit seat. I sat in a seat ahead of it. No one was there, so it was exactly right. And no words were spoken about the emergency seat. The bus stopped and I walked to the house. I got inside, and the bald man said the same type of words—

"I was hoping he'd be late."

I stepped into the room I slept in and closed the door behind me. Clothes off, into bed, eyes closed. And dream…? I'm not sure I've ever dreamt. Have I ever dreamt? Dreamed? Maybe when I was much much younger. Dreaming…

Eyes closed.

Eyes open.

The lunchroom air chilled around the empty table and chairs surrounding me. Noise and conversation swelled. My hands held each other in front of my face as my eyes stared blankly. I leaned forward in my seat with no reason behind it. I wasn't thinking deeply or anything. Just sitting. Nothing special. Only sitting, waiting for the lunch bell to ring and to get the day over with. It would be kind of hard to think with all the noises around, chatter, chairs scraping the ground and all. Simply just sitting. A chair scraped the floor loudly, not so disruptive to cause a scene, not out of place. The scraping sound was just hardly louder than the usual chair scrapes on the ground. It was the kind of volume increase that happened when the sound happened closer.

Wait.

I didn't change where I was staring; however, I focused on my left peripheral vision. Everything outside of the empty chairs and table were like an out of focused camera as usual.

Wait.

There was a slight contrast. Across the table, to the left, the last seat at the very edge was now a blurry silhouette. No, the silhouette was bigger than the seat and different in shape.

Did that just...?

It's whatever.

A person was probably just wasting time or wanted to be left alone. Or something else. That is what it usually was whenever this happened from time to time. The air stayed chilled. The noise in the room picked up. More chatter, conversations.

"What are you doing?"

It wasn't silent. Nowhere nearby. Yet, it suddenly seemed further away from silence. A person's conversation must have been louder than the rest.

"Oh, I get it. You're shocked by my unlimited power. No one can take me on."

The empty table I sat at slightly moved as a person leaned on it. "Not even the banana overlords can take me on." The table slightly moved again as a person took their weight off it.

That was the second time in the last few seconds that some words in the room were louder than the rest.

Wait.

Did that just...?

Is a person...?

"Wah ha ha!" A cartoonist laugh was aimed in my direction.

Is a person...?

Are they..."

Wait.

I'm overthinking. It's either a conversation with a person or a jokes were trying to be created that were about me. The noise in the room picked up. The air stayed chilled.

"Not even the mole people can take me on."

This voice is slightly familiar. What person does it belong to? It doesn't matter. I'll stay out of it.

"I can see why you're terrified."

The voice. Young, so a student at this school. A male's voice. Comical tone, but for what reasons? Still, familiar. Why?

"Who wouldn't be terrified by the awesomeness I have? Mwah ha HA!"

Familiar. The sound in the room swelled. When's the bell going to ring?

"I can understand why you decided not to sit in the emergency seat anymore."

Sound died in my head.

Wait.

Emergency seat.

Sound picked up.

I have heard this voice before. The emergency seat on the bus. So, this voice is in fact aimed at me. Perhaps not, and I'm just overthinking. The problem is that the voice being aimed at me is the only conclusion at this point that makes sense. Most definitely, I should never sit in that emergency window seat ever again.

"So, what is your name, you heathen?" Said in some dramatic way as if it was trying to be said in a medieval voice. "I must know the name of my enemies before they are vanquished! Wah ha haaaaaa!"

Riiiiiing!

The bell. Should have rung sooner. Immediately, I stood up and turned my back towards the voice. I slowly stepped away from the table, away from the situation, and away from anything such.

Back in class, then the bus. Of course, I did not sit in the emergency seat. The bus stopped, I stepped off, and was at the front door of the house where I take residence in. Turn the doorknob, push. Step inside—

"I was hoping for a little more time."

Walk to the room I take residence in,

"Make sure you don't cook as much tonight. You don't need to eat today." He laughed at me.

turn the doorknob—

"Yeah." He laughed with someone else.

step into the room—

"I just don't feel like seeing him today."

Close the door behind me. Take off my clothes, fold them, put them down, crawl into bed. Thin sheet over me. Eyes close.

Dreamt.

Dreaming…

Eyes open.

I sat by myself on the bus, waiting to get off. Eyes close. On the bus. Eyes close. In a classroom. Eyes close. Lunch. Eyes close. Cooking dinner for the rest of the residents in the house. Eyes close. Classroom. Eyes closed. Lunch. Eyes closed.

Eyes open.

The air was chilly in the lunchroom. The table and chairs where I sat were completely empty. A normal day. My hands were in front of me as I stared forward blankly. I put my hands down slowly and leaned back in my chair. Air pushed past my hair, making it wave slightly. I leaned my body forward. Both of my elbows were placed on the table with my hands curved towards my body. I stared blankly at the table. Not straight down, not particularly up. The air pushed through my hair some more. I could just barely see a few white strands blowing at the top of my left eye.

I just noticed something about the table. Although the top was an off-white color, there were very small black dots scattered throughout. A scraping noise as a chair slid happened across the table towards the left. An outline of a person, the same one from days ago, same place. No, not the same place, a seat over. Not a seat in a farther direction. Now, closer. Why didn't I notice these black spots before?

"Look, I just wanted to say last time I was only joking."

Same voice. Definitely the same person.

"You can sit in the emergency seat, it's chill dude."

The chill air pushed through my hair more.

"I'm just a big jokester. You know what I mean?"

Jokes. They all joke.

"Not saying it excuses it, don't get me wrong."

The black spots were very noticeable.

"What's your name though? Now I gots to know."

Where's the bell?

"I'll tell you my name if you tell me yours," said in a smirking manner. "You ain't ready for a name as handsome as mine."

Riiing!

Good.

Names. Name's. Names'. Giving out mine...Giving out mine? Giving out mine. I don't know about that. Eyes close.

24

In bed. Eyes close. Bus. Eyes open.

Air pushed through my white hair again, as if on cue. The lunchroom had nothing except activity and conversations. It was busy. Chairs scraping around. One scrape was closer than the others.

"You didn't sit in the emergency seat again."

Again.

"Dude, don't worry. Like I said before, you can sit there, no problem."

Bell. Where is it?

"Do you know why I like that seat?"

I do wonder, but there's no need. In the sense of the long run, there's no reason to know.

"Eh, you probably don't care about that," the person laughed off.

Not necessarily.

"I never caught your name, though."

Riiiiiing!

It was slightly cold with the bed sheet over me. I pulled the thin sheet even further over me and had my eyes halfway closed.

Why try and talk to me? I don't understand. Eyes closed.

In bed.

Dreamt.

Dreaming...

Eyes open.

Lunchroom air chilled through my hair. My eyes almost felt dry. Chair scrape. Right on cue. Silhouette close, yet far. Time passed. Then more. And more.

No words?

That's...not normal...Oh well. Back to an old normal.

Chatter among the people spiraled through the air.

Riiiing!

Eyes closed. Lunch. Chair scrape. Silhouette. Eyes closed. Bed. Eyes closed. Class. Eyes closed. Turning a doorknob.

Eyes open.

"Does he ever say anything?" People turned and stared at me in literature and history class.

"Back to work," the teacher's voice instructed in a respectful, reserved manner.

Eyes close. Lunch. Eyes close. Outline. Eyes close. Bell. Eyes close. Bed.

Differences are the same. Some differences are only different.

Silence...

The bed sheet felt cool to touch.

Name. Talk.

Eyes open.

Lunch is lunch. Lunch was lunch. Air pushed through my hair, chilling my entire being. Conversations swelled around me. Voices of all pitches exploded through the room. Trays clicking on tables. Chairs scraping.

Wait.

I haven't heard a chair scrape, not a close one I mean. What? The last few days he's been here. Sure, he hadn't talked, however he was still present, sitting in the same spot. Conversations.

Talking.

Why does he talk? Why do all these people talk? Do people have to talk? Is it a requirement of some sort? Perhaps I'm overlooking the amount being overlooked. As redundant as that phrase might sound, it must be emphasized. It could just be my perspective that is so focused on a particular angle that the whole picture cannot come to light. Isn't that an argument that is a one size fits all?

Dreamt.

Dreaming.

Why don't I do that? Life is life. Lunch is lunch. Lunch was lunch. Life...was life...?

A tray clicked the table so close in front of me I almost

flinched. A chair scraped in front of me, and a silhouette sat down in it. The silhouette leaned down and began cutting up something on the tray.

Here.

The air pushed through my hair some more, harder even. The silhouette stopped cutting and pushed the tray forward. It went towards me and almost touched my left knuckle. I looked at the tray and the food on top. It was a usual school lunch, today being a chicken sandwich with a side of fruit. The difference in this lunch was the sandwich being cut in half, and the two fruit cups instead of the usual one.

"I have not seen you eat a single thing at lunch," he said plainly. Some seconds passed. "Ever."

I stared at the table. His fingers tapped the table as if to respond to my lack of response. He stared forward. "Look man. It's cool if you don't like talking. I can talk all day, but the last thing Imma do is make someone talk."

The table, I stared at it.

"But here's the deal. I'm not going to eat my half until you eat yours. I don't know, I feel like I freaked you out and this is the least I can do."

He didn't freak me out.

Wait.

He's, he is, he's. Offering me food? My stomach punched me from the inside in realization. When's the last time I've eaten? I don't know. Recently when I cook, they would eat it all without leaving any for me. They just haven't been in the mood lately.

"I have the stamina of a cheetah and sexiness made from the cosmos. Mwah Ha haa! The cosmos, I'll have you know. I'll wait all day."

Why?

Why give me food?

Why give me anything?

What is the motive?

What is happening?

"I'll tell you this," he leaned forward and straightened his back. I took a look at him for a second.

Messy. That's the first word that came to mind. Messy.

He had a plain white T-shirt that had fresh stains on it. Not nasty stains, or any stains unpleasing to the eye. It kind of matched the shirt and his overall style. It looked as if he had blue jeans, dark blue to be exact, and old gray shoes. It was all unkempt.

"I can tell you don't like giving your name, so I'll give mine." His skin was dark brown. Dark eyes to match. His dark 4c hair was unkempt, like a kind of beardless Fredrick Douglas, just a slight split in the middle, more forward, and mainly consisting of extremely tight curls. Some hair stuck together like it was in the process of locking up, perhaps in the process of forming freeform locs.

Kind of indescribable. It was like a crazy unkempt hair style that only happens from working for days straight without sleep and tending to one's hair, yet melodiously it did not look mangled. It wasn't crazy looking. Nowhere near as crazy as mine, and not in terms of color but in terms of style. It just wasn't the usual style anyone had. One just might see it on occasion. This was one of them.

He leaned back, his eyes sort of almost gleaming.

"My name is Asher Craft." He smirked and tapped his fingers on the table for a second. "And like I said," he just stared at me for a moment. I haven't met his eyes or anything this entire time. Regardless, he stared straight at me. He then, while still not blinking, opened his mouth to speak. "I'm not eating until you're eating."

Wait. What?

When is the last time I've eaten? It doesn't matter. I cannot eat someone else's food. That would be selfish.

Wait.

Isn't it selfish in this circumstance not too? He said he

wouldn't eat until I ate. If I don't eat, then I'm forcing him not to. I looked back and forth, contemplating.

But.

Should I or should I not?

Plus.

I can't just eat and not say a word.

Silence…

Silence..

Silence.

It's not that I'm fearful. This is just life.

All routine.

Admittance and Acceptance.

All the above…?

This above is different. It's full of dreams and dreaming as if I've dreamt. Although, I guarantee I have not dreamt. So, what is this? In conclusion, what? What is the above? The routine? The admitting? The accepting? Life is life. Life was life. And—

Life is now life.

I'm going to have to talk. That is a must. I'm going to have to eat that half so I won't be rude to him. I never wanted and still don't want to be. Just living, just existing. What about existing at this moment? This is bound to happen on occasion. It's bound to end soon as well. This is life. I won't have to worry about it. I'll do what needs to be done.

The air pushed through my hair more.

Eat.

I stared at the cut in half sandwich.

Eat.

Dreamt. Dreaming.

Eat.

My hand raised. My hand very hesitantly moved through the air towards half of the sandwich. Was I blinking or did my eyes close?

Eat.

No. They've been open. Eyes open.

Eat.

My hand touched the sandwich. Carefully I grasped it. It started towards my mouth. My other hand gripped it as well. It touched the front of my mouth and there was a pause.

Eat.

I opened my mouth like my eyes. The sandwich went in, and I pushed my teeth together, closing my mouth.

I have taken a bite of the sandwich.

I didn't register the flavor. The action was enough for me. I took time to chew.

"Ohh, there we go," Asher grinned through the atmosphere. "Now that's what I'm talkin' about. Ohhhh yeahh." He began clapping, making it more dramatic than it was. He clapped as if he had won every gold medal in both the winter and summer Olympics simultaneously.

I just ate. Now, talk.

Should I...

Talk.

Push. One step. Two steps. Push.

Talk. Don't be rude.

"Not too shabby, broski," Asher smiled.

Talk.

I finished chewing.

Talk.

Swallowed.

Talk.

Eyes open.

Talk.

Dreaming.

Talk.

Mouth opens.

Talk. Talk. Talk.

Inhale... here it goes.

Talk

"Why do you sit here?" Plainly. Calmly. More layers than a field of multifaceted thoughts of past, present, and future. I looked past the sandwich patiently waiting for an answer. Time ticked. Tocked. Seconds passed on all clocks.

Silence.

Riiiiing!

Explosion. Of. Noise.

I placed the unfinished half of the sandwich down and slowly stood. I stepped from my seat and turned around, walking away from the table and the whole of the indescribable.

Eyes.

My bed sheet chilled in the dark room against my skin.

What was that? That whole…I wouldn't even call it an exchange. Whatever it is, I'll be cordial to an extent for now until life goes on its course. Interesting.

"Wooo, oh boy, man…It's gonna be a long day today." Asher stretched in his seat and relaxed. "You know what I mean?"

I didn't look at him. Talk. "Day by day." My eyes contemplated the lunchroom, it all being chill and blurry.

"I feel like you say that whenever I come by," Asher started laughing as if imagining some elaborate scene. "You're like low-key trying to learn how to teleport or be invisible."

I looked at the table placing my hands underneath it. Asher leaned in for a second.

"I now realize you have the true power." Asher leaned even more forward. He started acting like a fictional character, making his voice sound like a stereotypical knight. "Sensei, what must I do to learn the teleportation technique?" He smacked his hands together and made a sign like he was some ninja. "Must my chi be balance?" He started quietly yelling like he was a battery charging for energy.

I looked at him and raised my eyebrow.

He held his hands up with a pure smile. "Don't judge me."

"I'm not." I turned my head right and looked at the immediate wall.

"I'm a bit surprised." His tone didn't change, still I could tell this wasn't a joke.

I turned back and looked at him. "Why would you say that?"

"Well, you never really talk." He put his hands up in a shrugging gesture.

I thought about it for a second. "Judge? Why Judge? People are people." I slid lower in my seat and turned my head right. "You all have lives to live."

The chill air hit my hair again. Asher made a quiet clicking sound for a second. "Makes sense. And I'm not talking about the pennies in my pocket."

The cool air. "Day by day…"

Eyes.

Bed.

Interesting.

"So, what's your name?" Asher's shirt had more stains on it. Or less?

"Jason." I looked past him, looking into the distance. "Jason Side."

"Side." That hung in the air for a few seconds. "Cool." He leaned forward, grabbed a part of his lunch and bit into it. "Cool like cold. Your hair though." I looked up, staring at my hair.

Here it goes.

"Whiter than snow." He paused and shifted in his seat. "You don't look biracial at all, mixed or anything…but…" He shifted in his seat.

"I'm completely Black."

Asher paused. "Same here. The hair is why I asked. My bad dude." He whispered the word "Anime" to himself for a second.

Oh my.

"I mean now that I think about it, even if you were, that doesn't really explain the hair and eyes," Asher said. "You're literally the only one with that."

"I'm fully aware."

"So, is your hair dyed or?"

"It's natural."

"You legit my dude?"

"That's not a fallacy."

"And your orange eyes?"

"And my orange eyes."

Asher sat back and got quiet. Of course. This is how it always is. First, they question. Then, the questions extends to everything. Assumptions are made. Watching through a window. Zoo animal. All rou—

"Bro, that's hella cooooool!" Asher voice shook the air and every foundation of every single existence of everything possible.

Wha-Wha.

He leaned back in his seat. "Wellll...not as cool as me of course, but ummm," he started flexing in a humorous manner. I couldn't pay complete attention. My focus was elsewhere.

What is this?

What. Is. This.???

I need to know. I need to know. I need to know.

"Why didn't you answer my question?" Those words hung into the air for a second.

"Wait, you asked me a question?" Asher looked confused.

"Days ago. Or weeks? When you gave me the sandwich."

Asher sat and looked up like it took extreme thought to figure out what I said. "Ah you mean days ago?" He sat straight up like it hit him. "Ohhhh that question. HA HA!"

I just stared at him, my eyes narrowing a bit. "Yes. Why do you sit here?"

Asher laughed for a moment. "Why not?" He answered

quickly. I just looked at him in confusion. He must have noticed my face and looked straight into my eyes. "Why not?"

I still am confused…Wha--

Asher sat up and leaned back in his seat. "I don't see an issue with you or anything. Why not live life? Be ourselves?
You even said it yourself."

"I said?" Is he serious? Is he truly serious? This doesn't
sound…normal…This is…what is it? I'll need to learn. I
need…I'm not sure.

"Yeah. You sure did." He assured me.

He leaned forward looking me straight in the eyes. Straight.
Nowhere else. Why is this different? I see. He wasn't staring
like he was looking around a zoo. This isn't all routine anymore, what is this? What identity does he see? Then why else
is he staring? What is the meaning? What--What. What is all
of this?

Asher didn't blink once. He continued to lean forward. He
inhaled, about to say something that must be different. Will
be different. Something indescribable. "Why not. You even
said it yourself. 'Judge? Why Judge? People are people. You
all have lives to live.' I agree. I don't see the problem in sitting
with someone or talking to someone. People are people. We
all have lives to live. Why not live it? So, what's the big deal
with doing this or that and talking to whomever? In other
words, don't overthink broski, it's all good." He hit the table
to emphasize his point.

I said that? Oh, I did. But I meant it differently. How did he
get that from my words? Where did that meaning come from?
A meaning from an entirely different meaning.

Life is life. Life was life. Life.

Life.

Life is…change. Life is ever moving. Life is…life.

This probably won't last forever. This is the now. Yet, I'll
live life, changes and all. It'll go back, I think. I'm sure. This is
all…

"Who in here read the assignment for today?" The teacher's voice hit like abstract art. Pleasantly with force. Respectful. "It is almost the end of class. You might as well tell the truth, whatever it is." The voice said from her desk. "Come clean if you will."

No one spoke up. The teacher sighed. "Nevertheless, the homework is still due. Next class, turn it in." Right on cue, the bell rang as if she told it to not ring until she was finished. Chairs shuffled; noises carried in the air. The door opened and closed repeatedly until the room was empty. I still sat in my seat right where the four desks connected to make the L shape.

"Jason Side, class has concluded. What are you still doing here?" The teacher's voice was at a lower volume and still had the same respectful polish to it. It wasn't just a matter of her voice; it was her very being. I could tell she wasn't even looking at me. The sound of papers filing was to my right.

"I actually do have a question," I said from my seat.

There was a very quick pause in the paper filing as my words rang in the air, continuing soon after. "Do you now?"

I slid my chair back and stood up. I turned to my right and walked to the front of the teacher's desk. She continued to look at her papers as I approached.

"Have a seat, Jason." She said, still eyeing papers.

I dragged the nearest chair over and sat right in front of the desk. She looked like her mind was on a million things at the same time, however she could easily deal with it and controlled all those thoughts at once. I already knew what she looked like. Still, looking face to face deepened the details.

She had dark brown skin that matched her eyes. Her 4c hair was an extremely coiled afro-texture. It was either dark brown or black in color and was pulled in an afro ponytail with multiple cornrows in the front that led into it. She was thin.

In front of her eyes were her usual black frame glasses. She also wore a black button-up shirt with tan colored brown buttons. The shirt also had a floral design with light brown and pink flowers that did not overpower the core blackness. She wore black pants to match. Beige flats. Stockings, I think that's what they're called, that were also black.

In front of her, on the edge of her desk, stood a dark brown name plate with the name itself engraved in a shiny gold metal. Her name.

"Ms. Grey—"

"Ah ah," Ms. Grey interrupted. "Did you finish the chapter for tonight?"

"I already finished the book."

Ms. Grey stopped filing papers and placed them gently on her desk. She made eye contact with me. "Continue."

"Change."

Ms. Grey looked at me and gestured with her hand to say continue. I sat up in my seat and scooted it back a bit. "What is change? I mean how does one define it?"

Ms. Grey sat silently and looked at me, intently studying me like there were subtitles for every syllable I gave. Her face didn't change, not conveying any emotion. As abstract as it may sound this somehow still made her feel more real and less like some emotionless creature. "How would you define change?"

Blank. That was my head. Blank.

"I'm not sure. For example, Okonkwo's descent was all because of change. Which is why, as the title says, 'Things Fall Apart.'"

"You finished the book because of this idea of change?"

I nodded my head.

"You still haven't answered the question, Jason. How would you define change?"

Silence.

Blank.

How would I?

"Do you know what I see?" Ms. Grey unwaveringly looked at me, not waiting for a reply. "Change is perspective."

I looked off to my side for a second, thinking, and returned to her face. "What do you mean?"

"I'm not talking about the very definition of change itself. I mean change is any shift that is different or even similar, if it is not the exact. You focused on Okonkwo. Out of all words, you used the word 'descent' for a reason."

Blank.

"What your real question is, is how to react to said change. Change is natural to life. What you need to decide is how you perceive it and act accordingly."

"I don't know about that..."

"Jason, we're now in the middle of August. We've been in school for about half a month, and this is the first time you've talked. Take your time. Open up." She moved some papers to the other side of the desk. "Thursday next week, I will hold a small afterschool event with arts and crafts, engaging other aspects of the mind. Speaking of aspects, an aspect of the event's theme will be the *Alkeeb Gods*." She said those last two words like there was much more meaning to it. Meaning that could split the very foundations of even the molecules in the air. More meaning than I could ever in all my life comprehend as if there was some kind of reality to it that I didn't and couldn't fathom.

"Alkeeb Gods?" I repeated questioningly.

"Yes. The *Alkeeb Gods*."

"I've never heard of them. What are they?"

"They're a very ancient set of Gods, older than Mesopotamia and other foundational civilizations."

"Why have I not heard of them?"

"They are a relatively new discovery, found mostly in the regions of Africa, some in the Americas and Caribbean, exceedingly small sections of Greece. As days go by, more of their stories are being excavated and understood. Information on them has not been released to the public as of yet. Since I am also in that field, I am privy. We're beginning an Alkeeb God section in class soon, doing a small touch upon them." She tapped her desk with her papers. "The afterschool event starts at five in the evening and ends at six. It's more of an art and crafts event that is for de-stressing students. The theme just is the *Alkeeb Gods*. Come along to it."

"I. I don't know…"

Open up. Open up?

Gah- no-Wah-Gah-

"Think about it and come." Ms. Grey said.

Think…

"What food is this?" His voice hit my eardrums. He looked the same. Bald head, penny brown skin, ordinary-looking. In his forties, not skinny or fat. He wore clothes that any other person would wear, mainly red plaid with darker blue jeans or something—

"Where are you at? You're not at school now. You're here. Serve me."

I grabbed a pot and pulled it along. It was kind of heavy, full of beans, peas, and other vegetables. I grabbed a wooden spoon, dipped it in, and pulled out—

"Oh, my goodness," said a woman's voice with an English accent. "I had such a long day, Calvin. You wouldn't believe."

"Why don't you try me," the man smiled, only able to match half of his wife's glee.

"Hey," he turned to me, snapping his fingers at me. "Stop daydreaming, I said 'serve me.'" He looked straight at his wife. "You know, Elizabeth, we could trade him in."

Elizabeth sat and thought for a second. She was dressed like she was above every class, yet not flaunting it around. It wasn't anything exactly fancy. It was probably the air she gave off. It matched the house itself, which was just a house in an average neighborhood. She was just there and didn't clash, yet it could be differentiated that she wasn't from here.

She had dark twisted afro-textured hair that stopped above her chin. She was dressed casually but professionally, wearing a shirt that mainly consisted of black with some pink. She also was in her forties to match her husband's age. What differed was that she was larger in size, rotund in shape. Her skin was a light pecan brown—

"No," Elizabeth replied to Calvin. "Leave him."

I finished serving them dinner. They ate their fill and left the kitchen. Once they were gone, I ate whatever was left. Usually there wasn't much food left, if at all, but there was a little bit more this time. I finished and started cleaning the dishes.

The water was warm and moved around my hands along with the soap. I scrubbed a plate and put it on the drying rack.

Think…

Scrub…

Think…

Scrub…
Think.

I think that I'll do what needs to be done. I'll live life regardless of a change or changes. Perhaps…Perhaps I'll go to this afterschool Alkeeb Gods theme crafts night thing. Step by step. Day by day. It'll end the same or somewhat close to that. I'll sit back and see, kind of like from a distance. I'll try this out. Live life and do what is needed per circumstance.

Live.

Is There A Change In The Slightest, Or Is It A Word That Holds Emptiness?

"How many times are you going to run into me on the way to lunch?" I said while looking ahead as I walked. "Already a few days of this. It's starting to make me think I should add 'supposedly' to what I said."

"Randomly, yes. That's how I live life. Woo!" Asher took bigger steps to get closer to my side and began walking with me down the hall. "You know how it goes." He started air guitaring. "You always walk alone any— Aah." He abruptly stopped along with his air guitar. I rotated my head discreetly to see what made him make that reaction. That poster. No. Some of the few people walking by? All the different faces. The smaller girl. No. The smaller guy. No. That other person. No. Someone else. No. Is it an object—

"There you are." A deep voice. Dark like an abyss. One that created its own world to whomever it was directed towards and trapped them inside. It wasn't overwhelming, but it was impactful, like a word having a depth to its definition than it seemed to have.

"What are you doing in this hall?" The voice encased an area of the hallway. Around us, people began filing out. The surroundings were practically empty, leaving Asher, me, and the embodiment of that voice. Just. Three.

Who's the third?

I looked to my right side. Standing in front of Asher was someone I've never seen. Tall, broad shoulders. He wasn't buff nor big but he was built. Brown eyes. Low cut afro-textured hair. Dark brown skin. He wore a gray shirt, a black leather jacket, blue jeans, and black athletic shoes. He looked older than me and Asher. He gave off an air of importance.

And something else. The atmosphere off him was...was—

"Choking?" The person snorted. "You can't talk now?"

Asher looked annoyed.

The person narrowed his eyes. "You think you're it or something?" He scuffed. "Even I have to admit, that sounded corny."

I looked slowly back and forth between the two. The person turned his head and his eyes locked onto mine. I don't know how to explain the feeling. It was just pumping through me, acting like adrenaline. The feeling was small, basically nonexistent. Perhaps it was the epitome of nonexistent, and I was just overthinking. The point is, it was like something was telling me there was more depth here. Perhaps, it was just the feeling that this person was giving off.

What is this?

"You..." He stared for a second and walked over, leaving Asher. The look he had was as if glass shattered, erupting a voluminous sound, all within the confines of his head. Each step he took was like a controlling action that made everything around him the exact environment he wanted. He stopped, looming so close a shadow engulfed me. He stared me up and down like he saw something he recognized but was confused about. "You look strange."

I'm used to those types of words and phrases. This presence...his presence...that's what's different. He didn't blink. He silently stared, then opened his mouth. "Where are you from?"

"Woah woah woah there broski," Asher stepped between me and him. "Let's get lunch." Asher placed his hand on my shoulder and lightly pushed me forward. I stepped in the direction he lightly pushed me, then walked towards the lunchroom with Asher, leaving the person behind.

"That wasn't the first time, was it?" I stared at Asher as he and I sat at the lunch table. He was in midbite and looked up across at me from my sudden question.

"Naw. If I'm being honest, I don't get it." Asher eyed past my head, thinking. "His name is Pericly."

"Pericly? Unorthodox name." There was something about him. Something off. Like...*off*. I can't explain it.

"Yeah, it's a weird name alright. Not sure where it comes from." Asher went back to his tray and picked up half a sandwich. "That's the first time I've seen him interact with anyone that wasn't me. Looks like he always acts like that. I thought it was just me, but." He chewed his sandwich.

Why? It's not my business, so I shouldn't ask. I sat leaning forward in my seat.

There was a pause as he chewed. "That was the third time. The first time was a few days ago. It's like he sought me out specifically. There was some aggression to it. I mean, you just saw what I'm talking about. It's like he was waiting for a fight, waiting for something. And it's like sooner or later he's not going to wait. And for no reason. I don't know, I don't get it."

It was a feeling. Something deeper. Something that was past my knowledge and everything I've ever known. A feeling that made it seem like needles were pricking the skin along my back and down my spine. Something. Was. Off. I could tell just by looking at him. A certain energy.

"Put Calvin's shoes by the door," Elizabeth ordered. "We're going out. Stay here and clean the house." She put a jacket on over her pink short and shiny dress, and went towards the door—

"I will not repeat myself," more of the English accent came out with a tinge of acid to it.

I grabbed the shoes and put them next to the door and—

"Mop the hallway." Bald head, dark eyes, now in a suit and tie. He went next to his wife and opened the door—

"We'll leave at this time and come back at eight for the next few weeks. Do anything boy…I hope you do. I want an excuse." He went through the door first, his wife following—

Door closed. I pushed water along the hallway floor and mopped. Next, I'll do the main room. Out late the next few weeks.

Next few weeks.

I stopped mopping for a second. The next few weeks. In that time interval. From around three thirty in the afternoon until eight. The next few weeks. I get to the house I take residence in from school around three, about thirty minutes before they will now leave for the next few weeks. The next few weeks…I might be able to go to that afterschool event thing. The Alkeeb Gods themed crafts event. Should I even go? There's more of an option now.

Options.

That's not normal.

Sit back and see from a distance.

"The Alkeeb Gods," Ms. Grey said as she wrote it on the chalkboard, turning to the class once she was finished writing. "They are a relatively new discovery. Not much is known about them. It's such a new discovery that if you were to try and research them, I'd be surprised if anything came of it."

The students looked at each other, some confused, some making small comments.

"There are references to them throughout the world." She began taking small steps around the front of the class towards different desks where students were sitting. "Parts of Africa. Very few parts in Europe." She stopped in front of a student's desk. "The Americas." She took some steps back towards the center of the board. "The Caribbean. The little information that we have has shown these Gods predate any that we know. American, Haitian, Ghanaian, Egyptian, Greek, Meso-potamian. All of these, and more, are younger," she under-lined "Alkeeb" on the board, "than the Alkeeb Gods."

The classroom was silent as students mulled over the in-formation.

"Now in your readings, there was mention of a man who ascended from being a mortal to becoming one of the Alkeeb Gods," Ms. Grey emphasized.

The class exchanged glances silently. A hand raised. "How did he become a God?"

Ms. Grey was standing in front of her desk. "Gods each have their own powers and abilities. There was once a God who had the power to give up his immortality and Godliness in exchange for his own life. The God saw that there was a man worthy of becoming a God and ensured that he took his place."

"Why did the God see him as worthy?" A different student asked.

"During a war. Although he is underrated and overlooked, it is also said that he fought bravely. Considering he was the one to become a God, it is highly probable that he more than adequately accomplished such brave actions." Ms. Grey leaned back on her desk. "It's okay. I did not explain the Alkeeb Gods or the beginning of their stories, so you would not know. We'll go through that soon in time. However—" She lightly pushed herself off her desk. "Does anyone have a guess at who this man I speak of is?"

The class certainly was quiet now, all confused and wondering who she meant. Ms. Grey looked at me. Her eyes met mine for at least three seconds, then she sighed. "Very well. Class dismissed."

Riiing!

The class piled out of the room. I stood to leave—

"You know the answer, do you not?" Ms. Grey was leaning back on the front of her desk again.

"Ethnone." I said without looking at her. I grabbed my bookbag and took some steps away from my seat.

"Ah. I see." She waved her arm at me as she smiled. "You knew Ethnone was the answer. Why not say it?"

My hand tightened on my bookbag. "I'm not one for talking."

"We're talking now, are we not?"

A pause.

"Yes." I walked towards the door and turned the handle.

"Think about coming to the afterschool event. It's in three days. On Thursday."

I pushed the door open and stepped into the almost empty hall.

The dishes done. The main room clean.

A math class dismissed, and the people piled out of the room. I waited until it was empty, then stood up. I grabbed my bag and walked away from my seat and out into the hall. It was vacant, maybe one or two people here and there. I needed to walk to my next class. I went past a corner towards a stairwell. It was the darkest corner out of all the hallways. I went into the stairwell entrance—

"Aye." A dark voice. I looked up and saw a cocky person who stood at the top of the stairs. His presence engulfed the area. "What are you doing around here?" He smiled. Pericly.

"No words again huh?" He halfway laughed, walking down half the steps and stopping right there.

I put my foot on the first step and moved tentatively up. As I passed, the energy around him whipped back and forth. I started turning to go up the next set of—

"You got something in you, huh?"

In me? I stopped with those words. What was meant by that?

"I can't tell who." His hand cracked as he made a fist. He narrowed his eyes more. "Who's your parent?"

Parent.

His eyes locked onto mine. All I could do was stare back. No words. Just staring. Finally, he leaned back, straightening his posture. "You're an interesting one." He turned down the stairs slowly, taking his time walking from the situation he had created. "Let's do this another time." His presence was gone. The feeling vanished.

That was weird.

Parent...

Whatever, though.

Life is life.

Watch from the distance and see what happens.

Asher made airplane noises as he literally played with his food. The chicken tenders were attacking the fruit, obviously to show that meat is the greatest of all the foods. He threw in some puns here and there, such as "Why don't we meat in the middle" and "Orange you glad I didn't bring bacon." His chicken tenders kept shooting at the cup of pineapples. The pineapples shielded themselves using willpower and imagination.

"Nooooo!" He put the tender in his mouth and savagely bit into it. "It's overver naow." He chewed his food like the tender was fighting for life. He swallowed and looked up. "You good?"

What?

I let out a puff of air from my nose.

Asher looked at me in a humorous manner. "I know you don't talk much, but you look like you're thinking of something specific."

"It's nothing."

"Just making sure dude." He picked up two chicken tenders and put them on a napkin in front of me. "Here you go broski."

"Oh no you don't have to—"

"Dude, don't worry. Live life. Be free." He bit into his other chicken tender. "Do you," he tried to say through his chewing as politely as he could.

Watching from the distance. That's what I do. I'll still keep a distance. However, shorten it a bit. Not much. Just slightly. Regardless, it will not shorten up anymore. The rest of this distance is solid. Keep it for protection. That being said…

"What day is today?"

Asher swallowed his food. "Tuesday."

I see. I think I will go to that afterschool art de-stress event Thursday. No. I have definitively decided.

I unequivocally will go to the afterschool Alkeeb Gods event.

Five in the evening.

At this time, I'm never here at school. This is kind of alarming, interesting in a sense. They will be out late tonight, so I won't get caught. I already prepped dinner yesterday so I could quickly warm it up when I get back. And I'll get back before them. This event ends at six. It takes about an hour to walk to the school from the house I take residence in. They'll come back around eight. A thin margin still within the threshold of possible.

Both of my bookbag straps relaxed around my shoulders. I walked towards Ms. Grey's classroom to see what this Alkeeb

Gods afterschool event was. I saw the dark classroom door. Nothing unusual. I looked back and forth. No one in the halls. Hmm. Well, I might as well see what's inside. I reached for the doorknob. Before I even touched it, the door swung open. I took

a step back to dodge.

Some girl that was maybe younger than me had pushed the door open to exit the room. She held the door open, turning her head away from me and continuing to converse with someone inside, smiling and giggling from the conversation. Behind her were desks that were moved to the edges of the room to create space in the center. There were a good amount of people around. Art and construction paper were every-where. Color pencils, markers, and more of this accord.

This was the crafts de-stress night.

I passed the girl and went inside. The lights were dimmed, which I didn't know was possible to do with plain old class-room lights.

"This was about to start." Ms. Grey. I turned to see her standing nearby.

"I thought I might as well see what you were talking about."

"Ah." She walked towards the front of the class and snapped her fingers. The room instantly gave her attention. "Welcome to the '*Alkeeb Gods* de-stress night.' Now that enough time has passed for you to come in, you all can now begin. Do as you like. Draw, paint, fold, build. If anyone is interested, you can try and make art of the Alkeeb Gods. The point is to de-stress."

The room was filled with a medium volume. The people around were chattering as they colored, folded, and created. I leaned over a desk and started folding a red piece of paper. I was trying to make...I'm not quite sure. It came out as a snowball. I failed.

Try again. Another ball. Fold some more. Another ball.

I looked at Ms. Grey, who was sitting at her desk, flipping through papers that were not for art. I looked back down at the ball I had accidently created.

How can people make swans, or any type of origami for that matter?

Either way. Folding papers.

The rest of the event was like this. Folding, a little bit of talking around me. It kind of peaceful. It was kind of nice.

Probably around seven in the evening.

The night sky was clear and quiet. No clouds, no wind blowing. The area was ordinary with no sound coming out of a single house. The one sound shuffling through the air was the sound of my shoes scraping against the sidewalk as I walked home. Both straps of my bag braced on my shoulders from each step. It was kind of a long walk back to where I take residence since no buses drove this late after school. I was close, just a few more minutes and I'd be back.

The feeling I had was contained yet building. It was like a chemical reaction, a small explosion almost, that was closed tightly in a jar. Freeing. I had a small smile on my face.

That was de-stressing. It was a lot of buildup and a final release. This was a release. Free. Sure, only for a little bit. But this moment. Walking outside under the night sky. The calmness of the environment. Doing something stereotypically normal that wasn't in my normal. That build up inside the jar was reaching the jar's limits. I looked ahead and saw the house coming forth. The buildup accelerated inside. I can't believe I did this. I—

A bolt of lightning, bigger than the utility pole nearby, shot down from the sky. An electric sound rippled the air. The bolt crashed into the sidewalk right next to the utility pole and made dirt, gravel, and small amounts of debris flipped feet off the ground. The light illuminated the immediate area. It was bright like a solar flare, and so quick I couldn't even close my eyes. The pieces of the sidewalk finally trickled down. They bounced off the ground and laid motionless. The lower side of the utility pole was charred in the most noticeable manner.

I didn't realize I was standing still until the bolt was completely gone. I hadn't moved. I stared at the area. The sidewalk was scorched and had a small crater. The utility pole was very, very, very slightly wriggling back and forth. The wires connecting to it were slowing down in their bouncing movements. The electric sound was still barely there but vanishing swiftly.

What the.

The sky was clear without a single cloud.

Where did that come from? Weird.

I walked past the scorch and crater and continued to the house. The build up feeling in me had died down after that sudden bolt. A calmness was in the air. I made it to the door, turning the doorknob, and stepping inside. It was nice. No one was there. All quiet. Just as planned. I smiled and closed the door behind me.

"Before class is dismissed, let us see the extent of this class's knowledge of *Alkeeb Gods*." Ms. Grey said with absolute certainty.

There were mixed emotions in the class.

"Who here knows each name of all three generations of Gods?" Ms. Grey tested the waters.

"His hair color's from an old generation," someone said as they pointed directly at me. The class broke out in laughter. Ms. Grey simply looked at the person and the class became quiet. It's not the worst one I've heard. I have been feeling good, especially ever since the afterschool event yesterday. It didn't affect me.

"I see that your minds need a break." Ms. Grey picked up a long ruler and held it like a staff. "The three generations of the Alkeeb Gods are the Primordials, who are the oldest of all the Alkeeb Gods, the Behiims, the second generation after the Primordials, and lastly the Kauzations, the current generation. We'll focus on the Kauzations comparatively more than the other two in future classes. Class is dismissed."

Riiing!

The class stood up and chattered as they exited. I parted through them and walked out the door. The hallways were piling with people. I walked past them and went to a darker, emptier hallway. I had to get to my next class.

"That was you, wasn't it?"

I looked over my right shoulder and saw an outline of a tense figure. Its fists were clenched. The voice it had was dark. Darker than the hallway. Oh great.

"Last night." The outline stepped forward and light off the floor hit its face. Pericly came into view. Oh great.

"Don't act like you don't know what I'm talking about, he said, walking quickly and closing the distance between him and I. Oh—

His hand lurched forward and wrapped around the front of my hair. My scalp burned in response. He pulled me forward, yanking my head with my body staggering after. Centimeters kept him and I apart. He stared down, looming over me, his presence engulfing the area. It wrapped around me like his fingers wrapped around my hair.

"That Surge last night." He breathed through clenched teeth. His fingers tightened and yanked again. My head and body followed. A burning sensation cascaded down my head to my neck. My blood pumped with heat.

"What are you talking about?" I grunted.

"I knew you could talk," he smirked with anger still flowing off him. "That Surge. You got it in you, don't you?" He stopped smirking immediately as his fingers gripped tighter around my hair.

"Have what?" I tried pulling my head back. My foot

stepped backwards to try and get leverage.

"What!?" He yanked me sideways and slammed my right into a wall. Blood was popping off inside. He put his face closer to mine. "You know what! Come on! Show me!"

Pericly stumbled forward a bit, his grip on my hair slightly loosened. There's now space. Use it. I pulled some of my hair away. A hand clamped down on Pericly's wrist and pulled backwards to get him to release his grip.

"No need to do this dude." Asher stared at Pericly. He was trying to pry open Pericly's fingers but to no avail.

I met Asher's eyes. "Asher, what are you doing here?

"Walking late to class, heard the noise." He pulled Pericly's hand harder, clearly to the hand owner's annoyance.

"You'll get in trouble if you get caught." I struggled against Pericly's grip.

"Aye don't worry. Let's just go—"

"You're gonna keep touching me?!" The air seemed to swirl with energy. Pericly stood hunched over in anger. "You know you have it in you too. I can tell from your Aura." He looked at me when he said the last sentence. "Neither of you are going anywhere."

Pericly lurched forward and let my hair go. He quickly rotated, grabbing a ball of Asher's stained white shirt at the chest. Pericly picked him up by that ball and slammed him onto the floor— hard. Asher didn't look hurt. Still, the situation was bad and getting worse.

Situation.

How did this happen?

"I'm someone you can't stop." Pericly held Asher down.

Why did Asher come out?

Wait.

It's like before. Why did he give me that food? Why did he sit at my table? Why did he and does he talk to me?

Life.

Life is change; it's all about how one reacts to it. It's just-it's just-it's just—

"You know what you have, don't you?" Pericly stared down at Asher as he kept him trapped on the floor. "You at least suspect it."

I can't let Asher get hit for me. I can't let anyone do things like this for me. Plus, there's a large chance of getting caught. I can't. Not for me. It won't last anyway…

Once I fight, I'll get in trouble of course. Back at where I take residence…It would end off with things going back to normal. All routine. I might as well admit and accept that. I said I'd watch from the distance. What I said exactly was that I'd sit back and see, kind of like from a distance. I already knew it would end the same or somewhat close to that.

"It was never going to last," I whispered to myself as I looked down. I ran over and shouldered Pericly off of Asher. Pericly didn't even stumble, but he did let Asher go.

Pericly took some steps away, grinning. "Now you're showing something." He turned completely to face me. "Good!"

I reached down and pulled Asher up with his right hand.

Asher looked surprised. He stood up and stumbled back two steps. He put his hands on his knees and looked like he was out of breath in an airless room. "Thanks—"

"Stay back." I said to Asher while looking ahead at Pericly. "You're stumbling. You should sit down. On top of that—" I looked away from Pericly to make eye contact with Asher. "You don't need to get in trouble with your parents."

"What about you?"

"Pay attention!" Pericly charged forward. I moved to the side and felt a grab on my arm. I wasn't fast enough. Another hand grabbed my hair and yanked my head way too far back. "This white hair of yours!" Pericly's grip tightened, and he began spinning around. He tossed me across the hall and more into the more brightly lit area. I tumbled down onto the hard floor and screeched to a halt.

My blood was pumping to a new heightened level. Something was swirling inside ready to burst. I slowly tried standing up. I was hunched over—slammed further into the light farther away from the dimly lit area. A hand pushed me again, this time into a yellow locker. A large bang was created when I collided with the metal. I turned and was pushed back first into the locker. The metal creaked on my back from the sudden pressure.

"And these orange eyes," Pericly sort of grinned. His glaring eyes locked onto me. His hands went to my shoulders and I instantly grabbed both of his forearms. He moved his head closer, "Let's see what you got."

Something was going to explode out of my body and it was going to have a form of its own. I pushed forward to get him off me. He shoved me back while smiling. I pushed. He shoved me back into the locker again. The feeling was taking over my body; it was going to burst.

"Get off me," I grunted.

"You're gonna have to do it." He shoved me harder into the locker, making an imprint. "You got to have something." Shoved me even harder.

"Get off."

Harder. "Come on."

Going to.

"Push me off, then." He shoved me in the locker more. "If you really want me to."

My grip on his forearms tightened. My knuckles cracked. Going. To.

Something in me barely cracked open. But it was enough. Arms struggled. Then, slowly, I pulled his hands off my shoulders. I started getting space between him and me.

"What the…" Pericly's face changed to confusion. "I'm not trying, but still—

Burst.

I pulled his arms completely open and thrusted an open

hand towards his chest. It impacted him for only a split second. A split second. It was more than enough. Energy coursed through me and around the area. The thrust threw Pericly straight back. He was in the air a few feet and slammed into a locker across the hall. When he collided with the locker a burst of energy waved through the air. He slid down and looked at me in stupefaction.

The air was still. My blood, that feeling, too stilled. Afterall, it was released. Asher was trying to come closer while taking his time. He still looked like he was gaining his composure while also suppressing something.

It was quiet.

What just happened? What did I just do?

"Hey!" An older Black man, balding, shorter, in a dress shirt and an orange stripe tie was running over. "What are you doing!?"

Pericly stood up. He glared at me, turned, and disappeared down the dimly lit hall.

"Who was that!" The balding man ran up. He turned to me. "Who were you fighting! I heard the noise and saw you push that kid." He got closer. "I know you were fighting!"

"Hold on," Asher came walking up looking better.

"Did you see what happened? Did you take part?" The balding man, definitely a teacher, stared at Asher questioningly.

"I don't know who he is." I said, staring at Asher, letting him know not to say anything. "I haven't seen him."

Asher must have got the message. His mouth was still slightly open like he wanted to say something. "Bu—"

"Then just you," the teacher grabbed me by my shoulder. He led me down the direction he came from. "Come on. We're going to the office."

"Detention for nine days. Wait out here for your parents to pick you up. I'll call them."

I waited. Hours. I sat in the principal's office as the rest of the day unfolded. Classes passed. Lunch, multiple of them. Next period, next ring. I sat in the office outside of the principal's room. Hours. I sat. The chair grew uncomfortable. Hours. Three in the afternoon. The bell just rang. Hours. Five in the afternoon. It'll get dark soon. Six in the evening. It's starting to get dark. Seven in the evening. Dark.

Eight in the evening. The clock ticked further.

They aren't coming. I already know. They want me to walk back. They won't pick me up. I'm going to have to walk back to that house. And when I get to that house...I will have to anyway. Can't change that. I'm going to have to walk home. I stood up, grabbed my bag, told the principal some excuse for them not coming while making certain I could walk home, and left the office.

I walked. How much time? Not sure. A walk is about an hour, maybe more, maybe less. The night was eerie. Perhaps that was just my stomach. Anticipation. Step by step. Closer to the house. I finally made it to the area I take residence in. Step by step. A strange calm went through me as if to counteract what I knew was going to happen now and the future. All routine. Admittance and acceptance.

A twig broke under my shoes, snapping me out of my thoughts. There was some chill in the almost autumn air, a few days shy of September. The wind picked up and made my baggy clothes flap crazily. I stopped and looked ahead. Down the street, ordinary looking as ever, with the kitchen lights on, was the house.

Here it goes.

I stepped towards the house, the house I take... a house, taking it all in as I went ahead. Step by step. Second by second. I got closer to the house. My shoes scraped the ground. Gravel bounced around my steps. Closer and closer to the house. Only a few feet away. Step by step. At the doorknob now. I gripped, twisted, and pushed it forward. It should be much past nine, if not ten by now, in terms of time—

"The boy's here," a man's voice said. "I guess you finally walked home." He laughed for a second. "Go cook, boy!"

I set my bag down and went into the kitchen—

"How was that walk?" The man laughed from the other room. "Pretty long, huh?"

I grabbed a dish and put it in the sink—

"It must have been good getting that energy out." His voice was softer now, deadly serious. He stepped into the kitchen slowly, like a bomb was about to go off. "I heard you let it out in other ways."

I scrubbed a dish—

"A fight!" The bald man, his face, and all came out of the corner looking like he was going to run into me as he yelled. "Do you know how that makes us look!?" He yelled to new degrees I've never heard from him. His veins were popping out of his face and neck.

"I expect that from someone like him," Elizabeth's English accent broke past the man as she walked into the room. "Are you stupid? Keep cleaning."

I turned and grabbed a dish—

"Ungrateful," the bald man eyed me, sneering to the point his clenching teeth could've snapped. "You're going to do this after we took you in!?"

I scrubbed—

"You were living in the gutter before us!" He looked at Elizabeth. "You wanna trade him in?" He raised the proposal to her quietly.

Trade me in—

"I'm not sure," her voice said sneeringly. "Maybe he'll make it up to us?"

Why should—

"Do you realize what position you're in?!" The man yelled louder.

Position—

"And you're going to do that?!"

Do—

"A fight! I bet you lost."

Fight—

"Course he lost," Elizabeth added.

Fight—

"Why would you do that, boy?"

Why—Why?—Why!

"Why didn't you pick me up?" I looked forward through the curtain above the sink that was halfway open. I was calm with a seriousness in my voice. It was said in a matter-of-fact way. It was nothing obnoxious. It just had full clarity and meaning behind it.

There was a long pause. Then finally, the bald man opened his mouth. "What?"

I dropped the spoon I was scrubbing. It instantly made a clattering sound come out of the sink. I turned around and directly faced the bald man. "Why didn't you pick me up?"

Elizabeth looked surprised. The bald man didn't even look at his wife. He looked straight at me. "So… you talk now?" His face changed, letting me know he was fathoming what was taking place. "It was a punishment. The beginning of one."

"When have I ever not been on punishment?" That hung in the air.

"Now listen here boy—"

"Day in and day out constantly."

"You're going to cut me off?" He looked confused and enraged. "Me?!" He stepped closer. "After I took you in?! You?! A child
like you!" His voice lowered suddenly. "We could give you a permanent punishment."

"The best days are when you're both out late."

His head went completely still. "What did you just say?"

He stepped closer. "I didn't participate in foster care for you! Boy!"

"You're going to talk to my husband like that?!" Elisabeth spat out.

The bald man, Calvin, didn't break eye contact with me. "We allow you to live here—"

My words came out quickly, "This isn't a home—"

"You don't have a home!" He slammed his hand as hard as he could on the table nearby and stepped closer to me. He and I were only inches apart. "You never did and never will!"

Emotion started building inside. I was trying to hold back, but it felt like it was just going to explode out. My fists clenched. Something was going to come out, no, break out, no, crack out, no, burst. All of the above.

Calvin stared me straight down and got dangerously quiet. "You want some truth?"

My entire body tightened. My face grew tough. Inside me was a jumble of everything as someone with only two arms was trying to hold it all together. Sooner or later, that some-one was going to drop one thing, some of it, or all. And the way this was going, it was going to be all, if not more.

Calvin suddenly became calm. "That's one of the reasons we took you in two years ago." He paused for a second. "You had just turned fifteen and already no one wanted you."

I was breathing louder. I was trying not to explode.

"How many foster families have you had by that point?" He continued without a thought. "We're just the latest one. You had about five or more before us. I forget which."

My insides were contracting.

"You even ran away a few times from the other families," Calvin laughed a bit. "They must have not really wanted you." He stepped closer. "Same as your biological parents."

"What's your point?" I looked at him waiting. "Tell me something new."

"The point is we just wanted a servant that we didn't have

59

to pay. One no one would believe or take sides with. At least it's less likely." He stared down, nostrils flaring. "You're a flight risk. You're on thin ice. With your age and track record, you and I both know if you do anything else they'll probably just put you in some group home." He stepped closer. "I know you don't want that."

I was breathing harder. "Your. Point?"

"You're stuck. And it's all your fault."

"Your. Point?"

"You can't do anything about it."

Something was cracking. Something was breaking loose.

Elizabeth started cackling behind Calvin. "Babe, it's like he's in quicksand."

"That's a good one," Calvin laughed. He stared directly at me, suddenly more serious and louder. "So, you know your place now, right?!" He leaned down, his face centimeters from mine. "You're just here to serve."

Something cracking inside me-breaking loose—

"There is nothing else you can do!" Calvin yelled louder.

cracking— building—breaking

"You should have only been quiet and cooked dinner!"

Cracking. Building.

Breaking

Loose

"And the disrespect you gave!" Calvin threw his hand behind him and swung it forward. He smacked me with the back of his hand, making a loud sound jerk through the air.

Breaking

Loose

"Don't touch me again," I stared at him with anger starting to bubble to the surface.

"You think you can give orders around here?" His hand once again swung through the air and smacked my face.

"Don't. Touch me. Again."

"More disrespect, boy?" Calvin again threw his hand back

and swung forward connecting it to my face.

Breaking

Loose

"You act as if this is the first time I've hit you," Calvin smiled and threw his hand back once again.

Breaking. Loose.

He swung his hand forward. My left arm went up to block it. The second his hand touched my arm, a flash of light engulfed the room. A shockwave pushed through the entire house. The sound was loud, sudden, and earsplitting. It was like when two microphones were slammed into each other. It was alarming and broke the entire atmosphere. Calvin went flying back. He blasted through a cabinet and part of a wall. Calvin stayed there, halfway inside the wall, halfway on the ground, and wasn't moving. He was unconscious.

What just...

"Calvin!" Elizabeth ran over to Calvin. "Babe!" She held his face and leaned in. She shook him shyly to see if he'd wake up. He didn't. He was out cold. He didn't look too hurt, but nonetheless was not waking up any time soon. Elizabeth twisted her head quickly. Her face scrunched up to an intense sneer, shock, anger, sadness, confusion, and more. "You! You pushed him that..." She looked shocked. "You—"

"Don't worry. I'll take my leave." I turned and started walking out of the room.

"You will Do NOTHING!" She was breathing hard. "Until Calvin wakes up!"

I walked into the hall and turned towards the front door.

"DON'T YOU LEAVE THIS HOUSE!—"

I grabbed my bag and walked out the door.

Does The Mind Cloud From A Lack
Of Understanding Or Overprocessing?

"No talking," the supervisor said. He sat behind his desk waiting for the time to fly. "This is detention."

I sat at a desk in the middle. The classroom was mainly a tan color and completely empty except me and the supervisor. I was the only one here. First day of detention. Now another eight days of this.

"It is a bit cold here." I looked at Asher across the table. "And you're saying you're not cold?"

"I mean when you got that supa hot fire, know what I'm sayin'?" He put his fist forward and kept it there. What is he doing? Wait, is this a fist bump?

"Oh," I said in realization. I fist bumped him, then returned my hand under the table.

"I've been thinking," Asher started off his sentence.

I looked at him waiting for him to finish.

"We should just wear alpacas," Asher continued. "Put grass on our shoulder so they won't starve."

"What goes through your head?"

"Couldn't I ask you the same thing?" There was a pause in the air. "How is that detention thing going? This is the third day—"

"It's alright."

"Just making sure. I could've helped—"

"It's fine."

Asher just sat there. I could tell he didn't know what to say. "Well, how are your parents reacting?"

Reacting...

"Are you in trouble or good?" Asher added to his question.

"Asher," I looked straight at him. "If I'm being honest...I don't know."

I walked through the front door of the house. It's been days since the incident, yet nothing has happened. The night it happened, I found an isolated tree to lean and sleep on. I did this an additional day. The third day, I quietly walked in and I slept in the bed I usually use. Elizabeth didn't say anything. Since returning to the house I take residence in, Calvin hasn't looked at or talked to me. I'm unsure if I'm getting kicked out or not.

"Go to the main room," Elizabeth said as she came from the corner of the hall.

I looked into the main room. There was a couch, a television in the front, a dark fancy-looking carpet stretching through the whole room. The room was more dimly lit compared to the rest of the house. Calvin was sitting on the couch. He didn't look hurt. He was just sitting waiting to say what he wanted to say.

"Hurry up," Elizabeth spat out.

I stepped into the main room.

"Grab a seat," Calvin said calmly.

I sat in a chair next to the couch and looked at him. "Look, I'm not sure—"

He looked at me. "I'm talking. Quiet. I don't know what that was in the kitchen. I didn't realize you have gotten strong enough to push people back that far. But, you're still weak. I woke up the next day like nothing happened." He looked at me. "I have decided what to do for the future." He cracked a smile. "I was trying to figure out how to show you what you have done is stupid and infantile. Then I thought of something. It's simple."

Does he mean what I think he means?

"The subsidies are a small profit with how little we have you consume," he smiled as he said that. He leaned back. "I've decided you'll use even less. Eat even less. Have even less. And we will make even more."

I didn't know what to think. It had some normalcy to it though.

"It's not like you have anywhere else to go," Calvin said plainly. "You're going to have to deal with it."

I thought about it and stood up. I started walking out of the room knowing what life had unfolded.

"One last thing," Calvin said across the room. "Boy." He grinned. "I want you in this house less. Come later. Stay away more. You don't even have to sleep here. As long as Elizabeth and I don't see you as much or at all, …then all is fine."

I understood and stepped further out of the room.

"If we end up seeing you more," Calvin said. "We'll take more of your rations."

I stood still then finally completely exited the room. The punishment I just received was nothing I'm not used to. I most definitely can deal with it. I walked down the hall hearing the echoes of my shoe steps.

"The oldest and first of three generations of the Alkeeb

Gods, the Primordials, reign ended abruptly. Zon, the youngest of the second generation, known as the Behiims, overthrew his father and took the throne. This successfully ascended the Behiims into stature and power." Ms. Grey looked around.

"Like, how was he able to overthrow his dad?" Someone asked.

"With the help of four of his older siblings and mother. It was actually at the anxious behest of his Primordial mother, Ay'ya, that Zon took a stand. His father did not treat his mother and siblings in a just manner, to say the least. To his Ay'ya's anguish and Zon's fear, he even confined some of Zon's siblings in Infern. Zon's father, Ay'ya's husband, is an extremely strong God. If four of Zon's siblings hadn't assisted in the overthrow, there would have been nothing except failure."

A hand raised.

"Yes," Ms. Grey looked at the one who raised the hand.

The hand went down. "What is Infern?"

"Infern." Ms. Grey repeated, saying the word more softly than the first time she spoke it. "Infern. It's not a matter of darkness when it comes to Infern. There are few places where no one, no God, would ever dare step in. Pain, punishment. That is what that place dictates. All nine circles of Hell are somewhere you'd rather be. What I am saying is not to prove a point. What I am saying is not hyperbolic. It is not a matter of would or could. It is. It is a deep abyss of torment and suffering."

"And that king put his kids there?" A girl asked, appalled.
"Yes."

"I can see why they overthrew him," someone else added.

"Speaking of overthrown." Ms. Grey stepped around the room as she talked. "In fear of ending up overthrown like his father, Zon began imprisoning his own children."

A hand raised.

"Yes," Ms. Grey looked at the one who raised the hand.

"So Zon imprisoned them in Infern?"

"No. He imprisoned them in an entirely different location, and there is not enough time to elaborate. The children that Zon imprisoned were Dittial, Telzyia, Missoa, Letnos, and Orthantehs, the last three names I'm sure you recognize from the readings." She stepped forward. "What...about...Zon's youngest child?"

Quiet in the room. Ms. Grey stepped around the desks some more. "He escaped. How?" Still quiet in the room. "X'stayn couldn't have done it by himself as an infant."

"X'stayn's mom," a girl's voice answered.

"Zriheia, who was a Behiimess, yes. Zon had imprisoned every child of his himself, until Orthantehs. Zon had one of the Minor Gods born from his siblings complete Orthantehs's imprisonment. Orthantehs was the last one born right before X'stayn. Zriheia noticed. When X'stayn was born, she tricked the Minor Goddess that Zon ordered to imprison X'stayn and hid him away. Zriheia now raised X'stayn in secret. Once X'stayn had grown enough to be on equal footing with his father, he tricked Zon into showing him where his siblings were. Zon had no idea the one he was showing was his son since years before his son was supposedly imprisoned. Once X'stayn found where his siblings were, he freed them and confronted his father, revealing who he truly was."

Ms. Grey walked to the front and grabbed a yard stick. "In a quickened synopsis, it was from here that a vast war, called the Behiimmach, transpired between the Kauzations and the Behiims. Ultimately, it ended with the Kauzations being victorious and the majority of Behiims being cast into Infern as their prison." Ms. Grey walked back to her desk and grabbed a stack of papers.

"We are out of time." She put down a stack of papers.

"Next subunit we will talk about the Gods individually instead of various random *Alkeeb Gods* stories. Class dismissed."

The bell rang right after Ms. Grey said it.

The class stood up going out the door. I stood up as well and the day went on. Class. Lunch. Detention. Somewhere. Class, lunch, detention, bed. Days and days and days. Time and time and time. It all passes by like a blur.

Detention was quiet. The clock ticked. I think it's day five into detention. A few days left. The supervisor had walked out needing to use the bathroom. Completely alone.

Tick tock.

Now I just had to wait for detention to end. My seat didn't make a sound as I leaned forward. I was getting bored.

"Ah, so you're the source."

Who was that?

Standing in the doorway was someone my age…perhaps a bit older. He stood straight up with his hands at his sides. It felt like he was the type of person who knew something everyone else didn't. His skin was dark brown. His afro-textured hair was cut low with some waves in it. He wore a solid, dark navy blue-colored bomber jacket and a gold-colored shirt under. His cargo pants and boots were both black.

And there was something else.

Something.

Else.

It reminded me of Pericly a little bit. No. Not the same energy. Yet. Yet. Yet. It was similar. There was more to him than anyone could ever remotely fathom.

He strolled on inside the room, knowing exactly his motives and a complete belief system to back it up. It was all confidence. "About time I found you."

The room seemed more silent than before. The clock ticks were nonexistent. He walked forward and stopped at the side of my desk. The room had nothing else except for him and all he presented.

"Kind of a long trip to Baltimore. Good thing it's pretty close to what I need." He looked around the room casually and brought his attention back to me. "Yep. Quite the strong Aura you have." He began nodding. "And a lot of it."

He suddenly looked at the doorway, hearing something. He turned back to me. "In a couple of days, I will return. Pack. Get your stuff in order." He turned and walked towards the door.

"What? Wait. Who are you?" My eyes felt like popping out from the randomness.

"Get ready," he said over his shoulder as he exited the room.

"For what?" I had entirely no idea what was going on. "What are you talking about?" I leaned forward in my seat trying to comprehend what had just happened. "For what?" I questioned louder after the mystery that vanished as quickly as his appearance.

"Hey," the supervisor was in the doorway looking directly at me. "I said no talking." He walked to the front desk and sat down. "You talk anymore, you'll get more days added. Who are you even talking to? There's no one here."

What in the actual-What? I was perplexed. For what? I wanted to know what just happened. I wanted to know what he meant.

A few days? Pack? It was here I knew something was - I don't know the words for it. What was going on?

"You seem tired," Asher said plainly. "But there's like some energy coming off you at the same time. Must have been a long day." He was looking at me as he was cutting something on his tray. The lunchroom was loud and almost blurred, but some blurs were taking actual shapes for once. The air swept through my white hair per usual. Things still felt a tad bit different; however, it wasn't in a bad way.

"I'm fine," I tried to wave off. I was in thought.

"Prove it with this chicken!" He slid his lunch tray over, showing a chicken sandwich cut in half.

"Asher, thanks but."

"Don't make me assume my ultimate form!"

"Well, when you put it that way." I slowly picked one of the halves and bit. I chewed slowly thinking about what happened yesterday. He said in a couple of days he'll be back. I had no idea what was going on. I had no idea what was about to transpire. Yet, I felt like I was at the edge of life as it compacts, expands, and morphs. It was strange from my point of view. Watching from the distance, seeing what happens. The anticipation, the confusion, the randomness, the timing.

I literally had no idea what was going on.

"You good? What are you thinking about," Asher looked at me.

"This chicken's kind of cold."

"I know, I gave you the cold part," Asher smiled.

"You know what."

Asher began laughing hard.

I shook my head in reply. There were other things on my mind. Maybe I'm just overthinking. I don't know. I just didn't know what was going to happen. And I still don't.

"X'stayn, King of the Gods," Ms. Grey stood in the front as if presenting. "A sky God who uses lightning at his disposal." She pointed at a random student suddenly. "You."

The student looked freaked out. Ms. Grey continued to point. "What about Orthantehs?" She asked the student.

"God of the sea?"

"Correct. One of the strongest Gods. You." She pointed at a different random student. "What about Letnos?"

"God of...how do you pronounce it? It started with a P," the student was snapping her fingers trying to remember. "Ah, I don't know."

"Parditont."

"Parditont!" She repeated. "That's it!"

Some chuckles went through the class.

"Letnos," Ms. Grey continued, making the class quiet down. "Lord of the Parditont. He is the God of death and shadows."

"So, is he like a grim reaper?" A student from the far back asked.

"Nothing of the sort."

"Ms. Grey?" A student said with their hand raised.

"Yes?" Ms. Grey responded.

"What's the Parditont?"

"The Parditont" — she wrote the word on the board — "is where mortals go when they pass on, with the possible chance of reincarnation. It is the afterlife. That is why Letnos is known as the God of death. It is in conjunction of his lordship over the Parditont, and his figure. He became Lord of the Parditont after the Kauzations's victory in the Behiimmach."

"You told us about Infern being worse than Hell." Someone said.

"All nine circles," someone added.

"All nine circles," the person who brought up the subject repeated. "What's the difference between Infern and the Parditont?"

"Infern is something else entirely different. The two are not comparable."

"Isn't Letnos bad though?" Someone asked and the room became quiet. "Like based off the readings he seemed…there wasn't a lot about him, but it said ssssomething about how he got his wife by kidnapping her."

"Oh yeah!" Someone else said, remembering.

"Yo, what?" Someone else.

The class became quiet. Some students leaned towards Ms. Grey for confirmation.

Ms. Grey stood and looked at the room itself. "He's still

one of the Thrice; although, he isn't of the nine Empyreans, which we will talk about later. He has committed some good acts of fighting in the wars. However, he has also committed egregious acts. I would consider him leaning more towards evil on a spectrum after what he did to Sprielia and Dittial."

"What did he do?"

"Dittial is the Goddess of vegetation and agriculture. Her daughter is Sprielia, Goddess of spring. Letnos, entranced with Sprielia's beauty, abducted the Goddess and took her to the Parditont. A distraught and heartbroken Dittial wandered the earth. Across lands. Across Apez Kauzus, the home of the Gods. She searched for her daughter tirelessly. She had absolutely no idea where Sprielia was, until Cresate came along. Cresate is the Goddess of magic, sorcery mostly to do with one's senses. She was also a close friend of Sprielia and a friend of Dittial. Cresate told Dittial what had happened."

The class was silent from her passage. Someone raised their hand. "So, did Dittial get her daughter back?"

"In a way."

The class was confused. Ms. Grey stepped around again. "Letnos is a very powerful God, especially within his own Realm. One cannot simply walk into the Parditont. If she found a way, she would then need to make it through the environment, find her daughter, and fight Letnos. Finding a way is already a difficult enough task. What could Dittial do? Dittial could only cry. Now, what was Dittial the Goddess of?"

"Agriculture, plants and stuff," someone said.

"Correct. With Dittial's in such deep despair, the vegetation on the entire planet began to die. Dittial might be the Goddess of vegetation and agriculture, but no one calculated her despair would cause such a dreadful degree of damage. People on earth began to starve and, even worse, die. This reached the rest of the Gods. They decided that Letnos had to return Sprielia. Lehgots, the God of speed, sound, and music, was dispatched to initiate this return. But there was a problem." Ms. Grey paused, showing the magnitude of the what was to be said next. "Sprielia had eaten six of the Parditont's African mangosteen seeds. You eat any food or drink from the Parditont, you are doomed to stay in the Parditont for as long as based on what you have consumed. Letnos tricked Sprielia into eating those six seeds. She is now stuck as the bride of Letnos, living six months of the year with him in the Parditont."

"But what about Dittial?"

"Since Sprielia can at least now come back for half of the year, the entire earth is no longer affected. It is now only the vegetation around Dittial that feels the effects of her despair. Half the year, the agriculture and vegetation around Dittial acts as it should since Sprielia is free to be with her mother, and away from Letnos. The other half, the agriculture and vegetation around Dittial are vastly affected as she cries. All because Sprielia is stuck in the Parditont coerced to her husband, Letnos."

"That's messed up."

"Therefore, I see Letnos as leaning more towards evil when looking as good and evil on a spectrum." She stepped in the front of the class. "Let's return to the main point. X'stayn, King of the Gods. Orthantehs, Lord of the sea. Letnos, Lord of the Parditont. It is the three of them together, these three brothers, that form the Thrice, the three most significant Kauzation Gods and three of some of the most powerful of all the Alkeeb Gods."

Ma. Grey looked around the class. "We are now out of time now. Class dismissed." The bell rang, and everyone stood up and began exiting the room.

I grabbed my bag and stood up, walking out slowly, then stopped. "That story sounded familiar."

"Did it?" Ms. Grey asked.

The classroom emptied until no students were left.

"Yes." I said processing the familiarity. "There are similarities between that kidnapping story and the one from Greek mythology."

"What do the Bible and the Epic of Gilgamesh have in common?"

I looked off to the side then back at her. "The flood."

"The flood," Ms. Grey confirmed. "A flood of such a magnitude was not mentioned only in those two mediums. There is mention of it within other significant words of substance in historical, cultural, and other sacred proportions. Other sources have shown that that flood must have been a real event. Although, the realism of the flood is not the subject of this conversation. The subject is the influence of one upon another. The Greeks have a kidnap story. Have you ever wondered where it possibly originated? Examples of this type of origination can be found by examining that same region. The Roman mythologies. A significant percentage of them come straight from Greek mythologies. As you know, the Alkeeb Gods predate all this."

I sat on the bed and looked at the room itself. Empty. Basically empty. Only a bed, which I'm sitting on, and a skinny, chest-high, dark brown drawer. Inside were a few clothes, all too big, and all I had. What would I even pack if I was going to? That thought made me smile and see the ridiculousness of the moment. Why was I thinking so much about it? That's what was so funny. I laid in bed and started drifting to sleep, leaving what happened behind, including the past, that person, packing, what he was talking about, and all. It was the last time I was ever going to see him.

Or so I thought.

"I can't wait to go home," Asher said. "I'm a bit tired."

"Yeah…" I trailed off.

"I feel you," someone said next to me. I slowly turned and

saw the same one, the same guy that appeared in detention days ago. Dark brown skin, and afro-textured hair with some waves in it that was cut low. Solid dark navy blue bomber jacket and a gold-colored shirt under. Black cargo pants and boots.

"Did it have to do with those Surges?" He asked me.

"Woah, woah, woah, who are you?" Asher looked confused to the point his head could've popped off his neck.

I couldn't register if this was real life or not. Where did he come from? He appeared out of thin air, sitting right next to me. He sat there casually, but with a posture of business. His convictions weighed and showed on his shoulders.

"I see you're trying to bring him along," he gestured at Asher as he talked to me. "I was going to talk to him later, but now's as good of a time as any."

The person looked back at Asher as he still talked to me. "He does have some Aura coming off him. Not as distinct as yours, but still."

Asher and I met eyes, then he and I looked back at the unexpected stranger, as more confusion started to bubble in my head. "What are you talking about?"

"I mean the parent," he said so simply it was as if I was already supposed to know. He looked at Asher. "Which parent do you have?"

Asher looked confused, as anyone would be.

Without skipping a beat, the person answered his own question. "You don't know, it's cool. Most don't until later. Who's your parent?" He turned towards me, and the question hit like a ton of bricks. That was and is a hard question. Parent...Parents...Don't think about that now.

"Okay, who are you?" I looked at him and needed to know this more than anything else in the entire world.

The person stared at me. He stared at Asher, then back at me. "Neither of you know what I'm talking about."

Silence.

"Is that right?" He seemed to say more to himself. "This complicates things."

Stares.

He sat silent for a second, formulating something.

Silence.

He sat up and leaned forward in my direction. He stared directly at my face. Nowhere else. Pure concentration. Pure conviction.

"Get ready to go soon," he looked at me blankly while having more meaning behind those words than anything. He turned his eyes towards Asher. "You as well."

Asher looked disgruntled. "I can't go anywhere, I have..." He quieted. "How do you expect someone to go with you out the blue like this man? What are you talking about?" He chuckled a bit.

"You can't?" The person said inquiringly to himself. "Let me guess, you have to stay for someone?"

"Yeah, I'm the man of the house, dude."

"Taking care of your mom?"

Asher became silent. "Y-yeah." He nodded his head.

"Did something happen to her? Is she in the hospital?"

Asher looked shaken. He breathed a little harder. "Don't you...Don't."

"So, something did happen." He looked at Asher wholeheartedly. "It was out of your control."

Asher's mouth was open, his bottom lip hanging lower than it should. "It-wha-how-?"

"You probably still don't understand it. Whatever happened, it wasn't your fault. I can tell it wasn't on purpose."

"How-how did you..."

"I know it's out the blue, but you need to get ready to go."

"Go for what?" I butted in. "What is going on?" I questioned with all the confusion bouncing around in my head, trying to make sense out of nonsense.

"No time to explain," the person said. He leaned back.

"They're coming."

That felt as if it literally hung in the air.

"They...?" I looked at him motionlessly.

"I would pull the both of you out immediately, but I can't pinpoint their location. I don't want us to end up running straight into their direction without us even realizing." He turned to Asher. "And now I know something I need to attend to."

"What?" I tried to ask. "What...are you talking about?... Who...are they?"

"No time to explain. You wouldn't believe me." He stood up and scooted his seat into the table. The person placed a paper on the table. "You dropped this." It was an assignment with Asher's name at the top.

Asher looked at it, silent.

"Pack essentials. I'll be back in a couple of days." The person walked away without looking back.

There was silence at the table. Asher kept looking off in the direction the person had walked away from. "Who was that guy?"

Silence. Air breezed through my white hair.

"Did you ever talk to him before?" Asher was looking at me with curiosity.

Nobody needs to know. I shrugged my shoulders and went back to my thoughts. They...?

I walked into the kitchen and looked around. Everything was silent since no one else was in the house. They were going out late again. A sliver of the dark night sky seeped through the crack in the kitchen curtains above the sink. The room itself looked clean. Untouched since...

I had my hands in my pocket and looked at what I came in for. The gash was very noticeable with pieces of drywall sticking out. Just a gaping hole, not circular or even. It was more long than wide. Part of the gash was bent and halfway off. It didn't break all the way.

Calvin and Elizabeth were surprised by the push I did. Somehow, Calvin didn't end up injured as far as I know. Pushing him through the wall was sudden for me as well. I wasn't trying to and wasn't thinking about doing it. That's the thing. I don't remember pushing. They said I pushed. But. I don't remember pushing.

They…

Who is that guy? He talks about packing bags, leaving, no explanation. Then he brings up "they" like I'm supposed to know exactly what he means. Parent…Then he figures out something going on with Asher's relatives, or something, right on the spot. He meant to talk to me more based on what he said.

What is this gash? Who is he? What does it all mean? I'm not sure. All I know is that the confusion from here will broaden its scope.

"The nine Empyreans." Ms. Grey stood at the chalkboard ready to write, her skin and hair shining in the classroom lights. "They are the main nine Kauzation Gods that lead the world from Apez Kauzus, home of the Gods. They each have a throne of their own." She grabbed a piece of chalk and faced the board. "You all already know a few."

The class settled and quieted.

"X'stayn, Orthantehs, and Dittial" Ms. Grey wrote their names on the board. "Letnos might be one of the Thrice Gods. Still, being the Lord of the Parditont and with his kidnapping of Sprielia, he isn't one of the nine Empyreans."

"Is it also because of Dittial?" Someone asked.

Ms. Grey wrote down "Dittial" on the board. "Yes. Dittial is an Empyrean. Of course she would not allow Letnos to be one. Ms. Grey turned her head to view the class. "Who is another Empyrean?"

"Missoa."

"Missoa," Ms. Grey wrote down Missoa's name on the board. "We've discussed her before briefly. She is the Goddess of marriage and family." She stopped writing. "She is also X'stayn's wife and sister."

"That's gross."

"I concur; conversely God genetics work differently. They're able to do this without the negative connotations and consequences."

"Doesn't X'stayn cheat on her a lot?" Someone else asked, but asked in a way they were more so saying it.

Ms. Grey stopped writing for a second. "When does he not, is the real question."

The class chucked while Ms. Grey raised her chalk. "Who else?"

Someone spoke out, "Isn't Nayleeuh one?"

"Ah yes," Ms. Grey began writing down "Nayleeuh" on the board. "Nayleeuh, Goddess of history. She is the daughter of…" Her chalk stayed connected on the board even though she finished writing the name. "That's a story for later." She faced the class. "Another God?"

"Zound?"

"God of war and blood. Son of X'stayn and Missoa," She wrote down Zound's name on the board. "Zound is very high on the hierarchy of the Alkeeb Gods, but he is not an Empyrean. He is a Major God. Name an Empyrean."

"Alytra."

"Goddess of love and beauty. Daughter of X'stayn and Missoa. She is an Empyrean. Who else?"

"Bracktius."

"Bracktius," Ms. Grey said as she wrote "Bracktius" on the board. "God of blacksmiths, metalwork, and forges. His parents are X'stayn and Missoa. Bracktius is an important Kauzation God yet is not an Empyrean. He is a Major God. Who else?"

"Telzyia."

"She used to be an Empyrean. Telzyia is the Goddess of borders and home. She is the eldest of her siblings X'stayn, Orthantehs, Letnos, Dittial, and Missoa. She gave up her Empyrean spot for a different God."

"Lehgots."

"Lehgots," Ms. Grey said as she wrote down the God's name, "the God of speed, sound, and music. Son of X'stayn and Missoa. He became an Empyrean after taking the spot Telzyia gave."

"Mynzonus."

"Another Empyrean, yes." She wrote down his name as well. "Mynzonus, God of archery and healing. Son of X'stayn and the gentle Behiimess, Lumoonah. Lumoonah was pregnant with twins, Mynzonus and his sister, a little before X'stayn and Missoa married. X'stayn was once more having an affair."

"What happened to Lumoonah?"

"She was cast aside because her twin brother tried to betray the Kauzations."

"Wait so they cast her aside because of her brother?"

"Not even because of her." A different student commented. "Yo, that's weird."

"Like this dude!" Someone pointed directly at me. "He never talks."

"Who else?" Ms. Grey asked, returning the subject to the Alkeeb Gods. She stopped writing. "Who's Mynzonus's twin?"

The class was still silent. "Oh, oh," someone raised their hand. "Ahlayniss."

"Ahlayniss," Ms. Grey confirmed as she wrote the Goddess's name down on the board. "The huntress. Goddess of the hunt. An Empyrean." She paused her writing. "One of the two Maiden Goddesses."

The class concentrated further on her words.

"Ahlayniss's beauty rivals that of Alytra's, if not surpassing hers." Ms. Grey almost said it in a way like a thought was occurring to her.

Someone raised their hand. Ms. Grey gestured to the person, and they cleared their throat, taking a breath after. "What do you mean by the Maiden Goddesses?"

She put down her chalk and turned to face the class. "Ahlayniss and Nayleeuh. It's as the name states. The two Maiden Goddesses. They do not marry or engage in anything intimate with men."

Some chuckled, others made different sound effects.

Ms. Grey paused to let the information digest. "Nayleeuh, as we know, is the Goddess of history. She wants to make sure her head is clear, with no other thoughts or distractions. Nayleeuh made no oath. It was a choice, her will."

Ms. Grey waited a second, signaling whatever came next was major. "Ahlayniss." Ms. Grey looked at the class. "Ahlayniss...is a different story altogether. Ahlayniss, to a certain extent...detests men. This started at a very young age. It was at age three she had decided to take up chastity. It, too, was a choice, but it would be an understatement calling it such. What Ahlayniss did was akin to an oath. Rumor says she killed men who have approached her, regardless of their interaction or intent."

The class chuckled as others were a little shocked.

"Did Ahlayniss ever fall in love?" Someone asked.

"No. Ahlayniss did not. She never did."

The students became quiet from the sudden information. No noise passed for a moment.

"Ahlayniss was arguably the main maiden of the two Maiden Goddesses," Ms. Grey continued. "Some think that she swore her oath of chastity to the River Z'yieh. That is the ultimate oath anyone can take. The ultimate."

The class whispered, processing the condensed information.

"Now, we are almost out of time." Ms. Grey waved her

hand, and the class went quiet. "In synopsis, the nine Empyreans are the most influential and arguably important Gods who also live on Apez Kauzus. These nine Empyreans are *X'stayn, King of the Gods and God of the sky and lightning, Orthantehs, God of the sea, Dittial, Goddess of agriculture and vegetation, Missoa, Goddess of marriage and family, Nayleeuh, Goddess of history, Lehgots, God of speed, sound, and music, Alytra, Goddess of beauty and love, Mynzonus, God of archery and healing, and Ahlayniss, Goddess of the hunt.*" Other important Kauzation Gods, who are Major Gods and are not a part of the nine Empyreans, are *Letnos, God of death and shadows, Telzyia, Goddess of borders and the home, Zound, God of war and blood, and Bracktius, God of blacksmiths, metalwork, and forges.*"

"How are we supposed to remember that?" Someone asked.

"It'll come up again. Class dismissed."

Riiinng!

Lunch was a little quiet. Asher wasn't here. Lunch just started but he tends to appear early on. Did—

A lunch tray clicked in front of me with food cut in half. "Yo bro," Asher smiled as he took his seat. He grabbed some fruit with his fork and scarfed it down.

Perfectly fine and normal.

My head hurts. Too many Alkeeb Gods and storylines. Too much school and writing. Too much living situation. Too much cold air breezing through my white hair. Too much confusion in general. I laid in my bed trying to doze off. It was storming outside. I could hear the rain plopping on the walls and roof. The pitter patters. Splish splashes. Running down the walls.

I can't sleep.

My mind feels jumbled.

The rain seemed to hit the house harder. Raining harder

outside.

I sat up. The room was practically pitch-black, but I could still see. It felt cold. And hot. Not median. Those two at the same exact abstract time. It should be around eleven, or close to midnight. Those two within this house I take residence in should be asleep. I need to walk. Around. I can't though. They don't want to see me or hear me. I can't risk waking those two up... then there will be no house to take residence in.

What has been going on lately?

Push or no push. They. Him. What?

That guy randomly shows up. Get ready to go...Go where ...? Nowhere. Somewhere?

What would change...?

Question.

Stagnate

Who is the "they" that guy speaks of? What was he talking about with Asher? It sounded like it was aimed more at Asher's relatives. His mother. A parent. Something happened and they got hurt, or something. I'm just guessing. It's not my business. No one is my business; however, how did that guy know? That's what I'm wondering. They're coming?

They...

What is going to happen in a few days?

I'm probably overthinking. Probably? Oh I am.

Possibly.

Maybe I shouldn't worry about it. Maybe. I'm not sure.

How does all of this add up? I tossed and turned in my bed as if there was an approaching feeling that was progressing closer and closer.

Sleep

I just don't...

I just don't...

Sleep

The guy.

Closer
I just don't
Sleep
Connections.
I just don't...
Sleep.
sleep
sleep
doze

Is There An Edge Of Possibility?

"Just to recap, there are three generations of the Alkeeb Gods: the Primordials, the Behiims, and the Kauzations. Ay'ya and her husband gave birth to the Behiims, who were ruled by Zon after he overthrew his father. Zon and his wife, Zriheia, gave birth to Telzyia, Dittial, Missoa, Letnos, Orthantehs, and X'stayn. Zon was eventually overthrown by X'stayn and the other Gods from the Kauzation generation, who are the main Gods we think of today." Ms. Grey stood in front of the class.

"Why are you telling us again?" Someone asked.

Ms. Grey continued without skipping a beat. "I'm making sure you all understand the foundations of *this* world so far, so the next part is not complicated. There are also Major Gods and Minor Gods, which are titles that can be mutually inclusive with the Kauzations, the Behiims, the Primordials, and Spirits. Spirits are also known as Lesser Gods, which is not a term that should be used when referring to them. In the *Alkeeb Gods'* world, there are also *Monsters*."

Ms. Grey stopped talking and looked around at the students, emphasizing her last words.

Some students started grinning, others making sounds of intrigue.

Ms. Grey kept her same demeanor. "Monsters can sound exciting in theory. Imagine the horror in real life."

The class fell silent, taking in the prospect that is the oxymoron of a real fantasy.

Ms. Grey walked to her desk and sat down. "Now we are out of time. This shall be continued. Final Note: remember, there is a senior year assembly in the auditorium next week on Monday. This class will be overlapped by that assembly."

The class cheered somewhat.

"Homework is still due. Class dismissed."

The bell rang exactly then. People stood up to leave. I did as well. I grabbed my decrepit bag and walked to the door.

"Jason Side." Ms. Grey said, feet behind me. I turned my head to see she was shuffling, filing, and organizing multiple types of papers as she usually did. The papers reflected a bit off her black-rimmed glasses. Without looking at me she continued. "Hang out after class for a moment." She grabbed a stapler, stapled a few papers, put the stapler down, and went back to filing and looking through papers. "Isn't that what the kids say? 'Hang out'?" She moved papers aside and grabbed other ones.

I walked back to her desk, pulled a seat in front of it, and sat down. "I don't know, actually."

Ms. Grey straightened a stack of papers until they were evenly on top of one another. "Acknowledged." She put down the stack and put her hands on top of a bare part of her desk. Her hands held each other as she simply stared at me through her black-rimmed glasses.

"You had your last day of detention yesterday, if I'm correct," Ms. Grey said more so as a way to start a subject.

I looked at her puzzlingly.

"Others talk more than necessary, and I was within range. Not purposefully. Others can be loud, or just loud enough."

It was kind of unexpected of her to ask. I wasn't sure of what to say.

"How do you feel?"

"Alright." I sat waiting since she would more than likely continue.

"Good, good." Ms. Grey looked down at a stack of papers, shuffled it, and put it back down. "You've been different lately. At least the air about you has been."

"Different?"

"I'm just checking in."

"Ms. Grey, I'm fine."

"Good, good." She moved some papers over and wriggled her glasses to fit them better on her face. "You're free to go."

I stood up, grabbing my bag as I went to the door.

"Make sure you do the reading, Jason."

I turned the door handle and walked out of the room.

How does one feel when going through the motions and then something just...

I was cleaning the last few dishes in the sink. Just a spoon and plate left.

How does one's heartbeat? Slow. Steady, as it should. However, what if there's something more to that beat?

I cleaned the spoon and rinsed it in the water coming out of the facet.

Like a buildup. An anticipation.

I put the spoon in the white drying rack.

A shiver down one's spine and body for its entirety.

I grabbed the plate.

How does one explain that feeling? The entire time I was washing dishes, I felt a weight on me. Like some feeling of buildup.

I grabbed the dish soap.

Beating.

Shiver.

Pumping.

Build.

The dish soap dripped onto the plate.

Shiver.

Beating.

Adrenaline.

Anticipation.

I turned the sink on.

What is this feeling? Why do I have it?

Scrub the plate. There were some specs on it. It looked like—

"Ah!" I gasped out. It felt like a sudden discomfort throughout my whole body. Not a pain. An irritation. A heat. It went through all my blood. All my veins. All muscles. Bones. Organs. Everything. Vision became fuzzy. It was like an electric shock. It was a blinding white light that engulfed my sight for a split second. All of this, my vision, my body feeling this sudden extreme heat, was all within a short second. And it all stunned me.

I dropped the plate onto the kitchen floor. It shattered instantly with an almost dramatic crash.

"What was that, boy?!" Calvin yelled from a different room.

My vision was already back, and the discomfort left.

"You're already on thin ice!" Elizabeth yelled out.

It became quiet and I looked down at the shattered plate. What was that...

That feeling. And the sudden spark and drop of it. The thing is that it hadn't completely left. There was still a slight shiver. Anticipation. It felt as if it was some sort of warning. Why, or for what, I'm not sure. I'm just sure of my confusion. Absolute, complete, without a single doubt or digression of confusion. What in the world is going on?

The feeling didn't fade. Not even during the weekend. Not even when I slept. Not even when I cleaned the shattered plate. Not even on the bus going to school. Not even during my first class. Not even now when the announcement went off to dismiss this first class to the assembly.

"Attention," the audio system crackled to life. "Senior year group one, you are now dismissed to the auditorium for the class meeting."

"Only fifteen minutes here," Ms. Grey commented. "You may go. Turn your homework in at the front on the way out."

Shuffling and chatter filled and started leaving the room along with the students who created the sounds.

"Jason Side," Ms. Grey said close by.

My head snapped from the sudden voice directed at me.

"Why are you still sitting?" Ms. Grey rhetorically asked. "Head to the auditorium. If you haven't already, place your homework in the front bin."

I realized that I was still sitting. "Oh." I stood up and walked to the door. I grabbed the handle, turned, and pushed the door open.

"Jason." Ms. Grey said from across the room. I turned and met eyes with her. Her dark eyes always conveyed thought, more meaning behind all her words. "Stay focused." Ms. Grey and my eyes stayed locked until I finally turned my head back to the doorway and walked out of the room.

Focus? My head was a jumble. Like I said, the feeling hadn't left. It felt like a weight on my shoulders, similar to the buildup before getting punished. That was throughout my body. That feeling persisted. Even when I went down the hall past the sea of people. Even when I saw the double doors to the auditorium from the lunchroom.

It.

Did.

Not.

Leave.

The room was set up like any other auditorium. A high ceiling that rose to around twenty feet. Rows of chairs stuck to the ground, divided into sections. Each section had a space and stairs between each. There was a stage in the front. The closer one sat to the stage, the more downward the stairs descended along with the chairs. The chairs in the back were higher, including the stairs that ascended upward to get to those chairs. The stage curtains were a dark red and closed.

I stepped out of the lunchroom and into the auditorium. A wave of sound hit me. Students were seated throughout, excitedly having conversations. People were in all rows, the upper and lower halves of the room. There were significantly less in the lower half, closer to the stage. That made choosing my spot easy. I walked past conversations, random words, gestures, and people to make my way to the front. There was an empty seat in the middle of this very front with no one around. My hand gripped it, and I sat down, quietly waiting for whatever the presentation was going to be about.

My mind wasn't, in contrast. It was nowhere near quiet. There were side thoughts that couldn't be made out, words that were too far to see. Still jumbled. I felt uneasy. I felt like there were flashes of heat on me that could pierce the soul. They were piercing to get my attention like someone was tapping my shoulder. Not even someone necessarily. Something. And the tapping was getting harder. And harder. And harder. And har—

"You must have bad eyesight if you have to be this far up front," someone jokingly said. I turned and saw Asher, this time wearing a jacket, leaning down smiling.

"Eyesight's fine." I responded.

"Well, I might as well sit with you."

"No, you don't—"

"Ah naw, it's all good." He chuckled.

He slid over and sat next to me on my left. I leaned to my

right. I needed space. In general, I need space. But today. To-day. Something was…

"Quiet down students," A teacher's voice broke through the air. "Get in your seats."

There was more shuffling with a little less chatter.

"Fill in the front rows," a different teacher's voice said.

More shuffling and movement. People filled the rows until teachers were satisfied. Small chatter went on around me, with a quiet amount from a random person who sat in the chair to my right. Asher was humming to himself to my left, waiting for the class meeting.

A teacher in a suit went on stage and opened the dark red curtains, revealing a large and wide white screen that descended from the ceiling. Attached to the ceiling was a projector that turned on once the thin screen was in place. On the screen was a presentation about the evaluation of overall letter grades.

"Good morning, seniors!" A man in the suit stood on the stage with a clicker in one hand and a microphone in the other to project his voice through the room.

The lights dimmed even further to a few tones above complete darkness. The room became quiet. I couldn't focus on any of it.

"Wow! It's a couple weeks into September! I say we're getting close to being halfway done with the semester."

Any of it.

Something else was…

Like I felt a constant anticipation.

Like a glass bottle was about to drop and shatter into infinite pieces, signaling something so far past comprehension, that not even a fragment of its properties and attributes could be fathomed within the complex imaginations of the very essence of fantasy.

Fantasy.

But

This
Is
Real…
What is this…?
"These are the grades for this class so…
It felt. It feels.
It felt like something about to hit its impending target.
Wait
Impending.
"Aye."
Coming.
The room shook slightly, like a small earthquake occurred for a second.

Asher tapped my shoulder. "Aye, you okay? You're a bit jittery. Like bruh, you neeeever move. What's up?"

I just realized my leg was bouncing. I needed to move. I needed to go somewhere. Somewhere else. Coming

Coming.

Who are they? The "they" that was spoken of.

The entire ceiling crackled above as it shook. Some people around let out yelps in surprise.

"Woah woah settle down," the presenter up front tried to say.

What was that?

Whatever, it doesn't matter. I –

Boom!

My ears split. Outside of the auditorium, it sounded like a truck crashed through multiple walls. Glass shattering, concrete breaking, pipes bending, the entire building shaking, cracks trickling. And then… Nothing. Just pure silence.

What?

Was?

That?

Screams seeped through the auditorium's closed doors. Everyone slowly turned to their left, looking directly at the doors. It seemed like a full minute passed. The screaming did not stop.

The teacher that was presenting pulled out a walkie-talkie and pressed a button on its side. "What's going on out there?" He whispered and let the button go. Static was the response. He pressed it again and asked the same thing. Nothing but static.

The other teachers in the room ran up to the presenter and whispered quietly. There were about six in total. The room started filling up with nervous reactions. Small chatter and scared gestures were exchanged throughout—

More glass shattered and concrete broke outside the doors. The screams became louder. And louder. The auditorium suddenly went silent.

Then, as if a pen dropped—

EAAAA!

Lights throughout the dim room flashed. The shrill punched the eardrums from the sudden existence of it. Someone had hit the fire alarm. Or something... The lights flashed from the alarms from parts of the room.

"Oh my god!"

"The hell's going on!"

The room grew louder from nervous words. Screams inside and outside the auditorium were stifled by the deafening alarms. I looked down and realized my leg was still bouncing. My leg never bounces. I really needed to move. I turned to Asher to see him looking a bit nervous.

"What do you think is happening?" He asked me.

I'm not sure. I just know I need to go. That feeling hasn't left me at all. In fact, it has only built up. Accelerated. Increased. I felt nothing except that. That anticipation, warning type feeling. My leg bounced more. I looked around, past the screams, past scared faces, past it all to try and see what was happening.

"Students!" One of the teachers in the front yelled. The

people in the room hushed, trying to decipher what to do.

"What's going on!" A kid's voice yelled out. More voices added on to this notion.

"Class!" A teacher yelled out to make people quiet. Astonishingly, it worked. Everyone went quiet. The only thing left was the blaring fire alarms and the screams outside the doors as everything possible was breaking. The teachers all in the front too looked nervous and scared but were trying to hide it. They were gathering themselves. One stepped forward, squinting through his glasses and facing everyone and me. His dark brown skin was hard to see in the dim room and disorienting flashing lights.

"This is what's going to happen!" The teacher who stepped forward yelled out in the crowd. "We think there is an intruder in the building—"

The class screamed while others yelled out profanities.

"Quiet down! This is important!" The voices hushed instantly in fear as the teacher continued. "It might be a terrorist. This is no time to lose our heads. I know you're all scared. We are going to leave the building and regroup elsewhere. We aren't going to take the doors to your left that lead to the lunchroom. We're going out the exit that leads outside to your right."

I looked to my right where the teacher gestured and saw a single reddish door at the back corner.

"We are going out through that door in a single file and we're going to regroup outside. Understand?" The teacher looked around to make certain there was no confusion.

The kids fearfully whispered and nodded.

Wait. Something's...

"Stand up and follow me." The teachers up front turned and went towards the exit door. The entire student body stood and stepped towards the exit door.

Something's off.

Anticipation.

Buildup.

I feel it all over. Something's—

"Hey dude," Asher nudged me. "Stand up. We have to go."

"Something's wrong." I whispered as I didn't stand. I'm not sure when, but my leg had stopped bouncing.

"What?" Asher looked baffled.

"Not out of that door." I gestured to the exit door to my right and the crowd heading towards it.

"That door is the only exit. It goes straight outside. We'll be fine dude," he smiled per usual. "The other doors had all that crashing and other noises coming through it. Plus, it goes deeper into the school, it can't be safe." He pointed at the doors to the left. The doors everyone used to come inside the auditorium. The doors that lead to the lunchroom. The doors that were now closed. The doors where all the breaking, screaming, cracking, and earsplitting sounds started leaking through.

Wait. Wait. Wait.

Where are those sounds now?

I stared at the doors to my left and listened. There wasn't a single sound seeping through like before. No, there were still screams, but that's not what I'm talking about. The glass shattering, concrete breaking, overall destruction. Where did all that go? I slowly turned to my right at the people in the room about to filter through the closed exit door.

Why is it quiet now outside those left doors...?

The teachers grabbed for the door handle of the exit door. One teacher gripped the door handle as the mass of people waited behind them.

Unless... Whatever is causing this havoc...

Is somewhere else around the building now...

My eyes widened and my head pivoted right. I looked at the exit door and the people around it. What are the chances—

A teacher barely cracked the door open when it snapped off its hinges and slammed into him. He flew backwards, crashing into a section of chairs. He urgently grabbed a chair, trying to pull himself up, clearly hurt but moving. Fog from the outside floated in from the now open and broken doorway. Outside light also beamed inside a bit. A monstrous roar blasted through the room, blocking even the sound of the still blaring alarms and innermost thoughts. My thoughts felt like they stopped. The shriek was animalistic. A rumble, throat rupturing. Beastly, fear inducing instantly. There has never been anything sounding like that before.

The roar stopped. No one moved. The world itself didn't move. That too stopped. Only a couple of seconds paused. Only. It was a heartbeat that had a day of its own. The anticipation, warning feeling was gone, as if to say there was no need for it now. Time zoomed back into the moment.

The doorway cracked as something slammed into it, making the wall connected to the doorway also crack. The wall, from top to bottom, nothing less than twenty feet high, all bent inward from the force. It was slammed again from the outside, creating more cracks. Whatever spot the doorway and wall were being slammed at was just at the right point to affect the entire room. Small amounts of debris trickled down.

"We need to get out of here!"

"Move! Move!"

People started shoving themselves out of the way, moving from the exit door and more inside the middle of the room. They flooded the place with their disorganization and fear of the unknown. The alarms and flashing lights continuing added more to the distress. Asher scrambled up from his seat. More people pushed their way inward as they screamed and yelled to get the direction they wanted.

The attack against the wall stopped briefly. The room fell silent as people were trying to see what was going on. Quiet. Everyone craned their necks towards the exit that no longer had a door. More fog streamed in through the gap. Other than the fire alarms still flashing and blaring, all was quiet.

I slowly stood up, staring at the wall and the outside light beaming through the doorless exit.

The wall erupted from a force. A gash was thrashed open in the wall. More outside light streamed in. Concrete, metal, copper, and more went soaring into the room. Sparks flared. Little spots of fire popped in the air. Half the wall cracked. It snapped in places and parts that started lightly swinging while hanging from the ceiling. The ceiling couldn't take the weight and it too started snapping. Small amounts of debris sprinkled down.

Whatever can't fit through the doorway to come inside is trying to create a new one to be able to fit.

A spark of fire floated down in front of my face. Metal creaked above me. Whatever was above was going to plummet. I stood frozen, almost dazed at what was happening. Something slammed into the wall again. The entire wall crackled. More sparks rained from the ceiling. The ceiling itself started caving in.

"Time to go." I told Asher as I shook myself from my slight daze. I sidestepped through the crowd of people and started running. I could hear Asher huffing behind me.

The mass of people flooded away from the former exit door towards the double doors that led to the lunchroom, which was now seemingly quiet. People frantically swam through chairs, running in fear pushing others out the way as they screamed. Quickly, there became a pile-up of a blockade of people all trying to escape through the double doors, a blockade Asher and I were in the very back of.

"What is this!" Asher yelled at me as people hurried around him and me like a raging river. A large yellow spark spiked out centimeters over my head. It popped and almost hit me directly in the eyes. Bodies pressed against each other, including mine. Breath literally and figuratively gasped out of lungs. The air grew hotter and hotter. I squinted behind me at Asher through the dim room and flashing alarms. He looked like a detailed outline.

The monstrous roar shook the very foundation of the ground. Another force slammed into the wall. I turned and saw a bigger gash was created. The large chunks of wall hanging from the ceiling were finally starting to win their battle. The ceiling was starting to buckle under the pressure.

Everything was all over the place and disorienting. People pressed against me who I could hardly make out. I could hardly move with how tight everyone was pressed to each other. It was similar to being in quicksand from the neck up. My chest, back, sides, legs, shoulders, and all were pressed. Cries and screams filled the air. The dark ceiling above was slowly collapsing down upon everyone and me. The fire alarms kept flashing as they screamed, and they did not cease. It was blinding and forcing people to move at the same time. Yet, people couldn't even move because everyone was pressed into one another, trying to escape through the same set of doors. It was the concept of nerve-racking being bottled up with a mixture of confusion. And then what was—

A long, thick piece of glass shattered on some chairs nearby. The monstrous roar grew louder. A force slammed the wall again. The whole room itself felt like it was tilted. A spark fluttered out as more debris fell. The ceiling was coming this way. I looked behind me. Asher was pressed against people, looking distraught and uncomfortable.

What caught my eye was something past Asher's head. On the other side of the room, the wall had some cracks that were kind of connecting. They were making the shape of a large, oddly circular doorway. They connected in a way to have space of over ten feet high and over six feet wide. There's no way...

I squinted to see Asher better and started straining forward through the people towards the lunchroom doorways. Asher did the same. Step by step, inch by inch, I had to use my shoulders and elbows to force space. My arms and hands stretched out as I literally swam in the flood of people. I slid past a girl who had tears streaming down her cheeks. It shined from the constant flashing alarms beaming on her face every few seconds. She wasn't the only one.

"Get off!" Cries.

"Hurry! Hurry!" Yells.

"What is that!" Screams.

"Out the room!" Panic.

It was weird. I felt as if I was and wasn't there because there's no way any of this is happening. People began to scramble quicker out of the room. About five feet away were the crowded double doorways.

Almost there.

A light fixture crashed on some stairs. Glass splatter covered the floor. The smell of dirt, concrete, and sweat engulfed the doorways. Everything and everyone was going in the same direction.

"Watch out!" Blubbered someone.

A large slab of metal smashed into a set of stairs to the left as the monstrous roar echoed through the room. I glanced behind me for another second. There were more holes in the wall, and the connecting cracks became more and more connected. Perhaps a couple more hits and it'll breakdown, making a big doorway. Then whatever is making it can enter.

That's not good.

Another light fixture crashed into some chairs. Glass showered down, sprinkling on everybody. More sparks fell and broke out as everyone advanced closer to the door. The alarm flashes blinded my eyes before I moved forward, slightly out of its range. There was maybe fifteen to twenty people left to go through the door and four behind me and Asher —

A part of the ceiling collided with the floor behind everyone, close to where the wall was being slammed into from the outside. I peeked behind my shoulder to see the severity of the situation. The ceiling was completely giving up. It was all falling.

Right now.

It was falling like a cascade, a set of dominos. It was plummeting from the wall that was still being slammed and it was coming this way. And nothing was going to stop it.

"Move!Move!Move!"

The last ten people ahead of me and Asher were shoving themselves out of the room. Concrete accelerated downward. Dust leaped in the air from the ceiling crashing into the ground. The doorways were about four feet away. I pushed forward, looking behind to make sure Asher was there and to see how close the ceiling cascade was. The cascade of metal, glass, concrete, and essentially all possible objects was only twenty feet from crashing on top of everyone.

No time left.

I strained forward. Pushed. Five more people. The ceiling was like a predator chasing its prey. Metal crashed. Glass shattered. Sparks upon sparks expanded and popped. Nine feet from everyone. Glass and metal crashed centimeters to my right. Dust bounced in the air and sprinkled on me. I concentrated forward. Someone tripped out one of the doorways rushing to get out of the room. Two people left—

A chunk of concrete bashed into the ground two feet behind me.

Gooooo!

I hurtled forward with Asher right behind me and pushed through one of the doorways. The last few people, pieces of concrete, and glass followed. Sudden light hit my eyes. I immediately closed them and tripped forward rolling onto the floor like a log in a lake. I rolled roughly on my shoulder and came to a stop.

I need a pause. I need...

I laid there. On my back. Eyes closed. Heavily breathing...

…Not moving.

I just-I…I just can't.

I sat up. My left shoulder and forearm burned in irritation. I touched them instinctually. Wet. Sweat, of course, but it felt thicker. Dry. My tongue was so dry. Water. I need water. My spine cracked as I sat up on the ground. I looked at myself. There was more than some dust on me. Shards of glass stuck in my oversized clothes. The blueish thermal-looking cotton shirt I wore now looked more like a gray. There were slashes on my decrepit black shoes. My large grayish pants had a few rips and tears I didn't realize were there until now. No. They weren't there until now. My legs were sore. That I could tell without getting up. That's why I didn't want to get up. Pains, aches, discomfort, burning all over. My vision was blurry like a camera out of focus.

I can't focus. Everything that just happened is indescribable to say the least. I know I'm confused. I know I'm in pain. I don't know exactly how I feel. It's all over the place. Neutrality. Nervousness. Surprised. A small amount of fear. Adrenaline. A daze. Exhaustion. Blocked, walled-off. I can't see where the point should pin. All the above? Sweat beaded on my forehead. I have no idea how to process anything around me. I feel like I'm sitting in a pitch-black place with no relative walls, ceilings, floors, or boundaries. I'm there, but at the same exact time I'm not. It feels like that shouldn't and isn't possible.

What is possible though?

"Gah—" I tensed trying to stand up. My brain was waving from the inside of my skull back and forth. I put my hand against a wall to leverage myself. I slithered my right side on the wall and put my back against it to straighten my standing posture.

I had to…pause. At least for a second. Breath: In; one, two, three. Out; one, two, three. I somewhat shook my head. Good. My brain stilled. My body relaxed a bit. My eyes opened and were attentive. I looked ahead and was shocked to see my surroundings.

A scream cut through the room, a girl, very young, by the sound of her shrill.

There were people hastily running, the fear obvious. Teachers, students, some from the auditorium who had managed to escape, were quickly making the surrounding lunchroom vacant.

The lunchroom? I wouldn't describe the room I was in as a "room" anymore. At least, what was left of it. I know the auditorium was now in shambles, and that's me being nice with the description. But this room... I'm not even sure it's the lunchroom. Is it? This can't be emphasized enough because it felt like the same room I just rolled out of. The comparison between this room and that, the auditorium now and the lunchroom now, is what took me by surprise.

Trashed? Wrecked? Demolished? Devastated beyond belief? Ripped wires hung from the ceiling like a field of grass. Little sparks discharged from them without any sort of pattern. Tables were thrown out of the way. Most to all of them were smashed as if meteors had crashed into them. Some were smashed uncleanly in half with the wood splintering across the floor in agony. Chairs bent. Burnt. The smell was in the air, and it showed its source through parts of the walls being burnt. The room used to be mostly white. It was impossible to tell now. The lighting was sort of dim since the lights in their fixtures were broken with a few flickering.

My toe inched to the left. I heard a crackle. Glass. The floor had large scrape marks and depressions randomly throughout.

Another scream, a male's this time. A teacher was running across the room. They were not leading students to safety. A full panic.

The vending machines across the room were unrecognizable. They might as well have exploded. One of them was in half. In half. Another was bent at an impossible angle. The glass from each was of course shattered and scattered across the world. This here, this can't be the lunchroom. It cannot. But it is.

What could not be overlooked was the amount of light coming from the back to the left side. Natural light. Natural. Light. A large hole, a gash really, leading straight outside was in a wall that was maybe one foot away from where the hallway intersected at the back of the room. Whatever destroyed this room created that hole to come in and out…then whatever it was also more than likely went to the outside of the auditorium doors, making the whole place cave in.

What was outside the auditorium doors?

I gradually pushed myself off the wall and walked more so to my left. I had to find Asher, check in on him.

Feet pounded the floor around—

"AHHHHHHH!" A girl, running down the hallway at the back of the room, also had tears on her face.

More shoes pounded and echoed, more people ran, and more tears sprinted through the hallway in the back.

Stop gawking.

Move.

Asher couldn't have gone far.

Soon enough, I saw Asher kneeling down, staring intently at the doorway that used to lead to the auditorium. It was now caved in by debris like a landslide had attacked. That basically is what happened.

"I see you're not too scratched up," Asher turned his head to look at me. He went back to examine the caved-in doorways. "Everyone made it out somehow. Even that teacher that got smacked by the door and went flying." He turned his head to look around, then went back to examine the caved-in doorways. "They're gone now, just kept running. I think teachers would usually stay for the students, but this isn't elementary," he let out a puff of breath from his mouth. "And with what we're in the middle of." He shook his head. "I can't blame them."

I looked around the room again. Have I ever stopped looking around? The room was mostly empty of people, outside of the ones running through to escape to another part of the building. They're either hiding or running.

More screams came from the back.

All of this transpiring…

"This is crazy, huh?" Asher asked. It sounded more like words to be said than an actual question. His face conveyed it all.

"…Yeah…"

A lightbulb above him and me burst, making Asher and I flinch. A small amount of glass shards sprinkled down. Fire alarms throughout the school could be heard abruptly like a sound director finally decided to put them into focus.

"Okay, time to depart." I brushed my shirt for a second. "There are multiple exits towards the back of the school. That seems to be where some people are going. Find an exit. Get to your house." I turned from Asher and took steps through the lunchroom.

"Whoa, whatcha doing?" Asher ran up to me.

I turned my body halfway and looked at him. "Getting out of here on my own. There isn't a close exit nearby. I'm going down a few halls to find one."

"Without me? I need to find an exit too and neither of us know what's going on here." He stepped forward.

"You saw what happened in that room back there. What made it worse was all the people packed into one place. Whatever happened in that auditorium could happen anywhere else in this school. This is dangerous. All of this is dangerous." I turned from him and took two steps away. "It'll be better to stay separated." And you actually have a family to go back to.

"Dude don't worry. I got you."

"I'm not one for people." Got me? Got? Me? Irrelevant.

"But that doesn't mean…" Asher trailed off. I could tell he was focusing on nothing except what was said. Exactly. Focus, which is what I needed to do. Focus. It felt like something could be following. That's a terrible thought.

I went a couple more steps forward into the room as it went silent between him and I. "You'll be fine. Find one of the exits." I called back to him.

I walked forward going towards the large hole in the wall.

Screams and footsteps ran through the hallway, passing me who was at the edge of it.

I looked outside through the giant hole, easily being feet tall and wide. The early sunlight. The extreme fog. I started to take a step. Stop, my foot did just that in midstep. Something felt…whoever made this hole, I shouldn't use it as an exit. I turned away from the hole. I'll go through the school towards the back.

I took off, turning left down a hall. I stepped on broken glass and various liquids that I couldn't identify. There were some people still running, not a large number, but an amount that couldn't be ignored. They passed, fear on their faces. What were the options? I skirted to a halt and looked back and forth. There were two options. Either go backwards to the lunchroom or keep heading down the long hallway I didn't exactly plan to use in the first place. I was just aiming to get to the back of the school. Keep heading down the hall it is. Without the flashing lights, the hallway was dark as night. One or two lights down the path flickered with a buzzing sound. The fire alarms vibrantly flashed making the only sufficient light source constant blinding spotlights straight to the eyes. Sounds of quick movement, scuffs, broke through the air, some from people who ran past, others from what seemed to be the air itself. Eerie. It reminded me of those horror movies. However, this was real.

"AHHH!"

More people rushed out of the darkness. Eight in total. At full speed they ran straight past, around me without a single look anywhere else. Shoes skirted down the halls disappearing from sight and sound. I ran deeper into the hall. Each step the path grew darker. It wasn't anywhere near pitch black mainly because of the flashing alarms. Still, the interior itself was sinking further into darkness. Somehow, the yellow lockers to my left and right stood out as I ran. What made everything jarring was that it was a late evening inside the building, but hardly ten in the morning in actuality. No, it wasn't really that. It was a feeling. A presence. I'm not sure exactly where but it was there.

More people rushed past my right—

The building shivered like a house would vibrate if a door was being slammed shut with full force. I slipped to my right, hearing my shoes squeak the whole way. My hand held out and made contact with a locker. I stood there, feeling the shiver's aftershocks.

"OH!" Some people in the hallway grunted and screamed. "PLEASE!"

What in the world was happening?

A monstrous roar trembled the very air molecules, making the building shake once again. Drop ceiling tiles and a thin plastic bar landed on me. Instinctively, my arms went up to protect my head. Fluffy blueish-gray insulation followed. None of it hurt. It just came out of nowhere. I brushed it off and looked around. Soundless, outside of the alarms and people. And the roar... I need to keep going. However, I should be careful. Running blindly isn't a smart decision considering the circumstances. I started walking deeper into the hall.

There were less people around. There hasn't been a copious amount I've encountered since the auditorium, and the number keeps dropping. The hallway was becoming further emptier than before, now being practically completely empty. If anything, it was making the hallway feel longer. Nothing has felt this long before. In the distance there was another horrific roar. Animalistic was a word that couldn't do justice in describing it. Wait. Not in the distance. Closer. Closer to me? For me? What is that? It wasn't as close as when I heard it in the auditorium, but it was closer than when the drop ceiling tiles hit my head. What was making that roar…? I didn't think about it much in the auditorium. Now, as I walk down this dark passage, I am truly wondering.

Each step was a weight of unexpected. There wasn't enough air in the world. My body heated up. A stream of sweat went down my face. Was I lost? There was nowhere else except straight. No other choice. Some sparks flickered in the ceiling. Wait, that wasn't me getting hot. The area was heating up. Wait what's that—

Three lockers to my left dented outward, looking as if someone's stomach, in a cartoonish manner, had filled with a large and perfectly circular bubble. It was as if something hit the lockers abruptly from the inside.

A yelp came from a girl rushing past with a guy.

No, not inside. Slammed…from the outside of the school walls… The lockers were slammed again from the outside. One of the lockers a metal door flew off. Automatically, I ducked. The metal door spun over my head and bashed into lockers to my right. It bounced off the locker and hit an alarm killing the light spinning in it. A monstrous roar filled the area, giving an invisible presence that made it all the more penetrating. It wasn't right on top of me. But. It certainly was closer. Go!

I rushed forward. Monstrous roars echoed through the building. As I ran, the lockers on my left continued to be slammed into. It wasn't just that. The slamming was following my direction. Sparks in the ceiling flickered harder from the force. A locker door flipped over me and banged against the lockers to my right, almost hitting the few fleeing people left. I kept charging forward. The locker dents and door crashes followed. Alarms screamed and flashed constantly. The sparks in the ceiling expanded further.

The wall outside of the school, where the lockers were attached to the left, slammed in rage. That slam was stronger than the others, shaking the ceiling. Yellow sparks exploded, pouring downward. My skin was singed instantly. I felt stings racking down my neck. Another slam. White sparks broke out from the impact. They popped off, spiking the right side of my body.

Go!

I pushed forward. I squinted and saw light ahead. It wasn't the alarms flashing. It wasn't sparks. It wasn't a newly lit fire. It was outside light. A large amount shined on the glistening hallway floor. I concentrated on the light ahead. Rectangularly shaped. Long. Thin. Four sets of them. It was only a few feet away. Push! I dashed the last few feet forward to the light sources aimed at the floor—

Gah! My feet tumbled over each other. I rolled and ended up sliding forward into the light on my back and conveniently away from the lockers. The light sources were emitting from four long glass windows to my right.

Decide where to go. To my left was the entrance of another hallway. That should lead to the back of the school.

Perfect.

I sat up quickly, taking rushed breaths as a car siren went off. Pause. Why would I hear that through all the noise? The siren noise became louder. I didn't move. It wasn't because of some volume increase. I looked to my right through the glass windows. The windows were the type that didn't open and didn't connect to the floor. Through them, I could see the foggy, darkish, cloudy sky. It was hard to believe it wasn't ten in the morning yet. Also visible outside those windows was a car—an incoming car—

I scrambled myself up. My shoes intensely scuffed the

floor. Come on, come on! That car wasn't driving. It was hurling through the air. My legs were in heat and pain as I pushed myself forward down the hallway leading to the back of the school. Faster! Come on! That car was picked up as if it was some toy and tossed. There were only a few seconds before—

The car crashed through the windows and concrete behind me. Glass flew. Debris scattered. Odd patches of dirt rained down. Specs of everything pelted my backside. My shoulder blades ended up with most of it. The backs of my legs were hit especially with concrete clumps. I slipped again, this time going feet first and sliding across the floor on my spine. The car siren gained massive ground along with the car itself. I couldn't get up. Then, everything laid motionless.

Not resting. Gaining my bearings. The car siren died along with its headlights. The crash must have been too much for it. My blood was pumping. It was cold and hot at the same time. It? No, I was cold and hot. I rolled on my side. Shards of concrete pricked. Ouch. My right hand went down to help me stand. The floor was cold. Hard. I looked up, then back down. I managed to get to my hands and knees. I peeked my eyes up and stared at a scene.

Stuck would be an understatement. Practically molded into the wall and remaining glass on the windows. I breathed in harder, taking in my demolished surroundings. The car was stuck, front first, midway through the wall and windows. It was scratched, torn, with pieces falling off. The silver paint wasn't noticeable through all the other damage unless it was pointed out. Cracks spiderwebbed through the windshield. One of the side windows was nonexistent. The walls and windows surrounding the car were relatively intact, making the car look like it wouldn't budge anytime soon.

I pushed myself up, standing weirdly on my own two feet. I searched around the car for any spaces that I could use. The small gaps between were exactly that. Too small. There was no safe way to slide past the vehicle into the outside air. On top of that, whatever tossed the car was in that direction… I needed to leave as soon as possible.

What's shaking? Oh, that's me. My stress and confusion encompassed all. No breaks were in sight. I was too tired to run but I knew I had to keep moving. The alarms hadn't stopped blaring and flashing. My blood hadn't stopped spiking. The building hadn't stopped feeling cold. The odd presence of something unexplainable hadn't stopped.

What

was

going

on

?

I turned around and looked once again down the hallway that led to the back of the school. Ahead, some hundreds of feet, was a door. A door with a small rectangular glass window. A window showing the foggy, dark, morning outside. A door leading to the back of the school.

All this running, and the end of it was right there.

I pushed my legs straight forward, jogging further down the hall towards the exit backdoor. My body was too tired to run fully. Lockers lined both sides of the hallway. It was like most hallways, with a different hallway that intersected ahead. I didn't focus on that. The intersecting hallway was there simply to pass by. Nothing mattered except that exit door straight ahead. It wasn't too far now.

I stepped into the intersecting hallway about to quickly pass by—There were footsteps to my right running towards me—

"Oh, there you are. Good timing."

I recognize that voice— I automatically turned and saw Asher coming up. What? I stopped running immediately, standing in the middle of the intersection. What? I looked straight at Asher and nowhere else. What?

"Aye, you cool?" He asked.

"What are you doing here?"

He looked a tad taken aback. "I heard all that noise in the same direction you went, so I came to check."

"You don't need to check." I turned my face away from him, looking forward towards the end of the hall. "It's too dangerous. This school is caving in."

"Couldn't leave you hanging."

"I can deal with it." I turned back to him. "You should have been gone by now or close to finding an exit."

"Well, I'm already here," he answered like it solved all the questions in the world. Nothing else was exchanged. The only thing interrupting the lack of exchanges was the still blaring alarms.

"Alright," I finally concluded, turning from him. I started jogging straight down the hall, continuing my way to the exit. Asher followed, being a step behind me. "The closest exit is right there."

There was about forty feet to go. The door was shrouded in darkness, juxtaposed by the dark, cloudy, foggy sky streaming through the small, long window. Although both were dark, one was darker. It made it feel like a spotlight, a sign. It was the only thing of importance. The only thing in sight.

And something else.

What was that? I stopped jogging and squinted down the hall around the door. Something was off.

Asher stopped right behind me in reaction. "Why are you stopping?"

I squinted harder. There was an outline. A silhouette. It was of a large person towering at the end of the hall, right before anyone could get to the door. I know this silhouette.

"It's about time," said a dark, deep, cocky voice. It engulfed the surroundings. Instantly all the blaring alarms in the area shattered simultaneously.

"What the—" Asher blurted.

The hall was practically pitch black now. It was quiet. Only alarms from afar could barely be heard. "I've been waiting." I know this voice. Darkness filled the room from the voice alone. It held all attention, forcing it all to be held upon whatever was making the voice. Nothing else.

I know this feeling. The silhouette stepped closer, making it much clearer. It was built. The silhouette kept taking steps closer making the silhouette itself disappear and a person took its place. He smiled cockily.

"Pericly," I whispered to myself.

"All the other exits and pathways are blocked off," Pericly announced with glee. "That's my fault, that's all on me. There are no other ways to go."

I stood there in complete disbelief. There was no possible... My blood pumped with more intensity. What is —

"They're still trying to find you two outside," Pericly sneered around.

Words wouldn't come out.

"Weeeell all three of us." He straightened his head and stared directly at me. "Especially you."

A strange quiet went in the area as the building shook from some impact.

"Round two," Pericly continued stepping forward. Closer and closer and closer —

He doesn't mean —

The building was struck again, shaking at its very foundations. I spread my arms out to gain balance. Asher almost fell, veering his arms onto a locker to the right. Pericly didn't flinch. He continued stepping closer and closer and closer.

"Pericly, we don't want any trouble." Asher abruptly exhaled.

"You wait." Pericly continued taking steps forward, seemingly darkening the world around him. Closer and closer and closer. "First it's that white-haired one."

My blood prattled. I'm not ready for this. Not at all. Last

time he wasn't trying. Last time all I could do was push him. This here. This—

The building convulsed. Asher grabbed a locker, almost losing his footing. I slipped and ended up in a partway kneeling position. My hands gripped my knees to steady myself. I eyed the ground, still feeling off-balance. Contrast this with Pericly. He was taking his time, tasting himself in the moment, barely ten feet away. Closer and closer and closer. It felt like there was no way to stop this. No way to run. No way to hide. The one thing that was certain was being trapped.

"This is happening," a closer Pericly's sneered. "Now."

"I agree."

That's a different voice. Not Pericly, not Asher, not me. Who is this?

Confident slow movements. Each boot step could shake the ground just off conviction alone. The steps stilled, boots silenced; yet, it said more than anything else today. It took command of the situation instantly. There was an engulfing feeling that Pericly created every time he showed up. This was not that. The difference here was the execution, the reasons behind it, the intent. The person it came from.

Standing two feet in front of me was someone my age...perhaps
a bit older. He stood straight up with his hands at his sides. He wore a solid dark-colored bomber jacket, and black cargo pants and boots.

It's dark in here, so it was difficult to tell. I couldn't get a full glimpse since my hands were still on my knees to steady my balance, making me lean downward. His back was towards me as he faced Pericly unwaveringly. There was already enough tension in the air. Adding this stranger's appearance made Pericly visibly exasperated.

"Come on!" Pericly snarled. A circuit must have broken above making white sparks rain down. "Course-eh it doesn't matter." He unexpectedly calmed. "You know I'm not here for you. I'm not here for you at all. Don't make this take long."

"I'm one for winning races," the stranger said. "So, let's go slow and steady." He took two steps forward, unyielding.

Pericly laughed. "You have little Aura coming off you. How do you expect—"

"Pericly," the stranger cut him off. "There are four of us in one spot. One of us is a beacon enough. Four is a spotlight's version of a nuke. You and I both know there isn't enough time. There's probably three minutes at best before they tear this school apart to find us."

Pericly gritted his teeth and narrowed his eyes. He looked like he wanted to be in denial but understood the truth far too well to be consumed by that river.

"There are only two options," the stranger said. "There are three minutes, max."

"Three minutes is enough," Pericly frowned—

The building was struck once again. One of Asher's feet slipped. He ended up gripping a locker door handle to not fall completely. My knees buckled making me bend further down and gripping them tighter. The stranger and Pericly didn't even tilt. They didn't even flinch. Pericly's face narrowed in annoyance.

"Two minutes," the stranger simply said. He took two steps to the right. "Or less."

Pericly noticed and became increasingly agitated. It was the look of someone waiting for something they now knew was even farther away than first anticipated. Pericly exhaled aggressively. He breathed heavily, brooding the circumstances. He took slow steps backwards into the shadows. "You white haired." He continued taking more steps, now being replaced by the silhouette once again more and more as he stepped further back. "Jason, was it?" The silhouette shrank. "And you," he aimed his "you" at the stranger. "You're always like this." He spat, sinking further into darkness, his silhouette completely disappearing.

"I'll postpone this." Pericly's voice echoed through the hall. It was the last trace of him.

"You guys alright?" The stranger asked. I finally breathed enough and looked up at him. He was now facing me.

I know this face.

My eyes widened slightly as I was taken back a bit. "You're that." From detention. From the lunchroom. From days and a few weeks ago. From him telling me to get ready. From this very moment.

The person grabbed my arm and helped me stand up straight. He looked past me, towards Asher. "There's no time to pack anything," the person announced.

He went to Asher and helped him stand up. As he did so, the school was struck again. I stayed standing, almost losing my balance. The person was holding Asher's arm, making sure Asher did not move as much this time.

"We need to leave," the person said. He looked at Asher and turned to face me. "Now."

From those words alone, I knew that the situation was ever more perilous, confusing, and dire than I ever thought before.

Is There An Edge Of Impossibility?

"Out this way quick," the person held the rear exit door open for Asher and me to use.

"Where are we going?" Asher stared through the doorway at the foggy, dim, morning outside air leading to a rear parking lot that felt as eerie as the atmosphere.

"No time to discuss," the person said, still holding open the door.

"Look I can't go," Asher quickly said. It was quiet for a second. No one talked. The person just looked at Asher with no expression.

"My grandma isn't back yet," Asher rushed his words through his mouth. "She's still on a cruise and is going to be gone for months. My mom is-I-I can't leave my mom—"

"I healed her," the person casually said.

There was a short and long pause somehow put together at that very moment.

Asher narrowed his protruding eyes to keep them in his head. "What? What!? What? Wait-what do you mean?"

"She's still sleeping but will awaken in a few weeks completely in full health, back to her old self. I left a vague note so when she wakes she'll be able to piece together what's happening with Asher without the world finding out, so don't worry about that either."

"Healed her…" Asher whispered to himself in a small voice. "A-a note, but h-healed her… How is that…"

"She'll be fine," the person assured Asher. "Something we won't be if we don't go." The building shook slightly. "Now."

"Healed…" Asher was still shocked. His entire body was motionless and facing the door as if nothing was around him. "Oh-Okay." He took a few baby steps trying to return his mind to the present. Still looking a little dazed, Asher quickly walked through the doorway and into the outside air.

The person looked at me and motioned with his head to go through the doorway. Who is this guy? I quickly walked through, passing him and into the outside air.

It was an old parking lot, probably not taken care of for being in the back of the school. Cracks and potholes littered all over the place. Some cars filtered throughout, a portion of which looked abandoned based on the circumstances. A few people frantically entered their cars, turning them on, or were in the process of entering. Foggy morning air. Dark grayish-blue sky. Eerie. There was the edge of a forest barely visible in the distance.

"This way," the person directed. He walked past me and curved left, walking slightly faster, as if something was coming. That's not an if, is it? Who is this guy? I walked after him with Asher ahead of me.

"Usually we'd go on foot," the person randomly said as he pulled a random door handle of a red car.

Click.

The door wouldn't open and he quickly went to the next nearest car to do the same.

Boom!

The school building shook.

A person jiggling their keys lamented.

Click.

I turned back to see the car door he tried opening stayed closed.

"Not this time," he grabbed another car's door and pulled.

Click.

It didn't open.

Boom!

The building shook again as a monstrous roar went off in the atmosphere.

A person ran into the parking lot, just having escaped the building.

Click.

Another door didn't open. The person went to the next nearest car, a dark teal blue that was small and practically decrepit—

Boom!

Some of the paint was fading off-

Click. A different type of click.

The person pulled the driver's door open, finally finding an unlocked car. "Good, I was about to bust a window." He grabbed the top of the door and pulled it farther out. "And we might need that window." The person reached over for the unlock button.

Click-Click.

Now all the doors were unlocked.

"Hold on," I looked right at the person, right at him, right at the stranger, right at someone who seemed to know everything in a humble way but wouldn't divulge a single one of those facts. He looked right back at me unwaveringly.

"What's going on exactly?" I questioned calmly with some more push in my tone.

"What's going on is that either we all get into this car, or we're going to die," the person simply answered.

Boom!

Part of a school wall nearby cracked as a monstrous roar rang out.

"'Die'?" Asher stammered out.

Boom!

More school cracks.

"So, get in the car to go?" Asher asked.

"Out of here," the person leaned into the car and pulled on the wheel. Hard. Somehow, I couldn't see from my angle, he gripped some wires that sprung out from under the wheel because of how hard he had pulled it. Wait is he— tiny yellow sparks flew and the car rumbled to life.

He just hotwired the car.

Boom!

Something collapsed in the school building.

"I'm guessing neither of you drive," he said to Asher and me without looking. Silence supported his claim. "One in the passenger, one in the back."

Asher went straight to the passenger side of the car and grabbed the door. He opened it and went straight in.

"Quickly," the person said as Asher closed the door.

I stood. Seconds hadn't passed, I was just assessing if I should get in that car with that stranger...wasn't like there was a different choice given the circumstances...

"Just this time," I whispered to myself.

I grabbed the backdoor, opened it, stepped in, and pulled the door shut.

"Buckle up." The person shut his door exactly after mine.

A monstrous roar echoed through the air.

More cracks and groans came from the school building.

The person revved the engine, and the car's tires screeched as he shifted its automatic gears.

Hold on. The car approached a concrete curb with grass on top, a road behind that, and the edge of a forest beyond that—the car veered straight ahead, screeching on the parking lot and lurching forward.

My entire body fell into the front black leather seats from the force.

The back of the car bumped, coming on top of the curb as the front came off. The tires screeched, pushing the car even further and flying off the curb itself—the car was in midair-sloping towards the empty road-seconds-minutes-hours seemed to pass-how does this all happen?—

The car slammed onto the road. The person veered left, speeding away from the school with the forest to the right. It all was hardly seeable through all the fog and dim morning light.

Or was my head just dim and foggy?

Probably both.

Boom! A different type of boom.

What was—

Monstrous roar

"Ah hell," the person eyed the rearview mirror.

Asher looked in the rearview mirror in front of me and freaked. "What is that!"

I turned around to see concrete flying above the school that was now hundreds of feet behind. There was a silhouette of something... something big...it's moving-

Coming this way

Boom!

Roar!

"Here we go!" The person announced. His foot slammed on the gas, shooting the car more than sixty miles faster.

My body pressed into the leather seats of the back.

Asher turned, looking at me while also looking past my head. His face told me exactly how far whatever that thing was. "It's getting closer."

"That's it," I gripped the headrest of the driver's seat and pulled myself up. I could see the forest zooming to the right, becoming a blur of green and brown. That didn't matter. The road didn't matter. Whatever that was didn't matter.

Answers matter.

"Is this the 'they' you talked about—"

RoaR!

A part of a tree slammed nearby the left side of the car, causing the person to veer suddenly, making my head slam against the passenger headset with my body flying forward, falling between the driver and passenger seats.

"I know I said buckle up," the person gripped the wheel. "Hang on," he pressed the gas harder, going speeds unimaginable.

My body jerked into the back leather seats from the sudden increased force. Maybe seat belts were a good idea. I shifted myself into the middle of the back seats and grabbed the middle seatbelt, clicking it into place.

RoAR!

"We might need to go down the main road instead of this side road," the person commented.

"Is this road more dangerous?" Asher asked.

"It's dangerous regardless. It might just be a better choice. If we can even get there."

"Who are you?" I stared into the rearview mirror eyeing the person driving. He looked at the rearview mirror catching my eyes. He seemed to be trying to understand who I am as well.

No one knows me besides myself.

What is identity?

Tree pieces exploded onto the rear left side of the car. They're from the forest right next to the road. What in the!

Asher let out a surprised gasp.

Glass splattered on my face and body as the left side backseat window broke into millions of pieces. My body tossed against the right side of the interior. Shards of glass continued to rain somewhat downward on my left.

Wait, rain downward?

The car was tilted and was only driving on its two right-side wheels. I could feel the wind whipping inside the interior with its abrupt exposure.

Everything was loud.

My head turned to the rear windshield. Cracks spiderwebbed across the surface. It was hard to see through. But there was something. I squinted hard to see an outline of that something. It was something difficult to make out through the dim lighting, fog, and cracked window. Something much closer than before. Something yards away.

Something catching up.

The person's forearm pressed against the steering wheel as his left hand gripped it tightly. With one quick movement he twisted his grip and shoved the wheel to the left, forcing it to turn. The car followed. The left side jolted down on the road as the entire vehicle continued to speed. Everything in the car bounced. I hit my head on the ceiling.

Asher quickly turned back at the rear windshield. "It's catching up!"

RoAR!

A few cars were ahead as the single lane began to merge into two. The person stepped on the gas, speeding up to the cars trying to pass them.

Boom!

A lonesome wheel trampled to the left ahead. The nearest car ahead swerved in surprise. Monstrous roar. It was louder.

Much closer.

The car rocked, something smacking it.

The person pivoted the car into the right lane, turning onto a bigger road that was even closer to the ever-expanding forest.

Boom!

The side of the car tipped for a second and stumbled back on all four wheels. The same thing that hit the car, a large chunk of tree, was flipping over the car. Seconds seemed to pause, nothing passing-

Asher froze-

the person gripped the wheel-

shadows cast from the chunk, making it even darker-

another flip-

it passed forward above-

then another flip-

Smash!

The large chunk crashed onto the road, rolling into the back of cars ahead, causing some of them to shift and crazily swerve on the road. One car spun in complete forever loops, screeching and scratching for the entirety of the endless action.

The person gripped the gear shift lever. He pushed it into the N spot. Neutral. With the car's speed and momentum, the car screeched forward even faster than expected. The person grabbed the wheel and swerved right. The entire car curled past the tree chunk and the car that had been spinning—it was too fast. The car was about to hit a different car ahead by mere inches.

The person's foot went off the gas pedal, barely touching the brake pedal. He then pushed the shift into the R spot, reverse. He grabbed Asher's headrest and turned his body to watch through the cracked rear windshield. He hit the gas pedal. The car jerked from the sudden change in a gear opposite in the momentum.

The person pulled the shift back into the D spot, drive. The car jerked while trying to regain its speed, lurching forward and literally bouncing for a second into the left lane. The person swerved the wheel right, forcing the car to drive straight forward down the left lane. He stepped on the gas, passing the car that almost collided into and leaving the rolling tree behind. The person pivoted the car into the far-right lane and sped up.

My body was contorted. It was stuck in one place because of the seatbelt and pushed into other places because of all the forces at hand. It didn't hurt, it was just uncomfortable.

Not as much as this situation.

RoAR!

A car that was somewhere hundreds of feet behind slid and swerved on the road, having been slammed by something.

And whatever it was, it was still far away to an extent. But it was gaining ground.

The car that had been slammed into had its hood detached, which bashed onto the road. The car was slammed into again, this time swerving completely off the road from the strength of the large outline of whatever was chasing—

Boom!

Another car was smashed and swerved off the road. Some parts of it toppled into the air.

Closer this time.

Boom!

I turned and saw the outline, blurred as it was, being dangerously closer than ever before. It's still unclear what it was.

What was clear was how close it was getting.

Boom!

Another car swerved.

The outline closer

RoAR!

"Find a glass shard," the person told me without looking away from the road. "The biggest one you can."

Glass shard? I looked down and searched for the biggest glass shard.

Boom!

A car somewhere behind swerved completely off road.

There was a big shard of glass by my left foot. I carefully picked it up and held it forward between Asher and the person.

"This works," the person said, grabbing it and putting it in the cup holder next to him.

RoAR!

Closer.

The person reached his right hand towards his back while still gripping the wheel with the other.

RoAR!

Closer.

No wait - reached between his jacket and shirt by going over his shoulder.

Boom!

He gripped something and pulled it out from between his golden shirt and dark navy blue bomber jacket. I couldn't exactly tell what it was.

RoAR!

Closer.

It was a very dark gray that looked similar to black jeans after multiple washes. It was thin but had structure to it. Foundation. It wasn't flimsy. Hard. Smooth. It wasn't exactly long either.

Boom!

The person stepped on the gas. He let the wheel go and tossed the object into his left hand. His right hand swiftly gripped the wheel. He stared at the rearview mirror, back on the road ahead, then the mirror again.

He was readying himself for something.

Boom!

A car spirals behind.

RoAR!

Closer.

The person looked out of the window to his left in thought. What was he-

RoAR!

Closer

I turned around to see the outline on the verge of revealing further details. Whatever it was, it was dangerously closer, maybe less than a few hundred feet away.

RoAR!

Maybe.

CRack!

The side of the car jolted as a car part bashed into the back windshield, causing the existing cracks to spiderweb further. Everyone inside staggered. My face hitting the sides and backs of the front seats. As the chaos ensued, everyone and I pushed and pulled to reset themselves in their seats. The person gripped the wheel with his right hand tightly. He stared out his window, and then back at the rearview mirror. He shook his head and looked at both me and Asher, nodding his head in thought.

It was loud. Just loud. It was hard to hear anything. Hard to feel and not feel at the same paradoxical time. It was hard being in that moment since no way reality is like this. What is this?

What is all of this?

"I need you both to listen real quick," the person said through the rushing air, cars, roaring, and indistinguishable sounds.

Asher and I just stared at the person.

"I already told you buckle up and hang on," the person continued as if it was any other morning.

What is he about to do?

With the object in his left hand, he hit a button on the driver's car door.

Click.

The person's car door window started lowering, making high-speed air and ear-slapping noise come into contact with both of their and my ears.

"Do just that. Nothing else," the person continued.

RoAR!

Closer

Boom!

Closer

A branch hit the top of the car.

Closer

"Watch the wheel," the person suddenly told Asher.

Asher, of course, was shocked and confused. "Wait what?" He was staring at the person and the opening window. "Wait! What?!"

The air whipped, the sound flooded, but the person was totally unfazed. He moved his head towards the now completely opened window.

RoAR!

It was even louder.

Closer…

The person used knuckles to steer with his left hand since the hand itself was still holding the dark gray object in it. His right hand let go of the wheel and hovered over the large glass shard that he had placed in the cup holder earlier.

Why did he need that?

RoAR!

SmasH!

A tree chunk was thrown into the side of the car.

RoAR!

That's even closer.

I turned around, peering through the spiderwebbed cracks of the back windshield. The silhouette was a little more than a couple hundred feet away.

Just a little more.

It still wasn't clear exactly what it was through all the morning fog, the cracked windshield, and the intensity of the moment. But it was hulking.

The person's grip on his object tightened. He turned it in his left hand until the back of the hand was pushing against the wheel to steer. He flicked his fingers and wrist, and the object made a makeshift snapping noise. Then, it kind of snapped. Like opened.

The object jumped outward from itself. It got slightly wider, but definitely longer. The entire thing was now partially curved, like a crescent moon that didn't quite extend to where it was supposed to be.

There was something else on it. Something else thin, like a string. A string connected from the top to the bottom, making a straight line through the curvature of the object. The box, once thin, was now something completely different.

A dark gray wooden bow.

What in—

SlaM!

The car tilted from the impact of a tree limb. Asher's head hit the passenger window. My body strained against the seat belt. The person struggled trying to steer and hold the object all with just his left hand. The person's right hand hovered over the glass shard as he gripped his bow. He nodded his head, thinking to himself, and turned back to the road ahead.

"Keep limber," the person said looking through his side window. "Stay fluid. Tensing up will cause more damage when there's sudden movements or in a crash."

What is he talking about?

What is he about to do?

"What do you mean by movements?" Asher gripped his seat as he stared at the person, beckoning for an answer. The person continued staring through the window poking his head out looking behind the car.

"I mean." The person gripped the wheel tightly with his right hand, the leather of the wheel scrunching and making a small whine. "We're about to go for a spin."

The person thrust the wheel to the left intensely. The car spun on its axis in complete and utter circles. Asher gripped desperately to his seat. I was forced right, crushing against the backseats.

The person grabbed the large glass shard,
air whipped,
He put it against the string of the bow with his right hand,
sound increased,
Pulled back hard – far making an arch,
the spins continue,
A small amount of yellowish-golden light came off his fingers, at least seemingly,
air whirling,
A feeling emitted off him along with the seemingly light,
The world mixed in sight,
The person stuck his bow out the window,
forces pushing everything to one side,
Aimed glass shard at the road the opposite direction the person was originally driving from,
tire screeches,
Aim,
silhouette gets closer,
Aim,
closer,
Fingers pull string back slightly further,
silence,
Eyes narrow,
spins and spins and spins,

Aim,

blur,

Aim,

blur,

Pulls glass shard back further,

blur,

three, two,

The person let the glass shard and string go. The glass shard soared out of the open window, flying down the road at whatever was coming.

Tires were still screeching.

RoAAAAAAARR!

"Got it," the person whispered to himself. He pulled himself from the window and turned to face forward. He gripped the wheel with his right hand and shoved it to the right and maneuvered it in a way to where the car wouldn't flip over. The car instantly slammed, bumped, screeching from its sudden force into the opposite direction it was spinning, making it slow down and stop the rotation. Without skipping a beat, the person slammed his foot on the gas and sped forward back down the road.

"You two okay?" The person asked as he gripped the wheel right-handedly. He flicked the bow in his left hand. It went back to its thin, long, box shaped state.

The surroundings were loud. They felt silent with all that happened seconds ago. I was stuck to my seat, frozen in intense...I don't know. I can't think.

What is that thing? The thing chasing, getting closer? The thing that can flick to a bow? This whole car situation? This? This?

What is going on?

"Okay? Okay?" Asher couldn't stop staring at him. "What was all that?"

"That shouldn't stop it. But it should slow it down by a few seconds." The person slid the object in between his shirt and jacket on his back, returning it to its original place.

The air swirled through the car as the speed continued down the road. The forest to the right zoomed by, making the trees hard to make out. The deep green color was the only thing not gray outside.

Talking…is…but.

but.

but.

Answers were needed.

"Only a few seconds?" I questioned. "'It'?"

"Being limber wouldn't have helped," Asher commented in a shocking manner looking around.

"It did in this case," the person rebutted.

The car was silent as what just happened was still trying to be grasped. The car sped like something was chasing us, but there wasn't a single noise. Not a crash. Not a roar.

That still didn't ease the tension.

"What is this case?" I stared straight ahead.

The person stared into the rearview mirror staring at me.

"This entire case?" I added.

Air rushing.

There was just looking. Eye contact. Not intense. Not uncomfortable. It was a moment of understanding that things must be said sooner or later.

"Look," the person's eyes went back to the road ahead. "Once we're at a safer spot, I can tell a bit more. For now—"

CRAsH!

The car tilted, driving only on its right wheels-

It swerved onto the very edge of the road-

The seat belt slashed at my throat-

Asher grunted-

I looked to my right through a cracked window-

the car tilted further-showing a deep drop into the forest-

at least forty feet down-

at least-

has to be more-

"It's back!" Asher's eyes widened and narrowed at the same time in fear.

"That didn't take long," the person gritted. He gripped the wheel tightly and swerved it down to the left, forcing the car back on all four wheels. He stomped his foot onto the gas—

SLAM!

Glass shatter-

Glass flew everywhere as the car tilted right then landed on all fours again-

ROAR!

Can't see what it is-

Can't see what's slamming into—

ROAR!

SLAAM!

It's throwing things, obviously angry-

The car tilted again-

The speed slowed and it tilted more and more-

at least a forty feet deep drop-

at least-

I could see nothing but green through the right cracked window.

"Hang on," the person's voice went through the vehicle.

The car kept tilting.

Gears cracked-

Engine whined-

Wheels screeched-

Tilting-

"Come on come on—" Asher lightly voiced.

The wheel strained under the person's grip. "Hang on."

"No-no-no—" Asher cut himself off.

I turned left looking through the cracked window. The sky was visible as if I was looking upward into the air. I basically was by this point.

ROAR!

SLAM!

Something smashed into the left side.

It was then that the wheels gave out.

"Hang on!" The person's voice rose slightly.

The car swept further, falling right off the edge.

ROAR!

The world flipped from grays to greens.

The seat belt dug deep into my skin.

Air rushed through the broken window.

Plummeting down and down and down.

Asher gripped the door handle, yelling slightly.

Plummeting.

The person grunted, gripping the steering wheel tightly.

Plummeting.

Glass flew upward, passing my face. I looked behind me. The ground, all green, was approaching quickly.

Here

grip-

It

plummeting-

Comes

CRasH!

Metal crashes onto the ground.

CRusH!

Metal bends.

The car slid from the high impact and skirted across the forest ground by a few feet. Finally, it came to a stop.

All motion came to a stop.

Breathe.

Just...

Inhale

Breath.

Exhale.

Breathe.

Eyes...ache...

Ears...ache...

Legs...

Arms...

What doesn't ache...?

Blurry... Everything... Everywhere...

My eyes tried to focus. Sore. That's the key word.

Sore...

It all seemed...

Out of place...

I was out of place. This whole situation was out of place. What is in place? It was hot and cold. No in-betweens. It was just all like a daze.

I groggily shifted my weight and head. All of it hurt. All of it burned. All of it was cold. All of it—

"Is everyone alright?" The person questioned quickly.

Everything was drooping right.

The person was hanging on by the wheel, gripping it tightly with his left hand as he looked around. His seat belt was the only thing holding his body from falling to the other side of the car. His other hand was gripping the console in the middle between the driver and passenger seats.

Asher was lying flat on his right side against the car door. The one thing holding him back from his whole body being on the door was his seat belt as well. He didn't seem hurt, but rather confused, groggy, and not completely focused. Objects were hanging downward towards him. Debris fell. Glass flakes landed next to him. Dirt. A patch of light shone down.

The car had landed on its right side.

"Is everyone alright?" The person asked again. A little louder this time.

Asher coughed and moved on his door. "Yeah...yeah," Coughed again. "Not too bad." Coughed once more, laying still on the car door. "Not too shabby."

The person turned his head and looked at me. "What about you?"

What about me?

The seat belt might have kept me from falling to the right side in the back of the car, but it felt like it was going to pierce my skin. It felt like I was hanging from the sky since I was in the middle seat. Open air was above and below me to my left and right. My arms were still as I took in his question.

"Are you alright?" The person added.

ROAAR!

-the person looked through his window upward

-Asher stilled suddenly

-listening-

the monstrous noise came from somewhere-

-not close, not far-

"We have to leave," the person said, looking around the car. "Now." He started moving towards the left side of the car, upward towards his door. He grabbed the door handle and was using it to halfway pull himself up. "Get up."

Asher started trying to pull himself to where the person was.

"We need to move," the person pushed his door upward with one hand. It didn't want to budge. He pushed it harder.

It budged.

The door flew straight open and the dark morning sky, past the trees and dirt, showed itself.

"Get up," the person urgently, yet somehow calmly, repeated.

The air was shaking.

Asher started stirring, grabbing for the chair he was partly on.

Click.

The person undid his seat belt. He was now halfway dangling by one arm with most of his body still in the driver's seat. His left hand was already gripping one of the sides of the car door opening that he had pushed open seconds ago.

Click.

"Ah," Asher fell completely on the right side's door now that he undid his seat belt.

The person managed to get his right hand on one of the sides of the opening.

"Hurry," the person pressed. Asher turned to face upward where the person was currently in the process of escaping.

The person began to pull himself up out of his seat, grunting a bit as he did so.

Asher began grabbing the seats and other parts of the car to pull himself up.

I should move.

I put my right foot against the passenger seat and grabbed the middle of the seat belt tightly.

Here goes.

Click.

I undid my seat belt and dropped by a few inches. My right foot pressed against the passenger seat, and my left hand's grip on the belt itself were the only reasons why I didn't fall all the way down. Tensing up, I was struggling with my footing and grip. The back seat door I had to use to escape was closed above me.

Pull.

My hand strained as it gripped the seat belt. I began pulling myself up while also pushing off the seat with my foot to leverage myself to the door. I reached for its door handle.

Out the corner of my eye, I could see the person was halfway out with just his legs left dangling.

Asher was right below his feet.

My fingertips stretched forward, gripping the door handle and pulling it down in the process.

Now I had to push.

I kicked off with my right leg to push the door up and out. With a rushing sound, it flew open. I reached for any side of the open car door.

Ting. It was a bit warm to touch. My left hand gripped the side tightly.

The person had already pulled himself out. He was just waiting for Asher to follow.

My right hand stretched out and gripped the side right next to my other hand. I let out a little breath. Noise to my right told me Asher was close to escaping the car.

Roarr!

distant-

but still-

"Hurry," the person urged from outside the car.

Focus.

I gripped tighter and started pulling myself upward. My biceps burned, getting hotter per second.

My head popped out of the opening. It was still dark outside. Foggy, damp, gray this morning looking like it was on the verge of rain. There was no rain in sight.

I pulled myself further out, my arms crawling forward on the sides of the car. Slowly, my legs emerged from the vehicle. I pushed myself up, standing on the crashed car.

Roaarr!

"Here we go," the person grabbed Asher's hand, grunting as he was helping Asher pull the rest of his legs out.

Asher kneeled on top of the car.

"Get up," the person patted Asher on the shoulder.

"Don't have to tell me twice," Asher heavily breathed, bewildered, and ready to escape absolutely everything.

"This way," the person turned towards the darker part of the forest, leaping off the car, and landed into ferns, vines, and other vegetation.

Asher jumped off the car with no hesitation.

Of course, I had hesitation.

My body ached. My mind ached. Sore all over. Confusion was life itself. No reasons given for all the above. Yet there really weren't any other choices to make. There was only one.

I jumped off the car, landing next to the person and Asher.

"Let's go." The person turned sprinting into the leaves and trees. Asher sprinted after him. With no other choice, I too sprinted.

"Where are we going?" Asher heaved out of breath.

The person kept his head forward. "Deeper into the forest." Shoes crunched on leaves and twigs.

Although the morning fog made it look like it was evening, the trees and the shades of green added to the effect.

"It shouldn't be following us right now," the person said. "If it was, it would've been on top of us already. It's probably resting." His shoes crackled some dead leaves and snapped some twigs. "We'll set up camp soon." He smacked a tree branch out the way.

Asher continued sprinting with no questions.

Snap.

I had questions.

Snap.

So many questions I couldn't count.

Crackle.

So much bottled up. Just so much. But not just. Not only. That was all. That is all. Every thought is a question. Everything needed is an answer. Every snap, every crackle, every breath, every step.

And there was only one way to find out.

Does A Lack Of Answers Build Questions Or Build The Plight At Hand?

"He slept quick," the person looked at Asher curled up and sleeping on a soft looking patch of vegetation a few feet away.

The forest was dark at night. The sky was hard to see through all the trees. It wasn't pitch-black. It was dark enough to not be able to make anything out past about fifteen feet away. It was only light around the small campfire that Asher quickly made before he fell asleep.

Maybe if I focus my eyes, I could see past fifteen feet. I can't. I couldn't. My mind was on other thoughts.

"In the morning, we move," the person said as fireflies, crickets, and other animals made their night sounds. Dirt patches layered here and there. There were two logs near the fire and short plants all around. The person sat on one of those logs. Asher was laying exhaustively on a dirt patch closest to the log I sat on.

That, I did. I sat. Thinking. Silent. Wondering. Silent. As

usual, but not usual. It's not a routine, but all routine. I need to understand this routine. I need clarity.

I need answers.

At least a few. A bare minimum. Something. A cricket chirped. Something. Fire crackled. Something.

I stared at the person. Eyeing him. Having to wait for words to come out of this mouth. Having to wait for answers.

This time, I cannot wait.

"Are you going to explain what's going on?" I questioned, breaking the atmosphere.

The person turned his head in thought. I sat there, continuing to stare at him. He turned his head more to meet my eyes. No words. Eyes.

Then, an inhale.

"You don't talk much," the person held my stare. "If at all."

Crickets chirped. The fire crackled. There were no other sounds outside of that. Maybe there were. I wasn't paying attention. I wouldn't attempt to. He didn't change demeanor. He didn't say a word. No movement. Nothing except him pondering.

"I won't tell everything," he clarified. "Plus, he's sleeping. If I do explain now, I'd have to wake him or explain it again later. I'll wait until tomorrow."

Is that so? My hands were in my lap as I kind of slouched forward.

"To be real, you're not ready"—he turned to a sleeping Asher for a second—"Neither of you are. When I arrived at that school, I was under the impression that you knew what was going on. At least to an extent."

Fire crackling sounds trickled into my ears for a second, then died down. "Why do you say?"

"There were three Surges created over the course of two days."

Surges?

"One is pretty normal," he specified. "More than two in

such a short period within the same area is when it becomes more than noteworthy. I followed the Surges in the direction they led. Baltimore."

This isn't the first time I've heard the word Surges in this framework. I know that much. No idea what it means though.

The person shifted on the log keeping his eyes on me. "Seeing you for the first time, in that room, with your Aura emanating off you."

Aura? He keeps using that word. Didn't Pericly also use that word?

"I come back days later checking in to see if you were getting things situated. Instead, I come to find you with another person I was going to check, both of whom did not know a single thing of what was going on. Not even a reference."

References were not even referred to until he appeared, walking in with his boots.

The person gestured at Asher. "Funnily enough, I found out about him by accident walking through the school halls. Felt his Aura. Good accident. Just in bad circumstances."

"'Felt'?" My arms crossed, debating what he was talking about. He was communicating in a sense that gave context without giving content.

"That's the point. You don't know. He doesn't know. Not even barely. I thought you at least had the basics." Fire flicker reflected off the right side of his face. "You don't have that either. If you don't have the basics, you're not ready to hear the magnitude of what you are heading towards." His eyes stayed steady. "Even at this very second."

The fire flickering drowned out all other sounds. That was in my head. I know it was. I was trying to understand, trying to grasp what he meant, trying to read between the lines, trying to see these lines, trying to see what these lines were made up on. Trying, trying, trying, but trying wasn't making it. I wanted to know these lines, know these spaces, know all the above. It wasn't just a want. What's going on, whatever that may be, definitely is a necessity regardless of how much I know the depth of such a necessity, and based on everything today, everything he said, and everything I can simply antici-pate, I most definitely need to know.

"I'll give the basics little by little starting tomorrow," the person said. "That way I can see how you both are taking it in, seeing how ready you are as we progress. No rushing it. No questions about it tonight. Tonight, we need to focus on resting."

Resting? Resting? Resting. Resting.

What is rest? What is resting? One person's rest is another's discomfort.

Not being ready? Not being ready? Not being ready. Not being ready.

What is ready? What is readiness? One's being ready could be another's already passed beginning, now in the middle much past the point of only being ready.

Slow down the thinking. My thinking. My thoughts. Per-haps he has a point. I don't understand anything that hap-pened the entire day, yet there's this innate feeling saying I should, I need, and I have to know or already know. Perhaps not already, but I have seen hints here and there that I haven't noticed are hints. Are there--were there any hints?

Slow down. Like I said before. Slow.

Don't overthink.

He said he'll teach the basics. The basics of what? As in ex-actly, to the detail, what are the basics?

Perhaps he has a point.

He?

I don't even know what he's referring to.

He?

I don't know if I'm ready for whatever it is, like he said.

He?

...He?

There was one thing in particular I, with less than a single utmost doubt, needed to know regardless of if I was or wasn't ready.

"Who are you?" I studied the person steadily. The stranger. A stranger, still after all that has transpired. Calmly. Patiently. His bomber jacket. His shirt. His cargo pants. His boots. His hair was cut low with waves on the top. Dark brown skin with dark brown eyes. A commanding air about him. All of the above were difficult to see in the low light.

But I for sure could feel. No doubt about it.

"I won't explain my entire reason for being here." Half of the person, this person, the only person in mind, face flickered from the fire's light. "That's when it gets complicated." His eyes held the fire, looking as if he was trying to see the shapes it created. He turned his head back to me, conviction looking into mine. "But considering everything that happened today, I do owe you that."

He inhaled, looked at the trees to his left casually, and brought his face back to mine.

"My name is Azmach." His name stayed hovering in the air, almost like an echo without the repeat. "Az sounds like Oz, with the letter A in spelling. Mach sounds like mock, also with an A."

Azmach. I'm not sure what to make of it. Never heard that name in my life. It felt almost like an answer that added more questions. I stared at the air taking it in.

"Last name's Washington. I would say more, but he's asleep," Azmach gestured to Asher, "Like I said earlier, I'll leave that for tomorrow.

Azmach Washington.

If that's all I can learn and have answered, no need to waste time. I crossed my arms and stared into the fire.

"There are a few things I've been wondering that I was hoping you could answer," Azmach addressed. He leaned forward, looking straight into my face. I could tell that he wasn't looking at me. He was looking at all of this as a whole, me and the plight at hand. What was strange was how casual he was about it, like he was trying to read a book that he didn't understand, but somehow had a feeling of what it could be saying. Unlike most, he wasn't stressed about not knowing. Not even a little.

"Your hair color is that naturally white?" Azmach inquired as the fire dance reflected off his pupils. Fire crackle and crickets.

I stared back at him, crossing my arms tighter. "Yes."

"Your eyelashes aren't white. They're a normal dark color that most people have. But your eyebrows are white."

Silence and beings meeting.

"For your hair being white, is there a reason?" Azmach speculated. "Any conditions, syndromes, disorders, illnesses, or diseases?"

"None." Haven't heard that one in what felt like a while.

Azmach's eyes narrowed in thought. "Yet...completely natural..."

The fire crackle seemed to suck the sound out of the atmosphere. Asher shifted in his sleep, inhaling heavily, then calmingly normal again. Azmach didn't notice. He appeared to be amid working on subjects he didn't know existed until now. That was astounding, considering the multitudes of knowledge and connecting concepts he seemed to possess, all of which I, to an extent I cannot measure, had not begun to learn in the smallest bit.

"Your eyes too?" Azmach concentrated on the subject of what he said, trying to find secrets covered in wraps. "Orange. A bright orange."

What is this sudden feeling? It feels normal, like everyday life, but what is it? Tension? No, it's pressure. This sudden pressure. What type of pressure? The looks of people. The comments. Their thoughts. He's studying me. The hair. Looking at me. The eyes. They look at me. No no no no, don't over read. See what the passage says first.

Heat from the fire emanated.

"You're a different case," Azmach's voice, echoed in thought. "A confusing… case…" Both of his fingers interlaced with each other and rested on his mouth. "Your hair's not likely. Let's say there's a very, very, very small chance it could happen. Even then, it's just not going to happen. Not like this. White hair. It isn't gray or blonde. It's straight up white. Like there's no way to get around it. Then the style."

Style.

"I wouldn't say your hair's all over the place," Azmach examined, "It looks more wild like…"

"Frozen fire." I suggested.

"'Frozen fire,' let's go with that. Bet that part's natural as well. It's the eyes that really get me. They're bright orange. It looks and is completely natural, no contacts, no nothing. That color's not possible. I don't care about stats. Having that eye color and for it to be that vibrant," Azmach hands went up in a behold sense directed at me. "Yet here you are."

Here. Doesn't feel like I am…Fire and crickets…why do I hear them…

"What's your name?" Azmach asked.

What? That shook my head up inside out. That sudden question is more personal than the last. I asked to learn and figure out what's going on. He's asking to…why is he asking?

"You haven't told me it," Azmach noted. "Or anything really."

Must I give it? I can't be rude. Yet, but, however, although, still, he's only given a name, not his age, not anything else himself. Why say what he says? Why say it in such a way? This is life. White hair, orange eyes, I grew up with this. Born with this.

Nothing new.

So why say it like that? Why? I feel as if there's a layer between the lines that I cannot read, yet that does not in any sort of, kind of, almost, or smallest, diminish the existence of what is said between such lines. Why does he need my name? It can't be a want. So why does he need it? What is he trying to pull? I have questions with no inferable answers. I have questions with no way to surmise. I'm stuck.

Stuck.

The fire crackle filled the lack of voice in the air. Crickets aided in the effect.

Give the name. If I want what I can't surmise. No other choice.

Name.

"Jason." I plainly half whispered. "Side."

"Jason Side." Azmach nodded, taking it in.

"How old are you?"

"Nineteen." Azmach shuffled into his jacket pocket and pulled out a black cloth. He fluffed it out, allowing the fabric to fully open. A black durag. No wrinkles. Soft, stretchy, polyester. Two long durag tails spilled over his knees, hanging barely two inches from the dirt right next to his boots. "This situation is going to be difficult," the fire crackle sound raised with his sentence.

"I've caught glimpses," I pointed out.

"You're not wrong. It's been a long day," Azmach placed the durag on his head, wrapping the tails twice around tying them in the back. "It's late." He pulled the knot tighter. "I'm sure we're all tired." Pulled the fabric down to press it against his waves. "We have to get up early tomorrow."

"So that thing won't catch up?" I prodded.

That's what was on my mind. I tried not to think too much about it since I had so many questions. I tried not to ask, but instead decided to see what he would say without being completely prompted. But, but, but, but. This is important. This needs to be explained. There's no other way to understand what's happening. After the auditorium crumbling, the school itself breaking, escaping out of said building, being chased down the road, the car crashing, and having to run deeper into this forest, all by some unknown… That's exactly it. Unknown.

Azmach let his durag go. He stilled as if he was caught in midsentence of a realization. "That?" Azmach's eyes showed just how grave the situation was. "Whoever said there was only one thing following us?"

The world stopped.

"I said 'they', remember?" Azmach heightened.

It dawned on me. Back at the school, in the hallway when going towards the exit door, Pericly had said something. *They're still trying to find you two outside.*

They're. As in

They.

This is no hyperbole. He too said it in an identical sense. Same context, same meaning, and now more fear-inducing.

What…are they…?

How…many…?

Take it in, take it in, yet it wouldn't compute.

…They…

"There's two chasing us," Azmach finished as if the knowledge was universal.

Two…

Two of whom…?

"Who… is doing the chasing?" I trailed off, my mind slowing down and racing at the same time.

Azmach's eyes laid upon the fire. It felt like a pin was about to drop and its sound was going to be deafening. Intently, the crackles grew as the world around dissolved into nonexistence.

"'Who'?" Azmach slowly turned from the fire facing me, the fire reflecting off him looking as if it were flicking in fear of his next words. "More like 'what'."

What…

No sound.

No air.

No breaths.

Yet, no pause.

Does that mean? It felt like I should have had a headache. Hot and cold blood avoided each other in my head, wrapping in my torso, flushing throughout my face and skull as an entity. This can't be right. This cannot be. What is what? In these circumstances, what is what? This was different. I don't know how to explain it. I'm not really sure what I was thinking. It was the feeling of being in the middle of concepts while standing on the threshold of subjects I didn't realize or knew I was on the edge of. I felt, I sensed, I was on the edge of reality merging with fantasy, making fantasy the new reality to perceive, whatever that might be.

What is what?

"You don't look shocked or scared," Azmach commented. "Well, you don't really show anything at all."

How is one supposed to react? He leaned closer, beckoning the importance of his next words, making me think in beats, the feeling of hot and cold blood pulsing through my system.

"I understand if you're mind's wandering," Azmach's voice lowered as the night darkened. "I understand if there's confusion. I understand the need to try and take it all in. Before we sleep tonight you need to know this."

The fire burned lower, consuming a great majority of the wood. Azmach leaned in closer. "There are some things you can't imagine, some things you can picture but not in a setting of what you know to be true. You're going to be forced to confront those things. Whether you're ready or not, you'll need to learn as much as possible. Because you must."

Processing. Tumbling thoughts. Reading through. Still, comprehending while not understanding. Must...

but, what does this pertain too

chasing, Two of not who, but of What...?

Must,

Azmach bent his head down, making sure his durag was

tight enough. He slid off his log, leaning his back against it. "We really should go to bed now." He leaned his head back. "Tomorrow, I'll start breaking things down. There's a lot to cover." His eyes closed. Simply said. Simply did. Simply, I was awake alone.

… I don't sleep well. I don't dream. Have I ever?... Do I dream and simply not remember upon waking?...? I don't know about that. How could I…how could I not?...Not simply…

There's a lot to process. What can be processed…? I don't know about any of this. In a general sense and total sense. In a specific sense and encompassing sense. What do I sense? What do I feel? Feel? That part doesn't matter. I can't tell anyway.

I slouched forward, not knowing what position to sleep in. It's not the first time outside, but around people…

Sleep…Think…Process…

They, what are those two? Not a who? What does that mean? A what? I don't understand. Is he trying to get me to think critically? What is critical? Is it how far one goes, or deep? Is it a distance driven concept or profound in the context of a copious amount of breakdowns? So many ideas. So many thoughts. So many ways. All confusion. All wondering. All trying to figure it out.

I can't even fathom a fraction of what happened today. I can't understand it in terms of reality, but reality is all there can possibly be. Right? Correct? Wr…wron- no it can't. Some concepts are ponderable. Frankly, they aren't possible.

Possible.

They.

I get stuck on that word. They. Seeing possibility right next to it seems to open doors to thoughts, ideas, concepts, fantasies that in actuality are reality. I don't know what. I don't know about that. It was just the feeling. The words between the lines. The unspoken, yet so loudly voiced.

The fire slowly crackled as my head filled with silence. Reality mixes with limitless possibility, contrasting with impossibility. I have no idea what I'm feeling. What am I seeing? But.

That's just it… but what?

Gah, I'm too tired to think. Sleep. No, I need to figure this out.

They. Two. What? How does it all add up? It sounds like it's not going to add up in a plausible way… it has to be possible. What am I standing over? Sleep…not now. Just exactly what am I looking down at? And must I go there. My foot's already over the edge. One foot only. I'm not sure if I want any more over this edge.

Must.

Sleep.

Must.

Sleep…

What's happening

Sleep…

Car crash

Sleep…

School

sleep…

chased

sleep…edge

sleep…fantasy

sleep…fantasy…sleep…meets…fantasy…sleep…fantasy…sleep…meets…sleep…reality…sleep…sle…ep…s…le..ep… sleep…

What Is The Possibility Of Fantasy Meeting The Truth That Is Reality?

"That was the best sleep in a forest I've ever had," Asher voiced, "I mean it was my only one, buuuuuut."

Eyes shifted, not open.

"I see you're up," Azmach's voice.

Aimed not at me.

"No, I'm down," sounding like he shifted on the ground.

"Ha ha, I'll give a couple more minutes, then we'll get moving."

Move where? Still not answered. What's the destination? I didn't sleep long. I don't feel like engaging, unless I have too, and I don't have to from how it sounds. I'll stay sitting, slouching. Eyes close. Don't start getting into the confusion of yesterday right now. Allow it to process naturally.

"Bro," Asher chuckled, "we moved all yesterday through trees and towns then trees again. I've never moved so much in my life."

"Speaking of yesterday, that was a nice fire you built last night," Azmach complimented.

"Ahhhh, it was no big deal, it was, ehhhh, saw it done before," Asher played off.

"How'd you do it?" Azmach asked as if he knew the answer. He asked as if it was simple and complex. He asked like it was much deeper than expected.

Eyes silently open, I looked to the right. It looked as though what Azmach had asked hit a portion of Asher's core. Asher looked lost, and trying desperately to stay buoyant, trying to keep a secret while living with said secret which was a burden, a weight on the shoulders and body as an entirety. His face looked loose but contorted. Clearly, he was keeping something to himself, and the pressure was building greatly.

"Weeeeell, well," Asher eyes widened, a thought occurring. His body loosened a bit from the pressure of before. He turned to Azmach, obviously wondering something that seemed to have been brewing in his head for more than just this moment. "You said you healed her?"

Azmach stood and took in what was asked. "Yes." Complete honesty behind such a simple word.

Asher looked like he was trying to read something in a foreign language he was pushing and pushing and pushing himself to understand. "Healed her?"

"As I've said yesterday, in a few weeks she'll wake up in her hospital bed fully healed and back to her old self. As I've also said, I left a vague note only she and people in our circumstance would understand so she would not be confused as to what's happening with you."

Asher head slightly cocked to the side. "At least she won't be confused. But I'm confused. How did you heal her?"

A sly smile came on Azmach's face. "That's what we'll begin to get into today." He turned from Asher to my direction. "I'll wake him—" I wasn't looking directly at him, but he certainly was looking at me. "Ah, you're awake. Good." He turned around, snapping twigs and shredding fallen leaves in his movements. "Let's get moving."

Asher's face reared back a second, looked at me, then at Azmach. "Where are we going, bruh?"

Azmach moved a low-hanging, skinny tree limb out of the way. "Deeper, somewhere a bit old. It's only a couple hours walk."

Asher blinked twice, turned his head looking at me, then back at Azmach, who had already begun the journey to who knows where.

Towards answers. I'll move for that only.

Must get up.

My body was sore. It was all in the back for sure, some in the ankles and thighs. What my body felt was a kind of stiffness. I slept in a sitting position on a log, so what else should be expected? I stood. Every single thing cracked. It seemed like blood rushed to every crease that was blocked, and life flicked me at all my pressure points simultaneously. I slid my hands into my pocket, looking at the ground. Dirt, twigs, outside. What is here?

Leaves crackled under my worn-out shoes. Green was everywhere. Or was it everything? Could it be everything? Dirt. I felt like I was covered in it, like a barrier or lining that was in no way the protection I needed or asked for. Sun rays were beaming. They illuminated through the trees, leaves, and covered randomized sections of my body. The clothes were always worn-out. It's normal, I just haven't noticed how obvious it was getting until now. Has anything changed?

My shoes stepped through the undergrowth, getting dirtier and dirtier. Were they ever clean? Everything I wore was old. The bagginess of it felt like it was dragging me down, a weight of something more…

Crackle. Shuffle.

Each step. Dead leaves, some colorful leaves, some tall vegetation. Sunlight scattered in abstract patterns and abstract directions. Details defined. There were things about Asher I didn't notice until now. Almost raggedy greenish tint, gray hooded jacket. Dirt patches and green stains sprinkled along the back. It flapped open occasionally from his movements, revealing his usual white shirt, stains and all. No, more stains actually. Not horrid looking, just noticeable. What I hadn't noticed before were the scratches on him and his clothes. Along with this, his freeform locs were growing. They grew more than I'd noticed before. They were just little springs out his head back in August, now the springs were up enough to see individual strands dreading.

Crackle. Shuffle.

How far is this walk going to go?

"Does he even know where we're going?" Asher asked more so himself as he stared intently at Azmach walking ahead. Azmach kept moving at his calm pace through the vegetation and chill air.

Chill. Cold. I didn't realize how cold it had gotten. Not unbearably cold, it was noticeably. Air that could potentially put frost on a window's edges was certainly present. A light chill seeped into my only pair of dark gray shoes.

Holes, strings, and the bagginess didn't help with the slight chill overall. More strings than before, much more. More holes on the right arm, some tiny, one noticeable. The pants were something else, oversized as always, dark grayish with scrapes, it certainly was ruffled. The dark, blueish-gray shirt had so much room that at times my skin felt no cloth. It was getting chilly.

Chill.

The sun warmed up the atmosphere, but there was still a chill.

I looked at Asher. He too had a couple scrapes on him. He stared intently at Azmach, not in anger, or exact curiosity. Just intently.

Azmach's boots crackled and shuffled the ground more than me and Asher. His face, head, and everything about him faced forward, leading on. Leading to? There wasn't a scratch on him. Not on his body. No, he had one scratch. It was a small scrape on the left arm of his jacket. That's it. Not even the durag that was casually waving in the air off his head and neck had a scratch. He plainly pushed low hanging tree limbs out the way, seemingly not even the slightest bit of exhaustion, as if this was everyday life.

What is life?

Step by step. Shuffle by shuffle. Crackle by crackle.

To somewhere.

Crackle by...

"Do you know where you're going?" Asher spoke up a little to reach Azmach ahead.

"Yes," Azmach didn't even look back, didn't even try to. Such a simple answer, clarifying and confusing, feeling abstract and precise. He moved a limb out of the way. "We're almost there."

Asher turned his head, looking at me with of curiosity mixed with confusion and concern. He turned his head forward again watching Azmach clearly looking like someone leaning on the edge of their seat.

Azmach stepped on a large rock, propelling himself forward. "We're almost there."

There?

Asher's head twisted. Even from behind, I could tell he had a pure curiosity with a hint of an edge of wanderlust.

Where?

Crackle. The sun beamed further. Ever so slightly, even so little, ever so insignificantly, yet so significantly, the temperature rose. Crackle. Trees were becoming closer and other vegetation sprung wildly. The woods were becoming denser. Crackle. Fewer light beams--crackle, but not noticeably less bright, crackle. Denser. Limbs, leaves, and other flora were weaving more, intertwining before the steps of the path, wherever it may lead. It was normal. It seemed normal.

What is this feeling?

crackle

The tree limbs slimmed down, twisting together from tree to tree, connecting more and making the denseness increase further. shuffle. What is this? I was a feeling similar to dozing off but still thinking deeply, so sleep and these deep thoughts mix, not creating a dream, but instead creating a world where the real has a drop of the possibly unreal. That feeling was what pumped through my veins. That was the air. That was the atmosphere. That was the energy. That was everything, yet nothing somehow being mutually inclusive.

shuffle

Azmach ducked under the increasing limbs, moving forward without a single pause for thought. The increasing denseness was enough reason for a pause for thought. It wasn't dense just in sight. It was dense from feeling. It wasn't claustrophobia being personified. It was more akin to a room full of a scent that wasn't strong, but definitely couldn't be characterized as weak.

crackle

Greens.

shuffle

Browns.

This fullness around...something was...not different...I think I felt this before...just not to this degree. Describe it...

crackle

Describing it... shuffle

It was on the tip of my tongue...

"It's closer," Azmach gently pushed another branch out of the way, stopping to make sure Asher and I were near. Asher stepped quicker and stopped straight behind Azmach's right shoulder, his face in wonder just like his mind certainly was.

What was ahead?

Vines, tall brushwood, limbs...shuffle...they intertwined, but done so in such a way it was as if they were making a disguised path, leading somewhere.

Where?

I stopped walking and looked past both Azmach and Asher two feet ahead. The two of them had stopped somewhat at the edge of a little dip in the ground. The intertwining vines, limbs, and other tall vegetation spiraled out, opening to what couldn't be called a field. It was a flatter part of the land that was encircled by trees and the intertwining vegetation. The intertwining met and crafted an almost cave-looking bundle a few feet into the flatter land. It looked simple. It seemed simple. But... ... ... It did not feel simple. It felt like there was a lightness and weight at the same time, like it was and wasn't there. And there was no other way to explain it. It just is. In depth and weight and absent and all. Perhaps a lack of knowledge on my part. Yet this phenomenon of a feeling was still here.

Or was that just the situation? As...a whole...?

What is it?

"Over there," Azmach gestured at the cave woven by the intertwined, as he took steps towards it and whatever he had in mind. Whatever he meant when he first wanted Asher to go with him. Wanted me to...

shuffle

Asher followed him. Where do I move? Forward

crackle

The beams of light dimmed closer to the intertwined cave. The entrance was about ten feet away.

What is it really?

shuffle The forest floor had a bit of that morning water layered on the surface. shuffle No leaves on it in front of shuffle Five feet to go. shuffle Three feet, Asher was a little behind Azmach. shuffle Two feet, the entrance was a wide arch leading to more interwinding, all brown with no leaves. shuffle

Fewer beams shone through. shuffle

Right in front.

Azmach walked straight inside. Asher behind him. I stared for a second and stepped forward. The air was…A small breeze swayed all the limbs, all the leaves, and my hair. I stared at the entrance once more then continued stepping forward. Finally, I waded through the entrance.

Inside, the intertwined cave was noticeably dimmer than outside, yet not dim enough to not easily see around. Less beams of sun were able to shine through the branches. It looked like a circular room made entirely of skinny, thick, or any other type of tree limbs with no leaves. They were all an ashy light brown. They swirled inside, making a ceiling, walls, and the edges of the ground. The branches, limbs, and whatnot swirled in the middle of the room, creating an almost circular pillar like desk. It was not too high off the ground, but it was high enough to lean against without having to constantly readjust. The ground would have been the same forest floor undergrowth, but from lack of sunlight and water there were few plants and mostly low dirt. Together, it all did not look like it happened naturally, especially the swirling of branches. Sure, it's possible. It felt like it popped out of the head of someone, and life decided to make it a reality.

Reality.

It was an interesting sight. There was something else. Something about the place. Something about the air, the atmosphere…

Azmach leaned on the circular pillar of branches. He ran his fingers along it, looking at it as if he was going down memory lane. "This used to be an old safe spot," his voice echoed. He took steps around appearing to inspect some more of the interior. "Before our time. It's a post for resting. Fighting. Anything else."

Anything else? This air, this atmosphere, whatever it was is something else.

"This place feels a little bit unreal." Asher had a bit of a smile as he took in the surroundings.

Unreal.

Wait.

…Reality

…so, it's not just me…this atmosphere…unreal…this air… Doesn't matter, some places just have a feel to them. Although, this air is…

"Speaking of unreal," Azmach leaned off of the pillar shaped circular limbs. "Let's get down to business."

Outside noise faded away.

"First off," he paused, staring down intently at Asher. "I know you didn't sleep without a durag, like bruh you're making our ancestors roll in their graves."

…

What?

Asher grinned excessively. "I meeaan when you're gettin' chased by god knows what, it's kind of hard to grab a durag in the meantime."

"More like 'Gods know what'," Azmach smirked.

"What?" Asher eyes squinted in a playful and confused way. "What is this man on?"

"This man has his durag on," Azmach eyebrow raised pointing out his black durag that was in fact still wrapped around his head.

Asher was caught in ice trying to decide to either fight to stay warm or give up. He chose the latter. "Imma give you that." Asher nodded, smiling. "Imma give you that."

Azmach let out a puff of air from his nose, smiling. "Never got your name formally, son."

"Asher, son!" Asher did a flex pose, stiffening his body. "What's your name, son?"

"Azmach Washington." He took his time saying that.

"Oh, we're doing last names nooow. Asher Craft."

Azmach stood for a second and took it in. "Alright, I feel it."

"I know, sexiest name you've ever heard, right?"

"I wasn't gonna go that far."

Asher broke out in lighthearted chuckles. "Aye, I'm just speaking the truth."

Azmach nodded, his face becoming businesslike. "It's time to get to that." His posture straightened, and he looked between Asher and me, readying himself for how he was going to explain.

Asher noticed at once and stopped his laughter.

Azmach looked between Asher and me as he was already trying to read any reaction to his words and subject. "I'm guessing neither of you know what happened yesterday?"

Quiet. Abruptly, voices, their corresponding echoes, dwindled off. A small, short breeze blew for a second rustling a few leaves outside the intertwinement at its entrance before dying off into the abrupt quietness. His question was answered with the utmost certainty, stemming from the lack of answers. It all said what entirely needed to be said.

Azmach lowered to the ground and sat with his legs stretched and spread comfortably. "You might as well sit down." Asher looked at me and sat down. I slowly lowered and sat on the ground, crossing my legs. My left hand rested on my knee while my right held my chin and mouth, its elbow resting on the other knee. I felt cold...uncertain about whatever was going to be said. It was not cold. It was a bit uneasy. What is he going to say?

"This is where I stayed while in the area before and after I found you," Azmach gestured towards me. "It was close enough to that high school and a great spot to plan." The air swayed and stilled evenly again.

"Three Surges in two days." Azmach's eyes waved past me. "That's what led me here. You guys know a little of what Surges are?"

"Surges?" Asher scratched his head. "Nnnnoooo...?"

"If I'm going to explain Surges, I have to explain Auras."

"Okay...what are auras?"

"When did you start feeling different?"

Asher stopped in the middle of his head scratching. "...In what ways?"

"As you've gotten older. How old are you?"

Asher's eyes shifted to me, to his right, then back in front of him at Azmach. "Eighteen since July."

"I'm guessing you're eighteen too?" Looking directly at me.

"Naw, he's seventeen," Asher answered.

Azmach nodded in acknowledgement. "That can still vary when it happens. It's an individual thing."

Asher took his hand away from his head, clearly confused. Still, he was trying to piece the puzzle together.

"It's like coming of age," Azmach deepened the explanation. "It started for me some months before I was fourteen," he looked off. "About five years ago. Time does fly."

"Are you talking about puberty?" Asher slightly squinted.

"Yes and no."

Asher's face and head cocked to the side in an expression that simply was asking every question possible in this context.

"Puberty, influx of hormones. They can bring out more of what I'm getting at." Azmach connected dots, but not all. "It can happen earlier or later than puberty."

"I think... we're all confused here." Asher's head was slightly cocked to the side as he was trying to visualize the metaphorical bush being beaten around.

"Have you ever been in a room where the feeling changed all because of the people or a person in it?" Azmach stared keenly. The wind blew then stopped as quickly as it appeared. Something changed. Not his tone exactly.

"It'll become cold or hot," Azmach continued. "The feeling. The energy coming off a person. Or simply, the energy somebody has."

Feeling. But it's a bit deeper than that. Energy. But I know he means more than that.

"Imagine a gene inside you becoming unlocked," and there at that point, Azmach snapped his fingers.

snap.

"And now you have a new energy," Azmach put his hand down. "A new feeling coming from you, inside and out. A presence, an air around you."

Unlocked…like a requirement.

Presence. That word sticks. Presence. In the hallways, covering the school, some presence was around. Yesterday, running through the halls, there was a presence. The auditorium, there was a presence. All in all, there was a presence. I don't know what, I don't know how to describe it. It was there. It was around, no doubt. A sort of feeling, a feeling coming off a person. Or was it in general? Possibly all the above? Isn't that normal? Although, he's talking about it as if there's more depth to it.

More depth indeed.

"This *Aura* you now have wasn't always there," Azmach looked between Asher and me steadily, making sure what he said made sense on the receiving end. "It will take some getting used to."

"Getting used to?" Asher queried.

"Adjusting. The gene might have unlocked, but you're not used to the Aura that accompanies. This Aura builds and builds and builds and builds. Until."

Snap.

Azmach held his fingers after the snap. "It has to come out somehow. Your body can't hold something it's never had and hasn't become Adjusted to."

"Aura…basically like the energy of someone?" Asher was clearly looking confused and annoyed.

Azmach turned his head more so to Asher, nodding once. "It's everyday energy. What we use to walk, talk, our hearts to beat. It's how sometimes we can possibly feel someone's presence in a room."

"Gotcha...So...Surges are...?"

"That buildup of Aura exploding out of someone."

Exploding...Burst...That sounds similar to...

"As I've said, it takes some Adjusting to." Azmach reminded me and Asher.

...feels like something...

"But it's not only about Adjusting." Azmach added.

...I think I felt...

"A Surge can happen after someone Adjusts to their Aura. Emotions can be a trigger. It's all about buildup." Azmach stopped. He wanted his words, his definitions, his meanings, and the metaphorical bush he was intentionally beating around to discerningly become wholly visible.

Asher scratched his fingers, rubbing them together. He looked off to the side with a face coated in confusion, deep thoughts, with specks of frustration. "Basically, it's too much energy exploding out?"

Azmach faced Asher, engaging in a silent exchange. Time passed, feeling short and long. Finally, Azmach nodded once.

"Couldn't you have just said that in the first place?" Asher plainly questioned.

"I could." Azmach shifted, pulling his durag so it would fit correctly. "There needs to be an added weight so when I get to the real stuff it's taken with the amount of seriousness it requires." He let his durag go, it now fitting in its correct position. "It's also y'all won't be buggin'."

"From what we've seen yesterday, I'm pretty sure we won't be geekin'," Asher pointed out.

"You might."

"Naw, we good. We got chased byyyy whatever that was yesterday, and we're still on people's energies and how it feels. I'm pretty sure we won't geek."

Azmach reached behind him to his right grabbing a broken twig. His thumb and index gripped a fraction of it, bringing it to the forefront. He held it at an angle staring at it normally, but with more worth than any twig should have.

No, it's not the twig itself.

Around and on the twig, a light was gradually emanating making it shrouded in yellowish-golden light. Lights in a house or sunlight would be brighter. No doubt the yellowish-golden light was dim. That wasn't the point. Most important-ly, it was there, it was existing. No explanation, no reason, nothing.

Wait, I saw this light before. When he shot the shard of glass out of the window at whatever was chasing the car, his fingers had light around them as well. So, I wasn't seeing things...

Asher was mesmerized, astounded. Bewilderment and a mix of...is that sadness? His eyes were wide and squinted at the edges. His mouth was partly open. He stared at the light, frozen in place, and I couldn't even see him breathing. The light hadn't changed, and that was the mind-shaking aspect in the first and last place. Light, no doubts or other concerns, was there around and on that twig. Azmach stared directly at Asher with a calm unwavering demeanor holding the twig shrouded in light. Half of Azmach's face was shaded, the oth-er half dimly illuminated in yellowish gold. One eye was un-seen in the shade, while the other reflected the baffling pre-sent. Azmach stared blankly at Asher's bewilderment. The light dimmed further and dissipated inward, like a star sucked into a black hole. As soon as it had manifested, the light disappeared without leaving any remnants, traces, or signs behind.

"Is that so?" Azmach tossed the twig like it had no mean-ing.

That cannot be nonchalant. Is that so? Meaning. Is that so. So casual. This cannot be casual. That, this, it's not...it's not...reality. No, wait it is. There's going to be an explanation. My eyes saw waves, not the ocean, not the sea...but tiny muddling waves in my sights...waves of reality.

"You," Asher cleared his throat trying to regain normalcy. "You said you healed her?"

Azmach looked at his fingers. "Yesterday, we got in a car driving as fast as possible with glass shattering around us and trees thrown at us. Then we fell off the road off a short cliff, crashing, totaling the car." He looked past his fingers at Asher. "Why do you think there's not a scratch on me?"

...I've taken pauses and stops, so I'm not sure what to call what this is now. This is, what this is... where are the words? A puzzle. Pieces scattered, some lost, some not even in existence; however, the puzzle is at the very least acknowledged, allowing the possibility of pieces to surface and connect. Indeed, possible seems plausible.

How? How and what? No scratches were on him. His face, hands, and barely on his clothes, just the one on the left arm of his jacket. Glass flying and shattering. The car falling and crashing. Not one scratch. Lighting up, illuminating a twig, was that him or a different phenomenon?

"Yes, I healed her," Azmach confidently answered Asher with nothing except truth and honesty.

"H-how," Asher stumbled.

"Time and a lot of Aura. I was surprised I could stand after."

Asher's eyes focused. "What else can you do?"

Azmach looked at me and Asher. "The real question is what else can *you* do?"

You? In what context? You in what ways? Why you at all? You?

"You, as in?" My question floated in the air.

Wind blew, quieting quickly after as two heads turned towards me.

"Has anything weird ever happened to you?" Azmach posed, fixed on my own question.

Weird.

"Has anything out of place, unexplainable happened?" He

asked as if there was a deeper definition to his words that could explain everything.

Out of place. All of yesterday. No, not just yesterday. Not just today. There's more. I know there's more. I feel there's more. There's more, a central piece of the puzzle that without the piece the picture can't even be halfway understood.

"What was that breaking the school apart?" I questioned. "What can chase a car for miles without rest? You also said there are two. You said it as if it's some sort of fantasy."

"Two?" Asher nervously repeated.

"No more sugarcoating. No more layering. Get straight to the point."

Azmach sat quietly, taking it in.

"Two of what?" I leaned forward waiting for an answer, anticipating whatever it could be.

Azmach let a small puff of air out of his nose, smiling. The smile shifted to a neutral face. His demeanor changed. Still calm, still serious. There was just even more seriousness to it, more seriousness in whatever the answer was going to be, more seriousness than ever before. Azmach inhaled, opening his mouth. "Monsters."

I can't move. I couldn't move. Is this some sort of joke?

"Monsters?" Asher was dumbfounded.

"Yes." Azmach laid out. "Monsters. Beasts. Creatures. Call them as they are. And they are Monsters."

There's something I need to ask. A question I should have asked by this point but has gone over my head.

"You mean like dragons and sea creatures and all that?" Asher shook his head, somewhat smiling. "You geekin'."

Azmach smiled, returning to his neutral face after. "Then what do you think is chasing us?"

…nothing said.

"What could break parts of a building into dust?" Neutral face.

…nothing said.

"I drove, what was it? An older car. As fast as an older car is, it might not have been able to catch up to us, but it was still able to give chase." Eyebrow cocked. "What could chase us at that speed?" Neutral face.

…nothing said.

"What could rip chunks off trees and toss them at the car like paper balls?" Neutral face.

nothing said.

"Roll it back, son, I just thought of it." His hand did a slow roll gesture. "What could rip off tree limbs, and even the tree itself out of the ground, then toss them like paper balls at the car while still giving chase?" Neutral face.

nothing said

"I'll give you this, the couple of whole trees that were thrown looked like older trees that were going to fall over by themselves sooner or later. But let's not forget. It also smashed cars and forced them to swerve off the road."

nothing

"And was still catching up."

"Keep in mind," his head cocked, "this is all at the same time." Neutral face.

nothing

It's on the tip of my tongue. There's a question I should have asked before.

"What do you think could do all of this?" Neutral face.

Nothing. Asher was trying to digest what was said and his own thoughts, his face conveying it all. Azmach's face stayed neutral, waiting for his meanings to soak in. What is soaking in?

"Monsters?" That's not the question I was trying to ask. Which one is over my head?

Azmach turned to me, looking in a way that answered what I just asked.

What question was filling the room, felt but unrecognized?

"We live in a world where the Alkeeb Gods are real," Azmach said. "So are Monsters."

Alkeeb? How does this connect? Tip of my head. Edge of my tongue.

"The Alkeeb what?" Asher questioned Azmach, seemingly himself and the atmosphere around him. "'Gods'? Scratch the gods part for a second, what is even 'Alkeeb'? You're just making up names now." His face scrunched up. "I've never even heard of them."

Something I should have asked.

"The Alkeeb Gods are the oldest of old," Azmach lightly added. "Any set of gods you've heard of the Alkeeb Gods are older. And are actually real."

"Now you're really just pulling our legs," Asher responded to him quickly. "I need to poke my head outside, see if pigs are flying."

"Then explain yesterday?"

Asher immediately went quiet. Nothing emanated from him except the look of freaked-out confusion. Azmach stayed silent, his face still neutral face.

Something I should have asked still stayed above my head. Something I should have already questioned.

"That thing on your back?" My words gestured, aiming to grasp that has been over my head, eluding me.

"Ah," Azmach reached between his jacket and shirt and pulled the dark gray thin rectangular object from yesterday. Wasn't flimsy. It was hard, smooth. He flicked it open, and it transformed into a wooden bow, still dark gray with a string connecting the two curved ends. "You mean this?"

My eyes examined the bow. Then, I examined him. Going over my head. One question I missed. Examined the situation. Over my head, dots connected. Light. Over my, no, on top of my head. A bow. Phasing into my head. "Alkeeb."

The most important piece of the puzzle shifted into sight. The metaphorical bush was becoming visible. It added up, but it couldn't equate to this. There was one question I should have asked, a question that should have been the first thing asked. No, I've somewhat asked it before. It was one of the first things I asked back in that detention room. I didn't, couldn't, ask like this. Not at that time. I couldn't understand the depth, and comprehend the fantasy shifting to reality. It's not possible. Regardless, the question needs to be asked, asked with an attachment of the depth needed to understand. So simple and complex. So real and surreal.

"Who are you...?" I asked. "Or rather...what...are you?"

"I'm what you are." Azmach answered with no hesitation. He kept eye contact, unwavering in his words and presence. "What you both are."

Asher leaned forward, listening.

A bow, healing, Alkeeb Gods, and monsters-"Which is?" I asked definitively.

Azmach closed his eyes while inhaling. His eyes opened. He exhaled.

Absolute silence.

"A Demigod."

Can Fantasy And Reality Intertwine To Create Truth?

"A Demigod."

Is that an echo outside or in my head? No, it's in my head. He just said it once. Why does it sound verbal? Why does it sound silent? He can't be serious. It has to be some sort of test, hyperbole, a concept along those lines. "A Demigod." So quiet and loud. What other truth is he getting at? A metaphor? "A Demigod" …demigod. Perhaps he's extremely pious. That doesn't sound right. He said I'm one too.

A demigod.

Asher hadn't moved. His eyes were wide and small, his mouth being partly agape. Quietness had never been so loud before, so impounding in my ears and head. No no no no no.

"A demigod?" I must have misheard.

"Yes. A Demigod."

"A demigod… As in…related to…the…Alkeeb…gods?" Or misunderstood.

"Yes. We are sons of Alkeeb Gods."

Asher's body and face had not moved….move?...I'm… surprised anything can move right now. This cannot be serious. It cannot be. I eyed Azmach, trying to figure out what possible double, triple, if not more, entendres existed in his words.

"So… what you're saying is…is that…" must be a sort of misunderstanding. "The Alkeeb gods… and any of the stories of them… are…the mythologies…" misunderstanding.

"I wouldn't call it mythology. I'd call it what it is."

"…Which is?"

"Real."

I think I'm done with words. I think I'm done in genera— what is all of this? What does he mean? What? Just, what? Slow down. I'm overthinking. I'll need to hear everything before I can see what he truly means. But reality.

Reality?

"Reality…?" I couldn't hold back that question.

"'Reality'." Azmach looked at me plainly like he was stating simple facts. He looked at me like he was confirming the answer with certainty.

It can't be simple. There has to be more of a meaning behind it, a depth I can't see. Nothing comes to mind. Nevertheless, there has to be a meaning. There has to be.

"I'll put it to you this way," Azmach flat out stated, his back straightening and eyes focused showing more conviction than I've ever seen from anyone in my life. "X'stayn, Orthantehs, Letnos, Missoa, Dittial, Mynzonus, Alytra, Zound, Nayleeuh, Ahlayniss, Bracktius, Telzyia, Lehgots, and the rest of them. The Empyreans, the Thrice, Major Gods, Minor Gods, The Behiims, the Primordials, Spirits, Dragons, Storm Harpies, Hellhounds, and that's just off the top of my head. Creatures, beasts, Monsters… They are real. All the stories, all the people, what we are, everything I just said and more. Every last bit is real, all of it, it's all real, I can't stress this enough. All of it. All. Of it… It's real."

There, he was quiet. Azmach allowed it to simmer in the atmosphere.

Everything given, filtered, filtered, filtered...There, it was quiet. In comparison, everything else must have been loud because this quiet was different. No, even the outside was now quiet. Or are my ears deaf? Real. My eyes blind. Real. My mind full, empty, spiraling,

real

demigod, those words cannot be in the same sentence. Why are they? How are they? Yet, he's serious. Azmach hasn't moved from his position.

Completely and utterly serious.

"Demigods..." Asher trailed.

He's a

"That bow," I pointed at his bow.

Azmach looked at what he was holding for a second, then back at me.

"That light you...had earlier...A demigod...Alkeeb. So...you're supposed to be...the...?"

"Son of Mynzonus, God of archery and healing." He had a small smile as he finished the sentence.

Quiet. "A god..."

"Yes."

"Real..."

"Real."

It felt quell and loud.

"M-Mynzonus," Asher stammered out. "He has healing powers? Do you...that's how you healed her...?"

Azmach looked at Asher as if he hadn't shattered entire perceptions.

"Demigods...?" Asher trailed off. "So... half God, half human?"

Azmach didn't change the look on his face.

"As in..." Asher continued to trail... "Half God. Half. God... Half God... Half human."

Azmach didn't change his countenance.

"So all of us have one parent that's a God," Asher tried to continually grasp. "The other parent's human-so my mom's human. That means for Gods... my dad—" Asher pointed at Azmach. "MMMMynzonus is your dad... and..." He turned and looked at me then turned back to Azmach. "Us all sitting here we're all... supposed to be Demigods?"

"Not 'supposed to,' we are." Azmach simply replied.

"We just can't be that," Asher abruptly stated. "Demigods?" He shook his head. "And you being Mynzonus's son, whoever that is." His face contorted. "That whole list of names you gave off too. Like come on. What's next? Vampires? Werewolves?"

"Those aren't real," Azmach said.

"Oh! So those aren't, but Gods are?! Gods?! And us being half Gods?! That's real!? But 'I vant to suck your blood', that's not real?! That isn't? Come on, man!"

"How injured are you?" Azmach's face was plain, turned towards Asher.

Asher stopped audibly breathing like someone had pressed pause on its sound. If ellipses were to be personified, they would be Asher at this very moment.

"How injured are the both of you?" Azmach compounded the question. "Let's keep count. Ran from a school that was falling to pieces, parts of it on fire. Tossed and turned in a car that had shattered glass everywhere. The car falls off a cliff. It was a short cliff; I'll give you that. But still, it was a cliff. The car crashed at the bottom. You both then pulled yourselves out, and ran through the woods you crashed into."

Asher looked at me briefly, returning his attention back to Azmach.

"How injured are you?" He asked again, now emphasizing the word "injured".

I glanced at my arms and hands. Scrapes, a few. Cuts, practically none. I could feel it through the decrepit fabric of my shirt. Mainly, my body was sore.

"There should be way more than a few scrapes and cuts." Azmach slowly looked between Asher and me. "Let's. Re. Count. School. Car. Cliff. Crash. Right here right now." He looked ahead at Asher and me at the same time. "There should be something broken."

Asher stared at his palm.

"A gash at the very least." Azmach didn't stutter, didn't stubble, didn't falter. "Cuts only?" He held that look. That look of fact. That look of conviction.

My mind just-

It was like reading a nonfiction book with everything on those pages being completely and utterly, without an ounce of doubt, absolute truth, yet my depth of the content, or lack thereof, crippled the absolution in my own head of the veracity of the possible facts. Is it a lack of comprehension or is it just supposed?

Truth, Reality, Fantasy, Reality. It can't. Can't.

"Has something ever happened to you," Azmach began the question.

Can't

"That you can't explain?"

Can't

"What do you mean 'explain'?" Asher eyes were wide in disbelief like he saw a ghost.

"You know what I mean."

Asher and Azmach held those words. They looked directly at each other, Asher looking at him like a cracked mirror. Azmach looked back, still as plainly as if the subject was so much simpler.

"Something weird." Azmach still. "Something you try to ration"—

Ration, perception

—"but cannot be rationed."

perception, Life

"Things that can only be explained" —
Life, reality
— "in ways you can't fathom."
Reality, Fathom. Fathom. How- How does one explain any-thing? All of what's happened? And now here I sit by two basically complete strangers in the middle of some forest or woods within Baltimore and and and and...I don't remember pushing him...in the kitchen...he practically flew across the room...crashed through that wall...regardless...regardless. Life is life.

"Look, man, I don't know about that..." Asher trailed off. "You say you healed her...It's just hard to-I don't know."

"What I do know is that we have Monsters after us. There is no time to stay stuck on this."

Silence gripped the air. Winter seemingly came early.

Demigods. This is. Demigod. What is? Identity?

...Identity...how to define...

"What if what you say is true?" I lifted my head to face Azmach. "What if I and you both are demigods." Thoughts. "What about all of this?" Connecting. "What then?"

"We move," Azmach stated.

"As in?"

"Outta here."

..."...As in?"

"You don't wanna be around here when the Monsters show up." He held eye contact for a second. "None of us do."

"Monsters... all this... I would ask...'Why didn't you tell us before?', but... that's just cliché and... why would we be-lieve until yesterday... plus now that I think about it...you said something of not believing you before..." Asher said, trailing while trying to grasp where his head was.

"I didn't have time. There were other things I had to get done."

Asher didn't reply, his eyes staring in the distance.

"Why did the monsters show up now?" I questioned.

"Why yesterday of all days? Why the school of all places?"

"It just so happened to be yesterday. And the Surges that led me there also led them. As long as the same basic variables were present, that could have happened at any time and at any place. There's something about that school, though."

"Since we're...Demigods..." Asher chimed in and trailed off, with more strength in his voice this time. "Couldn't we take the Monsters on? —"

"No." Azmach's eyes locked on Asher, unwavering on his word. "Not with the current conditions, not in the current circumstances, not with your lack of knowledge. Not at all. Whatever thrills you get from stories and fantasies– don't. Those stories are just stories. This is real life. You might have only gotten a few cuts and scrapes, but you still got them. You still got injured. You both are lucky to have just that. It'll get worse." He leaned forward. "These Monsters. This is something different."

"What's doing the chasing...?" I asked... just a silhouette... roars...

"That's the point. Something different. Something I've never faced. Something I've never seen, and I still haven't seen." Azmach inhaled, answering my barely asked question. "Two somethings."

...silhouette...

"Do you have any idea what either of them are, like cyclopes or a three-headed snake thing?" Asher anticipated.

"No. None of that." Exhale. "What I do know is that they are not the same type of Monster."

...hulking silhouette.

"What I do know is that we can't take either of them," Azmach persisted. "Even together."

"Well, we're still sitting here breathing," Asher pointed out. "Why haven't they gotten us?"

"They take breaks and sleep." Azmach gripped his bow tighter. "But you best believe they're still after us."

chasing…"…How is it…?… How are they able to…?" I trailed off, trying to ask.

"Aura." Azmach answered my question while looking between me and Asher periodically as he talked. "You don't need to Surge Out for them to sense you, but that definitely makes it easier for them. Since you both haven't Adjusted yet, your Auras keep spilling out. It screams you're a Demigod." He locked eyes with me. "Demigods are what these Monsters crave."

…crave

He turned to Asher. "Every last one of them."

…monsters…

He turned to me. "They will come after us."

after…

"Night. Day." Azmach reiterated. He breathed in deeply. "Demigods or not, we have to move."

"So… where?" Asher asked. Azmach tilted his head towards him. Asher leaned forward. "Where do we need to go?"

Azmach sat quietly for a second. He breathed in, deeply. "There's a place with hills, rocks, and trees." Held his breath. "A place safe for Demigods."

"Demigods…"

"Yes. Demigods." He put emphasis on the last letter in the last word he said to specifically emphasize the word being a plural. "Here's where things get interesting."

"It's not already?"

"It's where it's located."

…Located…monsters…demigods…where…

"How far?" …my mind trailed…grasping what I asked…

"Far."

"How far is far?" …mind still trailing…how far…

"States."

"Is that a joke?" Asher jumped in.

"Right now, we're still in Maryland. Where we need to go

is somewhere in the Midwest."

"Which state exactly?" …mind still trailing a bit.

"Illinois."

"Illinois!?" Asher freaked. "People in Illinois haven't even heard of Illinois."

"There are two Monsters chasing us. Not one. Two. This is the now, whether we like it or not. We're here and we need to get there, and it's not just a need, we must get there. There are no other choices." He held that look on his face, that look of fact.

"So get there or die." Asher summarized.

No other ways.

Azmach stayed silent, only nodding his head once. Just once. It was all that needed to be done.

"In that case." I began to ask a question, since there were no other choices. "Leave now or later?"

"This journey is going to be difficult. I mean this outside of everything else we talked about. We don't have a car. We can't take another random car unless, in that moment, it's a last second do or die situation."

"Isn't all this a 'do or die situation'?" Asher questioned.

"Driving away in cars seems to greatly agitate Monsters. They're apex predators. When you turn around and run, that's when they hunt you down and give a finishing blow. We've already seen what happened when one saw us in a car."

"Maybe a bus or train?"

"Who here has money on them?"

No answer.

"As I thought. If we had money, a bus and train can't take us all the way where we need to go. Even if we stow away, buses and trains still make Monsters act the exact same way as cars."

"That…" Asher trailed off.

"Let me be frank. You both are covered in scrapes and

some blood. Looks suspicious. Being in public too much looking the way we do…" He shook his head. "Add in taking a car. We don't need to add to this. Now, Demigod fingerprints and DNA are different. Our fingerprints have various subtle ancient African-looking symbols that make it hard for mortals to tell what's what. To them, it looks like somebody burned their fingerprints off. They can tell a person is there but not identify them. Our blood and DNA in general acts similarly."

"Similar how?" I puzzledly asked.

"Doctors will just think we have some rare crazy condition that can't be determined. They wouldn't be able to identify who and what we really are. We'll be fine with the crashed car. Even if they recovered it, they wouldn't be able to identify our blood and fingerprints because of the nonmortal half, especially since your God genes have started to awaken. Your God genes are going through your bloodstream as higher potencies as we age. Still, I'm not willing to risk the very minuscule possibility of being discovered."

"L-L-L-L-Look." Asher shook his head as if it was scrambled and shaking it would put all the pieces back in their place. "Aside from all that…whatever that was- Why don't you have a car in the first place?"

"Just don't. We're going to be traveling on foot. We're mostly going to be running. Jogging. We'll walk quickly when we need to cool down, but we're going to keep moving. For the rest of Maryland, we'll cut through some more towns and farms like yesterday as quickly as possible. We don't have much traveling left to exit this state. Once we hit West Virginia, we'll be traveling mainly through forests. There might be the occasional town, farm, city travel but expect these types of surroundings to be the norm for the next few weeks." He gestured with his outstretched arm.

"Few weeks?" I asked to make certain… just how long?

"About fifteen days, give or take. We'll be cutting through lots of areas, taking the shortest and least risky routes."

Asher was dwindling between trying to be calm and the opposite. "That's... a while."

"This journey, whatever you want to call it, it'll be difficult. It'll be draining. It will be daunting. This is nothing to brush off. We have no other choice. We must do this." Azmach focused on Asher and me, complete conviction on his face, it being stern showing tenseness in his jaw. He inhaled, inhaling all of the situation, all of the plight, all of the circumstances as a whole. Then, all of it, he exhaled. "If we are to survive."

Have to. No choices. No ways. This is it. Admittance... perhaps. Acceptance... that. That.

"For a few hours, we'll catch ourselves," Azmach reached between his shirt and bomber jacket and brought forth a skinny dark gray paper-thin, rectangular-shaped object. With one flick of his hand, it sprung in size, becoming a dark gray quiver. There were no arrows poking out the top. Glass shard yesterday... that's all he had.

"Rest," Azmach reached inside the quiver. "Heal." He pulled out a bottle of water, placing it in front of Asher. A second followed, placed in front of me. "And prepare ourselves."

Ready. How can someone be— water. When's the last time I had water?

Asher was already emptying his bottle's contents.

My mouth was dry. It was warm outside. Small beads of sweat were going down my sides. I reached forward. The bottle was cool to touch. It wasn't cold, but more like room temperature. I twisted the cap, taking it off.

Azmach flicked the quiver, returning it to its thin rectangular size and sliding it between his shirt and bomber jacket.

No choices, no ways. Admittance. But... acceptance?

"Before I forget," Azmach focused on Asher, who's eyes widened from the sudden focus. Digging in his jacket pocket, Azmach pulled out a black durag. "You need this."

Asher stared at the cloth. "You're not wrong." He reached for it.

Wrong.

He gripped the cloth.

So, this is all true? I could admit.

He placed it on his head.

Possibly...Reality?

He tied the tails around and up in the back.

Accept...that I don't...

He moved the tails and the durag as a whole around so it could fit correctly.

"Now I say we're ready to get ready," Azmach let his words lay down the situation. "In thirty minutes, we'll start."

Hours. More or less days more than two weeks total. Start, going. Do I ever move? Why do I feel in place? Stationary? I move but I don't.

Asher drank the rest of his bottle. I stared at mine. It's already twisted, the cap that is. Not. Moving.

shuffle

"It's starting to get dark, we'll set up for the night soon." Azmach said.

shuffle

crackle

All these leaves

crackle

shuffle

Lights fading

crackle

shuffle

Admittance

shuffle

"No more fires at night." Azmach. shuffle

But acceptance?

"They can be used to find us." Azmach.

crackle

shuffle

"It's hard for me to get cold anyway," Asher added.

crackle

shuffle

shuff…

"Here." Azmach.

shuffle…

"We'll set up." Azmach.

shuf…

"We'll get up in two hours." Azmach.

"Two hours?" Asher.

shu…

"We'll only be sleeping two hours at a time until we get there." Azmach.

shuf…

"I'll be sleeping as well, but I'll mainly keep watch."

shuf…

"Neither of you are ready for something like that under these circumstances."

fle…

"This is nothing to play with." Azmach.

"Yeah… I hear you there." Asher.

shuffle.

Lay down. quiet. silence. nothing. Laying down. Quiet. Silence. Light fading. Nothing. Today. Yesterday. Everything.

All the above.

Was it this dark before? Those two are asleep, laying down over there. I barely remember me laying down. Feels like no time has passed. On the contrary. What has come to pass?

demigods…Alkeeb. Tales wrapped in fantasy to present a supposed reality. And the presented reality… demigods.

I am a demigod. There should be a question mark, but that is a statement. All of the Alkeeb gods.

Mythology.

Admittance and acceptance? Admittance or acceptance. Is this an either or? All the above? All routine? There are two monsters chasing. Two in pursuit. Not a dragon based on what he said. What else could it be? That's not the point. Am I internally shaking my head? Shaking, yet still, yet same, yet different. All of yesterday. All of today. All…routine? It was so quiet. Just quiet.

Admittance, potentially. Acceptance…no. No.

I need evidence. I need tangibles. School demolished, roars, cars swerved off the road, trees thrown, the car knocked off the road. Proof of what, evidence of who, tangibles of essence are not found. They are not here. To fully accept, to fully engulf in this so-called possible reality, there must be something. Isn't there something…? No. Yes. Both of those answers. Admittance and acceptance with all of this being a routine are in hands but are not placed on the table.

However, there is a table. The table, the potential, stands on four legs. One, this guy is leading the way from Baltimore to Illinois, aiming towards somewhere in the Midwest. Two, whatever those two monsters are in fact are proven to be chasing, the proof shown by what happened at the school and car. Three, me in the forest with two people who, generally speaking, are practically strangers, one of them in particular. Four, explanations. Given the context, what other explanations would have made more sense? Any explanation would sound similar to that exact amount of lucidity, even in the confines of what is known as possible and impossible, before the potential new confines of what was told today, as well as what was possibly shown today and yesterday; yet, however, although, still, there is a table.

Admittance, the possibilities certainly. Acceptance, that I cannot do. It's still the same routine, a different table only inside the same room. That table could easily be the original table from days before, with alternative lenses, a change of perspective.

So quiet, like the edge of anticipation with no build up or tension, just the very existence of such is enough, and the fact of the possible potential of a plethora of perceptions past the publicized reality. End of the day, what is it? End of the day, how does it come together to the actual reality? So quiet. It can only come forth through time, through proof, through illustrations, through evidence; not something where there are only potential possibilities and nothing concrete. What is the one? What is concrete? What is the actual reality? The one given? The one that comes from the questions given? The same room with the original perspective of the table from before yesterday, along with what is in those hands that are now holding what was once on that original table?

Admittance. Acceptance... All this routine. All the above.

How Does One Prove Reality Seen From The Distance?

"A bit chilly," Azmach said to himself. Based on the sounds of undergrowth shuffling, he must have been sitting up. Seems he has awakened.

It is a bit cold, early in the morning. There was a bit of mist, a bit of dew on the leaves, branches, and other vegetation of various heights. It was almost the end of September, that much was evident. The leaves themselves were already beginning to change colors. Some were red, others yellow, some were halfway between two colors. A few were lying on the ground and on top of other vegetation. A significant number of green leaves were still hanging onto trees. Dim light blue rays were out, giving a tiny amount of daylight in the world like any usual morning.

I felt like I hadn't slept, a complete middle ground like a mind both processing and not. I didn't feel particularly cold. I felt... here and somewhere else. I looked out into the distance, leaning my right shoulder against a tree with my hands in my front pockets.

Some shuffling sounds behind. "A lot on your mind?" Azmach was walking up. The shuffling stopped. He must have stopped about a foot behind my left. My face stayed forward, still looking into the distance.

"Three days since we officially started moving," Azmach said in some introductory way. "And you still don't believe."

I turned my head towards him. He continued to look into the distance, his arms at his sides.

He turned his head towards me, a small smile on his face. "It's cool. Can't blame you."

How so?

"You have seen while not seeing." His smile faded into a blank expression as his head turned back to the distance.

I turned my head to look at the distance. My mind was empty and full, stagnant and moving. How does one describe such a feeling?

"Today, we're getting into real important stuff," Azmach informed, what he said hovered in the air. "Keep your eyes open."

shuffle

shuffle

He must have turned and walked away, the shuffling sound now coming from a distance from where it once was. Real stuff. The distance, I watched it. Looked into it.

"We're talking about Aura again?" Asher asked jokingly. He stood around some trees on the outer edge of a large field-like empty patch of dark brown forest floor. Surprisingly, the patch itself was short in height, only being a few inches tall, and surrounded by endless trees and several scattered autumn-colored leaves. The sun was beaming down through the afternoon sky.

"As a Demigod, some things are innate," Azmach stood in

the patch. "Other things take time to control. Aura is everyday energy. Whether you feel it or not, everyone has it. Mortal. Demigod. Monster. God. What you both are learning today is to control yours."

Asher's eyes perked up, considering it. "Aaaaand do what with it?"

Azmach instantly sat down, legs crossed, finding a stick in seconds and holding it. The stick began to emanate yellowish golden light, dim like last time, including a bit of the air around it.

Asher stared at the stick. "Well, that ain't a fluke."

The light stopped and Azmach placed the stick down. "Like me finding you both."

Asher lowered to the ground, now sitting next to him. "From Aura, Surges, and all that jazz."

"Why do you think Pericly noticed you?"

I looked up from where I was, sitting in the shade against a tree a few feet from the two of them.

Pericly.

"Remember what I said a few days ago? Right now, both of your Auras scream that you're Demigods. Any God, Demigod, and Monster within a radius will be able to sense you. Once you're fully Adjusted, it'll act normal like it did before your God genes started kicking in. For the most part, it'll act like it does for any God, Demigod, and Monster."

"And what does it normally act like then?" Asher asked.

"It'll feel as if you're completely human, except in certain circumstances."

Asher's head tilted, his eyes looking above as he took the questions in. "So, how do you Adjust?"

"By stopping Surges."

Asher had a face like he understood while also being confused by everything.

"A Surge doesn't just happen to happen. When the God half of a Demigod is starting to fully awaken, the body must

Adjust to something the likes of it has never encountered. Only over time does the body Adjust past the point of Surges occurring so easily."

Asher's expression remained the same, comprehension with an equal mix of confusion. "If it's about stopping Surges, then how does that go with Adjusting?"

"My whole point is getting you both to speed up the process of Adjusting."

"Come again?"

"The risk of your body Surging Out stops you from fully accessing your Aura. It's like a cap. You tap too much into that new Aura before you've Adjusted," he snapped his fingers, "you can Surge Out. As I said yesterday, you can also have too much of this new Aura build up inside you before your body has Adjusted," fingers snapped. "That can also make you Surge Out. And those aren't mutually exclusive. They could both happen at the same time to cause you to Surge Out. Only after Adjusting can you fully begin to control all of your Aura."

That makes some sense.

Asher's face had more comprehension rather than confusion. "So how do we stop Surges?"

"I know you've probably had at least one Surge before. You both probably have." Azmach's last sentence was louder than the rest. He must have wanted me to hear. Asher must have noticed. He turned to look at me with his eyes barely narrowing in curiosity, trying to see what Azmach was getting at.

"What pushed you to that point?" Azmach placed the question in the air.

Pushed.

"I said it days earlier," Azmach said. "Emotions." His head turned slightly in my direction. "Emotions can tap you into your Aura, which usually happens to most Demigods when their new Auras are first settling in. You don't need emotion to use it, but it can push more from within you. Since your

Demigod Auras have now started awakening, emotions will help jump start it until you have control."

"Emotions." Asher repeated that word.

"Yes. Trigger your Aura, push it to the edge of a Surge, then pull it back down. You're flooding your bodies full of Demigod Aura, then pulling it back down repeatedly until your body fully Adjusts."

Asher turned his head, looking at me, then returned his attention to Azmach.

"We're forcing your bodies to get used to it." Azmach finished. "We're speeding up the Adjusting Process."

Asher's face flickered like he understood everything. He readied himself for anything. I could only see half of his face from my angle, but it was more than enough to see how he was feeling.

"Like so," Azmach's hands rested on his knees as his eyes slightly narrowed.

Whoa. I feel something, something coming off him. His fingertips slightly had a very dim light, the yellowish golden color.

I felt this before. Detention, the day I first saw him. The energy coming off him, aura as he calls it. That same energy is coming from him now. It felt warm, calm, and solid. There was something else about it. Something doesn't feel...full.

Azmach's eyes didn't move, but they were slightly narrow. The energy he gave off was lowering as he looked at Asher.

Asher had the face of someone who was in the middle of building a structure with instructions that had skipped more than a few necessary step. "The light? Are we supposed to do that or something or?"

"I just showed a little light just so you could see while feeling what I was doing. When you do it, nothing should be showing since you're doing nothing specific with your Aura, except tapping into it. It'll show something if you Surge Out or you try and tap into some abilities. You got that?"

Asher seemed to be internally scratching his head. "Ah, kind of."

"First, you need to tap into your Aura. Think of something deep," Azmach highlighted to Asher. "Something personal."

Asher held his right hand in midair, staring at it attentively.

"Grasp it." Azmach said.

Asher's hand shook. The shakes were small, so incredibly small, but there. He was concentrating—

There's something there. Something. Nonetheless, I feel it. A small warmth type of feeling. It was interesting, like a candle being lit that hasn't been lit in a while, a warm energy that could possibly become warmer. No, more like an oven heating up after months of no use.

"Whatever hits your core," Azmach said to Asher.

Asher's hand continued its small shaking. That warm energy increased; although, it was not to an extreme extent. It also shouldn't be understated. There was certainly more.

"Grab it, and push it to the surface," Azmach encouraged.

Asher hand shook a little bit more, his face a mixture of concentration, ambiguity, and deep hesitation. Behind that mixture, the energy was building further. Hold on, what's that above his hand? It looked as if heat waves were around it. They were small, few, almost unnoticeable. Were they even there? For whatever reason, my eyes could be straining. No, they must be straining.

Warm energy built further within Asher, his face grimacing.

"Concentrate," Azmach encouragingly said.

The inside of Asher's hand looked as if a yellowish red light was shining through the skin. Dim, like a strong flashlight being lit under the hand. Wait, my eyes truly were straining. Or could be…

Asher grimaced. More warm energy was building up. His hand was shaking more and his teeth, now visible, were starting to grit.

"Concentrate," Azmach further pushed.

Asher's eyes were wide, staring at his hand shaking, the light being less dim than before. His head slowly shrank back from his own palm. Suddenly, his fingers clasped shut upon his palm, ending the sight as well as the feel of the warm energy.

"I don't know about this," Asher quickly said as he kept his eyes on his hand.

"It's cool," Azmach didn't flinch. "You were almost there. I was about to tell you to pull your Aura back down. We can't overuse and build up our Auras, or the Monsters will find us more easily."

"I...I just don't know."

"Don't rush it. I can tell it's gonna take days for your body to Adjust with the Speed Up Process." He stood up next to Asher. "Take a break for today."

Azmach walked towards me then stopped. "Once he gets further Adjusted, I'll get you started. I can't have you both start at the same time or it's going to increase our chances of being found."

Found. Monsters.

Azmach looked to his right at the trees, or rather what could possibly be behind them. "West Virginia, and I still can't tell where they're at. They have to be on our trail." He became quiet for a second. "But where?" He became quiet once again.

Where. Found and where. Regardless of what's true or not, two things are chasing and in this situation those two words sound... horrifying. Yet, and yet at that, whatever they are, they're out there... somewhere around... somewhere near...

Azmach looked back at me. "We'll move in a little bit." He turned and walked to a nearby tree, leaning against it.

There was something about him, something off. Like a little lie that's being kept. Azmach energy was different. It wasn't like it was from that detention day when he first appeared.

When he was building and pushing his energy out, not even five minutes ago, it was different. I'm not sure.

I turned my head and looked at Asher. He hadn't moved from the same spot. He was still sitting with his hand in mid-air. His hand in the air? Still?

Asher continued to stare at his hand. I could barely see from my position, but what I saw was enough. He stared at it like a historian would a relic. No, he stared at it with more meaning than some relic, more definite presence in the present time than an object of the past. Whatever it was, it is the now, coming from the now, affecting the now. It was all over his face back when that warmth was coming for him and especially presently. He stared at his hand, enwrapped in his thoughts and the convergence of what seemed to be the relic pulled to the current.

What is he seeing?

"It's gotten even chiller today," Azmach said to himself. He zipped his jacket up as he walked ahead of me and Asher, who was to my right.

He's not wrong.

"You said once our bodies Adjust, we'll be able to do stuff, right?" Asher questioned Azmach.

"You just started the Speed Up Process today now, and you're trying to jump the gun even further?" Azmach looked back at Asher as he continued walking through undergrowth, past trees with leaves now changing even more towards their autumn colors, and over other twigs and branches.

All routine.

"Aye," Asher smiled, "just wondering if we can do that light show you do?"

"Asher, you and I both know you have a bit of a light show of your own."

Asher's face slightly lurched back as he quickly looked down, then returned his attention to Azmach's back. He looked at me for a second then brought his face back forward. "So, will we be able to do your specific light show too orrrr?"

"Other things, most likely. Unless you're also sons of Mynzonus."

Asher's face froze with thought. A light bulb could've been over his head, and it wouldn't have been out of place. "How do we know which God is our parent?"

Azmach stopped in his tracks.

"That is an excellent question." He took a step forward, continuing to walk ahead.

Asher turned his head looking at me as he raised his eyebrows before turning his head forward.

"There are a couple different ways that can be used for identifying which God is your parent," Azmach began.

A couple?

shuffle

"They can randomly pop up for a second and straight up tell you." Azmach stepped forward, Asher listening intently behind.

"Or they'll straight up raise you like any parent should." Asher suddenly added. "Tell you sooner or later."

"Them doing either of those is the least likely to happen. At least, in the last two decades."

shuffle

step over a twig

"They'll give you some sort of sign." Azmach continued. "It could be subtle, like plants bending towards you in a kind of unnatural way. It could be apparent, like a red-hot hammer falling out of the sky and landing right next to you."

"A red-hot hammer out the sky? Is that a joke?" Asher asked.

"Not even. There's been a couple Bracktius kids I know who got that sign."

"Well I'll be. What type of sign did you get?"

"Not a single one."

shuffle

Asher looked at Azmach with a little disbelief.

"Most of the time, you'll have to figure it out yourself." Azmach kept forward, the sun starting to peer through the trees above.

Figure it out...

The wind blew, causing Azmach's durag and Asher's hood to flap for a second.

"How did you figure it out?" Asher stepped over rocks as a little more wind gently blew.

"Circumstances," Azmach pushed a low hanging branch aside. "It'll most likely be the same for you both."

crackle

Asher turned back and looked at me for a solid second.

"I do have an idea for who yours is," Azmach speculated to Asher.

Asher stopped walking like he was suddenly locked into place. "...for real?"

"We'll get to it. I want to confirm first." Azmach turned his head to face me. "For you, to be honest, I have no idea."

None?

"Give it time, we'll figure it out," Azmach turned his head back around.

Asher looked at me for a second, then forward.

None? Parents.

"I want to make sure I'm getting it," Asher started to reassure himself of his understanding. "So, nine Empyreans."

"Yep," Azmach assured Asher as he jogged, leading the way.

"And these nine are," Asher breathed in deeply as he collected his words and kept pace, "X'stayn, Orthantehs, Dittial, Missoa, Nayleeuh, Lehgots, Alytra, Mynzonus, and Ahlayniss."

"You've got it."

"There are four more important ones I think, uhhhhhh Letnos! That death shadow God dude."

"That's right that's right."

"And Telzyia and Zound. Oh yeah, and Bracktius, that blacksmith God."

"Can you say what each God you named are the Gods of?" Azmach ducked under a tree branch.

"On some, I'll probably mess up."

"Aye, it takes time."

"Do we have time?"

The rocks on the terrain increased along with distance traveled.

Azmach poured half a water bottle's contents on his face. Asher did the same. I poured water on my hands, rubbing them together, then scrubbed my face with my now wet hands.

"Push," Azmach instructed.

Asher's hand was raised just below his face, the energy coming off him— aura, they call it, Aura, no, no, energy. The energy coming off him was warm. The barely visible heat waves looked to be around his hand again. The energy level had increased, not substantially but noticeably, from before.

"Concentrate," Azmach encouraged from feet away. He was kneeling with one of his knees on the ground so he could rest while directing.

Asher's hand did tiny shakes as he seemed to be channeling something from deep within. The warm energy, his warm energy, heightened. Asher's face was what Azmach had encouraged, pure concentration. No, not pure. Something else was there, something else noticeably different from the first few times he did this process. Was there something different or something becoming more defined? Panic and hesitation were less prevalent now than the very first time. No, it was something else.

"Almost," Azmach steadied Asher.

Asher's hand tensed-oh, there's more of that warmness. Asher's hand shook further. Were there more heat like waves coming from it or was I staring too intently? It's barely there if at all, so it could be argued either way.

"Almost," Azmach pushed Asher.

Asher's hand shook, warm energy now at the edge of igniting.

"There it is," Azmach swiftly said. "Now drop it."

Asher relaxed his hand, the possible heat waves around it disappeared, all the warm energy vanishing from where it once existed. He continued to stare at his hand intently.

"Day two, and you're really getting the hang of it." Observed Azmach.

Asher looked at the forest ground for a second then stood up, continuing to look at his hand. Without breaking eye contact, he took steps towards Azmach, who was still taking a knee.

"You okay? Do you need anything?" Azmach asked without any hesitation.

"Uh, well..." Asher trailed off, finally breaking eyes from his hand. "I was wondering about if...how..."

Azmach smiled. "Go ahead and say it man."

Asher's face turned to the side as he was collecting his words. "Uh...When it comes to..." Collecting his bearings. "...powers..."

Azmach listened calmly.

"Uh, and all that...stuff..." continuing to collect and trail. "When will...how..." looks at the forest floor at an angle. He breathed in deeply and directed his eyes to nothing else except Azmach. "When will we learn how to use our powers?"

"Powers?"

"Yes." Asher nodded, more so to himself. "Powers."

"Hm," Azmach pushed off his knee to stand tall. "I wouldn't recommend."

Asher stayed quiet.

"Not now, not here," Azmach turned, stepping a few paces away from Asher, looking around at the surrounding endless onslaught of trees.

Asher had a forced blank expression. "...it's just—"

"We can't." Azmach turned back to Asher, stepping towards him. "I know you have a lot of baggage from powers, and you're trying the best way for you to grasp it, but—"

"I'm not talking about anything big." Letters overflowed in Asher's mouth, making him choose between forcefully chewing it up or just intensely spitting them out into words. "I'm talking about—" spitting. "I'm talking about..." chewing.

Azmach looked at Asher and nodded, a puff of air coming out of his nose as he held a face of pure understanding. "I hear you dude. I do."

Asher grew quiet.

"I understand." Azmach's palms faced the sky before returning to his sides. "We just can't risk it. Those Monsters, those things." He looked around for a second, seeing if something was near...or if something was watching..."They could be anywhere. And I mean anywhere."

...monsters...Anywhere...

anywhere...

Asher looked disappointed but was also mulling.

"That will be something to focus on once we get where we need to be," Azmach emphasized. "That I promise."

Asher stared at Azmach, taking in his words. He heard and listened, but his face was half empty. His demeanor was no different, if not comparatively, to the beginning of the conversation, like a cracked door to emotions. The very few finite differences were from fractions of traces of emotions tinkling from the crack more now than before the conversation.

Azmach nodded, understanding, and turned his head to

look through the trees and vegetation to see in case there was anything close. "It's getting dark." He narrowed his eyes, stepping through a world of green and uncertainty. "We'll get moving soon."

shuffle

shuffle- Azmach walked away from where he stood.

shuffle

shuffle- Asher walked closer to a tree while staring at his right hand again like he has been the past couple of days.

All these past days.

…anywhere…close…

I leaned my head further back on the tree I was sitting against.

…close…

The terrain became hillier and, to an extent, mountainous, thus quickening the danger of this plight. Danger has already been growing in this plight. The terrain, if anything, is symbolism, a motif even. How befitting. Where the fitting of the danger begins and concludes is based solely on the tangibility of so-called possible realities in a probable sense.

Azmach and Asher were sitting, tilting to one side since they were on a hill, surrounded by trees and leaves.

I sat a few feet away, leaning my back against a tree.

Is this reality extending to the theoretical depth explained days ago? Is it…

Azmach stood up. "Alright, that was our minute break. Back to it."

Asher stood up.

"And you," Azmach said, referring to Asher.

"Back to that speed up thing," Asher finished Azmach's sentence.

"You're right on it."

I stood and followed a few feet behind as Azmach and Asher jogged. Asher held his hand up and pushed out warm energy, or at least that's what was explained.

How do I explain the warm energy?

"How do you know where you're going?" Asher asked.

"This ain't my first-time trekking through this part of the country," Azmach answered. "I'm going down memory lane."

"When was the first time?"

shuffle

Asher stepped over a dip in the ground, the ground itself becoming rockier ever so slightly.

"Some years back," Azmach ducked under a tree branch, "I was surviving out here for like half a year."

"Aoh," Asher bent his head to the side to pass a tree branch. "That got real."

Azmach chuckled for a second and settled down instantly after. "Yeah. Then someone saved my life. He took me to where I'm bringing you two now."

"Who was he?"

"You might meet him. He's still there."

"Nice," Asher nodded his head, approving of the possible meeting.

What is possible?

What time is it? It's dark now. When did it become dark? Can't sleep. Another night of this? Why can't I sleep?

"Aye man, you've been quiet lately," Asher's head was turned to me as he walked to my right. He and I were following Azmach, who was a few steps ahead leading through the trees, other vegetation, and the evening's last bit of orange sun.

"Like quieter than usual," Asher added. "It's been days since you've talked."

crackle

I turned my head, looking at Asher for a second. Then, my head went back forward. Not quickly or slowly. It's just a matter of…

"A lot on your mind," Asher answered his own question. "I feel, man." Asher's demeanor deflated a small amount. "I have some things on my mind too—"

Snap!

Freeze! - Azmach threw his hand up behind him, signaling for no one to move a muscle. .

what was…

step step, small shuffle-Azmach gingerly stepped towards where the sound originated

is it…

a stick snapping to the right—Azmach kept his hand up - step step, closer and closer to the sound, he went.

closer…

behind a tree and some long green vegetation with autumn leaves already laying upon it. I can't see what it is.

Step step-Azmach peered forward to the right, forward behind the tree and greens…

Asher's eyes were slightly wide while he watched Azmach looking towards the tree and greens…

closer… step step- Azmach, inches away from where the sound originated, stopped moving. He was about to unmistakably check the tree and behind the greens.

Three-Azmach leaned a little more forward.

Two- Asher waited, barely breathing.

One.

Azmach whipped the greens out the way, aggressively checking what was around them and the tree itself. His bow had already been snapped open so quickly there was no way it wasn't in his hand before. His eyes focused, narrowed, scouring up, down, thoroughly. He stilled. He let out a puff of air from his nose. He relaxed, taking steps back away from the greens and trees. Instantly, a hare poked its head out and sped off into the distance, not once looking back.

Asher exhaled loudly. "Thought that was…"

"Better safe than dead," Azmach responded. He still watched the trees and vegetation.

"Look. We ran into a rabbit this time. But just in case, when are we going to learn other stuff…like powers?" Asher asked Azmach abruptly like a puzzle he had only seen glimpses of once had come to his mind again, and now there was a pounding need to know more than just those simple glimpses.

"In due time," Azmach answered as if he saw the question coming. "You're almost done with the Speed Up Process. "Then"–he turned to me– "you'll start."

"But what if—"

"It'll be fine." Azmach reassured Asher. "Don't worry."

Asher exhaled, nodding.

Azmach stepped away from where he was, going back in the direction he was leading before the snap. "Let's continue."

What does continue mean in this context? Is it in arm's reach or closer? Simply the unknown with very few references. Has one ever felt in the present and somewhere else indefinable at the same exact time? Like something so eerie one can't grasp, yet it's right there in arms reach. What is out there? On the edge? Or…closer than arms reach, past the fingertips, past the wrists? Up against one's beating heart inside of one's chest?

What is the possibility of…eyes open - walking behind Azmach with Asher to my left.

Where's the certainty… eyes close- another night, how many have passed total?

Regardless, that feeling is there. That low hanging feeling. Regardless of certainty or implicitness, it hangs low, low enough to impact more than the physical heart. Eyes open. Eyes close. Eyes open, Eyes close. Is it in arm's reach or closer?

Eyes...

Night's out. It's late. I sat and leaned my back against a tree as I prepared to try and sleep. Well...I still can't seem to sleep.

shuffle
shuffle
Another long day of traveling.
shuffle

shuffle
shuffle

"You feel any differences?" Azmach asked Asher.

"Normal...but I have to admit, looser. In a relaxed way." Asher started standing up from where he was sitting.

Normal. Routine. It isn't completely out of the ordinary, out of the question, that is. What is ordinary? Must it be explicit?

Azmach had his quiver was in hand. "I'll say you're very close to being fully Adjusted." He reached in and pulled out a water bottle, passing it to Asher. He then reached in again, pulling out an apple and passing it along as well. "Maybe by tonight."

Asher was already gulping down all his water, ready to devour the apple next. He suddenly stopped, looking down. "'Tonight.'"

"I haven't forgotten about you," Azmach tossed a bottle followed by an apple to where I was sitting. I caught both, placing the bottle down on the ground and holding the apple with my right hand.

Asher handed his finished water bottle to Azmach, who slipped it back inside the quiver. Azmach tossed his finished apple onto the ground to allow decomposition.

"We need to get moving before it gets darker." Azmach instructed.

Asher stayed quiet, staring at the inside of his hand per usual.

Usual...normal.

Walking, jogging, running. It changed based on how much time was in the day and how much time was wanted to be stripped from the journey. Over rocks and vegetation alike. Asher bit into his apple, tossing it to the side once finishing.

Azmach stopped ahead, seeing something. "We'll have to take a boat."

Asher stepped ahead and saw a river past the trees. "Here we go again."

"A good number of states have rivers that border them, like West Virginia and Kentucky..."

"So we have to find another boat."

"We have to find another boat." Azmach's eyes tightened as he peered around the area. "Taking a boat is risky in the same ways as taking a car. It's also way too out in the open, anything could see us." He eyed the waters, his face tightening in thought. "I didn't make a fuss last time since we had no choice, and it's the same thing this time. That river's way too wide to swim, miles long. We'll have to do this again to cross a river within Kentucky. That might not be the last time."

"Figured." Asher nonchalantly brushed off.

Azmach's eyes were slitted as he looked around. "We're in an isolated area. If we're lucky, someone was once here and left a boat. We got lucky last time, but I don't like counting on luck. Boats do get left more often than you think, especially when they're old, maybe stolen. Sometimes they're forgotten, sometimes they're left behind on purpose. Sometimes in this area. We probably could find an old one."

"Better than nothing."

"Exactly."

Azmach carefully stepped around. "Watch your six. There could be people."

"Or Monsters." Asher said in a low voice.

Azmach looked around, leaning his body forward, craning his neck. He stepped and moved lightly in his search. He crouched under leaves and stretched his neck to study the shore.

Asher peered past trees, leaning on some as he looked at the left side of the shore running into the distance.

Minutes passed.

Asher looked at the shoreline, waiting for-"There's one I think." He pointed at vegetation at the shoreline. Hidden under some was a barely noticeable old, dirty, white rowboat flipped upside down.

Asher quietly rushed over to it.

"So we are in luck," Azmach said.

Asher flipped it over and examined its condition. "What do you think?"

Azmach crouched down and eyed it. "Doable. Let's test it first."

The two of them put it on the river's edge and held it so it wouldn't drift away. So far, it didn't immediately sink.

"I see no leakage," Asher observed. "Can it hold three?"

Azmach stepped one leg inside it while making sure half of it stayed on the shore by pulling it further in so it would have a hard time drifting away. "We'll start with me." His other leg followed, and he sat down.

Asher observed and nodded. "Nothing." He stepped inside, keeping his eyes open for any water that could be flooding. "Looks good." He looked at me. "Come on Jason."

Come on...is this, this is real. The circumstances are how...

I stepped inside and sat down.

Azmach pulled out his bow and quiver, not snapping them open. "Let's get across to the next shore quickly." He used them to push the boat completely offshore, then dipped them partially into the water, using the unopened bow as the right oar and the quiver as the left.

The sun was dying down as Azmach rowed. Clouds grew in the sky. It was going to rain tonight or tomorrow.

"Basically, Kentucky," Azmach said through his rows. "So far, so good."

The unopened quiver and bow made small waves, pushing through the water. The rowing itself was beginning to be harder to see. The sun was still able to shine through the clouds, but with night approaching, and the clouds building, there was nothing that could be done to stop the incoming night.

Asher sat quietly, staring at his hand once again. He looked like he was somewhere else. Wherever he was, it was far, and it was deep.

"'Tonight'," he said to himself, softly.

"As of today," Azmach said in an introductory manner. He turned his sole attention to Asher. "Your body's fully Adjusted."

Asher sat a couple feet from Azmach as he looked through the darkness of the night then at the ground. "Hm."

Trees encompassed the area, making it even darker. Everything was in shades of black and dark grays. The sounds of night filled the air. Crickets, other insects. Open space.

"You're Aura isn't coming out as a screaming presence anymore," Azmach said to Asher. "It's a lot harder to feel. Now, it's normal like everyone else's. More subdued."

Asher nodded silently.

"I'll get you started in two hours," Azmach said to me. "Let's sleep until then." He made sure his durag was on correctly before lying down in a comfortable position.

I sat feet away from the two of them, my head now leaning back against the cool bark and my eyes closing.

Rest. Can I ever fully rest? Is it simply not within me? Am I even tired? Am I ever tired? Yes. Exhaustion, on the contrary of belief, doesn't guarantee an entryway to sleep. Am I even exhausted? That might be a hyperbole, however tired I am nonetheless—

Why is there sudden light? This isn't natural night light—

I opened my eyes and turned my head to see the inside of Asher's right hand emanating a reddish-orange light. His hand shook as he clearly concentrated, which was further shown by the light radiating his face. There was more warm energy coming from him than ever before.

Azmach sat up immediately. "What are you doing?!"

Asher was exhaling loudly as his hand shook harder and harder. The light was gaining more definition, more-

Flames engulfed the inside of his hand. Asher grunted.

…flames…actual flames…fire…

It wasn't just engulfing.

….fire…going…in his…hand…flames…

The flames whipped up like a reverse faucet at the fingertips.

…fire…actual…real…

Asher's face tensed in concentration as he grimaced, his eyes locked on the reddish-orange flames.

…real…

The flames started at the palm and were building up where the fingers connected to the hand. It looked like waves fighting each other to get to the fingertips first.

…real…

Asher's hand shook in a concentrated chaos. His hand then slammed shut into a fist, the flames extinguishing with no trace.

…reality…

"Do you realize what you've just done?" Azmach was incredulous.

…that…

"I get it." Asher.

…how.

"No. You don't," Azmach condemned. "And I guess not at all."

…how-how-how-how-How —

I stood up, walking away from…what that was. What was that? Flames, fire, sure. What was that? How. How did that…within the confines of reality. Usual…Normal…Routine? Perhaps, perhaps so, still concrete is needed. I just don't know. Like a head in the clouds with no clear sense of up, down, left, right, and overall direction. I just don't know.

But isn't that concrete?

The vegetation crackled, shuffled, and snapped under my feet as I walked further.

Mythology being the opposite of mythical. Gods, monsters, auras, all that being real? Demigods…me being a demigod…or rather a Demigod?

How? How did that happen? How did all of this happen? None of this makes sense, and now here I am stuck in an almost obliquely incongruent sense, a sense that, relatively speaking, doesn't change nor negate fact.

My shoulders scraped against trees, my fingertips feeling bark times.

Practically. Fact. Isn't what happened seconds ago enough to cement the concrete?

…

I stopped walking, leaning my right shoulder against a tree. Isn't it enough?

…r

Isn't what happened explicit enough?

…e

Evidence enough?

…a

Fantasy

…l

Meeting

…real

Reality.

I just stood there, quiet. Is this quietness in my head or out-side? I'm not sure. I was just quiet.

Reality. That's just it. Reality. Eyes. Reality. Eyes…Open. Reality… Open. Gods. Monsters. Not simply aura, but Aura. Demigods… A reality. The reality.

Quiet. So quiet…

Admittance? Yes. Yes, I can admit that. Acceptance? Yes. Yes, I say it all. All of this must be, and is, the norm, the real-ity.

Admittance and Acceptance.

All routine.

Quietness. No voices? Aren't those two still talking? It was pure quiet. How far away did I walk? I should go back. I pushed myself slowly off the bark and—

Wait. Why is it so quiet?

No crickets, no animals, nothing. Temperatures have been dropping a little, but that doesn't explain this drop in noise. Quiet doesn't describe it well enough. It was just silent. Com-plete silence.

Silence itself doesn't even describe it well enough. It was just soundlessness. Absolutely soundless. What is this? This feeling? It's like a soundlessness to the extent that it made it conceptually not soundless, the absence of noise being a noise itself.

Something is wrong.

I stepped away from my spot slowly and looked around. Leaves crackled and vegetation shuffled from my move-ments. That just made it worse. Those were the only sounds now, as small and barely existing as they were. Sounds within the absolutely soundless.

Something is very wrong.

It felt like a heart stopping that somehow didn't cause

death. Instead, life continued without the continuation of a heartbeat.

No heartbeat, which would make no sound...

What is this feeling? Where? Don't know. Is something even here? What's this feeling? Over there. Why over there? What's over there? It was all difficult to see with it being dead in the night, dead in the dark. I crept a few steps forward, peering around as I did.

...what is...

...this feeling.

I soundlessly stopped and squinted ahead.

That tree. Far, nor close, it was ten to twenty feet away. It was barely visible, only a silhouette. Kind of tall, thick, surrounded by tall underbrush with other trees very nearby. What's with this feeling? Why this tree? I stared. I stared... This tree... This tree...

... Is it moving?

The tree creaked in resistance. Middle and some higher branches and limbs were slowly being pushed to one side. Wind must be trying to pass through.

My mind went blank...because there was no wind...

Branches, limbs, parted further, creaking and snapping, some breaking through the soundlessness. They bent further. Something started poking through the gap of the parting. An outline. It poked further. No. Horns. Two of them. Further. Nose poking out. Animal nose. No, I wish it was just an animal. Creeping forward, branches were creaking further with a few snapping. Ten feet high? No, more than that. Big and large. Can't see its width. Concealed by the tree and darkness. Concealed by vegetation and darkness. Concealed... I'm not sure I want to see it. It poked further forward. I know this one. I read about this one. I've seen this one before. Not in real life.

I don't want to see it in real life.

Horns of a devil. It stayed there. Snout of a beast. It turned its head downward. It's looking at me. It's glaring at me.

Monster…

Branches snapped as it pushed forward. Its glare continued. Absolute soundlessness…

Run.

I don't even remember turning around. My shoes were already pounding against the ground as I sprinted back to the sleeping site.

Snap! More limbs broke from the tree it was at.

Snap!

It's coming.

Come on, where are those two?! They must have been too deep in their conversation and didn't notice me walking off or the noises yet. Hurry, Hurry! It's hunting me. The ground shook with each of its steps. I could feel it. Feet behind me. Go! Go! Faster! I slapped branches, leaves, and more out the way as I ran.

"One misstep and we're dead," Azmach's voice. Tiny, small, barely distant. Over there. Behind some trees and—

Snap!

"Listen," same voice, Azmach's, closer, now obviously hearing the branches breaking.

Almost tripped. It's still behind me. Closer or farther, I couldn't tell. I rushed forward, vegetation slapping me as I surged, the ground shaking. Faster! Over there!

I skidded past a tree to a halt a few feet away from Azmach and Asher. The sound of me breathing loudly from all the sudden running was all I heard. Asher stared at me, obviously noticing something wrong. Azmach turned his face. He without a doubt looked alarmingly serious, leaving no query that he knew exactly what was happening. His eyes locked on mine, no words escaping his closed mouth.

One, quiet. Two, soundless.

"Let me guess?" Azmach asked without needing an answer.

Snap!

Asher jerked his head to the sound, eyes wide. Azmach reached over, heavily tapping Asher's leg. "Get up," Azmach said as he himself was standing up.

Snap!

Asher was an icicle in the dead of winter that was also trying to move. "Oh-oh I'm—"

"We'll talk about it later," Azmach grabbed Asher's bicep, pulling him up, and staring past me. He focused on the trees for any movement, moving his own self slowly forward towards where I just entered. Even with some natural dim moon light, it was practically impossible to see past the surrounding trees. Still, Azmach stared, trying to see past the impossible. Asher stayed where he was standing, clearly holding back an apprehension that didn't do the word justice.

I need to move.

Taking steps forward, I turned and walked backwards as I watched where the Monster had been pursuing. I've never thought of this Monster as a fear. I've seen this one, heard of this one, know this one, but it being here in real life, in reality... This feeling. It's here. For sure, it's here. But where?

Soundless.

RROOOOOAAAR!

No one moved. Such a vicious sound... a vicious scream. That scream was right ahead. That was nothing. That was barely any feet away.

No sudden movements.

Crack!-the tree yards in front of me was slammed into, the base of it starting to crack more and more. It's pushing the tree to break it.

I turned and rushed away.

Crack!-the tree had fragments broken off completely— Instantly I rolled to my right just as the tree fragments, branches, part of the base, crashed and rolled onto the ground. Limbs and branches scratched my left arm and side.

"Over here!" Azmach yelled.

Asher was already behind Azmach looking between the fallen tree and me.

Movemovemove. I pushed myself up rushing towards Azmach and Asher. The two of them turned and swiftly ran once I had caught up.

Snap!

I pushed deeper into the dense trees, rushing behind the two of them.

Crack!-a tree limb snapped and flew towards me, its branches scratching my back and nearly catching at my heels.

In the midst of running, Azmach whipped his bow out, already spinning around with a pointed branch. A little bit of yellowish golden light was added to the branch, barely noticeable. He pulled back and let it fly, shooting past my head—

ROOOAR!

"Keep going!" Azmach whipped back around, surging forward. "Turn here!" Azmach slid into a deeper, denser part of the forest. The trees became bigger, with thicker limbs. Some limbs and branches of different trees were weaving tightly next to each other. Some of this weaving was on the lower half of the trees.

I see what he's doing.

Thunder boomed in the clouds above.

Crack!-another tree limb broken. It was multiple yards behind. Still, too close for comfort—

Snap!

Azmach was breathing heavily as he ran. Hold on, he was breathing more heavily than he should've been. Asher was behind him, keeping up but wasn't breathing so heavily. A—

Cracks!-branches fell, scratching my left side.

Azmach was now leading upward. A hill. No. More like a

mountain—

RoAAAR!

It had been getting hillier and rockier over the last few days—almost tripped. Asher noticed, making a face that said it all.

Some of the tree branches and limbs were stretching even lower to the ground, twisting further together to make an almost makeshift barrier. It was hard maneuvering around, literally forcing me to run in circles and spin. I shifted right, leaping and ducking under branches. Azmach slid past a tree with a massively thick trunk then weaved past another. Asher hurdled between two trees standing close together, scraping his right shoulder—

Crack!-pieces of a tree base were shot towards my direction, the pieces being much bigger than hail. I felt some of them, the sting. Move. I slide right to avoid them— gah I'm slipping back down the hill. My knees scraped against rocks as I slipped further—my body turned until I was sliding on my back. Quickly, I reached up to stop myself from slipping more. Quickly grab something anything hold onto the ground, I just barely did—

Right there. The denser trees, with branches and limbs twisted and bundled together, concealed the Monster below. And it did not allow this concealment any longer. It tore at the branches and trees, snarling. For its size, some of it needed to be broken. It all slowed it down, but it was still gaining.

Crack!-closer.

Those. Those horns. Two long horns. Two enormous horns like a demon. Fangs sharper than anything in existence. Salvia dripped from each long one. Each fang looked corroded. Still, nothing could break them. Fur covered its body. Pure hunger, hatred. Right there. Barely twenty feet from me down the hill. I could see it. Oh, I could see it. The darkness, trees, and twisted limbs holding it back conceived it somewhat.

Still, I could see it. It stared at me, and I stared back wide-eyed in disbelief.

ROOOOAAAR!

Right in my face. I could feel its breath. Worse, I can taste it. Rancid, fermented. I can hardly breathe. Sweat streamed down my face and body. I could feel it all, but not as much as I felt its stare, its contempt, its-its…I'm frozen. Move! Can I? Move! Move! Breathe and Move!

I turned away to pull myself up. A hand clasped around my wrist.

"Come on," Asher urgently pulled me up.

Azmach was ahead, halfway up the top of the hill, pulling back a pointed branch on his bow. He's taking its attention, buying time.

Get up.

I stood and rushed up the hill. To my left, Asher looked behind his shoulder eyeing the—

Crack! Snap!-it's forcing its way up. It must be angrier. It'll break everything possible.

Azmach let the branch fly, shooting above my head. Already, he was shooting another one. The branches he shot had no light on them. The Monster paid no mind. An assortment of cracks and snaps were breaking through the air.

Asher and I caught up to Azmach and stood next to him. Azmach's eyes locked on the Monster. He turned his head to look up to the top of the hill behind him. The other side past the top couldn't even be seen. Then, he turned back to the Monster forcing itself forward, pushing and breaking dense tree limbs, back down the hill. "Seems there's no choice."

What does that mean?

Thunder exploded harder above.

"This way," Azmach turned and rushed forward away from the continuous cracks and snaps. Of course, I and Asher followed.

Thunder exploded above louder than before.

Shoes pounded against the ground. Cracks and snaps broke further through the air. It's breaking out of the denser part. There's no time. Go! Go!

I rushed forward, the top of the hill coming closer and clos—

RrOOOAAR!

Snap!-tree limbs scattered and spun above, flying in every direction. I looked behind my shoulder. Its arm shot forward, breaking past more trees and limbs. Four fingers, one of them a thumb, all of them were horrid, raggedy, beastly, sharp claws at the end of each, all were razors—

RROOOAAAAR!

CRack!-a part of a tree was broken off. Some seconds will hold it back in the denser trees longer.

No time. Look ahead.

I focused forward, the top being feet away.

"Here we go," Azmach put his bow back in its place, stopping at the summit of the hill. The air in front was now an opening in the trees and denseness.

Cracks and snaps broke out.

Azmach looked downward.

...Hold up. Downward?

I stopped next to him and also looked downward.

Downward?!

This was a mountain. In this situation, this plight, that's drastic. It was a steep mountainside that was basically a drop into even denser and bulker trees. Jagged Rocks, dirt, some low vegetation, and many trees of all sizes. A pure mountainside. It might as well have been a cliff.

Thunder became common, exploding above.

Asher stared down the steepness. "Maybe there's a different way—"

RROOOOAAR!

"Does it sound like there is?" Azmach looked at Asher, already locked into the decision.

Thunder.

Cracks and snaps.

Asher looked back down the hill where the Monster was. He then looked forward down the steep incline as he rubbed his hands together, inhaling sharply. "This is going to hurt."

Crack! RROOOOAAAR!

-booming steps-it's free-out the denser trees-it's coming

"Now!" Azmach urgently yelled.

The both of them and I jumped.

My ear drums rushed from the air scraping by-Gah! My back scraped, sliding down the mountainside. The world was spinning-

ROOOOOAAAR!

Tumbling and turning-Ah, side of my head hit-breathe breathe- my elbow-

ROOOAAR!

Cover my head! Cover my-

Explosion of thunder.

Arms around my head-Ah-my side, definitely a tree-Gah my chest- scraping and scraping and sliding and sliding-

Thunder.

dirt kicked up, close my eyes-turn turn feet out!-my ankle. On my back. Legs spread a bit. Slow down. Slow down! There.

The mountainside started to plateau. It was certainly still angled like any mountainside, but it was more manageable. I looked out below as I slid on my back. Asher and Azmach were a bit further down-

my heels-ankles-Gah-a big rock tilted me- Spread my arms. Ah-smaller rocks pelted my arms-No! I was flipped onto my stomach-tossing and turning. Protect my head!

Asher grunted from somewhere. Not sure. My eyes were

closed again—

Gah! I slammed into something thick and bulky, stopping completely. It all stopped completely except... Breathe... Breathe... Breathe... Nothing existed except... Breathe. No light or darkness existed. Just...Breathe...Breathe...Breathe...

...eyes open.

What I had slammed into was a tree. Thick, large, strong. The bark was rough, tough against my inflamed skin. I pushed myself up slowly, my body already sore—can't stand yet, not ready to. I leaned on the tree. Scattered leaves and tall trees were going down the rest of the mountainside. It wasn't as steep as the part behind me, but of course it was still angled. Or do I just feel angled? Probably both.

"Everyone good?" Called out a voice.

I stepped around the tree, leaning on it for support to see exactly who I heard. Azmach was some feet further down, covered in leaves, a few dirt streaks, some scrapes, and holes on his jacket. He was breathing heavily as he stood.

Thunder exploded, the loudest yet.

I pushed myself off the tree, stepping-ah, that's sore for sure-towards the two of them. I pushed myself, walking faster, getting within a few small feet of them-doable. This pain is doable.

Asher had managed to get up a few feet from Azmach, his hands on his knees, scratches and holes on his jacket and shirt, as he eyed back up the mountainside. "You think it's still chasing us?"

"Let's not wait to find out." Azmach answered swiftly.

Thunder erupted.

Asher nodded. Azmach turned, running further down the mountainside. Asher was right behind, clearly ready to do whatever to get away from death.

I was already behind the two of them.

Vegetation, branches, and all slapped as I hurried further downward, deeper into the forest. The feeling of the Monster still chasing at every step never settled. All of this, the horns, the claws, the fangs, the Monster still chasing, yet being left behind, yet feeling as if it was exactly right here, did not leave. This feeling, now solid and persistent, built stronger and stronger.

How Does Death Factor Into Responsibility?

"You think we're safe?" Asher crouched underneath an outstretching rock mass, hiding from all the rain pouring down.

"We ran the entire night without stopping, and faster than we usually did. I say we're safe. For now." Azmach also crouched, his clothes partially soaked from all the rain coming down.

The rain showered harshly from above, pouring seamlessly from the early light of the morning sky.

"Look," Asher slouched deeper under the natural rock, already soaked to the bone. His face was pained, squinted up in guilt as rain droplets ran down the sides. "This was all my fault—"

"Asher," Azmach calmly said. "It's not your fault."

"Naw, I should've listened. Instead, I got stuck in my own thoughts, my own... fire, my own..." He inhaled deeply then exhaled just as hard. "If I didn't do it, we wouldn't have almost been killed."

"And we weren't," Azmach said as if it was that simple.

The rain pouring down sounded louder as Asher was silent as he was either taking in Azmach's last three words, rejecting them, or a combination of both, all of which seemed involuntary.

"It was already in the area," Azmach added. "It was going to find us last night no matter what."

Asher stared forward at the rain, looking for encrypted messages inside the droplets.

"Now, I'm not gonna sit here and front," Azmach said, his tone having slight agitation coming in. "You shouldn't have done that."

"Yeah," Asher despondently agreed.

"I warned you over days.

"Yeah."

"Days, man. I understand why you did it. Just don't do it again while we're out here. Alright?" Azmach held his hand out to him.

Asher nodded looking at the hand. "I can't be calling you bro if I'm not being that." He reached out and shook Azmach's. "Alright."

The handshake was firm, lasting seconds, shedding away any of the unspoken.

Azmach nodded, pulling his hand away after the handshake ended. "Like I said, there were more factors than you using your powers. Don't put all the blame on yourself."

"You should do the same," I spoke. "You're more tired than you're letting on. Exhausted would be an understatement. You've been like this since the car crash, possibly before. In addition, the lack of sleep, the fact that even during the sleeping intervals you're mostly on watch, the times you forced yourself to use a little of your powers. You have been getting progressively worse."

Outside of the rain, nothing. My eyes watched it pouring down over the rocks sheltering from the ocean falling above.

The rain hadn't changed, but the sound seemed to be quieter yet more present. I turned my head and looked at the two of them.

"It's been days since you've talked," Azmach pointed out, calm as ever. "I wasn't sure how to react, but since Asher didn't say anything, I thought it was normal. The first time you talk, in days, is about something that calls me out." Azmach smiled, laughing a little. "You're not wrong." His smile quickly faded. "I didn't want you guys to freak out, especially considering how deep we're in it." Azmach shook his head, disappointment and regret lightly showing under his calm expression. "I should have said something. I held you both back from learning what you need, and it almost cost us."

Asher looked like he wanted to protest, but those last words subdued a portion of his internal conflict that was still rioting.

"That's why I decided," Azmach suddenly said.

Asher questioningly perked up, his eyes slightly narrowing as his obvious internal conflict mostly paused. "Decided on what?"

"You both need to learn. You both need to train. Last night was proof of that. We barely got outta there. I can't really do anything until I fully recover. And I'm not going to recover anytime soon. We can't wait for that."

The words mulled over in the air. Training.

"...you're saying..." Asher trailed off.

"Yes," Azmach nodded. "Powers too."

Asher sat quietly, taking in the words, diction, connotation, denotation, and all.

"We can't go crazy though," Azmach added. "They would find us more easily. Stay cautious."

Asher inhaled sharply. "I still—"

"It's on me," Azmach said.

Asher stared at the rocks quietly, still grasping what he said and his internal conflict. It was a little better than before, but the conflict was obviously still there.

"Slowly, you'll start learning to control your powers," Azmach concluded with Asher.

Asher looked like someone ready and not, wanting and avoiding, deciding and already decided. His face had little expression with these clear emotions switching between each other underneath. After taking it in, he simply nodded his head to Azmach's words.

"You'll start the Speed Up Process." Azmach said.

Said to me. I'm doing what?

I turned and looked at him. He was already looking at me, forthright.

"Let's see if you can Adjust innnn....not quite sure. It's hard to tell with your Aura, but we'll see." Azmach added, nodding his head now with a small smile. "We'll start whenever this rain dies down," Azmach finished saying as all words grew quiet.

There was nothing but rain. The rain seemed to pick up as soon as there was a gap in sound to fill. Raindrop splatter echoed. It was full of noise. Unlike last night before...

That Monster.

Why that one?

That one I've heard of throughout the years, different renditions like the echoes of the rain drops around? That one that seemed so outwardly orthodox in concept, yet so perplexingly unspeakable in reality. That one I never deeply thought of until this now grave relevance? That one I heard of so many times before? That one...

Why that one?...

Out of all the Monsters, why the minotaur?

"Are we not going to talk about that Monster being a minotaur?" Asher questioned.

"Not 'a minotaur.' The Minotaur," Azmach corrected. "There's only one." Azmach looked off to the side at the ground. "And I can't believe it's that one."

"Isn't it from Greek mythology?"

"Where do you think the Greeks got it from? They probably saw it and added it into their stories." Azmach took off his jacket and laid it on his left shoulder.

"It's been alive this long?"

"That's what I'm wondering." He took his durag off, brushing his waves forward with his hand.

"And there's still a second Monster," Asher deliberately took two steps away as he talked. "And we have no idea what it could be."

A second Monster with a variety of possibilities could probably be anything.

"But it won't be werewolves or vampires," Asher almost smiled before it almost faded into nowhere. He grabbed the bottom of his shirt. "We're going to be soaked for hours."

My left side was mainly soaked. I was cold. The weather had been chilly before, but with my left side and the morning air, chill had elevated to cold. It wasn't cold autumn weather yet, but it certainly was not summer. I might need to take this shirt off. I reached for my shoulder—that's sore.

"Welcome to Kentucky." Azmach walked over to a tree and broke a long and wet branch off. "At least it stopped raining. This is perfect."

Asher looked at him puzzlingly. "Our wet clothes?"

"Yes." Azmach shoved the stick in the mud, making it stand tall. "Let me see your jacket."

Asher stared at his partially soaked jacket and immediately took it off, showing a used to be white undershirt. It was now dark beige, stained with mud, dirt, and some specks and a few small patches of blood.

Azmach looked at the state of Asher's shirt for a few brief seconds. Small concern showed on Azmach's face. He looked conflicted, looking at his hand for a split second. He resumed his original point and grabbed Asher's jacket. Azmach placed it on top of the stick, the jacket now somewhat being held in the air. "Dry the jacket."

"Dry it?" Asher was confused by the abruptness.

"I think about this for a second, Asher. With or without the jacket, are you cold?

Asher eyes slightly narrowed, looking off to the side, thinking of the question. "Nnnnnot really. No."

"When was the last time you felt cold?"

Asher stopped moving, taken aback by the question. His eyes widened a bit. "Not sure..." He softly said, looking off to the side, trying to pinpoint the exact time. "February..."

"You're from Baltimore, wouldn't it still be cold in March?"

Asher looked over at Azmach, who was already looking back.

"It's chilly outside right now," Azmach added. "We're soaked to the bone. You're not even a little bit cold?"

Asher looked off to the side, eyes narrowing. "I never thought about it too much."

"February is most likely when your Aura and your fire first awakened. Your body probably keeps at a certain temperature unless it passes a threshold, December, February, that deep winter weather."

Asher slowly nodded his head, taking it in. "I can see that."

"You radiate heat a little bit. Usually it wouldn't be noticeable, but out here in this type of weather. If the temperature was any lower, the bit of heat radiating off you wouldn't help." Azmach gestured to the surroundings. "It gets chiller at night. Haven't you wondered how the rest of us stayed warm? Jason doesn't even have a jacket."

Asher looked at me, inspecting my lack of a jacket.

I hadn't even realized it. Not even a thought.

"When it comes to using your powers," Azmach brought the point back to Asher.

Asher focused straightaway.

"That heat," Azmach underlined. "That Aura. Concentrate

on it. Control. Push it out towards your hands."

Asher held his right hand up, his palm facing the sky.

"Key word," Azmach said. "Control."

Asher's hand shook, just barely.

"Push it out slowly," Azmach instructed. "Your Aura's there so you don't need force. Gently push."

Asher deeply inhaled. Then. Exhaled. Flames sprung to life on his hand, jumping up about a half a foot up.

"Control," Azmach repeated.

Asher exhaled loudly, his hand shaking almost violently. Then, the flames shortened, restricting closer to his fingertips and away from the edges of his hand. His hand shook less and less as the flames died down. The flames became a small fire that was more towards the hand's center. It still ran above his fingertips in height, but it was more subdued, more structured. Asher panted, a few sweat beads gliding down his face. His control certainly was taking a lot of energy.

Or Aura rather.

"There you go," Azmach encouraged approvingly. "Now, focus on the jacket."

Asher stepped to the jacket, crouching to be the same height where it was being held up by the branch.

"Don't burn it at all," Azmach instructed. "Just dry it. You need to keep that fire under that control for as long as possible."

Asher held his fire hand in close range to the fabric, eyes narrowing in concentration.

"Let's get closer to Asher," Azmach said, turning to me. "We might be Demigods, but things could still make us sick."

Being sick in a situation like this...when was the last time I was sick?

Azmach and I stepped closer to Asher, the heat emanating from his fire immediately warming up the nearby surroundings.

I was still feeling cold, but it definitely wasn't as present.

This shirt... Can't risk it. My body ached as I tried peeling it off. The damp and few soaked patches clung to my skin. Its grip started loosening as it sloughed off my lower back. Soon, it was only covering my left arm. My back, my shoulders. Soreness, especially my shoulders. I pulled the rest of the shirt off, twisting it tightly, causing water to drip. Asher's fire warmed up my right side, the chill and the cold were decreasing further.

I looked down at myself. Cuts, scrapes, and bruises were at various places, mainly the shoulders and forearms. They weren't big or many in number, they were just noticeable.

Asher looked away from his fire to Azmach. His fire flared up, making him turn back to it, exhaling loudly under his concentration.

"Alright, remember what Asher had to do?" Azmach asked to make sure.

I nodded my head once.

"Good," Azmach said. "Now. Dig deep."

What do I dig for exactly? I narrowed my eyes, trying to dig for... dig for...

"You need emotion," Azmach added.

Emotion...feeling...dig...grasp at...least....

"Seems that way's not going to work for you," Azmach observed. "Let's try it differently."

As in?

"Find your Aura," Azmach conveniently answered the question that I didn't ask out loud.

Find it?

"Feel for it," Azmach added.

Feel. I closed my eyes looking...feeling. Grasping. There. That's it. I can feel my energy, my Aura.

"I'm sure everybody can feel their Aura," Azmach said. "What you need to do is pull it out."

How do I...? Grab. With what?

Pull.

Energy, Aura, it's shapeless.

"Treat it normal, like everyday Aura," Azmach instructed. Normal.

"Because it will become that," Azmach said.

I'm not grabbing a ball. I'm not even grabbing. I as an entity am pulling a different entity- there. A thin line that separates the two Auras, the Demigod and normal, that haven't fused yet. Pull the Demigod to the normal.

"There you go," Azmach encouraged. "I feel something."

Pull, grip it. It feels like the epitome of the word burst, like forcing myself to get up when I didn't ready myself and was too exhausted, while also flexing all my muscles as I pulled myself up—

The air spiked and whipped suddenly. I opened my eyes instantly, seeing Azmach slightly crouching with his arms raised to his chest, and Asher almost losing balance and control of his fire. The both just looked at me.

"…that wasn't a Surge…" Azmach trailed off quietly. "…yours is going to be interesting …"

Asher looked at me, his fire whipping slightly more and more, becoming flames once again.

Azmach turned to Asher. "Concentrate."

Asher turned back to his jacket, the flames lowering to a fire. His hand shook slightly, obviously straining under keeping it controlled and keeping the fire lit.

"Try pulling some more Aura out," Azmach instructed, his eyes narrowing in a studying thought. "Slowly."

I closed my eyes. There. I feel it already. Grasp. Grasp it. I can't grab the whole thing-wait. Where is the whole thing? Does it end, I can feel it all but also not. Pull. This feels…heavy. Pull.

"Stop there," Azmach held his hand up.

Why?

Azmach's right fist was against his mouth and supported by his left arm. "…You're like…raw power."

As in?

"Every time you even remotely tap into your Aura, it seems to try and go straight into your powers," Azmach nodded his head, understanding his words as he said them. "That's… usually not what happens. Tapping into your Aura is not the same as using it for powers. All we're doing is starting the engine, but for you it keeps trying to go straight into drive."

My Aura is automatically… I'm not sure what.

"Your body still isn't ready for that," Azmach elaborated. "I'd be surprised if a full on power forms instead of it breaking partway like it just did. You need to fully Adjust before you can completely form a power. Even if you try to tap into your Aura past this breaking apart point, you'll definitely Surge Out. You'll probably have a better chance of a power forming if you Surge Out, but yeah," Azmach shook his head, "don't do that. You're not doing this to form a power, you're doing this to fully Adjust quicker. So you're going to have to be very careful. Just barely tap into your Aura. Barely."

Ah, I see.

"Woo," Asher said exhaustedly. His fire was completely extinguished as he breathed heavily. He was already crouching, but now he slouched more like he had just sprinted miles with no breaks.

Azmach grabbed the jacket off the stick, examining it. "About two minutes. Mostly dry. Not bad Asher."

Asher's breathing was slowly steadying as he held a thumbs up.

"Next time hold it for three," Azmach said.

With wide eyes, Asher whipped his head around. "Three?" He breathed heavily "Yo." More heavy breathing.

"Alright," Azmach said to me. "Once more."

It's becoming chiller and chiller. To what point will it become colder and colder? The night's sounds were softly around. Crickets, other insects, maybe animals.

A long day of Aura. This vegetation beneath me, this dirt and more, I do not feel. What I do feel is in limbo with little movements in a direction that is fathomable but questions the foundations of the perceptions of reality. Getting used to energy-Aura. Aura.

The night air breezed by. My body stiffened.

"Hey," a voice whispered out.

I turned my head to see Asher holding his jacket extended in my direction. Everyone should be asleep right now. At least I thought so.

"Take this," Asher extended his arm and hand further, extending his jacket towards me, his fingers tightly gripping its edge.

I know he's not- I looked at the jacket, then back at him.

"Our clothes might have dried," Asher said, "but I know it's getting colder. Take this." He gestured to his jacket.

I don't want to use someone else's; it doesn't belong to me. I can't be selfish. I'm fine.

"Dude, I don't feel cold at all," Asher added. "Not even a little. Take it."

I'm going to have to take it. He won't stop until I do. I reached for the jacket slowly, grabbing it, and pulling it back towards myself. Should I? I still don't know.

"Wear it at night," Asher turned over to sleep. "Give it back in the morning." And just like that, he was sound asleep.

I looked at the jacket. It wasn't thin or thick. It was one precisely for this autumn weather where the temperature drops at night. I guess. I guess. For now.

I slid the jacket on and went back to laying down.

For now.

shuffle
shuffle

"You keep saying Minor Gods," Asher pointed out to

Azmach as they walked. "What's the difference between them, the Empyreans, and those, what was it? Those four other important Gods you talked about?"

"It can get complicated, so I'll need to explain Major Gods so Minor Gods make sense," Azmach stepped over a gash in the ground. "In general, Major Gods have the most influence in the God world for that generation, and they usually helped set the rule of that generation."

"Generation?" Asher asked.

"The Primordials, the Behiims, and the current generation, the Kauzations." Azmach stepped over a big rock.

"Yeah yeah, you said something about that once." Asher jumped over a gash in the ground.

"Each generation has their own set of Major Gods. All the Primordial Gods are Major Gods, only some Behiim Gods are Major Gods."

"Like Zon?" I inferred.

"Yeah, like Zon."

"Now that's a cool name," Asher commented.

"Like the Behiims, only some Kauzations are Major Gods. An Empyrean is automatically a Major God. The Thrice are also automatically Major Gods."

"Hold on, what is the Thrice?"

"Those are the three brothers who are arguably the most powerful Kauzation Gods. X'stayn, Orthantehs, and Letnos. They were extremely essential in establishing the rule of the current generation. X'stayn and Orthantehs are also Empyreans, and X'stayn is the King of the Gods."

"The King of the Gods. Is he like the King of the North? King Arthor? X'stayn. That's an even cooler name. Hold on that's a rhyme." Asher threw his hands to the sides dramatically. "Bars."

Azmach smiled, tilting as he walked to dodge a branch. "Telzyia also helped establish the rule of the Kauzations, which is why she's a Major God. Other Major Gods are the children of Major Gods that are held to importance in some way, like Bracktius and Zound. It's the same with Lehgots, but he's also an Empyrean so there's another reason why he's a Major God."

"Yeah. I see what you mean. This can get complicated. Sounds like one of those things where you have string on a wall connected to pictures and whatnot. I'm thinking about the one that goes throughout the whole room."

"Verbatim, what is a Minor God?" I questioned.

"Gods who are not a Major God in any way. You mainly need to focus on Major and Minor Gods from the current generation." Azmach bent a tree branch aside to walk past, but it snapped and fell to the ground.

"And just to make sure I get it; the current generation are the Kauzation?" Asher eyes narrowed, his lack of certainty apparent.

"You got it."

"This really is like yarn connecting to walls."

The air breezed a bit as my grasp on my energy-Aura was lost. Again. Find it. Sense it there. Pull it. Grasp it. The air seemed to bend as I was pulling more and more of my Aura.

Heavy breathing rose in the background, deep inhaling and exhaling.

"Almost four minutes now," Azmach said to Asher. "Not bad progress from yesterday."

I could feel my Aura a little more.

"Next," Azmach said. "You'll be doing it for five.

Grasp it.

"Let's do it now," Asher sounded like he was almost smiling eagerly.

"No," Azmach flat out said. "Both of you listen. This is important."

I opened my eyes and looked at the two of them.

"Your body hasn't finished Adjusting." Azmach looked

back and forth at Asher and me. "Even if it has, never force Aura or a power out. If your body isn't up for it, don't force it out either. Neither of you."

"Or what happens?" Asher looked at Azmach shocked but smiling from the suddenness.

"You'll burn from the inside out."

"Like, a fire?" Asher's voice dropped in volume as well as his smile.

"Your body breaks down and just…destroys itself."

Asher's face had unease written all over it.

"That's why I had to stop using my powers when the Minotaur was chasing us, and I won't be able to use it anymore until I recover. It's too risky at this point." Azmach said to Asher. "Never force it. Take a break."

"Well, when you put it that way," Asher said.

Burn from the inside out…

shuffle
shuffle
rocks tumbled downward from steps
shuffle

Water poured onto my hands. They scrubbed each other, then my face.

The landscape had become more mountainous.
crackle

"Yo this," Asher grunted as he stepped higher and higher, looking more like he was climbing rather than walking. "This is abuse right here."

"I'm surprised you're this tired and can still talk," Azmach said jokingly.

"I don't get tired, you feel me?"

"You wanna hold a fire right now? Do it for an hour."

"Ooooo, ummmm, you see?"

Azmach laughed along with Asher.

Hold up. Tired.

"Shouldn't your energy have returned by now?" I questioned Azmach. "It's been around a week."

Aura. I keep slipping that word.

"You're wondering why I still seem more human than I should," Azmach surmised.

That's one way to put it.

"If I had used my Aura like usual, that would be the case." Azmach said. "But it was what I did and the extent of it that changed things."

"How so?" I asked.

"A lot was going on. I was a state over in the middle of a mission, kind of nearby where I found you two."

"Which was? Asher asked.

Azmach instinctively reached for the side of his hip before stopping midway. "Let's not get into it."

"Complicated?"

"Complicated."

"I feel you."

"I was already using up Aura from that mission, but what followed really did a number on me."

snap-twig stepped on

"Mm," Asher stepped on leaves, crackling them. "So, what followed?"

"Healing your mom," Azmach answered.

Asher nearly stopped in his tracks. "I've been meaning to ask. How did you even find her?"

"Pericly told me a bit of information that was hard to miss. It was also kind of small news in your county back in February."

News?

"Of course..." Asher's tone quieted.

Pericly.

"Healing...works a bit differently," Azmach said. "It

doesn't just take Aura to use that power. You're basically using your health and giving it to them."

"Waiwawawawa-wait," Asher managed to say. "You're giving your life to someone else?"

"No, not exactly. It acts almost like that. Think of it like this. Your fingers moving, your heart beating, your organs functioning, living. It takes Aura to do that. I have to tap into it. Not just the surface level but deeper, even deeper than any Aura that the body stores. After that, it takes days, weeks, for you to get back to normal, especially based on the extent of whatever you're healing."

Asher ducked under a tree limb.

"Giving all of that to someone... can put you on the brink of death." Azmach's boots crackled on some more autumn-colored leaves.

Brink of death? My shoes crackled on an assorted pile of leaves.

"She..." Asher trailed off.

"Is one hundred percent healed. I become more than just one hundred percent drained. It took almost everything I had down to the last drop. Your mom was lucky."

"Lucky how?"

"Her wounds weren't past the point of no return. Just because I can heal does not mean I can heal everything. She was at the threshold of what I can and cannot do."

snap- small twig.

"Until I'm fully rested, I'm running on less than empty," Azmach revealed.

"Alright," Asher said. "I think I get it now."

"Is that why you have a hard time sensing the Monsters?" I questioned.

"Yes," Azmach answered. "My body is at such a low point, it's similar to a regular human. I can hardly sense anything. It's only when things get close that I can sort of feel it. Not gonna lie, it's low-key frustrating."

"I feel that," Asher responded.

crackle

"All this to stress about...and this war's still goin' on..." Azmach trailed off.

"Yo, what?" Asher confusingly questioned.

Azmach's face went still, his eyes slightly wide. He said that out loud without realizing.

"You can't go past that like you didn't just say anything," Asher pressed. "What do you mean by 'war'?"

Azmach's face became blank, his demeanor silent. Finally, he turned to Asher. "Just a little frustrated."

Asher's eyes were on Azmach, questions clearly on the edge of his mind and tip of his tongue. He nodded, obviously not satisfied with the answer. He faced forward and continued walking upward on the mountainous landscape.

What was that last part?

crackle

Grasp it. The air moved around me, most likely blowing my hair a bit. I'm not entirely sure. My eyes were closed.

"Thirty more seconds," Azmach directed Asher.

Asher blew out air from his mouth, clearly sounding like it was straining him to hold his fire any longer.

It's getting easier but still... I'll just- Pull. Grasp more. Grasp a lot. Pull. Pull-

The air whipped suddenly around.

"Remember, don't overdo it," Azmach reminded. "And the Monsters could be nearby."

...okay. Maybe I shouldn't pull that much. Can't Surge Out here.

Grasp.

crackle
  shuffle
  shuffle

crackle

shuffle

I bit into the apple, chewing a piece as I walked.

Asher was slightly more ahead, finishing his water bottle. He handed the empty container to Azmach, who slid in in his quiver. Is that thing bottomless or something?

Pull.

"Y'all are making great progress," Azmach said. "Jason, you're not done Adjusting but your Aura is becoming harder to feel when you're not pulling it out. It's not so much of that screaming presence anymore. It's not normal yet, but it's getting there."

Grasp it.

"Asher," Azmach turned his attention to him. "You can hold that fire for a little less than five minutes now."

"I can't throw it or do anything really," Asher chuckled.

"Once controlling it becomes first nature, you probably could."

Grasp it.

"When do you think I could do that?" Asher asked.

"Not anytime soon," Azmach answered.

"Ah!" I puffed out. My eyes shot open to the night air. I leaned forward, away from the large tree my back was against. What is this? This sudden discomfort throughout my entire body. This heat. The night air now was fuzzy. No, my vision's what's now fuzzy. All of this was within a short second.

I've felt this once before.

"What happened?" Azmach questioned, sounding serious yet calm. "What do you feel?"

"A...heat," I answered. The heat feeling was persistent. The issue was not the matter of its persistence, it was its familiarity. When did I feel this before?

"My bad," Asher tried to stumble out.

"It's not you," I told him.

"This isn't the first time you've felt it, is it?" Azmach's eyes focused, studying me.

"No," I answered. The first time was...not in the forest. Before that.

"When was the first time?" Azmach looked at me intently, waiting for the answer.

The first time was, it was...not in the forest, it was, it was, the school? Around that time, it was, it was... in the kitchen. At night.

"A few days before the Monsters showed up at the school," I answered.

Azmach stilled, inhaled deeply, then started shifting his legs. "It's coming."

"You mean-uh-N-Now?" Asher stiffened.

"The Minotaur," Azmach pushed himself up to a crouch. "It's hunting you." He turned to me when he said "you".

Turned to me? Hold on, targeting me? Wait, wait, targeting-It's coming?

"Sometimes Monsters can do that," Azmach said quietly, looking at the surroundings intensely. "They send their anger, their malice, and all those feelings to their prey for a reaction."

Prey.

Asher shifted to a crouch as well, looking around.

Azmach looked around, scanning the surrounding forest. "They want you to fear," his voice was hushed. "They want you to know the end is near, to torture you for their entertainment."

Torture.

I started shifting my legs, trying to prepare myself. Prey, torture, entertainment, me. Hunting me specifically.

"Where's it at?" Asher's eyes looked back and forth as he

crouched, not making any sudden movements.

"Not sure," Azmach's voice was more hushed than ever. "They can send those feelings from miles away. But I know that's not the case here." He reached his hand to his hip. "Move." He moved while crouching away from me, leaves crackling under his shoes. "We'll draw it out," Azmach hurriedly whispered to Asher. "Jason, you stay right here and hide."

What?

"We can't leave him by himself," Asher whispered urgently.

"We just have to keep its attention." Azmach emphasized "we". "If I'm correct, it's less likely to kill anyone else before its primary. It's the best bet for our survival."

Asher swiftly looked at him, then at me and nodded, then back to Azmach. He followed him away from where I was.

Stay here? I need to hide. How? I shrunk lower against the tree to the ground, pushing nearby leaves to try and cover myself.

There weren't enough leaves.

Azmach and Asher continued to crouch feet away, each of them behind a tree. Azmach reached for his hip again.

Wait, what's that? On the lower inside of his jacket there was something. It wasn't his hip he was reaching for; it was this. It looked like a thick, round, brown leather bag. The thing was thin in size, folding against him, and medium length, long enough to need two maybe three hands to hold it—

This Aura.

Crackle.-Something large stepped on some leaves.

It's here.

Crackle-Step. Each step it took made a sound.

Crackle-Step. It's closer.

Something's moving. I silently craned my neck to the right. Tree branches bent as something moved past. Long, thick

horns, the points sharper than blades, protruded. What followed was the large snout of a bull. It exhaled deeply, sounding like it was holding back an uncontrollable impatience. Its
breathing was loud. It walked on fours, crunching leaves,
breaking twigs, and coming closer.

It stopped. Its eyes were too far away to see, looking like a
shadow was purposely cast over them. It inhaled. Deeply. Its
head slowly turned to its left.

It's looking at where I'm at.

How much can it feel my Aura?

It exhaled, sounding like anticipation was building inside.
It stepped in my direction-

Do I move?-don't move-do I move?-don't move

Crackle-Maybe more than ten feet away

do I move don't move do I move don't move

Crackle-Eight feet away.

Or less. I swear I can smell its breath.

Crackle

doImovedon'tmovedoImovedon't

Leaves rustled some feet away behind two trees. Asher
held a fire, nothing major but obviously there for attention.
Azmach already had his bow out with a random stick pulled
back.

The Monster stopped moving and focused on them. It
growled.

Azmach shot his stick, none of his light enveloping it. He
couldn't envelope or he would burn from the inside. The stick
connected with its shoulder but bounced right off its dark fur.
The Monster exhaled loudly. Its head turned towards them.
Sharp fangs were bare angrily.

Agitated.

It stomped over to the two of them. Steadily, it advanced
faster. It growled.

"Save your Aura," Azmach said.

Asher fire extinguished immediately. "What do we do

now?"

"Run."

The two of them turned and sprinted.

Roar! The Monster picked up speed.

Azmach and Asher slid behind some trees, disappearing. Soon, the Monster disappeared in the same direction.

I sat there, letting out a quiet breath. That was close-no.

I can't let people die because of me.

I silently sat up, crouching. I grabbed a twig and tossed it into some branches. The leaves rustled loudly, and the twig collided with bark, scraping past it and making more noise.

Come here.

Crackle- Right on cue.

Hide! Hide!

I walked around a tree I was nearby and a mass of under-brush while still crouching. I lowered further to the ground to hide myself from the line of sight of where the Monster went—

Growling. Low bellowing growling. Feet away.

Crackle- A step closer.

Still crouching, I lightly stepped around the tree, hiding further from view from where the sounds were coming clos- it's coming too close. Stop moving. Past the tree. I could hear it breathing somewhere past the tree I was at. It's somewhere just feet away. Just.

Only.

My palm felt the tree bark. Cold. Or am I the one who's cold?

Crackle

Where now? I reached down.

It growled.

Slowly reached down. My fingers felt a stick.

Crackle

Silently, I lifted it.

Growl.

I'm going to have to- I quickly threw the stick to my left.

RA!- It heard it. The Monster chased after the sound. Instantly, I moved in the opposite direction as quietly as possible.

Ahead, there was another tree encircled by an underbrush. Hurry! Behind that one. The Monster stopped moving and I did the same.

Good. I'm already out of sight, barely making it behind the tree, and I'm farther from the Monster. It's never been so hard to keep my breathing quiet. I didn't think about it until moments like these.

Crackle

It's coming.

How much can it feel my Aura?

Crackle

It keeps coming in my direction. But it seems unsure.

Growl.

There's light coming from somewhere, a small amount. Asher. Something zipped through the air and broke against something else. Azmach shot a stick, didn't he?

RoAR!

It's running towards those two.

I took some careful steps away from my hiding spot, aiming towards another tree. I clutched another stick and tossed it far. Very far. It rustled through branches and leaves.

Raaa!- A deep growl. It's more annoyed than-

Crackle!-SnAp!-A section of a tree in the area broke apart.

ROAAR!

It's ramming into trees now.

RoAAAR!

Snap!

It's finally losing uncontrollable patience.

A large tree branch flew into the air. Some of the trees are thicker here so it'll be harder for it to break-

Crack!

-to an extent. Well then.

ROAAR!

When did it get that close? It's a few feet from the tree I'm hiding behind. Don't move. Don't breathe. No, I need to breathe. Breathe slowly. Quietly.

Ra

Breathe-Stop

Stop.

...it's against the tree that I'm against.

I could feel...it's growl...vibrating through the bark... through the ground. A tree. The underbrush encircling the tree. These were the two things between me and it, me and that Monster. Me and this Monster.

Something zipped through the air, making a snapping sound from it hitting something.

Raaa... a deep dark growl.

Another zip and another snap.

Ra!

Azmach's shooting sticks again. Zip, and another snap-

It's inhaling deeply-

CRAck! SnAp!

What is this gust of air?—Multiple cracks and snaps—bark and twigs fell on top of me. That wasn't wind, that was air. Something moved so quickly that—

ROOOAAAAAAAR!

The bark, twigs, and anything else falling subsided... part of the tree I'm currently hiding at was gone... a whole gash from the lower left side... these trees should be too thick to break... but this gash here... it's like the size of half my... body... The Monster has already broken branches, limbs, and some cracked off pieces of a tree base... but this... this... Can I even say gash, it's more like a doorway... and this tree here is bigger than any of the ones it broke before...

Hide.

I crouched lower, staying where I was. I couldn't take a chance moving now. A gash like that at the base of a tree? Not cracks? Not just a few fragments or pieces broken off? An entire gash?

A growl, deep and low.

CRAck! SnAp!

A gust of air, more powerful than when the gash was created, shoved the atmosphere.

What's that noise?

It was like creaking, bending, resistance that was failing whatever it was fighting against.

I looked up—No way. The tree, the one with the gash, the one I was hiding behind, at the gash was falling. It was slow but surely snapping, falling to pieces like a thread at the seams. And it was gaining speed. It creaked, seemingly trying to resist gravity. This was a fight it was undoubtedly losing.

Boom!

The lower half of the tree smashed onto the ground, shaking the earth.

…what in the…?

It was so quiet now. It was silent…no, it wasn't. There was the Monster's deep breathing.

I looked up. The Monster was across the jagged tree stump it had created. It was looking back at me. No, it was glaring, pure hatred in those eyes. Detest. Disgust. It's heavy breathing lessened - it couldn't be heard anymore. It didn't growl. It didn't roar. Not a sound came from it. The minotaur…The Monster… was silent. Its head inched closer to me. Sharp fangs led the way. Hot breath. It's mangled humanly hooves clawed whatever was left of the tree base—

It's rushing around the base! I stood up—It stopped. Inches from me, it stopped.

Inches.

Its face was mere inches from mine, glaring from such a height. It stood on its hind legs, leaning downward at me. Its breathing got louder as it became more and more enraged.

Run. DO something something. Something. Run something runsomethingsomething

Its eyes were locked onto mine. Slowly, it inched even closer. It was now only an inch away, an inch from my face, one inch. One.

What do I do? What do I do? WHatdoIdo What do I do...?...

It breathed in deeply.

ROOOOOOOOOOAAAAAAAA—

My ears shattered. It was creating a whole gust of air that made my clothes flap and hair fly backwards. My body tensed.

—AAAAAAAAAAARRRRRRRRRRRR!

Silence returned. The Monster's eyes stayed locked as it inhaled deeply. Its body was more tense than mine but for horrifyingly different reasons. Its muscles were intensified all over, looking as if they would tear out of its skin and fur any second.

My heart was beating out of my chest.

The Monster started inching backwards, keeping eye contact. Slowly it turned, still keeping eye contact, still holding hatred. It took another step backwards, eye contact and hatred held. A low growl came past its fangs, vibrating the surroundings. The Monster turned completely around, its back now towards me. Suddenly and swiftly, it clawed off into the distance. Just like that, it was gone.

...Gone?

I stood there. I stood there in the same space. I stood...

What kind of world is this? How am I...alive?

Someone ran down a hill towards me. Asher stopped next to me out of breath, eyeing where the Monster had disappeared. "Why—" he breathed deeply. "Why would it—" still breathing deeply.

"So that's what's going on," Azmach commented as he cautiously walked over with his bow in hand, eyeing where the Monster left.

Tired and confused, Asher turned to him while his heavy breathing slowed.

"It doesn't care about me or Asher." Azmach stared intently at the trees. "It only cares about you, Jason."

…Me…

"When it was chasing us in the car, it didn't expect me and Asher, so it let us escape." Azmach continued to eye where the Monster went. "The second time it showed up, there was no way we should have been able to outrun it. It had to let us go."

"Why then?" Asher questioned, his face being the embodiment of what a headache would be. "Why not just—"

"It was testing us. After the car chase, it became cautious. It had to see what we could do." Azmach became silent, looking into the trees. "After knowing we couldn't do anything to stop it, it knew it could focus solely on you."

…me…

"That's what this third appearance was about," Azmach said. "That Monster wants you to fear. It wants you at your worst. Then, and only then, will it kill.—"

"Naw naw—" Asher said quietly before cutting himself off.

…kill…Death…

"Next time it comes, that's it." Azmach said in a seriousness that he never amassed until those words left his mouth. "It's over."

Asher stumbled his words slightly. "There's not even a—"

"No. It's done." Azmach ended all other options right there. "Splitting up like we did this won't work. Next time, it won't be testing or trying to only make you fear. Next time it'll actually kill. We need to leave."

I stood there. I stood there in the same spot. I stood...move. I need to move. Walk. Come on.

A jacket appeared in front of me. Attached to it was Asher's hand.

I didn't realize all this time I was cold.

"We need to get to Illinois before it gets us," Azmach shifted his jacket, the medium sized brown bag on the inside showing itself for a split second.

I looked at Asher as I wanted to wave his jacket away.

Asher's face was intent. He was going to give me the jacket regardless of my declinations.

No, I can't take it. I can't rely. Admittance and acceptance. All routine.

Walk.

I took steps away from Asher towards Azmach.

Azmach had already started stepping up an incline. Asher was putting his jacket back on and went in Azmach's direction.

I walked forward, walking in the same direction as them.

...me...

Death.

Is Death Placed In Suddenness?

"Should we go through some more towns and farms?" Asher tossed the idea out to Azmach. "The Minotaur never popped up when we passed through those types of places. Maybe it's just less likely too?"

"Have you forgotten about your school?" Azmach asked, already knowing the answer.

shuffle

The sun shyly poked back and forth behind the clouds above.

"Should we get a car then?" Asher asked. "I know it can make Monsters get angrier, but it's at that point."

"That's why we can't, now more than ever," Azma answered. "You saw what it did the last time we were in a car. The Minotaur would be on top of us before we even got to a door. It seems to chill a bit when we're on foot, and that's not a lot but it gives us more room to act. It's following us right now as we speak. I wouldn't be surprised if it's watching us at this very moment. It's better on foot. We can maneuver more instead of being trapped in one place. It is at that point, which is why we really need the movability."

Asher ducked under a branch. "Isn't a car mobility?"

"It might not seem like it but a car is a tiny place to get trapped inside. Imagine not being able to escape because the Minotaur's outside the doors." Azmach's shoes crackle on leaves. "If we're driving and it catches us, which it would if we use a car, there's nowhere to hide. Even if we escape the car, there won't be a lot of hiding spots around like in a forest."

snap-a very small twig broke under a shoe.

"More than likely, the roads we drive on will have more houses, buildings, open spaces, or places that are just impossible to hide if push comes to shove. Imagine trying to hide on a highway." Azmach moved around a tree and continued forward.

"Yeah that would be..." Asher trailed off.

"Houses and buildings sound good in theory, but they're pretty isolated. They're also more wide open between hiding spots when compared to forests and woods. You won't be able to maneuver around as much. It may not seem like it, but being on foot in a forest gives more options of moving from hiding spot to hiding spot, and giving cover to avoid attacks."

"What about a bus or train?" Asher asked quickly.

"They have the same issues as a car. Let's say they didn't for a second, where would we find a train or bus? Plus, remember, none of us have money. Even if we sneak on, we look suspicious. Let's say that wasn't a problem either, buses and trains won't take us all the way where we need to go. That's not even adding the guaranteed attacks from the Monsters."

"Couldn't we sneak into a car quickly?" Asher fearfully stammered out.

"Like I said, they wouldn't even let us get close, especially the Minotaur. The same goes for a bus or train." Azmach ducked under another tree branch. "Even if we took a car, it wouldn't be one we own. I don't like the chances of police also chasing us. But let's say police weren't an issue, I have to admit, I don't know the roads well enough here to drive from any random standpoint. I know it better on foot. Shoot, where would we even find a car that quick? A car usually wouldn't be a bad thing, except for agitating any nearby Monsters. We had to do it to escape the school. The situation now is worse than before. A car isn't easily available like it was before, and even if there was one, there's no way either Monster would let us near it. It did before, but now it has us within its sights. Using a car in these circumstances would be more dangerous. The two Monsters after us are too strong. They could probably take on Empyreans."

"Wait, they could?" Asher stopped in his tracks.

Azmach stopped and looked at Asher. "Why do you think I'm so adamant about our situation? We have no room for extra risks." Azmach turned around and began walking again.

Asher kicked a few rocks accidentally as he walked, looking around for a set of eyes full of the desire to kill. "Yeah, I feel..."

"There's still the second Monster that we haven't encountered," Azmach said, a bit of stress coming through his voice.

"I was just hoping it'd disappear." Asher said bleakly. "You know anything about it?"

"No. Not a single clue. I felt its Aura a little somewhere outside when the school was being torn apart. Felt like it was about the same caliber as the Minotaur." Azmach's boot almost dipped into the stream he walked next to. "Jason."

What? I turned my head towards Azmach, who was a few feet to my right and at the edge of the stream.

"Do you know anything about the Minotaur? Like a connection you share with it?" Azmach questioned, seemingly submerged halfway in his own thoughts.

The Minotaur. Those horns. That anger. That's something I could never forget.

I shook my head and looked forward.

"The Minotaur should be dead." Azmach said. "It was killed by one of the Gods inside the Labyrinth thousands of years ago. Yet, here it is, alive, sending you those feelings. Only the strongest of Monsters can do that."

"Is that so?" I asked, more so to myself.

"For Monsters to send feelings, there must be a connection. They have to have a reason to hate to such a depth. There's no way the Minotaur is just alive and hates you that much for no reason."

Then what would the reason be?

"It was killed inside the Labyrinth," Azmach said in a confused incredulous tone. "*Inside*. Do you understand what that means? The Labyrinth hasn't existed for hundreds of years."

"More years," Asher commented, "Now we have a time-line."

"What happened to the Labyrinth?" I questioned.

"Whatever God created and held its existence together no longer could. It disappeared, including everything inside. Even if the Minotaur survived the fight with the God that killed it, it still shouldn't exist since the Labyrinth no longer does."

My surroundings seemed to pause. Dead. Hundreds of years. Doesn't exist. This isn't adding up.

"It probably got out before the Labyrinth disappeared," Asher inquired.

"Probably," Azmach pondered, "but that's not the point. For the Minotaur to come out of hiding..." His boot almost dipped into the stream. "Why does it hate you so much?"

Me. The Monster hates me, no doubt. It does hate these two people, but only me to such an extent. They're just collateral. Because of me.

"If it shows up before you two and I get to wherever the

place is, you two must keep going." I told them.

Asher looked turned to me not a moment later. "I know you're not saying what I think you're saying."

"I'm saying there's no need to put yourselves in danger for something that is strictly my failing."

me

"Naw son. That ain't how it works," Azmach asserted.

"It's after me," I pointed out. "Not you two. Me. There is nothing that necessitates you two being in danger."

"What is necessary is that we're not going to leave you for dead," Asher said in a matter-of-fact way.

My jaw tightened ever so slightly. It seems there is an impasse. No, not an impasse. Those two are in agreement, and in the sense of proportion that would mean the majority.

"I understand your concern bro, but don't worry," Asher assured me.

It's not that.

I stepped on a weak dirt patch that caved in a bit under my foot.

Ahead, there looked to be a road that had more trees and other vegetation across it.

"There's one thing that can be done if there's absolutely no other way," Azmach ensured.

"You mean that bag?" I asked.

Azmach's walking slowed for a second as he looked at me before regaining his normal pace. "I see you've noticed."

"Bag?" Asher asked. "What bag?"

Azmach opened his jacket a bit, revealing the medium brown, round bag attached to the inside.

Asher eyed the bag. "That's kind of random. What does it do?"

Azmach stepped on a twig, snapping it. "I'm hoping that you don't have to see. You just take the cap off and point it towards a Monster. It's a one shot. That's it."

One shot. Everything here is one shot. Somewhere on the

edges, or closer, it's following. No, it's not on the edges. It's closer.

Asher stood at the edge of the road, looking both ways. He then jogged across. Azmach was right next to him while I was a couple of feet behind.

The cool night. I've never been good with sleep. I just feel on and off. Imprecise. What is off?

The air almost whipped. Gah, I could tell. I was pulling too much Aura or too quickly. Or both.

"Two more minutes," Azmach instructed Asher.

The Monster is after me. At least that specific one. I must not have anything be affected to such a degree because of my existence. And death. Death. That's a fact. A simple fact. The only fact. Admittance and acceptance. Eyes. Pull. Closed.

Walking across a road.

Jogging across an open field.

Open.

Why would…Eyes. Sit back and see. Close. This is just the now. Open. Pull. Eyes. Not the forever. Closed. Grasp. All routine.

Snap!

I froze. My heart was now subtly beating as if it too was trying to conceal itself. I lowered myself in a crouching position.

Asher and Azmach hit the ground, trying not to slide down the rocky hill side they and I were on.

It wasn't a loud snap. Is it the Monster or paranoia?

"I don't sense its Aura." Azmach said in a hushed voice. Already, his bow was out, as he stayed flat on his stomach, looking up the rocky hillside. "Do either of you sense it?"

Its Aura. There's nothing there. But it's not like I could feel it every time it appeared. Sometimes it snuck up.

It's after me.

I walked quickly up the hill while crouching. Rocks were sliding downward as I moved. I'll be the one to check, not them. I stopped in a place higher up the hill than where the two people were located. My eyes darted around, seeing nothing. It can't be here. It's too big to be concealed in this daylight and the lack of trees on this rocky hill.

"What are you doing? Get down." Asher whispered insistently.

Nothing.

I stood up straight, turned, and walked back down the hill.

"Looks like neither of the Monsters are here," Azmach said as he stood, returning his bow to its usual place. "But stay on guard." He and Asher turned to walk down the hill in the direction Azmach was leading.

The familiar but surrealistic veracity of this world. This monster, this thing. How does one comprehend the visual reality that conceptually, in a seemingly sense, lacks realism?

Deeper into trees. The sun is going down.

How long until the destination, and what is this destination? Why does it feel as if the destination is tangible and intangible where I can see it but my hand sweeps through like smoke? Is it all smoke and mirrors? I see the conceivable smoke but where is the idiosyncratic mirror? What is idiosyncratic about this? Is it broader? Is it normal? Routine? Mirrors. Mirror. What is in the reflection?

I sat, my back being against a tree. When did it become night? At my feet was a jacket.

Asher. When did the two of them fall asleep?

It doesn't matter. The point of the matter is the reflection. The mirror, whatever it is, reflects what exactly? Where does this mirror lie? Where is the angle?

What time is it? I cannot sleep but I know I need to…

I am possibly going to die. Two Monsters. One Monster specifically after me, targeting me, hating me, wanting to kill me. Death. Is my body sore or is it this feeling? This feeling of… is it dread? I felt this before, just not in this type of circumstance. I can hardly breathe. I need to breathe. I must breathe.   Breathe.

Inhale…Exhale…Again…Inhale…Exhale…Death. I probably will…Sleep. Yes, that's correct. I need to sleep. Sleep. Death. Sleep.   death.   sleep   death   sleepdeathsleep…deat sleep…dea…s.sle.s.

Something shook me awake. I dozed off? I guess I dozed off. Sleep is only supposed to be two hours, so how long did I doze? I opened my eyes to see early morning light seeping past leaves.

"Dude, you need to wear the jacket." Asher said, his hand on my shoulder. "I know it's getting colder."

Using my knee and forearm, I stood up. A water bottle was put in front of my face. My head is clouded in what feels like smoke, but what does the mirror show? I grabbed the bottle and drank. A hand gripped the now empty bottle and took it from me.

"Come on," Azmach said. "Let's start today."

Eyes.

Why can't I see myself?

Pull.

Too much smoke. My mind is jumbled. Eyes. Can I see the mirror? Can I see any mirrors? No. It's not a mirror or mirrors. It's just the smoke making it seem like there are mirrors. Clear it. Inhale. Exhale. Death. Death is the smoke. Death is the fog. Death. I can admit and accept it, but this smoke, this smoke still exists. Push it away. Push it away push-

The air whipped suddenly, making my clothes and hair flap. It was harder than it usually was whenever it happened. Stronger. Most importantly, there was less control.

"I already told you." Azmach strongly reminded me. "When it comes to Aura and powers, never force it out."

Force it? I wasn't even trying to use a power.

What can I even do?

I closed my eyes. Or are they open? I don't see the surroundings, but what do I see? Smoke. I was trying to push the smoke yet... squint. Narrow the eyes. See through it.

"We'll take a break and instead get moving," Azmach said.

"Woo, cause I couldn't hold the fire forever," Asher said jokingly.

"Let's see your running endurance then."

"Hardy har."

Why is there smoke?

shuffle shuffle shuffle crackle

"Quickly," Azmach said as he jogged speedily ahead. "Past this field then back to the trees."

"Being in the open feels weird," Asher said.

"It's not safe."

All this traveling.

I laid my back against rough tree bark, needing to sleep. The night sky was showing its presence. Think about it tomorrow in a few hours. Right now, just sleep and only sleep. Sleep. Sleep. sleep...

...sleep...sleep.s...leep...

What's that?

I woke and sat up immediately. The night sky was still about.

What time was it? What's this? This feeling? Oh. Here it comes. This Aura. So soon? So quickly? It hasn't even been close to a week. It hasn't even been a few days.

"Ah," I grunted. Heat trickled throughout my body and skin. My vision became fuzzy but quickly returned. An irritation. The Monster sent its feelings again, its rage for my fear. I was forced into the present, more than ever before.

A growl echoed in the distance.

Azmach was awake with his bow out.

Asher stirred, his eyes instantly becoming wide and narrow at the same time.

"Here it comes." Azmach intensely said.

I stood completely up.

Asher and Azmach stood up as well.

Roooar.

It was a low one. It's announcing itself.

I looked around, anticipating where it would appear. Where exactly is its Aura coming from?

"I was hoping for a few more days," Azmach gripped his bow tightly.

"I was hoping not at all," Asher nervously said.

Trees, branches and leaves rustled.

It's after me primarily, not these two.

I sprinted to the right deeper into the trees and darkness, leaving Asher and Azmach behind.

"What are you doing?!" Asher asked in disbelief.

"Stay together!" Azmach called out.

I slapped tree branches and tall vegetation out of the way as I ran further. I'll handle it. Asher has a family. Azmach seems to have more. This Monster is here because of me.

The smoke cleared away in my head. I—

Snap!

ROOOOAAAR!

The Monster's hairy arm jetted between two trees behind me where I had just passed.

Forward. I need more space—

Crack!

The Monster's whole body burst through the gap where it had shoved its arm through, and I could feel it staring down my back—

Crack!—

Left!

I slid left into an entanglement of branches, limbs, vegetation, and whatever else was there-it's catching up. Fast.

Its arm shot out just where I had slid away from, barely missing me. Those talon-like claws.

ROOOOOAAAARRR!

Move!

I slid heels first, gripping a tree so I didn't fall, and turned around the tree as I ran—

Crack!

I instinctively ducked as I ran forward—

SnAP!

It's coming closer for sure. What can I do?

Crack!-It's closer. Forward!

I rushed ahead and slid behind a thick tree- Oh, that was close. I almost kept sliding unwillingly.

Snap!

Silent. Don't move. Stay hidden behind this tree. I need to figure out something. Something before this Monster gets closer.

shuffle-a lot of shuffling in the opposite direction the Monster was just coming from. How did it get there!?

Snap!-wait, that snap was in the opposite direction of the shuffling. So the monster was still in the area I had just run away from. Then what is—

Azmach and Asher came running out, stopping about five feet in front of my hiding spot without realizing.

Oh, come on.

"He's not here," Asher said to Azmach.

Crack!

ROOOAAAR!

"That's here," Azmach said, readying his bow.

The Monster was coming into view. It charged forward. I can hear it. The two of them were right there in the Monster's line of sight, maybe twenty feet in front of it. It came closer to them, also being feet away from me and my hiding spot. It didn't know exactly where I was located, but it did know for Asher and Azmach. Since they were right there in its sights, the Monster was about to attack them.

Now or never.

I slid out of my hiding spot, which was feet from the right side of the Monster as it clawed towards Asher and Azmach. I ran towards it.

Get to it! Get to the Monster! Faster!

One step- Only three feet away from its side.

Two steps- The Monster just started turning its head, now seeing me only at the last second.

Three steps- It's turning in my direction, trying to at least.

Four steps- What am I even trying to do?

It's right there, centimeters away. Too late to think.

Jump!

I leaped, landing on the back of the Monster.

Grab something! Anything!

My hands wrapped around two hard stone pillars. No, not pillars. Its horns.

"Well I'll be—" Azmach tried to say.

ROOOOAAAAR!

My ears felt like they were splitting. It's always been loud, but being this close-

ROOOAAAAR!

The Monster started thrashing—Gah my chin. Keep my mouth closed. I can't have my teeth smashing together-Gah my legs were flying off. Grip! Tighter!

My hands tightened. They strained, barely being able to wrap around the horns-gah, it's moving too much—I can barely see anything— Sharp. Something sharp just scraped my arm. Claws. It's reaching for me, trying to pull me off. Move!

I tilted its horns to my right-

Growl

Woah. The Monster resisted the tilt. Does this mean I can—

"Wait for an opening!" Azmach called out.

What? I squinted my eyes, looking down to find him- oo it's bucking.

"And do what?" Asher yelled.

ROOOOOAAAAAARRR!

The Monster charged forward, and my head reeling back from the aggression. I squinted harder. The Monster was still belligerent and pursuing Asher and Azmach.

That's what I was trying to stop. I gripped its horns the tightest yet and yanked it towards a tree to my right.

ROOOAAAR!

It's so much stronger. It resisted and focused back on Asher and Azmach, racking faster towards them. Quickly, they slipped between two trees. The Monster turned towards where the two of them slid. I yanked its horns downward right. The Monster pulled back but didn't react fast enough to avoid the tree it was running towards.

Slam!

The tree shook. My head shook. The Monster was pushing itself off the tree, taking its time, clearly assessing itself. It was becoming closer to exhaustion.

Exhaustion. I don't have time for that. I need to get away. Let go of the horns. Quickly. Now. I did just that, pushing off it and sliding behind the tree it had slammed into.

Asher and Azmach were standing close by and turned as I landed on the ground. They began sprinting away from the Monster like I was.

Growl.

"You should have kept going," I told them between breaths as I looked ahead.

"Didn't we go over this?" Asher asked. Snap- he stepped on a twig as he ran.

Crack!- from where the Monster was at.

ROOOOOOAAAR!

The Monster's moving again.

"Alright," Azmach said. His bow was still in hand as he led the way. "We might be able to survive. If we keep moving, it might—" He suddenly stopped completely in his tracks. "That's not funny."

Asher and I also stopped, confused.

"Come on son." Azmach's eyes fixed on something in the direction he was just leading towards. "Come on son!"

"What's going on?" Asher questioned, clearly puzzled seeing Azmach's unease. His eyes searched around where Azmach was fixed on, attempting to decipher what was happening.

What is he...?...

I followed Azmach's eyes. Around ten to twenty feet straight ahead, tree branches were bending forward. No, there's more to it. The branches were bending towards the direction Azmach and Asher, and I stood. That's not where the Monster was at... it's back there... Then why would the branches be bending?

ROOOOOAAAAR!

I looked behind my shoulder to see the Monster. It was standing on the very edge of view only a few yards behind Azmach, Asher, and me. Wait, it stopped? It's not attacking? It was just watching. Wait. It's watching where the branches were bending. Anticipating. I looked forward to those branches.

The Monster? The? It's not "the" anymore.

An appendage with a sharp tip edged into view. It looked to be a large and extremely long scorpion tail. The body that was connected to the tail was big...bigger than the minotaur even. Between nine and eleven feet long... and proportionally wide,... its body was that of a lion...no, it was not just that. It was bigger than the average lion...with an enormous gray scorpion tail.

It inched closer into view.

Dusty gray fur covered it in most places. It had long legs with hooves in the back and talons in the front.

It inched closer.

Large leathery gray bat wings began to extend as it inched into view. In the midst of an unruly and dirty gray mane, its face was that of a calm lion. Fangs revealed themselves between lips that were pulled back almost to the edge of its face.

It inched closer.

The Monster behind growled at the new Monster ahead. In response, the Monster ahead stepped forward. Its tail snaked up in the air—it shot out—

Dive!

I dove right, landing and sliding on my shoulder.

Azmach and Asher did the same, moving out of the way.

I looked at where I just was. The scorpion stinger was impelled into the ground. Slowly, the stringer withdrew from the ground, slithering back to the Monster.

That's a long stinger...

The minotaur growled at the other Monster, its eyes confronting it. The Monster's scorpion tail pointed, aiming at the minotaur.

ROAR!

The minotaur rushed forward. Its claws were outstretched towards the other Monster.

"Over here!" Azmach immediately stood up, running towards some trees away from the Monsters.

Instantly, I stood up running in the same direction.

ROAAR!

Azmach and Asher, and I slid behind trees where the earth dipped downward like a short trench, hiding tens of feet from where the Monsters were beginning to fight.

Snap!

Dirt, branches, and more were knocked into the air, some of it raining down where Asher, Azmach, and I squatted down to stay hidden. I squatted down to hide further. The Monsters snarled, roared, screamed, and hissed.

"Is everyone alright?" Azmach asked. He continued squatting as he moved closer to be only a few inches away.

"What is that?" Asher questioned, upright on his knees.

RoAAAAR!

SNAP!

"That would be the Manticore," Azmach answered.

All of this...how does one fathom?

Crack!-the manticore's scorpion tail broke through a tree nearby. Bark and other tree fragments scattered about, showering over the area.

While fighting the minotaur, it was using its tail to look for Asher, Azmach, and me.

Or is it only looking for me? No, that's what the minotaur's doing. Still, I'm putting them in danger.

ROOOOAAAAR!

"Between a rock and hard place." Azmach said, more so to himself.

SNAP!

"Alright," Azmach began to say. He switched positions to be upright on his knees, placing his bow down, and reaching inside his jacket. "Go to southern Illinois. It'll be a forested area—"

Scrapes and snarls.

Asher eyed Azmach.

Dirt and leaves were kicked up.

"Find a map somewhere if you have to." Azmach continued. "Follow the roads. You'll both be able to figure out where to go from there."

261

ROOOOOOAAAAAR!

Crack!-the scorpion tail burst through another nearby tree, making bark and more of its fragments scatter.

"We'll be able to get to Southern Illinois, since you'll be leading the way." Asher accentuated Azmach.

ROOOOAAAAARRR!

Azmach's hand went further inside his jacket.

SNAP!-branches flew above.

"Here," Azmach held out the thick, round, brown leather bag to me. It was the one I had asked about a couple days earlier. It was cool to touch, rough, and big enough for two hands to hold, if not more. There was a cork-like cap at the top to keep it closed. "Bring this with you. Do not use it, unless its absolutely necessary."

"Isn't that time now?!" Asher poignantly pointed out.

"That would defeat the purpose for why I'm here."

SNAP!-branches flying.

ROOOAAAR!

"When you get there, give that to Lamonte," Azmach told me. "Tell him 'The Stromoios greatly number the cave—'"

SNAP!

"'—and there is only one opening to get in and out.'"

"Naw naw, you have to come with us!" Asher urged. "Let's go now!"

"The second they realize we're escaping, they'll just run us down." Azmach attested. "There's no way we can outrun one of them, let alone both. Not this time."

SLAM!-the world shook.

"We can wait until they're tired out." Asher intensely said.

"That's not going to happen. Neither of them is going to let us escape. They won't kill each other this time."

ROOOOAAAAR!

SNAP!

Azmach pushed the brown bag all the way into my hands, turning towards the direction where the Monsters were fighting. "They're too focused on us."

Growl

CracK!-a large chuck of a nearby tree was just gone.

"They'll keep coming after us," Azmach contended. "But, if I stay behind, I can slow them down, and you two could make it."

They'll. They.

ROOOOOAAAAARRR!

Have to. I know what I have to do. I know what I need to do.

"At least one of them is after me specifically." I told the two of them. "Not you two. Me. If anyone must stay, then I'll be the one."

The snarls and hisses were growing closer.

"You haven't even finished Adjusting," Azmach said to me.

"And you can't even do anything until your body restores itself," Asher retorted Azmach. "Get behind me. I can do something."

"You'll burn this forest down and take all of us with it," Azmach instantly said. "You haven't gained enough control for combat yet."

This Aura. Azmach's Aura. His fingers started glowing.

"You said you'll burn from the inside if you do that," I said, taken aback.

"Get going," Azmach said, gripping his bow.

Is he serious?

ROOOOAAAAARRR!

It sounded like a stampede was viciously thundering. And it was getting louder.

Crack!-the scorpion tail broke past a tree and slammed right next to Azmach.

They were coming.

Azmach stood fully up, his fingers glowing brighter while the inside of his hands also began to glow.

The scorpion tail whipped back. Azmach ducked, practically dropping to the ground to dodge the appendage. The tail smashed into a tree, breaking it almost in two, as it reeled back to the manticore's body.

ROOOOOOOAAAAAAAAAAAAAARR!

I cannot let this happen.

The Monster, the minotaur, was rushing forward. The manticore too was rushing forward, clawing as it galloped. They fought each other on the way, slowing down each other's movements. It was difficult to see from my angle. Still, they were getting closer and closer, right now only being some trees away.

Azmach positioned himself for the ensuing fight. "I already told you get going!"

Asher was in shock, his eyes and mouth agape. He shuffled and started standing up.

The Monsters were closing the gap between Azmach, Asher, and me.

ROOOOAAAAAAR!-the minotaur pushed the manticore towards a tree. The manticore eyed the minotaur, shouldering it back, but focusing on Asher and Azmach, as well as me. Both were getting even closer. Those Monsters. The minotaur and the manticore... the Minotaur and the Manticore... if any person is going to die...

Death.

I cannot let any person die because of me.

I looked down at the bag.

The scorpion tail shot forward, breaking a tree. The Minotaur's claws raked trees as it rushed. The two Monsters were still attacking each other, maybe sixty feet away. Sixty might sound like a lot, but it really isn't. It's far closer than one would think. They were way too close. Their stench filled the air.

Asher shuffled, trying to decide to stay or leave, clearly leaning on staying but also having an understanding of the situation and knowing the better decision would be to run.

"Get going! Now!" Azmach yelled.

Here goes.

I rushed forward, passing Asher then Azmach. I stopped and stood in front of them by a few feet.

Point it.

I aimed the top of the bag at the Minotaur and the Manticore.

Open it.

I gripped the cork and pulled.

Wind came gushing out. No. It's the reverse. The bag was pulling wind into where I took the cap off. The air looked to be fracturing as the makings of a somewhat transparent tornado was created and pulled into the bag.

Gah. My ears split hearing a wind tearing everything to pieces. It sounded like a howl and a freight train. The bag felt like it was trying to pull itself out of my hands. It inflated in size, now being completely round and robust rather than thin like it was before.

I squinted ahead, trying to peer through the wind. Branches and twigs were swiftly being broken. A few feet away, the Minotaur was clawing at the ground, trying not to get pulled inside the bag. The Manticore tried wrapping its tail around a thick tree limb. Having done so too late, the limb it chose was not strong enough. It was already breaking.

Stand true.

My feet dug into the ground. I can't fly off at this moment. My right hand gripped the top of the bag. My left supported the bottom. Both of my hands tightened, my body tensed, and when I say tensed I mean *tensed*. I held the bag the best I could against my chest.

ROOOOOOOAAAAARRRRRR!

The Minotaur's claws dug deeper into the ground. Still, it was being pulled by the strong wind. Long trenches were being carved into the ground as the Minotaur resisted.

Ah! It's getting harder to hold. Hurry!

The Manticore clawed closer to the tree which had the limb that was wrapped around by the scorpion tail. The limb was definitely going to break. Cracks grew where the limb where it connected to the entire tree. It was already halfway broken off—

My shoes slid a bit forward before I shifted my weight. That was close. I could barely keep my eyes open. My hair and clothes flapped from all the wind. I'm losing my grip.

CRAcK!-SNAP!

The limb finally broke.

The Manticore was dragged across the dirt, branches, and vegetation. It tumbled and rolled, nothing stopping it from being pulled towards the bag.

Here it comes.

I dug my feet in deeper.

The Manticore was sucked through the air. Its body faded from sight, only leaving a slight outline as its body was less than a foot away from the bag's opening. The outline faded more and more, looking as if it was transforming into the very tornado-like wind that the bag was pulling inside.

Oh. Outside of all the wind and forces, the bag felt heavier.

ROOOOOOOAAAAAAARRRRRR!

The Minotaur was being dragged closer and closer, deeper trenches being created as it resisted further and further.

It was less than five feet away.

Hang on.

My grip tightened.

The Monster, the Minotaur. It turned its head to stare at me past its shoulder. Its eyes locked on mine. I'm surprised that the Minotaur and I could see through all of the wind while being at the heart of this storm. The Minotaur's eyes were wide, its mouth clenched. Nearer and nearer, it was dragged. More and more, it resisted. Not once did it blink. Its eyes were locked and stayed locked.

Fear. I see fear in those eyes. Rage. Uncertainty. Anger. Possibly regret. Nothing but emotion filled those eyes, the eyes of a Monster. Suddenly, its eyes filled with rage more than anything else, snarling with no sounds that broke through the wind.

Could it escape?

The Minotaur lost its grip.

ROOOOOOAAAAAAAR!

The Minotaur was pulled through the air, its body fading to an outline as its roars faded to nothingness. The outline swiftly vanished, becoming a tornado like wind that was around the opening of the bag. The thick tornado was pulled inside, leaving only the heavy wind still pulling everything it possibly could towards the bag.

Is that it? That's it! Close it! Now!

I slammed the cork back into the opening. The wind died instantly.

I need to make sure. I pushed the cork further down in the opening, so it wouldn't accidentally pop out. Don't push it too far. I stopped my hand and froze.

Breathing. That's the first thing I noticed. I know it wasn't quiet with how hard I was breathing. Considering everything, my hard breathing was silent enough. Compared to that noise seconds before, it felt like even with my heavy breathing, there was nothing except pure silence. Am I even breathing? Inhale, exhale. I can feel that. Something feels shut. My eyes? No, they're open. When's the last time I unfroze?

I looked up from the bag— oh. Trees, branches, and the very ground were torn apart. It looked as if a small tornado ripped through the place while leaving the skeleton and the scatters of a forest intact.

Isn't that essentially what happened? Breathe. Admit and accept. That I can do.

In my hands, the bag felt heavy. It wasn't as thin as it was before. It now looked like it held something inside. My body felt heavy. The air felt light, yet there's a weight on me. No, it's within me. My muscles are still tense. That's why. Calm down. It's over. Right? Calm. I don't feel any Aura. It's over. Over... the smoke's gone. Eyes.

"Y'all good?" Azmach asked, breathing deeply in and out. "Asher?"

"...yeah...What is that?" Asher trailed off in a kind of raspy voice, astonished.

"That... is a Reverse Bag of Wind... from Levaveus." Azmach answered.

I continued to stare at the Bag as I was breathing heavily. This thing here. Fathom?

"Jason?" Azmach said my name for a response, his breathing close to fully normalizing. "You good?"

I need to answer. I turned to look at him, nodding my head only once.

"Good." Azmach stepped over, putting his bow back between his jacket and shirt. His hands appeared next to the Bag. None of his fingers were glowing like before. "It's fine. I'll take it now." His voice was quiet, calm.

I moved my hands, moving the Bag over to him. I felt robotic.

Azmach held the Bag, holding it with caution. He took some steps past Asher, stopping and turning to look at Asher and me. "Let's move."

"Right now?" Asher rightfully questioned. "You mean after everything that just happened?"

"That's exactly the point. All of that was a lot of commotion. People might come to check."

Commotion. That was more than simple commotion.

"We'll move for a bit," Azmach planned. "Then, we'll go to sleep."

"Look, after all that, I'm sure it's nothing to worry about. They'll probably just think it was some crazy tornado or something." Asher's body acted like a slug while he was standing, exhaustion obviously waving throughout his system.

"There could be more Monsters."

Asher couldn't look deeper within distress than that moment.

"Let's not stand around," Azmach turned and started walking, albeit slowly.

Asher breathed for a second. "That I can agree with." He followed, his apparent exhaustion increasing with each step.

I looked at the results of what the Bag did to the forest. The portrait of scars was illustrated deeply. Branches tossed. Limbs thrown. Trees weakly standing. A Reverse Bag of Wind.

I'm going to have to walk with those two.

I turned and began following behind, still feeling the weight of that Bag in my hands.

Can The Definition And Depth Of Reality Stretch?

"How long are we going to stay at the edge of this forest?" Asher asked as he took a sip of his water.

I turned my head left to see an older house across a grass field about fifty feet away from the edge of the forest Asher, Azmach and I were sitting at. It was old, small, and looked similar to a farm without a farmhouse.

I laid back against cool tree bark, the sun dimmed by the clouds. It was a bit chilly this morning, a few hours already passed from having to sit here.

"Hmm. Perhaps nightfall." Azmach thought out loud. "I don't like walking through all these farmlands. Of course, Kentucky's full of them."

"I'd rather have open fields than Monsters." Asher said.

"Too easily spotted, and the way we look, that's bad news."

"Speak for yourselves. I'm still handsome."

"Perhaps if I squint really hard. Naw, not even then."

"Don't make me be the next Monster you face."

"Because you look like one, exactly. Case dismissed."

"I'm 'bout to put a case on you and I'm not even Denzel. But you are Washington."

Azmach pointed at Asher. "You violatin' son. That's a good one."

They both laughed.

"That's a good one," Azmach repeated between laughs.

Once the laughter calmed, Asher looked down for a quietly for a second. "It feels weird laughing after everything that's happened, but I'll take it. No Monsters, less stress. Which is why I rather have open fields."

"There could still be Monsters lurking around."

Monsters. It doesn't seem possible that there could be more of that.

"Those two Monsters are out the way," Asher said. "Could we take a car this time?"

"I would agree," Azmach said. "With those two out the way, it's less risky taking a car. The Monsters out there are less likely to be as strong as the Minotaur and Manticore. But I'd rather not risk it when we're this close to the goal. Really, there's just no need for a car. Where we need to go is a bit past that farm. We're basically there."

"We're that close!" Asher looked excitedly past the farm. "How many more days?"

"About two." Azmach answered. "Maybe less." Crunching sounds were created as he bit the side of an apple.

"Two or less? Let's go!" Asher smacked his chest with a closed hand as he said the last two words.

Two days or less. What is at the destination? What even is the destination? I need more details. Yet, it is somewhat a bit late for those.

Azmach stood up. "For now, we'll train."

"Azmach," I said.

He turned to look at me. "Yes?"

"About that Bag," I started.

Azmach's face didn't change at the mention of the Bag as if

it meant nothing. His face had a plain expression.

I opened my mouth to continue. "You handed it to me. You didn't want to utilize it, meaning you were willing to give your life for it. And I used it. I might not have understood, but that doesn't change the fact that I still used it. You said you had a purpose to be here. Have I ruined that purpose?"

Azmach reached into his jacket and pulled out the Bag, taking a knee once he did. "No. I was prepared to use this Bag if I had to. I just wasn't sure if I could use it correctly. It's a one-shot policy and I'm not the only one here. I couldn't risk using it, failing, and basically getting all three of us killed."

"Wouldn't you fighting by yourself also end the same way?" Asher asked. "Like you said, taking on one would be impossible. But two? So, if those Monsters killed you, they would then come for us after."

"My mission was making sure the information I told you was given."

"You mean the information you said about 'the cave' and 'Stromoios'," I recalled.

"Yeah, 'the cave' and "Stromoios'. What does that mean?" Asher asked.

"Nothing you need to worry about. We're not going to get into all of that. I'll know more once we get back."

Asher looked as if he wanted to question, but after that last sentence Azmach gave, he let the curiosity die inside him.

"The point is with the circumstances; I chose what would give the best chance for that information to be passed along." Azmach slid the Bag back into his jacket. "It's a good thing you used it."

A small breeze blew for a second.

"The outcome we got couldn't have been better." Azmach finished what the breeze almost cut off.

"We are alive, so." Asher looked up, nodding.

"We only have a couple days left until we're there. Maybe even less," Azmach finished.

"'A couple days'." Asher nodded thinking to himself. "Whatever this place you're taking us is, I can't wait to see."

Information. A couple days. However the cave is defined in this situation, it would seem that regardless of the plight, Azmach either has a lack of planning about the cave and, with the caveat of an or, a lack of depth. With his response, it would more than likely be a lack of planning, which would mean there isn't an exact understanding on his part of what this cave would absolutely conclude. Ultimately, the information is not connected to me and thus, based significantly on his testimony, I have not ruined the purpose he held. This possible ruination does not matter since it was in fact not a ruination, and in the grand scheme of this transpiring I am irrelevant to it.

Still, weight. This weight. Exists, this weight.

I looked at the farmhouse in the distance. Until nightfall.

Pull.

It's easier. Still, it feels far away from tangibility.

Pull.

This weight I'm pulling. This weight in my hands.

My head felt faint and lighter. Still, something had a weight. I'm not sure where the weight kept shifting. The weight of the Bag wasn't in my hands alone.

"Ten more seconds," Azmach said to Asher.

Pull.

How long will it take me to Adjust? Not only to Aura, but including this weight? Admittance and acceptance. I have. All routine. It is. Then what is the prospect that does not allow complete enormity? The weight, what is it?

Pull.

I'm pulling Aura, grasping it to Adjust fully. Pulling the weight.

Weight. That's it.

Weight is the depth. I have admitted. I have accepted. This

is all routine. There's a depth to it that has never existed there before. Or perhaps I've never perceived it until here.

Pull.

"Not bad," Azmach said. "You're hitting a solid ten minutes now, Asher. Alright man, take a break."

This depth, this weight. That I can do.

Admittance and acceptance.

All routine.

"There's a couple more of these open spaces and streets here," Azmach said as he jogged slightly ahead. "Stick together and stay out of as much light as possible."

"Tell that to the moon," Asher chimed in.

"At least it's not full."

shuffle

shuffle

shuffle

shuffle

"Alright," Azmach stopped in his tracks "This is when it gets interesting."

"Like the Monsters didn't?" Asher sarcastically asked.

Azmach eyed Asher for a second before returning his focus ahead on something. "The Ohio river."

I squinted my eyes to see what he was gesturing at. There were trees and other vegetation surrounding the area, almost like being in the middle of a forest. It was enough to conceal Asher, Azmach, and me while also being enough to conceal whatever Azmach was gesturing at.

Wait, something's shining.

Ahead, past some smaller trees and vegetation, was a large body of water. It flowed far and wide and was reflecting moonlight.

"We cross it, and we're basically there," Azmach said as he took steps forward.

Asher looked at me then followed Azmach.

I passed trees and other vegetation as I got closer to the shoreline.

Azmach stopped just short of the water washing onto the land.

"You both know how to swim?" Azmach gestured towards the land on the other side that was hardly noticeable with the time of night and the dimness of the moon.

"You didn't ask us other times?" Asher asked, taken aback.

"Because we won't be using a boat this time and the water isn't shallow. I don't see any abandoned boats right now, and looking for anything that floats would take too long. The other side isn't too far." He turned to Asher. "You do know how to swim, right?"

"Ahhh a bit," Asher answered.

"How well?"

"Do I look like a guppy?"

"Yep."

Asher stared at him, not amused. "Your durag's lopsided."

"Seriously though, how well do you both know how to swim?" Azmach grabbed his durag, untying it with one hand, and slipped it into his pocket. His waves were less prominent than the last time I saw them, barely being there at all.

Asher looked up and thought for a second. "I'm alright."

"It's about a mile or more to cross. You're going to need more than just 'alright.'"

A mile or more. I looked across the river at the opposite shoreline. Swimming in this chill, that's going to be more of a problem.

"Calm night," Azmach observed. "It has a little bit of a current. It doesn't really pick up until it gets closer to the Mississippi river."

"IIIIIIt's doable," Asher responded.

Azmach reached between his shirt and jacket, pulling out his quiver. He then reached inside the quiver, digging for a few seconds. He pulled out a dark wooden arrow. At the bottom of the arrow, there was a long rope connected to it that was now circling the ground with its length.

Azmach grabbed his bow from the usual place, snapping it open. He grabbed the end of the rope and tied it to the front of the bow, making sure it was tight. "Let's make that for sure." Azmach aimed the arrow across the river, pulling back the bowstring. The arrow flew as he ever so lightly let it go, the rope looking as if it was trying to catch up. Due to the lack of light, it became harder to see the farther it flew.

Wait. How far is it going?

"Now that's far," Asher commented. "Can arrows even be shot that far?"

Vegetation, and short tree branches rustled a distance ahead across the river. The arrow must have gotten entangled.

"With me being a Demigod, yeah." Azmach answered Asher.

The rope was pulled to its limits, fully extending from the bow to wherever it reached across the river.

"Why didn't you ever use that arrow?" Asher asked.

"It's my last arrow. Ran out of the rest of them before the whole car chase. This one here is not for fighting. It's more for climbing and grappling. It wouldn't do any real damage. Even if it did, without my body being fully restored it doesn't matter what I have and what I shoot. " Azmach tugged the rope hard twice, making sure the arrow was stuck to something. "Good. Let's get across."

Azmach laid his bow on the ground and slid his hand into his jacket, taking out the Reverse Bag of Wind.

Weight. Admittance and acceptance.

He placed the Wind Bag next to his foot, taking his jacket off and stuffing it in the quiver then doing the same with his shirt.

"Clothes in here," Azmach said.

276

Asher started taking his jacket off.

"Whatever we don't take off, you need to dry up before we sleep," Azmach said to Asher as he unlaced his boots.

"Gotcha," Asher said, taking off his shirt.

I need to do the same. I took my shirt off. Yeah, it's getting chiller.

Azmach held his boots and shoved them inside the quiver.

Those can fit too? It seemed to be a tight fit, but they were in there.

Asher paused, looked at his shoes, then at the quiver. Azmach already put his own socks inside the quiver and started taking off his pants. Asher untied his shoes, looking at the quiver questioningly.

Shoes.

I bent down to untie the ones I wore. They were so rattled. I couldn't see details in the dark, but what I could see made me question how they were even still holding themselves together.

Asher handed his jacket, shirt, and shoes to Azmach, who had just put his pants inside the quiver. Asher was staring in wonderment at the quiver as Azmach pushed the clothes that were just handed to him inside as well.

My shoes were off, next the pants. Socks followed.

Asher pants and socks were off. He turned and handed them to Azmach, who once again pushed them inside the quiver. Asher eyes were locked on the thing.

I stepped over to Azmach and handed him my clothes.

Without all that, I'm trying not to shiver. I only had on underwear.

Azmach seemed to be cold too as he stood in his underwear pushing in the last bit of clothes. Asher was a different story. Even though he was also standing in his underwear, he didn't look the least bit uncomfortable.

"Alright," Azmach said. He grabbed the cover of the quiver that was connected to the quiver itself, flipped it over the opening, and pushed it inside tightly like a cork.

"There's no way that can fit all that," Asher said, gesturing to the quiver.

"After everything, that's what you're stuck on?" Azmach jokingly asked. "Don't be buggin' B." He picked up the bow and tossed Asher the quiver.

Asher caught it like he was trying to give a bear hug that was mainly using his hands. He stared at what held in awe.

"Time to swim," Azmach said as he approached the shore, bow in hand with the rope curling in front of his steps. "The quiver and the bow float."

Asher looked down at the quiver in his hands for a second.

"Now, the current isn't too strong," Azmach pointed out. "But hang onto the rope as you swim. We'll go two at a time, starting with me and Asher."

I looked at the dark river reflecting some moonlight off its surface. The shore across the river is about a mile swim.

"I'll swim back for you Jason and pass you the quiver," Azmach said. "Then we'll both swim to the other side."

"I don't need the quiver," I walked to the shoreline and stepped into the water.

Cold. The ground was cold enough, but this water is even more so.

My whole body submerged next to the rope that was touching the surface of the river. My arms stretched forward and scraped the rope as I began to swim. I just need to get to the other side.

Water was rippling and splashing a bit behind me as the rope was moving and jerked to my left. Azmach and Asher were swimming behind me, staying next to the rope to avoid drowning and being swept away by the current. It was a small current, but there was no need to take unnecessary risks.

I swam faster, making sure the rope stayed next to me. I don't need it next to me.

Through the water and dimly lit moonlight, the other side was coming into view.

I sat on the ground detangling my hair. All that water shrunk it some.

Asher held a fire in his hand, drying Azmach, himself, and me. Without that fire, there would be no source of warmth.

Azmach was completely dry, pulling clothes out of the quiver. None of them, not a shoe or a shirt, were wet. None of them had a single drop of water. Azmach sorted through the clothes, dividing them into three piles.

"Officially, we're in Southern Illinois," Azmach said as he continued dividing clothes further.

"Illinois..." Asher said tiredly with a slender amount of disbelief. "So, we're at the place?"

"Just about," Azmach said. He put his pants on and picked up a pile of clothes, placing it next to Asher. "A little more walking tonight and tomorrow morning. But, we're basically there."

"All this traveling. 'bout time," Asher said. He looked at the pile for a second and extinguished his fire, gripping his socks and pants.

An end to all of this. The edge of conclusion is a twist of a feeling.

Azmach dropped clothes next to me. "Where'd you learn how to swim like that?" Azmach asked.

"...picked it up." I answered. Not too many tangles left. My fingers shifted through my hair.

"Your hair has that same wild shape." Azmach observed. "Even while wet." His head tilted to the side and his eyes narrowed, a thought occurring to him. "After getting wet, most afro-textured hair stays shrunk until we do something to it. Without doing anything, yours looks like it's already popping back up to its normal size the drier it gets. And it's keeping its shape. Is that normal for you?"

All the knots and tangles are just about gone. "…Yes."

The night sounds surrounded the ears, but it was mostly silent. I laid on the ground, angled up because of a tree.

The two people were asleep.

I looked through the darkness as if I could see the edge of everything. What is everything?

I grabbed a few strands of hair and gently pulled them down in front of my eye so I could examine them. My hair was back to its normal size since it was dry, and long enough that when the front was pulled fully down, it would be at my chin.

White hair.

Orange eyes.

All routine.

Admittance and acceptance.

What is this edge I can and cannot see?

My shoes crackled on autumn leaves. Trees surrounded the area. A usual forest. It was a bit warmer today compared to yesterday. The sun was beaming down through the branches and leaves, which were still hanging on their respective trees.

"Almost there?" Asher asked Azmach.

crackle

"Not too far now," Azmach replied.

Asher inhaled audibly then exhaled. "Took us a bit more than two weeks."

"And now less than a—"—

What's this feeling? It was like pressure pushing me down. It wasn't actually a force, but it invoked that feeling. Strong. Something I've never felt.

Azmach had stopped dead in his tracks, cutting his words off.

"What's happening?" Asher looked at him, seemingly at least feeling a small amount of whatever that was, while also stopping to see why Azmach was reacting in such a manner.

Azmach's eyes widened as he breathed in and out deeply. He looked up, down, left, right, scanning the surroundings. Then, he stiffened.

"What is this feeling?" I questioned him.

"Aura…" Azmach answered softly, trailing off as his head snapped around. He scanned the surroundings further.

Aura. Oh. This feeling is Aura. It's on a higher scale than what I've ever felt before. It's something that feels unreal.

"Azmach?" Asher questioned.

This feeling, this pressure.

"We're running," Azmach apprehensively said, his eyes locked ahead of him. "Now!"

Azmach sprinted forward, Asher immediately running to his right.

I sprinted behind the two of them.

This feeling-wait. Is this—

Break!-an entire tree was cracked in half a few feet behind.

"Watch the sky!" Azmach yelled out.

I looked up through the trees. There was something up there. I could barely see. There was only a blurred outline with some colors on it. Something flying?

That's a person.

Slam!-something hard, something strong, a fragment of it smashed into the ground, breaking branches on the way down.

Asher quickened his pace as he looked ahead of himself, at the sky, and Azmach.

I looked up for a second. What is that? That person themselves wasn't flying. They were flying on something.

Cling!-the thing the person was using to fly was scraped by something else. That something else was a thing another one was using to fly.

Two people.

It was hard to see exactly what was what. But what each person was using, they were... One was standing on a small, golden, flat oval that seemed to be made of a somewhat thick liquid. Extremely sharp golden shards formed around him—

One shard shot out towards the other person, who was standing on a flat oval of red—

Scrape!-the shard was blocked by a newly created oval of hardened red liquid.

Crack!

There's yelling above.

The two flying people were fighting each other.

Crack!-an enormous red shard slashed downward, breaking a tree in half somewhere behind me.

A grunt, a monstrous one.

"Yo." Asher quickly staggered on the word.

Some kind of muscled Monster was chasing me, Asher and Azmach. It was coming from the right, yards away. It had no eyes, but it did have sharp teeth with a large lower jaw, hard brownish-gray skin covering its body, and long arms with three fingers on each hand, which it used to scar the ground in its pursuit.

"It's that kind of day," Azmach muttered. He ran faster, his shoes pounding the ground, with Asher and me right behind him.

The Monster gained some ground—

Slice!- an enormous red shard shaped like a blade cut the Monster in half through its shoulder at an angle. Blood spilled—

The blood wasn't spilling. It was floating, being pulled upwards and fast. The blood formed into a solid point and stabbed towards the person on the golden oval.

Crack!-it was blocked by more golden liquid formed into a quick shielding structure.

Gah, almost tripped. The hill had some slickness to it.

These Auras. They're entirely different from what I've felt thus far. No. The Monsters had a similar feeling, but not in the same way. The Monsters were subdued since they could easily take on two weak Demigods, and another notably weak one who hadn't even learned how to use whatever powers they had. What's different here is the intensity. It was the feeling of two people who knew they couldn't hold anything back because of just who their opponent was.

Crush!-some large golden fragment bits fell on top of a tree to my right. The tree was devastated.

Trees, trees, trees, when do they end?

Woah. It felt like I ran through a doorway filled with a ray of light. What was-

Crack!

When will the fighting end? —

Break!-a tree was pulverized, with shards and pieces of it scattering on Asher, Azmach, and I.

"Run for the hill!" Azmach yelled out. He continued to sprint forward.

The trees were opening up ahead. Wider gaps between each one appeared.

I sprinted faster, looking for the hill he meant.

Crack!

The landscape was leveling out, becoming a flat field. Far ahead, the field had curved upwards, forming a massive hill.

There it is.

Azmach slid past a tree and surged forward. He maybe was two steps ahead, knowing exactly where to go. Asher ducked under a branch, still rushing to the hill.

The further it went, the fewer trees the field had. It was opening up in space as the hill became closer. The ground, the vegetation changed. It became shorter with the color green popping out more —

Clink!

A twig snapped under my shoe.

Closer to the hill.

Crack!

Faster, Faster, Move.

Azmach sped ahead. Asher was still behind him to his right.

Halfway through the field.

Is that yelling?

I looked up. The one with the golden liquid leapt off their oval, slamming into the other person. The other person - tumbled, almost slipping and falling off their oval, falling like the entire golden oval was doing now.

The golden oval had solidified further and was falling right...

Run faster.

Twigs snapping.

I can hear the oval plummeting.

Halfway to the hill.

The oval was getting closer—

Its solidness sounded like it was bending.

Almost at the hill.

Asher's back curled a bit as he slipped but regained his footing.

Almost there. The hill was closer. So was the golden oval. I wasn't looking up. Still, I could feel it and hear it—

Hardness cracking and groaning.

Yelling in the distance.

Crack!-a tree must have broken nearby their yelling.

Groaning.

At the edge of the hill.

The sun's getting blocked. I'm under a shadow-

Dive!

I leaped right—

Crack SMASH GROAN!-the golden oval crashed onto the ground where I was at—

GROAN SMASH!- it was rolling destructively-

I also was rolling-

CLUNG!

SkydirtskygreenredgoldI kept rolling

GROAN!

Rolling.

Arms scrape. Stop.

Yelling in the background. It's getting closer.

I was on my back, motionless. Finally, I opened my eyes. Clouds on a sunny day. A couple. A few. A clear sky.

Yelling grew louder, grew closer.

"Come on!" Asher yelled, standing nearby.

I was on my feet and running again, now finally going up the hill—

Dirt shot up to my right.

"They spotted us!" Azmach yelled.

Yelling!

Dirt blasted up, like bombs hitting the ground.

"Don't look back!" Azmach yelled.

Dirt blasting-

Just up the hill, just up—

Yelling.

Dirt.

Halfway up.

Dirt-in my eyes-gah- I squinted, sprinting faster up the hill—

My foot—*Dirt exploding* - my foot. Something struck the ground next to both of my feet, making the dirt blast upward- I can't see it-*Dirt exploding-*

Asher grunted somewhere left of me.

Yelling.

Slams and clinging - they were still fighting each other - their grunts could be heard behind—

Dirt exploding-

A few more steps away, there was the top of the hill.

Dirt exploding.

Ten more steps.

Dirt.

Seven.

Azmach rushed ahead by inches, leading—

Dirt

Three.

Dirt

One. Top of the hill.

The ground shook.

Run! Straight forward! Run!—

Woah. This same feeling again. It was the feeling of running through a doorway filled with a ray of light. It was denser this time.

Faster!

The ground shook.

Azmach curved left.

"Hurry!" A voice yelled out.

People were running in the direction that Azmach was headed.

Wait. People? Doesn't matter, keep going.

The Ground Shook.

"Down here!" Another yell. Another voice.

Azmach curved right, rushing towards where a handful of people were running. People were heaving themselves down a rectangular opening in the ground roughly the size of a doorway.

Dirt blasted upward at the top of the hill near the area where I felt that ray of light feeling.

Azmach was at the edge of the opening. There were stairs

leading deeper into the ground. Down, the people and I went.

Dim. There was light, but nothing like how it was outside, like a cave lit by only candles and torches. The stairs were made of brown stone. There were echoes from the pounding of multiple shoes, but those echoes were broken by —

The ground shook.

Dirt and stone particles fell from above. The opening was far away by this point as Azmach, Asher, the people, and I descended deeper into the ground. Dirt and brown stone were the surroundings —

The ground shook.

My feet hit the bottom of the stairs. Panicked voices crowded.

"Anyone else?" Someone asked someone.

"A couple more are coming," someone replied.

It was a moderately sized room with a capacity that could accommodate multiple at once. The ceiling, floor, and walls were made entirely of brown stone.

The ground shook, the entire room followed in the trembling.

Dirt and stone particles fell from the ceiling, then subsided once the shaking settled.

There were some tables and chairs, but not enough for the amount of people. People filled the room. There was enough space to move around if needed, but the people were noticeable —

The entire room shook.

—as well as their words, gasps, and other sounds.

Azmach leaned forward on a stone slab that acted as a table on the right side of the room. The yellowish dim light made it difficult to make anything out clearly.

The room shook.

Particles sprinkled from the ceiling.

I walked towards the table, stopping just inches from it. I

think Asher did the same. I don't know, my mind's…
somewhere else…no he's here, I see him standing in front of a
different side of the table—

"Close the door!" Someone yelled.

The door for the room slammed shut at once.

My eyes concentrated on Azmach. Were they concentrated
at all? Concentrated or not, they were on Azmach.

Too much was going on.

All of this? What is it?

"It seems I owe you both an explanation," Azmach plainly
said.

Particles sprinkled down. Some gasps and shocked
comments went through the room.

"That goes without saying," Asher replied.

Seconds passed, no one, between the two of them and me,
said a word.

"The two men fighting in the sky," Azmach finally said.

The room shook.

Particles fell.

"Woah," someone said in the room.

"Back away from the door! It's not safe!" A different one
yelled.

"They are men, but I wouldn't say they're men." Azmach's
eyes were concealed from the dim light.

Particles.

I looked through the dimness at him. "You mean—"

The room shook.

"Yes," Azmach answered. "Gods."

The room shook, yet everything stopped, particles of stone
and dirt rained down, yet everything stopped, the people
around spoke and gasped with each shake and violent crash,
yet everything stopped, is it just me who stopped? Is it just
me?

gods. Where's the question mark?

Gods.

The room shook.

Gasps and other expressions went through the room.

"Gods," I said aloud, trying to let it process.

"Right now?" Asher asked in astonishment. He looked up at the ceiling. "Here?"

"Here," Azmach confirmed.

Gods.

In concept, it's perceivable. It manifesting into a tangible reality is … … … … … … … … … … … … What diction would fit this case? The conceptual becoming what, at least in this very moment, is seemingly but also completely factual, regardless of how I think and feel would be reality, is insurmountably beyond description. Yet here it is.

Particles rained down.

Gods…

"Why are those two fighting?" Asher questioned. His first few words were quiet as the events were beginning to sink in.

"Why are they all fighting?" Azmach rhetorically asked.

"All of them?

"The war." I whispered, having an epiphany.

Asher turned to look as well.

"You referenced it around a week ago." I shortly recollected as I looked at Azmach.

The room shook - particles sprinkled down.

Gasps and other exasperations went through the area.

"A war?" Asher questioned. "That war! I remember now. You said it like it was a slip up and you changed the subject real quick. What's this war about? Why are they fighting?"

"The reason why any war happens." Azmach said.

The room shook-Shook harder than most of the other ones.

Particles sprinkled down sounding like sandbags spilling open.

"Power," Azmach answered.

Asher stood there, looking at Azmach the best he could through the dimness, understanding everything said but looking as if core concepts were skipped over as the next step was pushed.

"Don't the Alkeeb Gods already have enough?" Asher questioned, his brow furrowing as irritation and anger partially came into his voice.

"Not since X'stayn disappeared," Azmach countered.

"X'stayn?" Came flying out of my mouth.

Shook-Shook-Shoo-Shook!

Particles pouring like sand.

"Ah!" Someone.

Others did the same, yelping and grunting.

"X'stayn disappeared?" I pressingly questioned.

"Yes." Azmach answered. "The King of the Gods is missing."

Knocks at the door. Four to be exact.

"That's the knock! Let them in!" Someone yelled.

Shook!

"Seventeen years ago, X'stayn vanished," Azmach explained.

Door slam shut. Footsteps about.

"Lock it!" Someone yelled.

"No traces. Nothing." Azmach went further.

"Any reason?" Asher asked.

"None."

Shook, not as strong as the others.

"He was just gone." Azmach went silent for a second. "It led to a power vacuum. Since then, most of the Empyreans and other Gods have been at war to take the Empiric Throne."

Shook.

"The Empyreans too?" Asher asked—

Shook.

Particles

Coughs broke through the air somewhere.

Azmach gripped the table. "Most of the Gods are fighting. The Empyreans are the main ones engaged in this war."

"What about the Thrice?" Asher said, that thought solidly bombarding him. "You said for they were the three main Kauzation Gods. If X'stayn is missing, wouldn't one of them just take his place? What about Orthantehs, the ocean God? Wouldn't he be next in line?"

"Orthantehs has been missing for decades."-

Shook-

"That one was strong," someone commented.

"Decades?" I questioned with emphasis.

Sounds of sand spilling broke through the noise, particles falling from the ceiling more rapidly.

"Decades," Azmach repeated.

"Letnos?" Asher questioned worryingly. "He's the other brother and the third Thrice. What about him?"

"He hasn't been seen longer than Orthantehs," Azmach answered, "Even if he was here, the other Gods would in no way allow him to be king."

Asher just stared at Azmach, trying to grasp solutions and finding no options to do so.

"You see why there's a power vacuum?" Azmach asked rhetorically.

Shook!

Grunts, and other sounds resounded.

Asher's head jeered downward from the impact.

Particles.

That one felt closer.

My hands rested on the table. I looked at Azmach, taking in the words and sounds around. My hands feel it, the weight.

"What does that have to do with you two, them,"—I gestured to the people in the room—"and me? None of you and I are Gods."

"We're Demigods." Azmach immediately said.

Shook.

Grunts.

Particles.

Azmach straightened his back as he gripped the sides of the table in seriousness. "Any threat they see to their power is something that cannot be ignored. The Gods have become paranoid. Some of them think we want to be the ones on the Empiric Throne, ruling—"

Shook!

Azmach jerked to his right.

Asher jerked backwards, his spine bending.

People were jerked in different directions.

I gripped the table as I was jerked left.

Grunts and other words broke through the air.

Particles continued to sprinkle down.

"That's why they started killing us," Azmach gravely said.

Shook.

ShOOK!

"And they continue to kill us," Azmach didn't flinch as he said those last words.

"Demigods… are being killed by the Gods?" I questioned. There was no way I heard that correctly. I must make certain.

The anxious and hasty words in the room seemed to grow more dense for a second right before suddenly returning to their previous volume.

"Yes. We're being killed by the Gods." Azmach answered.

I stood silently. Silently.

"Why didn't you tell us before?" Asher asked. There were traces of agitation slipped into his voice. He began looking around, his brow knitting. "Now we're here, whatever here is."

Azmach shook his head. "As we were running for our lives? I couldn't do that to either of you. You guys just found out you were Demigods and had to leave your homes behind, you guys had to sleep in forests and dirt every night, and only for two hours at a time because we had to keep moving, you guys had Monsters wanting to kill you, you didn't even know Monsters were real up to that point. And as you found out… I'm… not…at…my full capacity. I didn't want to add another thing for you to worry about."

"I get where you're coming from, but this is something we needed to know before."

Shook!

"And I get where you're coming from. My thing is you guys could have died at any day at any second. Last thing I was going to do was say 'There's a war where Gods are trying to kill us, not just those two Monsters'. That would be too much at once. I was going to tell you both no matter what. I knew to wait until the best time. So, I had planned to get you guys to a safe place, then tell you—"

Shook!

"I just didn't expect the day we come back, this would happen." Azmach looked around.

Asher nodded his head. "I do see where you're coming from, and it does make sense. There are just some things you should try and tell us sooner."

"There are some things I won't be able to do that with that I don't have a choice in. But for everything else, the necessary stuff like this, in the future, I'll tell you."

"I'll hold ya to it." Asher held his hand out to Azmach.

Azmach grabbed Asher's hand, shaking it. "Bet."

They released the handshake.

Asher was looking at the people and generally around the room. "Is it really safe here?"

"Yes, to a point."

"What is this place?" Asher stared at the ceiling then back around the room.

"Right now, we're in an underground room, used for times like these," Azmach explained.

Shook. It was smaller compared to the other shakes.

People stood around, looking at the door and ceiling as the two Gods outside continued fighting.

Particles.

"We call it a 'Railroad'." Azmach said.

"Who's 'we'?" Asher asked.

"Demigods."

I looked at the people in the room. All these people are Demigods? It's not surprising. It's fathomable in concept, but for it to shift from concept to existence so suddenly can be oddly discombobulating.

Surreal and yet reality.

Shook!

"Ah!" Someone let out.

"There are multiple Railroads throughout this place," Azmach added.

"And what exactly is this place?" I questioned. I gripped the table as the impact settled.

"Where we were heading all this time," Azmach said.

"Which is?"

Particles sprinkled down.

"You'll both see when we get up there," Azmach said with a weight to his words.

Shook!

Weight. My hands feel it.

Is Reality Truth When Further Questions Are Founded Upon A Lack Of Necessary Content?

"It's been quiet," someone said.

"I think they're gone," a different person.

Azmach straightened his back.

Asher looked away from the door and turned his attention to Azmach because of his sudden change in posture.

"Let's go," Azmach said.

The door used to enter the Railroad was pushed open at the top of a narrow staircase.

My eyes.

Sunlight poured in. I squinted, getting used to abrasive light. The people standing on the steps ahead of me blocked some of it, but it was still hard to see, coming from dimness to the sudden opposite.

Asher had his hand in front of his eyes, putting it down quickly after adjusting to the brightness.

It was quiet. No shakes. No eruptions. Not even a breeze.

"It's safe!" Someone nearby the doorway yelled out.

"Good," a different person.

People began exiting the stairwell, some talking in hushed tones as they went, but most were quiet. Tension was still hanging in the air from what had just transpired. Of course, the atmosphere of danger would linger. It wouldn't leave that easily.

Tension. Heaviness. Weight.

I walked up the stairs as more space opened from people continuing to file out. Soon, the doorway was within reach.

Azmach exited the staircase into the outside air. Asher was right behind him.

I followed.

"How long were we in there?" Asher asked as he walked next to Azmach.

"Had to be at least a couple of hours," Azmach estimated.

"That's more than enough."

"That! Was only two Gods." Azmach stopped walking and looked at Asher with pure seriousness. "Imagine if there were more."

Asher stood still, the meaning of Azmach's words starting to connect with him in an awful manner.

"What we just experienced pales in comparison," Azmach said. "That wasn't even a battle. That was barely a fight."

"Is that him?" Someone anxiously called out in disbelief.

I looked around. There were trees surrounding the small dirt pathway, more like a trail, that Asher, Azmach, and I stood on. In all of this, the person who had called out was nowhere to be seen. Where are they?

crackling, scraping

There.

Footsteps crunching leaves, breaking twigs, and scraping the ground were coming closer.

I turned to see four guys around my age walking up from around the trees. Each of them were different shades of brown. One had short cornrows that went to the bottom of his neck. Two had their afro-textured hair cut very short. The fourth had a small afro. All of them looked shocked and in awe.

The four of them stopped two feet away, staring.

Asher looked at Azmach for a second then back at the strangers.

The person with the cornrows eyes gawked.

"Yo, it is Azmach!" Said the one with the small afro.

"I could barely tell," the one with cornrows realized. "I hear no one's seen you in like two months."

"Felt longer," Azmach sighed, yet with the usual firmness in his voice.

"When did you get here?" One of the two with the shorter hair asked.

"Couple hours ago."

"You were in the middle of that?" Shock and realization set in the one that asked, then spreading to the entire group of four.

"We were," Azmach gestured to Asher and I.

The four of them looked over Asher and me as they exchanged looks of shock and worry, along with verbalizing it with sounds and quick comments.

"Have y'all been to the Infirmary yet?" The one with the cornrows asked.

Infirmary. That word seems foreign and far away.

"We were just heading there," Azmach answered.

"Good," the one with cornrows said. "We're about to check the Barriers."

"They do need to be checked. Be thorough."

"We will." The one of the two with the low cut hair said.

"Great to have you back." The one with cornrows said to Azmach. He then turned to his group, keeping his attention on them. "Come on, y'all."

The group walked past Azmach, Asher and me. Once again, Azmach began walking down the dirt pathway with Asher to his side and me a step behind.

The pathway was opening up.

What is this?

Feet away from the trees and the dirt pathway was a vast clearing of vegetation that had been cut very low. "Clearing" might not be the right word since it was full of people. People were walking, running, standing, and going about their lives. All of them were around my age, had various shades of brown skin, and were in the middle of doing something. Some of them were moving stacks of blankets around, others were holding vegetables and fruit in baskets. There were a few large logs on the ground that were being moved by people as well. Small conversations and other sounds softly filled the air. There had to have been more than fifty people, yet it was surprisingly quiet. I could hear each footstep I took. There was a rush and urgency in the atmosphere and behaviors of the people, but it was gradually calming away from this urgency. It was completely busy, teeming with activity, with stress and some fear guardedly leaving the area. I could also tell there was going to be more ahead.

The silhouettes of buildings could be seen in the distance. They didn't resemble skyscrapers or suburban houses one would usually see in a modern populace. I couldn't tell yet from how far away it was, but it felt out of this world while within.

I looked around, taking it in, while the two and I walked further.

"Azmach!" Someone voice called.

Some of the people moving around froze, all of them staring at Azmach and where the voice came from.

A person around my age, perhaps a few years older, was

walking up. He was tall, had dark blue jeans, a gray shirt, a brownish-red jacket, and dark shoes. His afro-textured hair was twisted on top and faded on the sides. A rough face sat on top of a matching neck. He had cedar brown skin with a small scar on the side of his chin. No, not just one, there were two - the second one extending to the top of his neck. They weren't very deep, but upon closer look, they were definitely noticeable.

Those scars were probably deeper as wounds before they astonishingly healed...

"When'd you get back here?" The person with the scars asked.

"When those two Gods were fighting." Azmach replied.

"Were they here for you? Did any mortals find out?" The scarred person's tone was stone, serious like someone who knew their entire life was constantly watched by omniscient eyes.

"Those Gods weren't here for us," Azmach said. "As far as I know, no mortal has found out from us."

"Aight," the scarred person moved his hand towards Azmach. "Good to see you back."

Their hands met, clasping each other's and sliding off, then switching to a fist bump.

"Can't be dying on you now." Azmach smiled.

"I see you brought two new ones." The scarred person looked past Azmach, and at Asher and me. "What about them? Did they get noticed?"

Asher looked at him confusingly.

"No mortals noticed." Azmach answered.

"It's going to take me a minute to get used to that word, but why can't 'mortals' find out about us?" Asher asked.

"Because the Gods will kill you." Azmach bleakly revealed. "Sometimes they'll also kill the ones associated with you."

Kill.

Asher stood silent.

"Gods won't even wait for a mortal to actually find out," the scarred person bluntly said. "They'll kill you if they see whatever you're doing as a chance of mortals finding out."

"That's the main reason why you didn't want to take any cars or drive them." I realized, turning to Azmach. "Or take a bus or train. You even stopped Asher from possibly burning a forest down when it the other options were abysmal."

Azmach looked at me, nodding once slowly.

"Because that could draw attention." Asher pondered out loud. "That...yeah that's something you don't spring on someone. I can see why you didn't tell that one yet."

"I can see wanting to know that information beforehand." Azmach nodded looking at Asher, the two of them sharing an understanding.

"Hold on. You didn't drive a car back here? I'm guessing you crashed the one we gave you, right?" The scarred person asked.

"You crashed another one?" Asher immediately asked.

"'Another'?"

"Let's not worry about that right now. "Azmach held his hands partly out.

"Oh no, we'll get back to it later." The scarred person smiled.

Azmach's eyes darted down.

"That aside for now," the scarred person continued. "None of you look like you're in the best shape. I'm assuming you're going to the Infirmary."

"Yeah," Azmach said.

"Let's go," he turned, walking next to Azmach. The two of them were side by side, now leading the way.

"Sorry about the interrogation," The scarred person said towards Asher and me. "We just can't risk it."

"Naw, I feel you," Asher brushed off. "It makes sense. I wouldn't call it an 'interrogation'. Too strong of a word, you know?"

"Eh- I like making sure. My name's Lamonte." He said, looking slightly behind his left shoulder to make eye contact with Asher.

"Asher," Asher extended his right hand and slid his fingers across Lamonte's right hand, gripping his fingers in a casual handshake. He then pointed with his thumb past Lamonte and Azmach's right, where I was walking. "This is Jason."

"What's good." Lamonte turned his head right and greeted. I nodded once.

Lamonte, that name. An old thought from what was heard...

The silhouette of structures in the distance was coming into view as more people appeared from the sides and ahead.

"Which two Gods were fighting this time?" Azmach asked.

"One was...my dad" Lamonte said.

"Controlling blood. Yeah, that would be Zound. What of the other one?"

"...The other one...I couldn't get a good look. He looked a little bit like my dad, I think. I might just be thinking that since he was controlling golden liquid.

"That is the real color of God blood. I can see why you're thinking that."

"But it was probably just gold itself or something that had that color. They were moving too much to tell exactly who he was. Probably a Minor God."

Woah. The architecture.

The ground itself was changing. The various walkways were now made of white stone with lines slicing through its top layer every few feet. They were surrounded by short and evenly cut green vegetation that barely passed a toe in height. It all looked new as if this was laid not a minute ago. It must always look like this. Everything looked perfectly integrated, matching each other without it feeling like a random shift from white stone to short green vegetation, miscellaneous rocks, and dirt. Buildings were coming into view. To the right, one building stood tall and wide, being made up of a dim bronze-colored stone. The architecture here had a modernized ancient feel.

"Is that Azmach?" Someone said.

"Azmach!" A different voice.

There were even more people around. This must be close to whatever was considered as the main area of this place. People were moving things, walking, talking, some looked busy, others carefree.

"We'll give y'all a proper tour later," Lamonte said to me and Asher. He led away from a more crowded area and the dim bronze building that was coming into view.

Other buildings were coming into view from the distance. More of them. People moved in and out of the line of sight as the structures continued coming closer. Off to the right ahead, one building was wide and tall, made of reddish-brown stone, and had an assortment of windows much bigger than the size of any person. A different building to the right of the reddish-brown building was more wide versus tall in stature. It was made of whitish-beige stone and had a grand staircase, which led to an enormous archway entrance. Both buildings were ultimately massive structures that had the same modernized ancient feel that the entire place held thus far.

There was one building that Asher, Azmach, Lamonte, and I were heading straight towards. The building was tall, but not as wide as compared to the other buildings. It was some hundreds of feet to the left of the reddish-brown and whitish-beige buildings. This building was made of golden beige stones with lines artistically slicing through the top layer of it all. The roof of the building was uniquely circular, unique in the sense that the building itself was more of a vertical rectangle up until where the roof connected. It seemed rather thin for a roof, but it also looked strong and reinforced. From where the roof connected to the building itself, it did not have a sudden change in shape, and it fit ever so perfectly that it created a normalized yet distinctive look. The roof's color was more golden than beige when compared to the rest of the building.

"Azmach!" Someone called out.

"Yeah, it is him." A different person.

A good number of people were going about their business, but there were some who were doing more. Chatter and murmurs went through the crowds of people who looked to be around my age. Some stared at Azmach, shocked at the sight of him. Their eyes widened as other expressions of astoundment illustrated on their faces and body language. Others had a mixture of curiosity and surprise as they took many glances at the group and me. Some stayed focused on their destination while simultaneously stealing glances here and there. A mass sense of relief exuded in the crowd as they stared at Azmach.

The building most likely to be the Infirmary was closer now, showing two detailed, thick, rectangular oak doors. Beige stones trimmed the outline of the doorway. The door-way itself was tall enough for two people stacked on top of each other and wide enough for four.

"I thought he was dead," someone let out a breath.

People started coming towards the group and me, mostly towards Azmach.

"When did you return?" Someone asked, walking up to Azmach.

"You haven't looked this bad in a while," someone else joked.

The questions and comments poured in as more people came over. Azmach casually looked around, having a re-strained smile at all the people.

"What's with his hair?" Someone asked.

Hair. That question was about me.

"Guys, we're heading to the Infirmary," Lamonte told the

approaching and nearby people. "We can all catch up after they settle in and finish healing."

The people trying to engage understood. They all began walking away.

"Good to see you, Azmach," Someone said as they walked away.

"Good to see you too," Azmach replied.

"Make sure to rest," another said.

"Will do."

People stopped approaching, but they continued stealing glances, mostly with smiles.

The group and I walked to the Infirmary's entrance. Its dark oak doors were smooth, having an almost glossy finish.

"Thanks," Azmach said.

"Don't worry 'bout it," Lamonte replied.

The group and I continued to walk, getting only a foot away from the door.

"Lamonte," Azmach turned his back to the door looking at the person he called out. "Before we go in."

Lamonte stopped walking immediately, looking at Azmach with candor. "Did you get it done?" His tone lowered.

Azmach's mouth clenched, he visibly exhaled. "Yes." He reached inside his jacket. "At a cost." The Reverse Bag of Wind came into the open air.

Lamonte's chest dropped, his breathing audibly escaping his mouth. "I see."

Azmach held out the Bag for Lamonte. Lamonte cautiously grabbed it with both his hands— Azmach fell to his knees, his breathing heavy.

"Yo!" Asher worryingly exclaimed.

"I'm…" Azmach took deep breaths. "I'm sorry…." His deep breaths didn't stop.

Lamonte stepped forward and pushed one oak door partly open. "Three wounded!" Lamonte called out into the Infirmary, holding the door in its partly opened position. "We have three wounded! Come quickly!"

Movement and commotion were coming towards the door. I couldn't exactly see since the partial opening was mostly blocked by Lamonte.

"I'll—" Azmach breathed heavily. His breathing lessened in weight but was still heavy.

" You can hardly stand." Lamonte said. "You can rest now. Worry about it after."

Both doors swung open. People around my age exited the building, rushing out towards Azmach.

"One's on his knees," someone said urgently to their in-coming group.

"Azmach," a different voice.

Instantly, six people accessed the situation, some already helping Azmach stand.

"He's completely out of Aura," one of them anxiously said.

"These two look bad as well," a different one anxiously pointed out, examining Asher while also looking at me. "I'm surprised they can stand."

"Can you both walk?" A different one asked Asher and me.

More hasty words were passed as they helped Azmach inside, with someone making sure Asher and I could walk inside the place as well.

I never realized how tired I was. It wasn't just sleep. My body was more than just exhausted. The body aches and the internal quakes as where I lay, I contemplate. Am I even here? What is here?

I'm in a bed. Am I really? How long have I been asleep? When did I even fall asleep? It was so quiet. This bed is so soft. A bed?

I opened my eyes.

An actual bed. I'm lying in one. The sheets were white. Clean? They're clean.

What's this room? It was small comparatively speaking

when taking into account the building it was within. Still, the length was the size of two bedrooms from the house I took residence in and it was the width of one.

Residence. The bald man. Calvin... Elizabeth...

I looked around and saw only one other bed accompanied by a desk on the left side of the room. The walls were dark beige stone with black lines gently swirling and straightening on the surface. This almost gave the room a wood-like look. A clock on the wall in front of me silently moved its arms. There were two doors, one being in the left corner of the same wall closest to my head, and the other across from me at the corner to my right. Both were made of dark oak.

What's that? A blurred outline to my left. I turned to see some folded clothes on top of a small desk right next to the head of my bed.

A doorknob's turning. The door across the room straight ahead of me opened. Someone stepped inside. She was around my age, tawny skin, dark eyes, long and thick braids stopping at her chin which also concealed the sides of her face.

"You're awake," she noticed as she pulled at her long dark gray cardigan, concealing a skinner frame. "You've been asleep most of the day. It's now nighttime."

Night. Although I could see the time on the clock, hearing that word hit me.

"Your name's Jason, right?" She asked with a tone indicating she needed additional clarification.

I nodded.

"Perfect." She took a few steps forward walking further past the doorway, the door closing behind her. "I'm Shanice."

"Where are the other two?" I asked.

"I'm guessing you mean Azmach and... Wasn't it Ash?"

"Asher," I corrected.

"Yes, Asher. You three each in different rooms resting, getting assessments, and treatments." Shanice answered.

"How injured are those two?"

"Asher wasn't injured severely. He was more tired and a bit strained. He said he's lost a little bit of weight. I don't know the details of your journey, but it's very fortunate that you're Demigods. Otherwise, you wouldn't have ended up with so few injuries. Asher will make a full recovery with a few days of rest. Mmmmm, as for Azmach… he'll take time."

I see.

"He'll be back on his feet," Shanice anticipated. "It's how he is. For you, you just need a little more rest."

"What if there's more severe injuries?"

"There's none, we've scanned you already."

My head snapped down to look at my clothes. They were the same clothes I had been wearing for weeks now. I looked at my hands and body. When did they-how did they?

"Don't worry, we have noninvasive ways for scanning," Shanice clarified.

The same clothes from the last weeks were still on my body. Noninvasive indeed.

"Now—" she clapped her hands. "As for you, since you're finally awake, we have to get you cleaned and change your clothes."

No, no, no

"I can do that myself," I said.

"Not a problem. You don't seem severely injured. I do need to make sure. Are you able to wash yourself?"

I nodded.

"Perfect. That's the washroom." Shanice gestured to the door at the left side of the room that I had noticed earlier. "There are washcloths, soaps, everything you need. Take those clothes"—she pointed at the clothes on the desk next to me—"and change into them. Fold your old clothes and put them on that desk"—she pointed to the desk closest to the bed I was laying in. The doorknob from the door she used to enter turned under her hand. Half her body was through the doorway. "If you need any help, just call."

Close.

Quiet again. I took it in.

I grabbed the clothes and stepped out of the bed, walking towards the washroom. The floor was a bit slick. Slick? I feel it myself. My shoes were gone. I could also feel soreness through my body. I walked to the washroom, opened its door, and peered inside.

Cream. That was the color of the walls and ceiling. The floor was closer to the color of the room I had just walked through, resembling a sandy brown. It was spacious enough to hold ten people with ample space for movement. In the back center was a walk-in clear glass shower, and next to it were white shelves filled with face cloths, soaps, and bottles for bodily cleaning. Positioned in the center of the right wall was a shelf filled with larger towels and an empty nylon bin to toss in dirty clothes. On the left wall's center was a sink with a mirror over it, and an additional long mirror extending to the left of the sink. To the sink's right was where a toilet was placed.

I walked into the washroom, closed the door, and started taking my shirt- ah, soreness and irritation went through my muscles. Pants and socks were off next. Where did they put my shoes? Later. For now, get clean.

I put the clean clothes I had down on an empty space next to the towels. I then grabbed a face cloth and a black bar of soap. This isn't mine, don't take much, if any at all. I stepped into the shower, closing its door, and turning it on. It warmed up quickly-hot. Hot water poured over me. It's actually hot, not cold like rain, streams, rivers. Rain and water bottles had been the only ways of staying clean. This feels strange. I put the soap in the face cloth, rubbing it around so the cloth would absorb it. The smell coming out was...good. Not sweat, not dirt. It was fresh. It was clean.

The old clothes were folded on the desk. The new clothes were partially thin, and a bit big on me like all the clothes I've worn thus far. No, I can't equate those two. It's not a good comparison because they're not as big as the clothes I've worn thus far. These clothes felt like they were designed to be a bit loose-fitting. The shirt and pants I now wore were smooth and soft on my skin, and off-white in color.

White.

My hair came into focus from the rest of me. It was already dry, but that's not saying much. I had lightly splashed a bit of water since I wasn't sure how much time I had to wash right now. I'll give it a good wash later tonight once I get the chance.

I looked at the door. That person was still standing outside of it. Sneaking past her wouldn't be a viable option. It was in the very back of my mind this entire time being suppressed by more pressing matters. The majority of my mind had been on Monsters, and worse, so the question was never outwardly asked, the question pertaining to the definition of what this place exactly is. I looked around. No windows, no other doors, no ways to escape.

Where would I go even if I did? Do I even want to?

Sit back, watch from the distance. All routine.

I walked over to the door. "Ready," I said just loud enough for it to be heard through the wood. I backed up towards the bed I had woken up in.

The door opened and the person, Shanice, stepped in with a smile on her face. "Alright. I'll do a quick assessment since you're awake to check for any further problems we might have missed. A couple questions. Sit down on the bed."

I sat on top of the white sheets.

"Roll your sleeves up," she said.

My sleeves slid down easily since the shirt was loose-fitted.

Shanice stared, examining. "A couple of scars. Some of them old, some healing. Is this all you have?"

"Some more. About the same," I answered.

"You're not frostbitten. Do you feel any pain? Extreme soreness?"

I shook my head.

"Do you have any difficulty breathing?"

I shook my head.

"Is your heart behaving naturally?"

I nodded my head.

"So no heart pain?"

I shook my head.

"Do you have any issues walking?"

I shook my head.

"Do you have full mobility of your limbs?"

I nodded.

"Have you had any sight or hearing problems since you've entered the God world?"

I shook my head.

"Any dizziness? Do you feel—" she shook her hands, trying to find the word "—off at all? Not including naturally being tired and some soreness."

I shook my head.

"So you're mostly at health. Perfect. At this time, there's no need to go deeper. Rest here for a few days just in case, then you're out. Sounds perfect?"

I nodded.

"Perfect," Shanice was already partially out the door, smiling. "Rest well. Call if you need anything."

Close. Quiet.

This routine is and is not. What is outside, inside, and deeper?

My fingers felt...this bed. A pillow. Clean clothes. Weight, my hands still feel it. Calm with the excess of noise with the excess of calm.

What is all of this?

I lay in an Infirmary. Nothing passes except everything and

naught. The walls, the floor, the doors.
  The lights dimming as sleep gravitates. Rest.
  What is all of this?

Does The Lack Of Information Mean The Lack Of The Person?

"It's been a perfect two days," Shanice said, sitting in a seat next to the Infirmary bed I was lying in.

I turned my body, starting to get out of the bed.

"Before that, I do have two questions," she said in a tone that was gradually hatching with curiosity.

That type of tone. It's not bad per say, it's just...

I stopped moving and looked at her.

"Is your eye color...real?" She asked, her face trying to keep intrigue hidden beneath a blank expression.

Orange eyes.

"Yes," I said.

Some of the intrigue slipped through the surface before being pushed back down. "And your white hair...along with its shape and style?"

"Yes," I said quietly.

All routine.

Her blank expression slipped as the intrigue danced beneath. "Hm. There are sandals for you next to your bed for whenever you leave." She walked to the door, opening it. "Be quick though." She turned her head looking at me as she smiled. "Someone's waiting for you outside." Shanice exited the room, the door closing behind her.

Someone? Who? I was going to leave anyway. Might as well find out who.

I stepped onto the floor, slipping my feet into black sandals, and made my way towards the door. I pulled it open to see a hallway stretching to my left and right with closed doors lining the walls.

"Good to see you, dude." Someone said.

I turned to see Asher leaning on the wall across the hall, a smile on his face. He was wearing similar clothes to me, black sandals and all, except the color of the clothes were a pure white instead of an off-white.

"Why are you waiting for me?" I asked. What does he have in mind?

"Yesterday, Azmach told me that he wanted to talk to the both of us whenever we got the chance, and I heard they were going to let you leave today."

Azmach?

"What does he want to talk about?" I asked.

"Not sure," Asher candidly said. "That's why I wanted to wait for you."

The door opened, revealing a room that looked similar to the one I was in for a few days. It had calming, dimmed lights and a single bed off to the side. Covered in a blanket with a pillow under his head was Azmach.

Asher walked through the doorway. I walked in after, closing the door behind me.

"Azmach," Asher said approaching him.

"…oh good." Azmach said with exhaustion that would not leave. "Great to see you both rested and well."

"Same to you, bro, same to you." Asher sat down in a

wooden chair next to Azmach's bed. "Looks like you're getting better."

"Yeah...I just need to rest for...a week."

"Nothing but that bed for a week."

"Yeah. Probably more. I can feel that I'll be sleeping for days... You guys got here just in time. I was about to knock out."

"I mean if you want, I can knock you out right now," Asher put his fists up in a playful manner.

"Give me some water, it'll be lights out for you." Azmach rebutted.

"Bro, you can't even get out of bed, you can barely talk."

"Now, that's cold." Azmach smiled as he held back his laughter.

"Is it facts or is it facts?" Asher was smiling as he nodded his head and raised his arms triumphantly.

"Now that's cold." Small laughter finally escaped Azmach's mouth.

"It had to be done." Asher joined in the laughter.

Their small laughter naturally died down after a few seconds.

"Why did you call for Asher and me?" I asked Azmach.

"Lamonte's coming." Azmach revealed.

"Lamonte?" Asher asked. "That one cool dude? Why, for what?"

"I'll tell you when he's here," Azmach specified. "There's something else I need to talk to each of you about."

"What do you mean?" I questioned, walking closer to the bed.

"Which God your parent is."

Silence thundered, weighing in the room.

Asher's playful demeanor evaporated. "I think you said you had a feeling or something."

"Yes." Azmach began. "It was either the first or second week of our journey..."

"To think all that happened in a little more than two weeks."

"Yeah. I remember…It was somewhere within the first week. Once you used your powers, I knew. I didn't say anything, I wanted to be sure, because if you are his son… you would be the only one."

Asher looked at Azmach with his anticipation swelling. "The only one?"

"Yes… and now I'm sure of it…"

"Who is it?"

Azmach inhaled, holding his breath for a second. "Soronos. The God of the sun."

Soronos. I recognize the name from readings.

"Soronos," Asher repeated. "I can see that."

"He's a Minor God, a Be…" He took a breath. "I've never heard of or met another child of Soronos."

"No others?" Asher said, curiosity filtering in.

"Not a single one. That's why I wasn't sure until sometime after you started training your fire. I couldn't deny the obvious."

Asher stared at his palm. "Mhm."

"Jason," Azmach said to gain more of my attention.

I looked at him, waiting for his next words.

"I have no idea which God is your parent," he said, his exhaustion exemplifying in his voice.

No idea.

Parent

No Idea. Parent.

No. Parent.

No idea.

No idea. It being said like this blatantly…

"You haven't finished Adjusting," Azmach tried his best to look intently at me. "Once you finish… it might be easier to tell." His eyes partially closed from fatigue.

No idea. No parent. No idea. Admittance and acceptance.

No idea. No parent.

All routine.

"You both need to keep training…" Azmach voice staggered off, his eyes now completely closed. "Tell no one what happened those two weeks…the Minotaur…Manticore…the Bag,…" His breathing slowed, deepening. "I should've said this long before…"

Said what?

Azmach breathed in and out deeply. "Welcome to…Numetus."

Numetus?

Silence. Azmach's breathing relaxed. He was asleep, and so deep in his slumber that nothing could wake him.

"Never heard that word before," Asher confusingly said.

Numetus? Meaning?

The door opened. I turned to see Lamonte walking in.

Lamonte stepped inside the room, his steps stopping once he saw Azmach's state. "Looks like I just missed him."

Asher nodded, looking off to the side at Azmach. "Barely." He turned his attention to Lamonte. "He said you were coming here for something."

"What is Numetus?" I asked.

"It's where we're at," Lamonte answered. "I'm giving you a tour."

"Numetus is a safe refuge for Demigods," Lamonte explained, gesturing to the surroundings. "Everything here, the ground, the hills, the Infirmary, those other places," Lamonte gestured to some other buildings in the area. "It's all of this."

The sun shined brightly as people walked around, some carrying things while others empty-handed. There were some who turned their heads to look at me, Asher, Lamonte, as the two of them and me stood with the Infirmary a few feet behind.

Lamonte pointed to the wide and tall structure that was

reddish-brown, had a short but wide staircase, and an assortment of windows. I had noticed it two days before when passing it. It was to the left of where Lamonte, Asher, and I stood, but to the right of the Infirmary, by a couple hundred feet.

"That's the Music Hall," Lamonte said as he was still pointing at the building. He then moved his arm again to point in the direction towards a darker building that was tall and wide, being made up of dim bronze stone. This building was hundreds of feet across from the Music Hall. "There's the Dining Hall down there." He added, his arm returning to his side. "There's more, but the point is if you notice, a lot of these places are on the edge of this big circle of white stone."

The ground was paved with large and wide white stone that formed pathways leading in multiple directions. These pathways converged, creating a massive circular area that was empty of structures. The circle had lines carving through it. Towards the middle of it, there were circular lines carved into the stone, with multiple circles nested inside each other. This created a pattern resembling a flat and even ripple. Other lines carving through the stone also intersected with these circles from all sides. Randomly situated around the outside of this massive white stone circle stood the Infirmary, Music Hall, and other buildings he didn't explain yet stood.

"This area here, it's called the Main Center," Lamonte said.

"Looks active," Asher commented.

"That's an understatement."

"Oh it's like that?" Asher smiled, looking around while nodding his head.

"It does get like that here. You'll get acquainted with it in time. We need to go somewhere first. We'll head towards Fabric's Quarters," Lamonte was already walking left, entering a crowd of traffic with Asher and I behind him. "Get y'all some fitted clothes."

"That, I do need."

I looked at my off-white, somewhat loose clothes and black sandals, while also looking at the slight looseness of Asher's clothes.

That's not the most important point here. A safe refuge? This place isn't adding up.

"What about Monsters?" I questioned, staring at the back of Lamonte's neck and taking in the surrounding scenery. "What about Gods and the whole war? Why didn't those two Gods take their chance to attack this place? Strategically, this would be the best place to attack. It's been quiet the last few days. Why aren't there Monsters and Gods constantly attacking?"

"Barriers," Lamonte said. "Two layers of them. Invisible to the naked. With those there, most don't try."

"Barriers? Now we're talking," Asher enthusiastically approved with a nod and a smile.

Two Barriers. That ray of light feeling. I felt it twice while running here when those two Gods were fighting. One of them was Zound, the God of war and blood. The other one, a mystery. This still is surreal.

My sandals scraped against white stone as the walking continued. Swarms of people moved in different directions, some walking in the same direction, others speeding in another.

"How do the Barriers work?" I asked.

Lamonte stepped around someone. "Only Demigods can enter. If mortals try to, they'll automatically pop way on the opposite end of the Outer Barrier without even noticing. They can't even see inside like we can. Monsters can see through both Barriers but can't pass either. Gods can also see through the Barriers. They can pass through the Outer but not the Inner."

"Now, that's nice," Asher said, clearly impressed. His sandals scraped against the ground.

There was a similarity between every person here. Their brown skin tones ranged, going from dark coffee browns to light tawny browns. All of their eyes were dark in color. The people passing illustrated a multitude of different hairstyles, not a single one of which being dyed, bleached, straightened, or manipulated in any extreme way. Every person's hair was coiled, afro-textured, and most of which were 4c and 4b. Everything was all completely natural.

Numetus.

That's unimportant.

There's something else I need to verify.

There's something else on my mind.

"I've been wondering..." I said looking around at people. "In terms of the Alkeeb Gods' connection to humanity—"

"You're wondering if the Alkeeb Gods created humans?" Lamonte's words came out quickly.

"Woah, wait a second," Asher chimed in. "You mean to tell me we're going to act like you weren't over here nonchalantly implying that the Alkeeb Gods created humans? Like Homo sapiens? Homo? Sapiens?"

"That's one of those not completely confirmed things," Lamonte quickly answered as one of his shoes scraped the pathway.

"But didn't you just saaaaaay?" Asher persisted.

"It's one of those things that we know they probably had a hand in. We just don't know how far back and to what end."

Asher nodded, slowly absorbing the information. "This is more complicated than Azmach's communication. He tells everything last minute. Make sure you can tell him I said that. I want to hear his rebuttal."

"You just woke up and chose to flame this man."

"I am the son of a sun."

Lamonte looked at Asher. "Huh?"

"That Soronos guy."

"Ah. You barely hear about him. It's wild he has any kid."

"I sure am 'wild'."

"Violating yourself now."

"Aye, everybody can get it. Like Azmach's communication skills. What's good!?"

Lamonte shook his head, laughing. He continued leading the way forward, walking past and around people. Tiny stone stalls with fabrics over their fronts began appearing on both sides of the pathway, with the pathway itself diverging to each one. People were entering and exiting the stalls, some empty-handed while others carrying various goods. A person walked passed with a basket full of corn. Conversations and sounds were in the air., but it wasn't overly loud.

Lamonte continued down a pathway that was about to intersect with another. The other one was a long pathway that ran across the crest of a long and large hill. Along the length of this long pathway there were multiple sets of stairs leading down the hill. Lamonte crossed through the long pathway, stopping once he reached the top of a set of white stone stairs. The stairs led down into a field.

In this field was a tall structure about two stories in height. It wasn't just tall, it was also wide and round. It was made of russet stone and had a high triangular umber roof. There were several small taupe stone huts scattered around, all of them being connected to each other and the bigger structure through white stone pathways. People were carrying piles of fabrics and clothes into and out of some of these stone huts.

"Fabric's Quarters," Lamonte addressed the view. "We'll head to Fabrics Mount, the main building right there." He pointed straight at the tall structure that was apparent.

Lamonte and Asher descended the stairs, with me following a foot behind. The two of them and I crossed pathways and huts, and soon arrived at Fabrics Mount's front door. Lamonte knocked on the oval-shaped mahogany door twice. The door partially opened and a person around my age peered out of the opening.

"Hello Lamonte," she greeted. Her voice was passive with a foundation of positivity. The person's eyes were dark and outwardly open to words and the world, while being balanced with realism. The sun shined off her carob brown skin. Her hair was put in a high afro puff. It reminded me of…

…Ms. Grey…

…where I'm at now at this moment feels like…

"What it do," Lamonte greeted. "These two are in need of clothes." He gestured to Asher and me.

"Okay," she replied, pulling the door all the way open and revealing herself to be skinny, wearing a long sleeve sky blue shirt, and black pants. She turned and stepped further back into the room. Lamonte along with Asher followed her.

I followed behind.

The walls were stone and olive green in color. Wooden panels, the same shade of dark brown as the oak door, were artistically woven on the wall's surfaces. The floor was made of beige stone with swirls of sand-colored lines, looking similar to marble that didn't have its extra shine. At the back was a stone staircase which led to another going upward in the opposite direction. Scattered around the room were a couple of desks and potted plants. A few of the pots were large enough that moving them required both arms. They were sitting on the floor showing their long stems and multitudes of healthy leaves. There was also an entryway on the right side of the room, which led to two connecting hallways. One hallway went left while the other one went straight ahead from the entryway. Through the dim lighting, there appeared to be different entryways to rooms on both sides of the hallway that went straight ahead.

"Layah just went into her room," the person said, her arm curled onto herself. "She's modifying her equipment right now, so she can only do one at a time," the person informed.

Lamonte looked ahead at the staircase. "Part of me would go upstairs or maybe even back outside to those huts, but that defeats the purpose. Trying to do two at the same time. And Layah's are good. Yours are the best."

"No, no, mine are just okay," the person self-consciously waved off.

"It takes a lot of time to make these types of clothes, and if Layah can only do one person right now, we'll split up," Lamonte decided. "Asher, you're with me."

"Sounds good," Asher put a thumbs up.

"Jason, you're with her."

"Down this way—" the person said to me while indicating the route by pointing out the left side of the room. In that direction was a one-way hallway that I couldn't see the end of from where I was standing.

Where does that hallway end?

Lamonte led Asher to the right side, disappearing down the hall.

The person walked to the left. I paused for a second before following her down the one-way hall. There was a mahogany door that she opened and stepped past to get inside of a room, taking her time as she did so. After she entered, she pulled the door wider so I could enter. I stepped through the doorway.

The room was larger than expected, being bigger than the room that was at the entrance. The olive-green walls did not have wooden panels weaving on its surface. There were a couple of chairs and desks around, all of which were made of wood and were a dark brown.

The person closed the door. "I should introduce myself," she said, letting go of the door handle. "My name's Mae. What's yours?"

I looked slightly down at her since she was a bit shorter than me. I can't exactly avoid this question in this context. "Jason."

"Jason." Mae repeated. "Welcome to Numetus, Jason," she turned, walking towards the back. "Follow me please. I need to get you measured."

Measured? I stopped moving to observe what she meant.

She walked towards two long tables in the back left corner. One of them had a short, lidless box containing something dark inside. The second table had some kind of thing sprouting from the top of it. Made from the same wood as the table, it looked like a sewing machine.

I stepped over in the direction Mae was walking, stopping next to the tables. She examined the wooden sewing machine.

"Okay," she said, turning her head to look at me. "Place your hands in here," she pointed at the lidless box.

The dark something inside the box was the smooth surface of clean soil. I stepped over, now standing in front of it.

"Palms face down," Mae instructed as she walked to the opposite side of the table.

On top of the soil? I did just that, not diving my hands in deeper.

"Push your Aura out a little," she added. "It'll calibrate the soil to resonate with you."

What if I make the wind whip? Push a little. I think I can handle that.

Inhale, push… Push. I need a little bit more… Grabbed it… Pull. Not too much. Little by little.

"Keep going," Mae said.

I pushed a little bit more out, after pulling small subsequent amounts.

"That's good," Mae said, as she grabbed something small and red from off the table. "The last step isn't a big deal, but please don't freak out."

In what sense? I eyed her.

"I just need to prick your finger to get a drop of blood into the soil"—she pointed at the soil as she said it—"and on top of this sewing machine"—she pointed to the sewing machine.

"What is all this for?" I asked.

"This helps with the measuring and making of clothes," Mae said. "Your Aura and blood make it an exact fit, and other things."

In that case.

I extended my index finger as Mae pricked it with a red tack, causing a small drop of blood to fall onto the soil. I stepped over to the wooden sewing, Mae stepping aside as I did so. My finger hovered above it until another drop of blood dripped onto the wood.

"Now we just have to wait," Mae said. "Layah was in the middle of working on her equipment so it might take her longer than usual. We'll sit for a few minutes while they get done."

She walked over to a sky-blue bean bag and sat down.

I looked at the two tables, the box of soil, and wood sewing machine. "Is that really soil?"

"Soil that I cultivated," she explained. "I can't make these types of clothes with just any soil."

"Cultivate it how?" I stepped forward, sitting down in a wooden chair a foot away from her.

"With my powers. I'm a daughter of Dittial."

"Goddess of vegetation and agriculture." I remember that. ...Mrs. Grey...

"Most of the people around Fabric's Quarters are children of Dittial." Mae grabbed a long, thick beanie and pulled it over her afro puff.

"Outside of how they're made, what is the fundamental difference between them and normal clothes?" I asked.

"They're much more durable. They stay in good condition longer than normal clothes, unless they receive a lot of stress. They're harder to get dirty, they stay pretty clean much longer. They're resistant to wrinkling, and when wrinkles do appear they naturally unwrinkled after some time unless the wrinkles were made because the clothes received a lot of stress. They also shift with the weather, so they can take colder and hotter temperatures. It'll try to keep you as comfortable as possible, but you'll still need different clothes if it gets too cold or hot."

"Weather regulation, unless it passes a threshold?"

"Yes. Oh, and your blood was used so it can take your powers."

My powers. I looked at my hands still feeling weight in them.

"If you're fast, they'll stay together. If you have some elemental power, they're able to resonate with it. I don't mean it makes you stronger or it acts like a magnet, I mean it can deal with your powers better than normal clothes. It can take it," Mae shifted on her bean bag. "They're not indestructible. If you overdo it, or the fighting gets too much, they'll rip. They get stronger with you, but if you get stronger too fast, it won't be able to take your powers as well and rip up more when you use them."

I shifted in the wooden chair, looking once again at the two tables. "Can the other children of Dittial make clothes like this?"

"Mhm hm," she nodded. "For the most part."

I looked deeply at the wooden sewing machine then around the room, my eyes trying to peer past the walls.

"I'm guessing you're the white hair guy everyone has been talking about?" Mae asked.

Talking about.

Already, if at all?

White hair.

I turned my head to face her.

She stretched the side of her beanie, her afro puff fighting it to return to the open air. "It's not everyday someone comes in with white hair and orange eyes. Especially with Azmach." She stopped stretching her beanie. "He's been gone for about two months. How is he? Is he well?"

"Yes," I answered. "Just exhausted."

My hair. White hair. Orange eyes.

What is identity? How does one define it?

"That's good," Mae said, relief in her quiet voice. "I know it had to be for the good of everyone here. Did he tell you why he left Numetus?"

Azmach said not to say anything about the journey.

I shook my head.

There was also the mission he didn't detail. Lamonte and Azmach talked about the Bag of Winds. I will not tell her since he didn't talk about it directly. Along with that, I know principally nothing. I'm only connecting with conjecture. Speculation is not nonfiction.

"No, he would have told me and since he didn't there must be a reason so it's very rude of me to ask. I-I guess a change of subject." Mae quickly said, almost stumbling her words and becoming embarrassed. "For the clothes, what kind of powers do you have?"

"No idea," I answered.

"So you don't know which God is your parent?"

...

...

Parent.

...

...

"I don't know." I said out loud.

Parent.

"Are your eyes and hair real?" Mae suddenly asked, un-rushed and calmly.

Hair and eyes. All routine.

I stared at the floor. "Yes."

Parent...

"I'm not sure there's any God that has white hair or orange eyes," Mae said. "It'll take time, but if they don't tell you or give a sign, I'm sure you can figure it out. What I was going to say was that the power could affect how much stress the clothes can take before they start ripping and tearing up. It doesn't happen all the time, but I thought I should warn you."

Parent. Even one doesn't feel corporeal. Who could it... if any... If any? There must be one to have this make sense.

...Parent.

None have white hair and orange eyes.

"I think they should be done by now," Mae peered at the door. "When the soil and wood have absorbed the Aura and blood thoroughly, you'll be able to get your clothes." She stood up.

I stood up as well.

Mae walked to the door, opened it, then exited the room.

I followed behind her.

"This is Ration's Quarters," Lamonte pointed around as he led the way walking.

Orchards of grapes vined to both the left and right sides. Other fruits grew next to the grapes. Strawberries, apples, pineapples, pears, and more. No wonder Azmach had so many apples.

How was his quiver bottomless?

Corn, wheat, carrots, my eyes soaked them all in. Sunlight illuminated it all, giving a tiny glowing effect. Everything was neatly in rows, and people walked along the pathways, some of which intersected with each other. People around my age carried baskets filled with vegetables, fruits, and bread.

There was something off about the people here. I'm not sure what it was. The more I looked at the people here the more the feel rose. It was the feeling of an important detail existing that did not have even a vague explanation.

What's the detail?

"There's no nuts, seeds, peas, and beans," Lamonte informed. "There isn't any meat here either."

"Hold on, I could've sworn I ate some chicken while in the Infirmary," Asher remarked.

"That wasn't actually chicken," Lamonte corrected. "It was fruits and vegetables, with seasoning."

Asher's head bent sideways, taken aback. "Naw fam. Looked like chicken tenders to me."

"You can cook and season it to make it look and taste like that."

"I know seasoning can make things taste different, but that's riidiculous. RiiDiclous."

Lamonte chuckled along with Asher.

"Alright let me get back to it," Lamonte said pushing his laughter back. "This Quarter is close to Fabric's Quarters. This is because a lot of Dittial's children sleep and work in both."

People continued to walk by, some giving curious glances at me and Asher, while others simply glanced without curious intent. Looking at the people, I couldn't brush the feeling away.

There was definitely something off.

"There's two Alytra kids in total at Numetus," Lamonte explained further. "Like Dittial's kids, they work and sleep mainly in both Rations and Fabrics Quarters. There's a building deeper in this Quarter, somewhere off to the left of us, where seeds are stored. For people who do their duties here, that place has plenty of rooms for people to sleep. It's called Rations Middle. It's kind of like how there are plenty of rooms where people can sleep on Fabrics Mount's first and second floor. We're not going in Ration's Middle because it'll take too much time to go through it."

"Well dang," Asher said in a monotone. "My dreams, thwarted."

As someone walked past me, they looked at my hair intently. The people around— what am I noticing? What's off?

"Alright, let's go to the Inner Barrier," Lamonte said.

"I've been waiting for this," Asher rubbed his hands together, a smile on his face and his eagerness evident.

Time passed as Lamonte gradually led the way through Ration's Quarters, pointing things out and explaining along the way. After a while, the Quarter was in the distance behind him, Asher and me. To the left of the pathway, there was nothing but a field that was cut short and stretched as far as the eye could see. Barely visible were structures far off ahead, showing there were even more places here.

This place is much bigger than I thought.

Numetus.

Lamonte continued walking and pointing things out along the pathway as he also provided more general information about Numetus. To the left of the pathway, there was a great green field that stretched as far as the eye could see. At some point, Lamonte veered left, walking off a pathway and through the field. The field was cut short, like all the other vegetation in Numetus that wasn't directly inside the more forested areas. Lamonte led Asher and me towards the towering trees that touched the sky. As the two of them and I passed through the forest, the dimming sunlight was being partially blocked by leaves and branches. Lamonte led deep into the forest, through undergrowth and more. Finally, he stopped.

"Here," Lamonte gestured at the open air ahead.

"Here?" Asher asked.

"You can barely see it, can't you? Look. Reach your hand out."

Seeing and looking. Eyes open.

Narrowing my eyes, and craning my neck, trying to see the unseen. There has to be… that.

Standing up close, I could kind of see the Inner Barrier. It was like looking through a clear glass window that didn't have a single blemish. Squinting and concentrating solely on certain angles of the Barrier allowed me to see a very subtle shine that confirmed it was there.

Trees, along with other vegetation and the ground, continued on through the Barrier and into the distance, as if it wasn't there.

I slowly put my hand out to touch the Barrier. It acted like a bubble, moving around my hand as I passed through. I felt like my hand was passing through a ray of light, with a bit more thickness to it. It was easy for my hand to go through, nothing resisting against it.

"Woah," Asher commented as he pulled his hand back through the Barrier. "That feels weird. It's not bad, just weird."

"You'll get used to it," Lamonte smiled. "Both layers of the Barrier stretch around for acres, miles, whatever you want to call it. It's the most important safeguard we have."

"Why is everyone in this place around the same age?" I questioned. Got it.

That's what it was. That's what I've been seeing this entire time, what I've been noticing.

Lamonte looked as if he was told specifically not to breathe.

"A small few looked like they're in their early twenties," I elaborated "But most look younger by a few years."

It became quiet, an absence of words. Trees echoed the absence.

Lamonte's eyes fixed to a patch of undergrowth before closing them. He took a deep breath, finally deciding the words he was going to say. "Has Azmach told you about the war?"

"Yeah," Asher replied in a serious, quiet tone, "A bit."

Lamonte looked off to the side, exhaling a long-held breath, before returning his face to the subject at hand. "Us Demigods usually don't live long because of Monsters. Still, there used to be more of us around, and there used to be a lot at older ages." Fear, and a depth of emotions bubbled up inside him. It took all of Lamonte's strength in order for him to hold it in before releasing a portion. That small portion filled his voice, but strangely, his tone was mellow. "What this war has done... it's a complete slaughter."

Slaughter.

Asher froze, his mind registering the situation further.

Lamonte suddenly inhaled. "Let's not talk about that right now." His voice was groggy. "That's a whole other conversation." He looked at Asher and me. "My bad for killing the mood."

"No, you're good bro," Asher said.

"You sure?"

"Yeah bro, you good."

"Aight." Lamonte nodded. "There's one last place to go before we go back to Fabrics Quarters."

Lamonte started taking steps.

"Where's that?" Asher asked. He stood still, his head following Lamonte walking.

"Commune," Lamonte answered, looking back at Asher.

As Lamonte walked out of the trees and returned to the open field from before, he turned left, moving as leisurely as possible. Moon light illuminated the area. The field transitioned into white stone the farther he left more forested area behind.

What's that? A silhouette of a large structure the size of a castle appeared. As the walking advanced, it became closer and the silhouette transformed to more than just an outline.

It was a massive structure with many components, standing a few hundred feet tall and wide. Just to get a sense of its enormity, I had to turn my head completely to the right and left. Hundreds to thousands of people could live comfortably inside. There were many adjacent structures connected to this main part, with triangular rooftops scattered about. A couple of turrets were visible. Some parts of the overall structure were flatter and shorter, one of which looked to be a corridor stretching into the distance from one adjacent structure to another. Walls encompassed the supposed corridor, so I could only surmise.

The structure wasn't a fort of any kind, with no drawbridge or stereotypical moat. It was much more casual in design. The entire structure itself looked like a modernized ancient castle, but it wasn't modernized in the sense of looking like any conventional building or house. It was clean, refined, looking like it was built recently with the intent of trying to revive and modernize a historical style.

"Woah," Asher admired it.

Details came further into fruition the closer it became. The structure was built with dark warm-toned materials; its walls being constructed of dark bronze stones while vibrant dark gray stone tiles made the rooftops. To the right, yards behind the structure, there was a big blue body of water, resembling a river or a lake.

Lamonte turned left, stepping onto a different pathway that led directly to the structure's front entrance. As he approached it, the body of water remained hidden to the right behind it.

"That building's Commune," Lamonte said, the entrance now only some feet away. "It's where everybody sleeps and stays whenever we're not doing anything else."

The double doors were rectangular, dark mahogany wood, much larger than any person. They had curves and grooves carved into them. Lamonte pushed it open, revealing a golden light projecting down like a sun onto the deeply smooth, tanned stone walls of the wide and large room.

How do I describe this?

There was definitely enough capacity for heavy traffic in multiple directions. The floor was made up of multiple smooth squares in two shades of dark brown that had an old feel to them. Designs were carved into the stone walls, so these surfaces were not simply flat.

To the right and left were large rectangular entryways. The left entryway led to a spacious room with some wooden chairs and tables. It looked like an area where people would sit for quietness. The right entryway led down a long corridor that curved leftward, at which point I could no longer see where it led.

Across the room, past the entryway on the right, was a long and wide staircase connected to the wall. It was a lighter shade brown compared to the floor, but darker than the walls. It had a simple stone column railing with the top of it being darker than the darkest brown square on the floor. The stairs themselves led to large, rectangular, dark mahogany double doors. Beyond those doors, there would more than likely be a corridor.

On the left side of the room, at the very back past the stairs, was a large entryway leading to a very long corridor. This corridor intersected with a large room that also began at the entryway. The room had a red carpet with dark tones, some wooden tables, and more that I couldn't see from here. This long corridor more than likely intersected with multiple large rooms and other corridors.

"The sleeping areas are mostly on the upper levels," Lamonte explained. "For the most part, people sleep in their own room. The rooms are divided up by keeping the kids of one God or Goddess around the same area or floor. It's easier to interact and work together when we know who can do what and where they're at. At least we try to, it doesn't always work like that. Rooms can be a bit randomly placed. Some Gods and Goddesses don't have designated areas or floors since they already have something."

"You mean like Dittial's and Alytra's children sleeping in Fabric's and Ration's Quarters?" Asher turned his face to look upward at Lamonte.

"Yep. Bracktius's and…Zound's kids kind of have their own places too. They can still have rooms here, but it's not like they have an entire floor."

"Who was Bracktius and Alytra again?" Asher asked. "Alytra's the Goddess of…?"

"Beauty and love."

"Yeah, and Bracktius was the God of blacksmiths and forges… yeah that was it." Asher nodded to himself.

"Where do you sleep if you don't know your parents?" I asked.

"Those are rooms on higher floors," Lamonte answered with no hesitation. "If you know which God's your parent, you'll be in a room by yourself. If you don't know, you'll be sharing a room with up to four other people. Rooming can be off the cuff, but we try to keep it orderly out of convenience. We don't need that confusion in the middle of this ongoing war." Lamonte's tone went down in volume as he spoke the last sentence. "Could be a battle at any second..."

I stared up the stairs at the closed double doors.

"I would show you more of Commune now, but the clothes should be done." Lamonte abruptly said. "I'll show you your rooms when we get back."

Lamonte knocked on the Fabrics Mount's door. Right on cue, Mae opened it.

"You took your time," Mae passively commented.

"Aye it was a tour," Lamonte said, stepping inside. "I still didn't get to show them everything."

"I was about to say," Asher playfully said, stepping in behind him. "I'm like there was a whole half we missed."

There were certainly parts that were unexplored.

Lamonte and Asher walked down the same hallway they did earlier in the day.

I followed behind Mae to the same room as before with the lidless box of soil and the wooden sewing machine sprouting out of the table. The door closed behind me.

"What type of clothes are you most comfortable in?" Mae asked, eyeing the sewing machine, gripping its sides.

Clothes...I like? Like?

"I don't know," I said.

"Really?" Mae asked playfully. "You don't have any go-tos?"

I looked down, off to the side. Primary. Core. A main set.

334

When have I ever…

I looked back at Mae. "Never," I said.

"Never?" Mae repeated as a question, the playfulness gone and replaced by surprise. She examined the sewing machine. "Besides underwear and socks"—she stepped over to the soil and gently cupped some with both of her hands—"you're going to need something to move so you can fight."

"Does fighting happen that often?" I asked, standing a few feet away from her and the wooden machine.

"It happens," Mae answered as she stepped towards the wooden sewing machine and hovered her cupped hands above it. She opened her cupped hands, allowing the soil to pour on it.

The soil looked like it was falling inside the wood without there being holes or crevices to fall into. No soil spilled over to the floor. The wood must be absorbing it all.

Interesting.

Mae brushed her hands over it, making sure all the soil was off her hands. She grabbed a nearby towel and whipped her hands quickly. Once finished, she put down the towel and started examining the wooden machine. She leaned forward and looked down at the sewing needle. She lightly tugged on it twice, then began gradually pulling a chunk of thin Black thread from it. Thread? It was no longer thin enough to be called that. Volume was beginning to increase as she pulled out more and more.

Is she pulling out clothes? Already finished clothes?

Half of one pant leg was complete, followed by the entire and crouch, leading to the last leg. There in her hands was an entire newly made pair of black joggers with their usual elastic cuff at the ankles.

I stared at the pants, studying them. Intriguing.

Mae set the joggers down on the table. Within a few minutes, a short-sleeved royal blue shirt was created. It had a casual look and appeared to be a mixture of polyester and cotton. A solid black hooded zipper jacket was next. Shoes followed. Shoes. The shoes surprised me. They were high-top sneakers with a casual look, also having the appearance of being made mostly of leather. The soles were black along with the shoestrings. The rest of the shoe was a toned-down indigo that was more on the dark blue side on the color spectrum. At last, Mae pulled out a pair of black socks.

"Try these on," Mae said with her hands full of the clothes she just created. She gestured towards a rectangular nylon container that was waist-high. "Put the clothes you're wearing in there."

"What does that do?" I inquired.

"Recycles clothes. It cleans them without a trace of anything. It can also break them down and can remake them into other clothes." She laid the pile of clothes she had created on the table in front of her and the shoes on the ground. She stepped away from the table, walking out of the room. "I'll knock to make sure before entering." The door closed behind her.

I looked at the pile she just created, taking it in. I picked up the shirt and studied it. It felt normal, just like any other shirt. It certainly didn't feel like a shirt that could handle a war, but that without a doubt was the case. The circumstances pointed directly to that conclusion. I placed it back on the table then took my clothes off down to the underwear. I stepped towards the nylon container and put my clothes inside. Then, I returned to the clothes that were just created.

Now to see how these clothes fit.

I slipped on the black socks, they both stopped mid-calf. The black joggers and royal blue shirt followed. The shirt was smooth and breathable. If any moisture got on it, it would most likely dry up within seconds. Water and sweat might now show up on the shirt, unless it was a large amount.

The black hooded zipper jacket was next. It was simple, soft, and fitted. The shoes were the last to be put on. It all felt comfortable. The pants, shirt, jacket, and socks were all soft. The leather-looking shoes could be worn in both summer and winter. Overall, everything looked casual.

Three knocks at the door.

"Are you good?" Mae asked through the door, her voice muffled.

"Yes," I replied slightly louder to make sure she heard.

Mae opened the door, walking inside the room, the door closing behind her.

"How do they feel?" She asked, walking closer.

I looked down at what I was wearing, examining it. "They feel like clothes." I spoke.

Where is she going with this?

"Okay," Mae said, walking over to the wooden machine. "What I'll do now is pull out some extras." She began pulling out a long-sleeved royal blue shirt. "Do you have a color in mind? Is this blue okay? I should have asked. It"—she gestured to the wooden sewing machine—"just did any colors this whole time at random that matched the other clothes it was making."

"Royal blue is fine." I said.

"This is royal blue?" Mae inspected the shirt. "Okay."

"Outside of that, if colors matter… then perhaps something that technically isn't a color."

"What do you mean?"

"Black."

"Oh, a shade." She pulled out a long-sleeved black shirt, followed by a short-sleeved one, multiple mid-calf black socks, and multiple black boxer briefs. "Over there—" she pointed to a table at the right side of the room, but to her left. "There are fabric bags you can use to carry these clothes."

I walked over to the fabric bags. They were black, thick, square in shape, and had more than enough room for the clothes just made. I grabbed one and walked to the table where Mae was still making some more clothes.

She pulled out four dark gray pants that looked to be pajamas, and four white short-sleeved T-shirts that could be for either sleeping or daily activity. Her hands distanced from the wooden sewing machine after the last shirt was finished. "That's it for the basics."

I grabbed the clothes and began putting them in the bag.

"If you need any more clothes, you don't have to get them from me or Layah. You can go upstairs, there's plenty of people who can do it. If you're in a hurry, you don't even have to go inside Fabrics Mount. A lot of the small huts in this Quarter store clothes, socks, underwear, shoes. They're in multiple sizes, types, styles, and colors. They're arranged in that order, so it's pretty easy to find. Those clothes are just standard. They're quickly made. They're not made specifically for you. They're not as durable and won't be able to take your power as well."

Powers. That word. I looked at my hands. Weight, I feel it.

Powers.

Parent.

"But I'm just letting you know there's more options." Mae added.

I slid the last sock inside the bag, then gripped the top of the bag itself, not its handles.

Parent.

"Are you ready?" Mae asked.

I turned to look at her and nodded once.

"It's getting late," Mae realized. "Lamonte and the other person should be ready." Mae began walking towards the door. "He'll probably show you your rooms at Commune."

I walked to the door, holding it open for myself just as she passed the doorway. I stopped moving right under the doorway.

Parent.

That there did and did not compute.

Parent.

Parent.
Finding out who my God parent is?
How would I even find that out?

Does The Lack Of Responsibility Within Accountability Lack The Person?

"We gotta get up," someone said.

"I need some food," a different person said.

"Should we wake him up?" A third one asked, referring to me.

"Been a couple days since he's been here and he hasn't talked like that," someone replied. "Let o' dude rest."

Footsteps departed through what must have been the exit, the door closing behind them.

I opened my eyes, shifting on a dark mahogany full-size bed. I was lying on a long white sheet and under a white blanket. There was a dark brown dresser next to the bed, which held the clothes I acquired a few days earlier. The room had another four of these beds with an accompanying dresser. A clock silently moved its arms on the wall across from me. The smooth stone floor was just like any other in Commune, made up of multiple squares that were two shades of dark brown. The walls were tanned in color like most walls in Commune, except the walls in this room had no intricate designs.

To the right of the room were two rectangular mahogany doors. One led to a room for holding clothes and fabrics, as well as cleaning them. It had tables and a rectangular nylon box that was waist height like the one in Mae's room. The second door to the left of this clothes cleaning room led to a large bathroom. I'm guessing each room is set up like the room I'm currently in. At least, the ones for people who don't know which God is their parent.

Sunset. Leaves on the trees were revealing more vivid autumn colors than just green. A gentle wind blew through my hair, making colors and branches wave as the breeze passed. I stood at the summit of a hill, leaning my right shoulder against a tree with my hands tucked inside my front pockets. Below the hill summit, as the land continued on, were more and smaller hills going into the distance. Trees covered the sides of them all, their leaves filling the vision with vivid colors. My hair, the leaves, and the branches swayed as gentle winds periodically passed.

"Didn't expect to see you here," someone said from feet behind me.

I turned to see Lamonte walking up the hill.

"Have you adjusted to your room these last two days?" He asked.

"What are you doing out here?" I asked.

"Taking a walk."

A breeze lightly ruffled through my hair and clothes. I was wearing black joggers and a long-sleeved royal blue shirt. It was odd; I was still getting used to wearing fitted clothes. It wasn't only the clothes I was wearing at the moment; it was all of them. Even the pajamas were fitted.

That's unimportant. There was something I needed to ask.

"How's Azmach?" I asked.

"Not bad," Lamonte answered without skipping a beat. "He'll be back up and running in a few days, maybe a week or two at the most. He needs the rest. He'll be busy once he gets up."

I paused for a second, my mind switching gears. "I'm guessing... because of that Wind Bag from Levaveus."

Lamonte looked like a fish caught on a lure when it didn't even bite on the hook.

"Azmach had said some information he wanted to be passed onto you. Due to the outcome, there was no need. I do have questions about it. What is the 'cave' and the 'Stromoios'?"

"He would be the type to almost pass on information," Lamonte confirmed. "Man don't die, and he better not."

"What is that Bag exactly?" I confusedly asked.

"That I can't say," Lamonte replied plainly. "You haven't even been here a week. Don't even worry about it."

There's more to that Bag. It's obvious. The cave and the Stromoios. Azmach gave that vague information as he handed me the Bag, and only a minute later I used it. What have I potentially caused?

I sat at a long, dark brown mahogany table that could easily seat ten people on each side. Around the room there were multiple of these clean and polished tables. The walls were a dark gray cobblestone that was shaped in squares and rectangles of various widths and lengths; however, none of them were excessively large. The longest and widest one would be just big enough to fit two hands on. In contrast, the floor was made of smooth taupe stone. The two very back corners each had a wide door etched into the wall, both of which I had never been behind before. They blended in perfectly, making them barely noticeable.

This place was the Dining Hall.

The room was massive, easily being able to seat hundreds

to thousands. At the moment, it was not filled with many people.

I chewed on a round piece of bread.

"Don't mean no harm, homes, but you gotta stop sleeping in your contacts" One of the people that uses the room in Commune that I take residence in said. "You could end up blind."

"They're not contacts." I said.

"Is yo hair not dyed either?"

I walked past trees, my shoes crackling on leaves as I looked at my surroundings. Trees, leaves, more trees and leaves.

"So those aren't contacts?"

I sat under a tree on top of a hill.

"I'm more stuck on the style." A different one said not out of rudeness, but pure observation. "It's all over the place."

I chewed on a piece of bread.

"How did this happen?" One curiously asked.

I lay on my bed late at night. The four people within the same room were all asleep. I could tell by their sounds, or rather the lack of. The presence around me did not feel good. Quietly, I slipped out of bed, walking through corridors, down multiple sets of stairs, and exiting the entire place. I took some more steps forward, then came to a stop with my back facing Commune.

What am I doing? I just don't feel like I fit. I'm out of place within myself. Has anything actually changed to bring forth this feeling? Is it a feeling of emotion or the mentality filtering through the body? I've done nothing. I've walked around, ate on occasion, slept on a bed. Back before all of this, I was going to school and planning or doing at least something. What about here?

What is identity?

A room seemingly designed for sitting in quietness existed within Commune. It could comfortably hold tens of people in their own separate seats. Two dark, warm brown carpets with darker tones of red at their edges adorned two walls, while a similar carpet covered a section of the floor. There was a black clock silently moving its arms on the back wall. In the center of the room was a dark coffee table with two thick and dark mahogany chairs in front of it. Off to the side, there was a long dark wooden table with mahogany chairs around it. I had noticed the room when I had first entered Commune, noting it would be somewhere to go for quietness.

The room's name was the Quiet Lounge.

I sat on a mahogany chair against the right wall of the room. I had woken up early enough that the people who sleep in the same room I take residence in did not yet stir.

The early morning settled. I sat leaning back in the chair with my eyes open, the time leisurely ticking- Is that? In my peripheral vision I saw... I turned.

Across the room was a book. The book wasn't remarkably big in size. If anything, relatively speaking, it was small. It was held in small hands covering parts of it. I peered at the cover, the pages. My eyes locked with it. Soft fingers holding the book flipped to the next page. There was no mistaking that particular book.

Things Fall Apart. Chinua Achebe.

If there's a book that means-

"Excuse me," I quietly said looking at the book holder.

The book holder turned their face towards me. Over her

head was a dark forest green hood, so her details were hard to make out. There were still some things I could see.

She was a sculpture personified. Feminine features. Soft. High cheekbones. Her eyes were soft and a very dark brown and her skin was the same. It wasn't just that, her skin was remarkably smooth. Her hair was long and went past her neck. I couldn't tell how much longer it was with her hood on, but what I could tell was that it was 4c afro-textured and stretched. The word "stretched" was used because her hair certainly wasn't straightened. It looked as if it was pulled out like someone had stretched it downward. It was as if her hair was blow-dried, but in actuality, that was not the case. Like her skin, her hair also looked soft. She also looked to be my exact age if not at least around it.

None of this is what stood out the most to me. There was something else.

Her Aura. That too was soothing.

Her dark eyes, quietly and patiently, looked into mine.

"Is there a library here?" I asked.

Holding the book in her small hands, she nodded faintly. As I thought.

"If you don't mind me asking, where is it at?" I asked.

Her and my eyes stayed connected, until she turned back to her book. The book was gently closed in her hands and placed on a tiny circular mahogany table next to her. She rose from her seat and lightly walked towards the door, right past me. She stopped at the side of the doorway and turned to look at me.

She wants me to follow her.

I stood up and followed her out of the room.

She and I walked side by side passing the Dining Hall and going through the Main Center.

While walking, there were some people that she and I passed. A couple of these people were standing with others, conversing, while others were mostly walking. There was one thing they all had in common, they all seemed stunned. I'm not sure. I get those looks sometimes, but this time it seemed different, more... elevated... and not entirely directed at me. As a matter of fact, it wasn't even mostly directed towards me.

I looked to my right at who I was walking with. She was slim and short in stature. The shortness of her stature was not excessive, but it was apparent. I couldn't tell with her hood on, but the top of her head was either level with or barely below the bottom of my nose. Pinpointing her exact height was difficult.

The hood was a part of a long and slick rain jacket that looked to be a modernized medieval archer style. The sleeves were a bit long, covering half of her hands. The jacket stopped at her knees, so I couldn't see anything else outside of her black mid-calf combat boots and black pants. The bottom of her black pants legs smoothly tucked inside the boots. With the jacket closed, her shirt was unseen.

There was a quietness surrounding her.

A depth.

The walk was quiet. Time passed with clouds in the sky becoming more evident, suggesting that there was possible rain on the horizon.

The Main Center and other significant structures were now left far behind me and her. The scenery began to change. The ground shifted from white stone to dirt trails. Clear green fields with vegetation that didn't reach past the toes in height were on both sides of the trails. There wasn't a single person around.

How far is she going?

The distance only increased as she and I walked further and further. After a while, a structure appeared in the distance up ahead. Details progressively came into view as it became closer.

It looked to be an older building made of dark red and brown bricks. A dusty dirt patch was in front of a tiny single-door entrance. The top was a dome with a historical feel. Without a doubt, it was an old library. It wasn't old primarily from time; however, it was old from lack of care. It looked on the verge of forgottenness and abandonment, age making a few cracks upon its face.

She walked straight towards the entrance of the library, stopping a few feet from the side of the door. I stopped walking and looked up, taking in the library.

She turned, starting to walk away.

"Thank you," I said to her.

She stopped in her tracks, turning her head to look at me. Her eyes and mine locked, holding each other in a simple pause that lasted for only a second which seemed to stretch. Once the moment passed, she turned her head forward and continued on her way.

I turned back to the library and stepped in front of its door. My hand gripped the circular bronze doorknob, turning it. The door required more force, like any older door. Finally, it creased open. It would seem that the door had only been open a few times in recent years.

The room was relatively clean, but due to the lack of light, it was hard to determine its cleanliness. Light stone made the floor, walls, and ceiling, while dark mahogany made various tables, chairs, and bookcases. There was an old clock silently moving its arms on the back wall. The room definitely had an older feel to it.

The bookcases were aligned next to the walls while the tables and chairs were placed in the center. There was a line of space leading from the doorway to the stairwell across the room.

The door closed behind me as I walked up the stairwell, my eyes adjusting to the dimness. At the top of the second floor, there was a large mahogany door with a circular bronze doorknob. I opened it to find a more spacious version of the entrance room. Several tables with accompanying chairs were placed in the center. There were even more bookcases brimming with books. The bookcases followed the walls, with some located near the center tables. Lamps were stationed around the room.

I stepped into the room with the door closing behind me and turned on one of the small lamps that was on top of a table. My head turned, my eyes noting the image for my mind to analyze. A library. It hit me. A library. It's been weeks since I last read. I looked back and forth to all the bookcases. Dust accumulated on their tops. This floor especially wasn't used. That meant there were more books around to be read. That meant I could read anything.

Anything.

What do I need right now? Comprehension. What is all of this around me? Not the library, I mean Numetus. What is the Alkeeb mythology in the sense of it being reality in actuality? Who am I? Who are my parents? At the very least, which God is one of my parents? What is the essence?

What is identity?...

The room never seemed so quiet until that thought occurred.

I stepped towards a bookcase, examining it.

This isn't the answer; however, there is the potential possibility in an unquantifiable regard that the direction of said answer could be led through these books. These pages. These words. These hypothetical tangible essences of the direction towards identity.

Where do I begin? If one does not know, one begins at the beginning, or the prologue to the beginning.

I stepped through the bookcases, finding a book that told the Alkeeb God stories of significance. The book felt smooth.

This will be the prologue to the beginning.

I walked over to a table straight ahead of the closed door

and sat down. I opened the book, beginning to read its contents.

I was walking down the stairs of Commune that led to the entrance room.

"Yo, it's been a few days," Asher said, standing at the bottom, dressed in a similar style he always did but now with fresh and clean clothes. "About time I ran into you."

I stopped in the middle of the steps, nodded, then continued walking down.

"Wanna get something to eat, bro?" Asher asked as I got to the bottom step.

"No, I have something to do," I said, walking to the front door.

"Want me to come?"

"No, it's fine."

"Hope it works out," Asher said as I passed. "Have fun."

The front door closed behind me.

After walking a long distance, the library door was in my sight. I turned the doorknob and pushed the mahogany door open.

Illumination. Someone had turned a few lamps on in the entrance room. That was unusual. Sitting at one of the tables, reading a book, was the person who showed me the library. A soothing Aura. Calming. Comforting.

She had her hood on, per usual, and she held the book delicately held in her small hands.

I walked straight ahead, passing her on the way, and went up the stairs.

Multiple books and papers were stacked on the table in front of me.

X'stayn and Orthantehs are missing. Additionally, Letnos essentially is as well. He hasn't been seen for decades longer than Orthantehs. A war. I must understand. Comprehend.

Identity. My fingers flipped through the pages. Hours must have passed.

I must sleep. I felt the bed beneath me, the room having no noise in it.

Early Morning arrived. I stepped out of bed, got dressed, and went directly to the library.

My fingers felt the pages, grabbing another book to open. Pages flipped. Eyes closed, eyes open, eyes, eyes, open closed, open, pages, sleep, outside, pages, pages. My eyes grew heavy... my head heavy... coming closer to the pages...sle.ep...

I woke up. My head was resting on top of an open book, the pages sticking to my cheek. How late is it? How late was I up?

I was sitting down chewing on a piece of an oval shaped wheat bread. It was late at night so the Dining Hall was mostly empty.

"Wait, you're that white-haired dude." A voice asked some yards away. "Not to be that guy, but I have a question." The sounds of his steps indicated the voice's owner was approaching.

More questions about my hair and eyes? Possibly.

I looked up at him as he stopped a few feet away from me.

"My bad for bothering you, but I just have to know," he said, scratching his right cheek. His afro-textured hair was cut low, and his left hand held two oranges. "I heard that a couple days ago you were walking with Ivania. Like, you were walking together. Is it true?"

...who? I've actually never heard that name in my life outside the parameters of it being a proper noun. As far as I know, at the very minimum, there has never been a single person with that name that has been within proximity of me.

A couple days ago?

I looked up at the person, puzzled.

He could obviously tell. "Remember? You were walking with her. She's like the most beautiful person here. No, probably ever. You know, her?"

I continued to look at him, puzzled, taking a bite out of my bread.

"Ya know? Short? Had that green jacket?" He reiterated.

"Green jacket?" I repeated.

"Yeah. She had on that green jacket. It was kind of long, stops" — he put his right hand just above the knee — "here."

Who wore-

It clicked. The person that showed me the library.

"Oh," I realized. "Green jacket."

"Yeah her. How did that happen?" He asked. "She's never talked. And she's been here for years, and no one's heard her voice. Ever. She barely interacts with anyone. Did you hear her talk?"

I took a bite of my bread, shaking my head.

"You didn't?" He stood silently, looking off for a second before looking at me once again. "I just wanted to know if she actually talked. Sorry for bothering you." He walked away and sat at a table where two other people were sitting and was off to the side of the room.

I took another bite of my bread, my mind on other subjects.

I stared intently at a diagram of the Alkeeb Gods' family tree.

X'stayn missing. Orthantehs missing. Letnos missing. It comes to reason that there could be other Gods missing. I must understand the stories, the realities. Have I even taken this all in? This reality? Gods? Aura? Death? Life?

I have admitted. I have accepted it.

That's not what's pounding in my head as my fingers flip through pages. That's not what makes me lack sleep. That's not the essence of identity. Regardless of the copious amount of stories and Gods there are, there is a specific thing I must acknowledge in order for the pages I've read to point more efficiently at conceivable general directions towards the answer. I don't know my powers, so there's no way to narrow it down. All I get is a wind that whips. There has been no sign of any sorts revealing parentage that I've found or have been given.

I sat at the table surrounded by books, lost in those thoughts, my eyes open when they should be closed.

Which God is my parent?

Does One Act As If The Utilization Of Importance Does Not Come With The Accountability Of Further Weight?

"Ooo," some voice quietly said.

Up ahead on my left, at the Infirmary entrance, the owner of the voice was putting on a jacket and looking surprised at the early morning chill. It was a little more than a week into October.

The sun wasn't completely out yet, a pale blue light casting over the area. I was on the outskirts of the Main Center and walking through it. Dozing off in the library was a regular thing now. Still, I needed some sleep in an actual bed.

Commune Quarters was somewhat close. The Dining Hall was ahead some hundreds of feet away, which meant that Commune Quarters was just beyond it. The two places were only separated by some hundreds of feet.

Something moved.

I stopped and looked to my left. The person who had put on a jacket was waving. She must be greeting someone behind me. I turned my head to see who stood —

No one was there.

…was she waving at me?

I turned back in her direction. There was no one else around… She had to be waving at me. Why? Regardless of her reasoning, I shouldn't be rude and inconvenience someone.

Without looking at her, I put my hand up for a second in her direction as a quick greeting. My arm returned to my side as I continued walking to my destination.

I only managed to sleep for another two more hours. Brushing off the lack of sleep, I got out of bed, dressed, and left the room. I was walking down corridors and stairs, I headed towards Commune's entrance. My foot stepped off the last step of the staircase some yards away from the front double doors.

"Yo, on the stairs again," Asher said somewhere behind me. It sounded like he was standing at the top of the stairs.

I turned to see him doing a small dance before he suddenly stopped like his body disconnected.

"Are you in the middle of anything?" He asked.

Last time, I barely talked to him. I shouldn't be rude and walk away so soon once again.

"Not exactly," I said.

"Cool," he said, like all the worries in the world did not exist. "Didn't want to hold you up. It's been a hot minute. How you feel about this place." He looked around as he said the last sentence.

How do I feel?

"It is what it is," I answered.

"I feel you. I do like this place." Asher smiled while looking

354

around. "Oh yeah." He stopped looking around, turning back to me. "Don't you sleep in a room with other people."

"Yes."

"Ah, gotcha. I sleep in my own room." He rubbed the back of his neck. "Turns out I really am the only kid of Soronos." An awkward smile drew upon his face as if he couldn't decide to smile or not, with it being both voluntary and involuntary. "It gets kind of lonely. But it's cool. The people here are very friendly."

Friendly. The wave from this morning—doesn't matter. It doesn't change the routine, what I have admitted, and what I have accepted.

The front door opened. Lamonte stood in the doorway, holding the door open. "You two? Good timing."

"For what bro?" Asher asked. "Free ice cream and a high five?"

"No."

"You better watch your back, Lamonte. This just got personal."

"So it's like that," Lamonte put his fist up. "It's a privilege for you to breathe." He put his fist down. "I'll let you, this once."

Asher laughed, before pushing it to the side. "For real though, why are you really here, man?"

"I was going to let you know about the duties you'll start receiving after next week, give or take."

"Duties?"

"Yeah, we give a grace period of a couple weeks for new people before they start being put on the schedule for duties. Cleaning, Barrier patrols, that type of stuff. It rotated in intervals, so it's not like you're always going to be on duty or doing the same duty. We play it by week or month, depending."

"Lamonte!" From outside, someone urgently ran up to Lamonte, covered in sweat. "There's four Monsters sighted near this quadrant of the Outer Barrier."

Lamonte's head snapped to him.

"They seem pretty strong." The same person added.

Lamonte's eyes widened. "Four?"

"Maybe more." The person immediately said.

"We don't need to take arms and start evacuating people to the Railroads yet," Lamonte directed. "Keep an eye out. Inform the Head if anything is out of the ordinary, or straight up outta pocket."

The person nodded, running off.

"Does this happen a lot?" Asher asked. He was bewildered, his arms away from his sides ready for action.

"Yeah. You were lucky there were only two Gods when you got here. We only evacuate and take up arms once they get too close to ignore."

"I wouldn't necessarily say lucky, there was also a Monster... No, maybe you could say lucky; it was killed by one of the Gods. That was crazy. He started controlling its blood, moving it around. You said that was your dad, right? Zound? The God of war, was it?"

Lamonte nodded his head. "War and blood."

"Blood's right for sure."

"The way you talked to the person that ran off about the Monsters made it sound like they could get through the Barriers. They can't get in, right?" I asked.

"It shouldn't," Lamonte stated. "Nothing like that has ever happened, but we're not going to risk it." He pushed the door he was still holding open further away from him.

"You also mentioned something about 'the Head'. Who is that?"

"The Head? That's the one person who leads this place. They keep things balanced and make decisions when necessary. There's also a group of people who help the Head."

"Like a cabinet?"

"Or the Knights of the Round Table." Asher pointed, smirking.

"I guess you can put it like that," Lamonte said. "They're called the Hands. There are six in total. They're the more stronger or resourceful Demigods around here. Right now, we're in the middle of planning something."

"Aye yo, 'we'?" Asher asked with a smile.

"Oh yeah, Azmach and I are two of the Hands."

"Now that's what's up," Asher nodded, a proud smile on his face. "Why haven't we heard much about the Head or the Hands?"

"Oh, you will. When things happen or events pass, you definitely will. You just haven't been here long enough. But it's mainly because of the nature of Numetus. Don't think too governmental about it. We all have input. We have to work together to survive. The Head is a step above just to keep things streamlined."

"You can't move if decisions aren't made," Asher inferred.

"That's right." Lamonte turned his head, looking through the doorway he kept open. "Now, I'm gonna need to investigate those Monsters." He turned his head back to the room. "Remember, you'll start to get assigned duties in the next few weeks."

"Looking forward to it." Asher gave Lamonte a thumbs up.

Lamonte turned and walked outside, the door closing behind him.

"I'm sure it's safe here," Asher commented. "But that's not something to get used to."

My eyes stared at the wooden door. Was I really looking at the door?

My fingers felt pages as I read. Read, should I read about Monsters—no. I must focus. Which God is my parent? I turned the page…

Levaveus. Between all the words, his name popped out. The Wind Bag. The screams of wind, the Manticore, and the raging roars of the Minotaur swept through my head.

Who is he?

I read deeply into the texts. A Minor God.

Stromoios.

This here...

I read further, grabbing more books off bookcases, and flipping through pages to find him. Levaveus. Violent storm Spirits. Bag of Wind. Now I'm getting somewhere. I must not jump to conclusions; however,... this is leading me...

Eyes open. Hands moved. Eyes. Fingers. Eyes. Levaveus.

Page.

Page.

Page,

Page,

Page Page Page Page. My hands moved books, my fingers flipped pages, my eyes examined it all.

Eyes open.

Knock knock. My index knuckle tapped the door twice.

"Come in," the person said from inside the room.

I opened the door and walked into the dimly lit space.

"Sorry to intrude at this hour," I said. "Well, intrude at all."

"Jason," Azmach smiled welcomingly from his Infirmary bed. "No intrusion at all."

"How are you feeling?"

Azmach sat up, looking well rested. "Chillin'. You seem good. How's Numetus treating you?"

"Not bad," I said, closing the door behind me. I walked to a wooden chair that resided next to his right side and sat down. "I have some questions."

"About what?" He asked.

"Levaveus."

Azmach went from a calm happiness to a neutral face, clearly shifting into seriousness.

"He's a Minor God, leader of winds. Violent Storm Spirits, known as Stromoios, are also subject to him. He is also the

King of Levoao, a kingdom on a floating island. It was he who created the Reverse Bag of Wind."

Azmach's face didn't convey anything. He simply listened.

"During those two weeks you led the way to Numetus," I continued, "at one point you talked about having a mission. That mission had to do with the Wind Bag. It had to do with the 'cave' and 'Stromoios' information you wanted to pass to Lamonte."

Azmach nodded.

"There's more than one Bag isn't there? I know those Bags pull in Monsters; however, their importance has something more to it." I leaned forward. "The 'cave' and the 'Stromoios'. What was that mission Azmach? What harm... did I potentially cause?"

"There is more than one Bag," Azmach calmly confirmed. "Whenever we leave the Barriers, those Bags are our last line of defense from Monsters. When we sometimes run low on food and need to get more, if we're in a battle with Monsters and we have no chance of surviving... And there's more to it. If the Barriers were to stop working one day... Some of us would survive, but..." He breathed in deeply. "And we live in a world of Gods, so the possibility can't be ignored."

It clicked. "That Bag I used; it was the last one. Wasn't it?"

Azmach sat silently, seconds ticking by. Finally, he took a breath to speak. "We were going to die. You made the best choice."

"And I have endangered every single person here because of that choice."

Azmach shook his head. "You did nothing wrong. The Bag was given to me in case anything like that were to happen. To keep it a hundred, using that Bag was expected."

"You literally handed me the Bag saying to not use it."

"Unless you and Asher had to." He immediately said.

"You were going to sacrifice your life for it."

"I was giving you two a chance to escape. Giving you that

Bag was just to make sure that at the very least you and Asher would both live and pass on the information."

"You somewhat explained it briefly in the forest, but learning all of this now, I don't understand why you didn't use the Bag yourself?"

"As you already know, each Bag has a one-shot policy. They can only be opened once, and the wind runs out if it's not closed after some time. One Bag can hold up to three Monsters based on how strong they are and how stable the Bag is being held through all the wind. With the state I was in? Shoo, I was basically mortal. I wouldn't have been able to hold it steady, and those two Monsters were dead strong. If I messed up even a little, that's it. I probably wouldn't have been able to pull in one, so that'd be a waste, but that was all I had. And I wasn't alone. I couldn't risk your lives by having no safety net, and I needed to pass on that information."

"What exactly was the mission?" I looked at him, feeling both flexible and rigid.

Azmach leaned towards me. "Levaveus's location resides around a cave in Pennsylvania. The mission was to scout the location. We needed to see what we're heading into before negotiating."

"Negotiating? How did you all get any Bags in the first place?"

"I heard it was seventeen years ago, around the time when the war first broke out. None of us know who the Demigod was that stole the Bags, at least the Demigods who are here now in Numetus. Before all the older Demigods were killed, a little bit after when this war first started, some of the surviving ones said that the one who stole the Bags never lived within Numetus. He was already much older than most of them. He's probably dead now like the others."

"Are you insinuating that Levaveus killed him because he stole from him?"

"Maybe. I don't know. Maybe a different God killed him,

or a Monster, or maybe old age. I'm not sure. I'm just guessing. But that's history." Azmach deeply exhaled. "It doesn't change our situation."

"I used the last Bag. I've changed the situation," I said as the full weight of the context slowly and suddenly fell on my head.

"No one knows you're the one who used it. As far as anyone knows, I'm the one who used it." Azmach reassured me.

"That does not change what happened, that does not change the facts, that does not change the truth. You might have taken responsibility, but that does not change my accountability. I've changed this situation. I've made it worse." The weight in my hands felt heavier.

"You didn't," Azmach said. "We haven't had contact with Levaveus since the Bags were stolen. As far as we know, he's never killed a Demigod. Stealing those Bags could've changed that. Levaveus might be a Minor God, but that doesn't change anything, we're still in a bad spot. That's why scouting his location was important. If negotiations fail, we need to know how to get outta there."

Reassurance. That I didn't feel. Weight. The weight in my hands, that's what I felt. This weight has built like storm clouds from a summer hurricane that has the absolute potential of reaching a magnitude of undefined proportions unexplainable by the diction existing in present time. And yet, here I sit. I'm the cause and here I sit, in front of one of the people I have put in danger with this weight, here I sit, in the place this person I have put in danger has led me towards that is full of people I have also put in danger, here, I sit. Danger is an understatement. Weight in my hands. Here, I sit.

"When do you think you guys will negotiate with Levaveus?" I questioned.

Azmach looked past my head, audibly breathing in then out from his nose, before returning his eyes back to me. "Sometime next week."

"'Next week?' Are you even healed enough?"

"About," Azmach smiled. "I'll be meeting with the Head and the other Hands for a couple of days to plan."

I looked down for some seconds, thinking. What am I thinking? I know what I'm thinking. I brought my head back up. "Using the Bag might have been expected, but nonetheless, I still used it. If I don't hold everyone back, let me go to the negotiations."

Azmach sat quietly looking at me. Slowly, he began to nod a few times. "To keep it a buck, you used the Bag well. Most people's first time, they can only get one weak Monster inside. You…" he said that last word with emphasis. "You were able to pull in two."

I looked at him with slight confusion.

"And not just any two," Azmach said as he pointed his right index and middle fingers up. "The Minotaur and the Manticore are two of the strongest Monsters out there. Sure, they were a little distracted with fighting each other and were pretty close to the Bag in the first place, but it's still basically the same thing. A good amount of people might not have been able to get in either one. You were able to do both, and you haven't even finished Adjusting. You were affected by all the Bag's wind. You just naturally dealt with it."

Naturally dealt with it. How so? Those four words didn't leave my mind, just as the weight didn't leave my hands.

"Although, that doesn't change anything," Azmach said. "You're nowhere near ready for stuff like this. You haven't even finished Adjusting. Most of us here are fully Adjusted and still aren't ready. Shoo, some of our more experienced people aren't ready. You never know what happens out there."

"What are the chances the negotiations will work?" I questioned.

Azmach sat quietly.

"Are you completely healed?" I asked. "Back to normal?"

"It's fine, it's fine," Azmach waved off. "We'll figure it out." He paused, leaning back in his bed and exhaling out of his nose. "It's starting to get late. I need to go to sleep. Everything will be fine. Remember, don't tell a single person about this. I'll talk to you later."

"Alright." I stood up and walked slowly out of the room, my mind aggregating and processing. I paused halfway out of the doorway before walking through, the door closing all the way behind me.

The bed felt... The bed felt? Felt what?... ...It felt nothing except existing.

The room was dark. Four people, aside from myself, slept in their own beds. It was one of many rooms for people who don't know which God was their parent... it was a reminder. Which God is my parent? The main thing on my mind up until now was figuring out which God could be my parent. Now it was jumbled. This negotiation is something that cannot be ignored. I learned of it not two minutes before I got into this bed. Gods, negotiation. I used that Bag, the weight still in my hands. My eyes were open as I tried to sleep.

Admittance. And. Acceptance.

The Dining Hall had two shifts in which cooked food was placed on the tables, these shifts being in the afternoon and early evening. The food consisted of dishes that looked and tasted like chicken and beef but were fruit and vegetable based. Pasta, none of which had cheese, was another staple. These foods were cleared off the tables before and after these shifts, which were the times in which I usually was inside the place.

This time, I sat at a table filled with these types during the afternoon shift. I chewed on a piece of wheat bread in the crowded Dining Hall before getting up to leave. My shoes scuffed as I stepped through the Main Center. Per the usual, people were walking in mass, making it look like an overflowing marketplace. Conversations and smiles gleamed. They knew of the dangers in this Alkeeb God world; however, they smiled through it, continuing to live their lives.

"Yo!" Asher had his arms arched out like he was going to hug someone. "How you feelin' man?"

"Fine," I said as I continued walking. "I have somewhere to go."

"It's all good. I catch ya! Live life!"

Breezes rustled through my hair as I sat on top of a hill with my back against a tree. It was the same spot I would come to on occasion that overlooked descending hills, the trees below covered in autumn leaves. The tree I leaned against was covered in autumn leaves, the breeze lightly rustling them. Another breeze brushed my hair, smoothly passing through. My head leaned against bark as I looked… looked. I looked. I looked onward. Eyes.

Regardless of if I feel here or not, existing or not, the people here seem nice. Can I admit that? I have already decided to sit back and watch what happens from the distance, and from my seat I can observe as much. Can I accept it? It looks to be all routine. The people here work together to survive here in Numetus.

"At a cost."

Those words echoed in my head. That phrase has been repeating in the back of my mind since I first heard it. Those words were spoken by Azmach when I arrived here. He said it as he gave the Wind Bag to Lamonte, referring to completing his mission. The weight of now knowing the context makes those words insurmountable. The last Bag being used was the cost.

I have cost these people their safety. I am the one who is endangering them. They don't know about the danger connected to the lack of Wind Bags. That is kept a secret, a secret

I have worsened. If there must be danger, put it on me. The people here have an entire structure, a whole community. They have all this, and me—… Me?... Doesn't matter. The people here have things that matter, and I've endangered them all. I've made it worse. Azmach might have taken responsibility, but nonetheless, it is my accountability.

A breeze flowed through my hair, pushing it gently aside. Breezed and pushed aside, my thoughts could not be. My thoughts were transparent, present, and nonexistent. Here, I sit with it. Here, I lean my head back against a tree. A breeze… with it. Admittance and acceptance.

…There was another poignant thought that had never left my head…

Sleep, exhaustion, weight, nothing stripped this thought from my mind. Regardless of everything, I must figure one thing out.

Who is my parent?

I pushed open the library door. My mind and feet were set with going towards the stairs. Seated at a table in the center-right was a person with a hood on. She was the one that showed me this place. Wasn't her name Ivania or something? I went up to the second floor.

Pages moved and books switched. A family tree of the Gods was stationed at the corner of the table. It seems no matter where I look, I find nothing that would signify a direction towards which God would be my parent.

I woke up with my head and arms lying on top of papers. When did I doze off? What time is it? At the minimum, it's probably dark outside.

… Am I doing enough? The most of what I'm reading are the basics stories, a lot of which I already learned from Ms. Grey. I've been reading through them again to see if there's something I've missed, something that would point in the right direction. Has doing this wasted time? Time is internal, so isn't the waste of the internal a matter of perception based off circumstance? What is my perception of the circumstance? I know this. My mind is also on other things. I need to take some time away from this.

My chair slid back as I stood up and walked down the stairs, the door closing behind me.

What Is The Main Aspect Of Fault And Solution?

"Oo," someone gasped as a basket of fruit slipped from their hands, causing it to fall into the middle of a pathway. The morning was early with a blueish-gray tint in the sky. There was a lack of people outside, which contrasted with the amount of fruit that fell.

I happened to be walking nearby when I saw what transpired. The person was on her knees as gathered fallen pears. I stepped over, squatted, and began placing fruit into the basket.

"Oh, don't worry," she said politely.

Without looking at her, I continued to pick up the fruit. The walkway was wide, giving the fruit plenty of space to spill out. Smooth wooden stalls used for quickly storing fabrics in distant areas from Fabric's Quarters lined the right and left edges of the pathway. They were called Fabric Storages. Some of the fruit that had spilled rolled over to the bases of these stalls. I gathered fruit from around them. Soon, all the fruits were inside the basket.

I picked up the basket and gently handed it to the person, immediately walking away after.

Hot water streamed down my shoulders as soap disappeared down the drain. I turned the water off, stepped out the shower, and dried myself off. I dropped the towel and the face cloth I used in a rectangular nylon bin within the bathroom. After that, I slid clothes on and walked out of the room.

Someone's in the room. It's not a danger.

I stepped further into the bedroom. To my right, one of the four people who sleep in the same room I took residence in was sitting on his bed.

"I never see you at this time," he said with a small, shocked expression. "Barely at all for real for real."

I looked at him with a blank expression before going across the room towards the bed I use. This bed was the furthest away one from the others in the room.

"Ain't nothin' wrong with that," he said, "I'm just surprised."

I sat on the bed, grabbing a pair of shoes next to it.

"I never really gave you my name," he realized. "Now that I think about it, well, I'm Jalen." Jalen raised his hand in a greeting. He was small in stature and skinny in width. His afro-textured hair was in cornrows, and he had copper brown skin with a small scar next to his right ear.

I had already slid my black socks on and tied my shoelaces.

"Your name's Jason, right?" Jalen asked.

I nodded my head once, standing up and walking to the door.

"Good, I thought I was trippin'" Jalen said more so to himself. "Well Jason, I'll see you later."

I turned the knob and walked out of the room.

The Dining Storages were a small number of one-room structures around parts of Numetus that were distant from the Dining Hall, lining the right and left edges of pathways just like the Fabric Storages. A few of the Dining Storages were placed nearby the Dining Hall for convenience. They held food for people to consume between the Dining Hall's afternoon and early evening food shifts. Each consisted of fruits, vegetables, and bread, with some even narrowing down to specific types of these choices.

I stood in one for bread, deciding what type I would eat this time.

The room was small, the walls and floor being rectangular and made of dark gray stone. The floor was a few shades lighter than the walls. Shelves lined the walls and were filled with different types of bread. I could see whole wheat, grain, and ones that were square and round in shape. White bread was the one type not that didn't exist within Numetus. There were also barrels filled with bread sitting on the floor. All of it was able to stay fresh as long as the door remained closed.

I grabbed a tiny circular piece of whole wheat bread and exited the structure, the door closing behind me. I walked to the nearby Dining Hall. The structure was hard to miss. It was large and constructed of dim grayish-bronze stone that matched the environment while also making it pop out. The very top was mostly flat with the corners and front of the building being the exception. Large and wide square stone tablets were stacked upon each other on these corners, and a triangular top stretched from the bottom of one stone tablet to the other at the very front.

Looking through its wide-open rectangular double door entrance, I could see the lively activity of the early evening food shift. It was vastly different from what I was used to, since I would usually only come in when it was very early or very late when barely anyone, if any person at all, was inside. Conversations and laughter flowed as people were seated or walking around from table to table. There must have been hundreds of people in there.

"You're on cleaning duty?" Someone asked, their voice breaking through the mixture of other voices in the massive room.

"Yeah, Imma be sore in the morning," an entirely different voice from another conversation said through the mixture.

"I need to get me a new jacket soon," another voice.

"For real, though," another voice in the same conversation about the jacket.

"I'll be back, y'all," different voice, different conversation.

I walked away from the entrance, going towards Commune.

The Quiet Lounge's lights were dim as the evening grew to night. I sat in a thick mahogany chair eating the piece of bread I had grabbed earlier. I was alone in the room. I leaned back in the chair, my eyes open.

Short, green vegetation made sounds under my shoes. My hands were tucked in the front pockets of my pants as I walked on white stone pathways. There wasn't a single person around where I was walking. It was obviously an area that wasn't traveled down as much within Numetus. That didn't change anything. I was just walking. I knew that in the distance ahead, the library was going to be off to the very far right. Going inside there was not a part of this walk.

"What you doin' on my block?" Lamonte jokingly asked somewhere behind me.

I stopped walking and turned to see just him a couple yards away. Seeing him wasn't expected considering the lateness of the night and the lack of people around the vicinity.

"I never see you in this area," Lamonte added. "You're trying to see the Summit House?"

I looked at him questioningly, my eyes squinting a bit.

"I guess you could say it's the center of operations here."

He answered my questioning face. "It's where I was just coming from."

The center of operations. That means that's where the negotiations are being planned. He's coming from there. He knew about the Levaveus scouting mission. Since he's a Hand, he's probably a part of the negotiations.

"I didn't show you the Summit House during the tour," Lamonte thought out loud.

"It's fine," I said.

"Maybe I'll show you some other time. I should get going. See ya." He walked forward, then turned left down a different pathway.

My hands shifted in my pockets as I continued walking, unsure of my destination. Later, I was in the bed I use with open eyes, thinking of the interaction and more.

My eyes opened to the fresh air of the room I take residence in.

"Yeah, they have me on moving duty," one of the four people who uses the room I take residence in said.

"What they got you moving?" A second one asked.

"Anything they need me to. I gotta get going."

"We all gotta go, I'm starvin'," Jalen said.

All four people went towards the door as I sat up.

"You're up," Jalen said, him and the other three stopping in their tracks either at the doorway, partially through it, or already standing in the corridor outside of the room. "Wanna eat with us?"

"No, it's alright," I said looking at Jalen.

"You sure?"

I nodded once.

"Cool," Jalen said as he and the other three people proceeded to exit the room. "Catch you sometime."

The door closed. I slid my legs out of bed and my feet touched the ground as I took in the quietness. I showered, walked down corridors and stairs, and stood in a Dining Storage, grabbing a piece of round whole wheat bread. The Dining Hall would not be a place to go. The people there could be heard from here. It wasn't excessively loud; it was just enough to exemplify the copious amount of people inside. The Quiet Lounge would suffice.

After a short walk back to Commune, I entered the Quiet Lounge, and saw no one in sight. The thick dark mahogany chair I sat in didn't feel hard. It felt normal... all routine...I started eating the bread. No crumbs fell as I finished eating. If any had, I would have cleaned them up immediately. I won't be inconsiderate. Time passed as I sat. Hours went by.

Time.

It's been a little less than three weeks since I've been here. The temperature has been gradually dropping with sudden shifts on randomized days at randomized times. It was like that in the middle of September, when all of this started with that day at the school. The journey to get here doesn't feel real. The two to three hours of sleep, waking up and immediately walking, jogging, and running, the push for the Speed Up Process, powers, the Monsters in pursuit, somehow were all real. The Wind Bag was also...

I pulled Commune's front door open, trying to exit. As the door opened, I made eye contact with someone who was trying to enter at the same time.

"Yo Jason," Asher exclaimed upon seeing me. He wore a clean white shirt, gray jeans, black shoes, and a light brown jacket with a dark grayish tint that had no hood. It looks like he changed his style a bit.

"Nice timing," Asher said as he stood to the side of the doorway. "You get your duties yet?"

I shook my head. "No."

"I'm not looking forward to cleaning and stuff, I'll tell you that," He chuckled for a second. "But I don't mind. I mean they are giving us a place to stay. It's safe, free food." He leaned forward, as if he were to whisper something secretive. "None taxed."

"Cleaning could be seen as a tax." I plainly said.

"You're right! It's a conspiracy! They thought they had us." He shook his fist dramatically, feigning intense emotions. "Nice try. Now, it's personal." He began talking in a raspy voice like an old man who had been through his share of gritty fights and a grainy life. "I will have my vengeance." He pulled back his dramatization after the last word. "I'm about to get something to eat. Did you eat yet?"

"Not hungry," I answered.

"I see I can't really force you to eat this time," Asher smiled. "I'll probably run into you again. Let's talk more next time dude." Asher walked past as I held the door open.

I turned to see him walking away up the stairs. The room he was going to was for one person because he knew which God...

"Live life, bro." He called backwards to me.

Live, life.

Sitting back and watching.

I stepped outside.

I was walking around at night, not in the usually more populated areas, such as the Main Center. I walked in places that less people would walk through like—Azmach.

There he was, walking across my path ahead. Wait. This was near the area where I last saw Lamonte. That means... the Summit House was nearby. He was heading there, going in the direction Lamonte appeared to be leaving from.

"Jason?" Azmach said confusedly when he noticed me, turning in my direction as he did so. "I never see you around here. What's going on?"

"Walking," I said.

"I feel that." Azmach nodded, smiling.

I had a feeling of what he was doing "When did you get out of the Infirmary?"

"A few hours ago actually."

"I'm guessing you have to plan the negotiations."

"That I do."

"… When do you leave?"

"The day after tomorrow."

The quickness of the date hit me. Two days? That repeated in my head. That's soon. That's extremely soon.

"We're getting the last details put together tomorrow morning," Azmach informed. "Then we'll start packing up."

I looked off to the side and nodded once, listening, before turning my head back towards him.

Azmach hummed after speaking the word, then opened his mouth to speak again. "I'm sure you have other things on your mind. I have to get goin'. Talk to you later." He walked away with conviction in his steps.

I stood there for some time, seconds or more.

On my mind.

The lights were dimly lit within the place at such a late time of night. It was mostly vacant, except for the few people eating by themselves and the few quiet chatter. Quiet. Excluding the few people around, the Dining Hall was quiet. Wait, the people are now gone, except for the one person cleaning tables up with a cloth far off to the other side of the room.

How much time has passed with me sitting here? There are just things on my…

Excluding that person, the Dining Hall was quiet. It was normal this quiet. Quiet. It was… other things on my mind… My mind felt cloudy with noise in the background. There was something of a clock ticking. At least it felt like it. At least… The person continued cleaning tables, moving closer towards my direction.

Other things on my mind.

"'Cuse me brotha man," the person cleaning tables said as he began wiping down the surface of the table I sat at, making sure to give me space. I didn't even notice him getting this close until he was right there. He cleaned the table thoroughly, moving on to the next upon next upon next. After cleaning the last table, the person drained their washcloth in a bucket and took their time walking out the room. Quietness was absolute in the room.

On my mind.

I continued sitting there.

The background of my mind.

Why am I even sitting here? I stood up and exited the place.

My eyes were open. In bed, my eyes were open. In the darkness, my eyes were open. With sleep not in the line of sight, my eyes were open. Were they actually open?

Early in the morning. Very early in the morning, sometime after midnight, the silent clock on the wall across the room showed.

Imagine there was no sleep without exhaustion to accompany it. That was this moment. It was still late, or early depending on disposition. Without a doubt, I couldn't sleep. Eyes, were they open? They were, but… but … other things on my mind.

Things. In the parameters of these exact contexts, the things dealing with the mind is the scope of the very definition of thoughts. Thoughts on my mind. What thoughts? I know what thoughts lie …Eyes. Were they open in actuality? Are my open eyes a fable, meaning there was the possibility of my thoughts being a fallacy? Isn't all this cloud within my head simply a personification of sorts for these fallacies, that were indeed not fallacies, and instead is acting as an obscuration to the more dense and significant thoughts?

Significant. That's exactly it.

The significant thoughts in the hand.

What is identity?

That isn't exactly it; however, it is concurrent to identity. It is one specific thought, one that existed in my mind since I could form thought and question existence, one that modified ever so slightly when the circumstances changed, one I pushed back for days now.

One thought.

Here I lie awake with that thought. Here I lie with that thought returning to the forefront. Here I lie, acknowledging the absolute fact of that one thought never truly slipping from my mind. Admit, this one thought I do. Accept, this one thought I have. All routine, this one thought is. Sitting back and watching from the distance, I had this thought regardless. All the above, this one thought.

Which God is my parent?

I was out of bed, dressed, and rushing through the Main Center before I registered all the detailed steps between. There was one place I had to go, one place for that one thought to receive one answer.

The library.

I pushed its door open, going straight to the second floor. Books. Papers. Family trees. Time shuffled along with it. I flipped pages.

Which God is my parent?

Turn papers over.

Which God is my parent?

I wrote notes down, the pencil lead almost breaking.

Which.

Page.

God.

Book.

Is.

Flip.

My.

Family tree.

Parent?

I stood there in front of the table, not reading, not writing, just pondering, just in thought, just in thought of that one thought. Of course, I haven't been through every single God and Goddess out in existence. Of course, I've barely scratched the surface. Where? Where do I go? What direction? There was no sign given. No signs. One thought.

Which God is my parent?

I have no idea with a lack of signs given from the God who is the parent. What do I know? Where am I at? I don't even have powers to point me in the correct direction.

My fingertips felt a book and slid it to the other side of the table.

Brarnet, God of Age and Wis- no. Z'yieh, Primordial Goddess of oaths and-doesn't connect to mine. Ethnone, not much information so possibly, but no- Ahlayniss, Kauzation Goddess of the hunt- no she wouldn't ever be with a man so I wouldn't exist- Cresate, Goddess of witchcraft- no, Heraba, Goddess of youth- no, Conzounce, God of wealth- no, that's nowhere near, Briariel, Kauzation Goddess of chance and destiny- no, Panyown, Behiim God of the wild- no, Jintos, Primordial God of openings and- I haven't even heard of some of these. Nayleeuh, no, Zon, no, Alytra, no, Sprielia, no, Cresate, Kauzation Goddess of magic and no. No. No.No, no, no, no, no, no

No signs, no powers. What can I infer, what can I hypothesize? I don't know. I hardly have any details. What are the details? No powers. What details? Nothing. What details? I haven't even finished Adjusting. What details? Whenever I pull too much Aura out at once, the most that happens is that the air whips. What details-

The air whips…the air whips…like a wind… like… Or is it just wind?...

My fingertips slid papers and books across to the table in

all directions as my eyes searched for what I thought.

Azmach has light.

My eyes scanned a paper.

Whenever Asher tapped into his Aura there was heat, and fire as his powers.

This is no mere coincidence for wind.

I pushed the paper away, not finding what I was looking for.

Wind Gods…Which Wind God? Only one came to mind. No. There's no way. That's no coincidence, yet it's too convenient. The probability of the possibility of such… Wouldn't this practically constitute the epitome of practically jumping upon a perceived conclusion? What constitutes the feasibility of what I am perceiving? I sat down, grabbing a paper filled with words. One particular God's name is inscribed somewhere within the multitude of sentences. Which Wind God? Is there only one? The words on the sheet scanned through my eyes. There. The name was right there, right on the paper, right in front of me, right where fantasy once again met possibility and reality.

Levaveus.

I stared at the name.

Levaveus.

I stared deeply.

Levaveus

Possible reality.

Levaveus.

Is it merely possible?

Levaveus.

Only possible?

Levaveus.

Or more…?

I gently placed the paper down, moving rigidly as I did so. Sat there. I sat there. Right there. Are there other Wind Gods? That cannot be overlooked. There are probably other Wind

Gods outside of him. Still.

My finger pushed the paper with "Levaveus" written on it away by a few inches-

Bag of Wind.

"You were affected by all the Bag's wind. You just naturally dealt with it." Echoed in my head, Azmach's words now layered with new meaning.

Perhaps I naturally dealt with it... because of parentage-

Think further. Azmach's Bag mission was to scout Levaveus's location in Pennsylvania. Pennsylvania is a neighboring state of Maryland, the state I'm-No, no that's still a stretch. Take a look at everything. Wind is certainly an attribute that cannot be ignored. I could naturally deal with the Bag's wind, Pennsylvania neighbors Maryland, Levaveus lives in Pennsylvania, what else is there? Must there be something else? This is all circumstantial.

Perhaps circumstance leads to truth.

...I sat there and looked at the paper with Levaveus name on it again. My right fingertips slowly dragged it back toward me. After releasing the paper, that hand went back under the table, into my lap...

Levaveus. It fits. It fits evenly, it fits justly, it simply fits. Admittance. That I have. Acceptance. This makes it so.

I continued looking at the name—

The negotiations. Wait, hold on. Yesterday, Azmach said they'll leave in two days. Tomorrow. If Levaveus is in fact my parent, then the negotiations could be— don't jump now, look where you leap.

There's been no confirmation of parentage. I haven't even finished Adjusting. The weight in my hands welled up.

I've caused this. I've endangered every single person here. As far as I know, the endangerment I have caused is long-term. The ramifications of what I did span. I know what Azmach said; that doesn't change what happened. I was the one who used the Bag. The people here, I cannot allow them to lose what they have. Not because of me.

I must go to the negotiations.

I stood up, rushing out of the room, running down the stairs, and continuing forward, passing the person who showed me the library. I exited and swerved left. I think it was this way. The sun was out, beaming down as I advanced. Azmach had mentioned that there would be a meeting in the morning, and since it's now around seven in the morning, that means the meeting hasn't started, or is currently going. If the meeting did pass, then perhaps if I find the Head and talk to— Just see if the meeting has started or has passed first.

I had never been to the place; however, Lamonte was leaving and Azmach was going in this direction-

Lamonte was walking down a walkway, merging onto the path I sped on.

Speaking of him.

"Jason," Lamonte said as he saw me coming. "Why are you in a hurry?"

I stopped in front of him. "Good timing. You're about to go to the Summit House, right?"

"...Yes?"

"Take me there."

"Next time," Lamonte started taking steps to his right, going straight on the pathway I stood. "I got to go to a meeting."

"So it didn't start yet. Take me to the meeting. I'm going there regardless. I don't know the exact way, but you do."

Lamonte had a small smile with seriousness slipping around the folds of his eyes. "Woah homes. That I can't do, and you can't come to this meeting. Nothing personal." He faced forward, walking down the pathway.

"The meeting has something to do with Levaveus, correct?" I asked rhetorically.

Lamonte stopped dead in his tracks, looking back at me with confused curiosity.

"I have details about Levaveus that will change the plight."

Lamonte stood, processing the information. Curiosity filled more than confusion. "...What are the details?"

"I'll say it at the meeting."

"Tell me now real quick."

"At the meeting. Accountability is on me."

"Do we by chance already know these details?"

"I guarantee none of you do."

A small hint of confusion was still on his face, but he was pushing to the side. He stood silently, thinking it over. Finally, he nodded his head in the direction he was heading. "You're lucky the Summit House is right over there. The rest of the Hands are pretty chill for the most part, but this is nothing to play with," he started walking ahead. "This way."

Lamonte led forward, sometime later taking a sharp left down a different path made of a multitude of small white stones that shone at certain angles in the sun. The multiple white stones that were stuck together essentially created a normal pathway that didn't shift under each step. The pathway was immovable and amazingly had a smooth surface.

Lamonte hurried down the path only because I was surging ahead. Short green vegetation trailed the sides like any normal pathway in Numetus. This pathway led to a structure.

The structure was made of smooth and vibrantly pure white stone, consisting of rectangular and square shapes. The roof was a large slab of thick rectangular stone extending past the rest of the structure by a few noticeable feet. At the very front was a large set of stairs leading to the entrance. Rectangular windows were placed on the higher floors with a few on the lower ones. A multitude of columns stood. They were smooth and had grooves in them, connecting to the rectangular slab of a roof. Grand in its size, it commanded the area.

I pushed open the large arch mahogany doors, its weight being nowhere near as heavy as the Bag felt since that night.

"Up here," Lamonte hurried past me going through the

vast open room made of smooth white stone. He hastened to a wide and thick beige stone circular bifurcate staircase. These stairs opened both to the right and left on the second floor. I followed Lamonte, passing some beige columns connected to the white stone ceiling and white stone floor. Lamonte ran up the stairs, taking the steps on its left side and curving along with it to the second floor. The stairs intersected with a hall-way.

I was right behind him.

Between where the right and left sides of the stairs led to the second floor, there were two large dark mahogany arched doors. Instantly, I turned left taking some steps towards them.

"Wrong way, that's the Head's Office." Lamonte came to a halt.

I stopped moving and looked back at him. "A meeting so important, wouldn't it be in this room?"

"Usually, but we wanted to make sure that this mission stayed a secret. We're doing the planning in a side room no one would think of."

"Alright." I turned, following him.

Lamonte was walking down the hallway in the opposite direction of the Head's Office. The hallway was long and wide with a couple of closed doors spaced out on both sides of its walls. Lamonte turned to one of the doors, grabbing the doorknob, turning it, and pushing the door open.

"The preparations—" A voice said, cutting itself off as its owner noticed the door opening.

Lamonte walked into the room.

"Lamonte," the voice's owner said. "Good of you to join us."

I hurriedly stepped into the large room, seeing a couple of dark maroon carpets with intricate designs and warm colors weaving through them adorning a few walls. There were also a few tables, with the one in the center currently being used.

"Who's this?" The voice owner said. He sat behind a large mahogany desk that had a stack of papers and a few pens. Only his torso and up was visible since the desk blocking most of everything else. He wore a red long-sleeved shirt and looked to be in his early twenties. He had to be the oldest person in the room and possibly all of Numetus by a few years. He was well-built, but not completely made of muscle, had a low-trimmed beard that was focused mainly on his sides, and had dark brown skin with a thin scar at the top of his forehead.

His hair drew attention away from his scar. Enormously long locs reached the middle of his back and were tied up in a lobster braid. It was difficult to view from the front, but some details were still noticeable. What wasn't hard to notice were the small amounts of confusion in his narrow eyes due to my presence. There was a bit of annoyance, not because of my presence, but because of the timing of my arrival.

There were another five people in the room. One wore a gray denim jacket, the second a loose-fitting elegant shirt, the third a dark gray blazer, and a fourth a black long-sleeved collared shirt. The fifth was Azmach, who sat at the left side of the table between the ones wearing a collared shirt and blazer, his eyes slightly wide in surprise. All five sat in the center at a large rectangular table that was some feet in front of the large desk. It was filled with maps, notes, and other papers.

"Why would you let him in?" The person behind the desk questioned.

"He said he has information to tell us." Lamonte answered confusingly.

"'Information'? Lamonte, there is no time for this." The person's voice was deep and stern. He looked at me specifically after finishing that sentence. "Whatever it is, we'll get it done on a later date. We're in the middle of something. I'm going to have to ask you to leave."

"I know something about Levaveus," I said.

Four of the six people sitting in the room had expressions as if life had personally told them to pause. In comparison, Azmach showed less of a pause, letting out a breath as he recognized what was happening. The changes in expression from the person behind the desk was subtle; he didn't move a muscle.

"My apologies for interrupting," I addressed the room. "I'm the one who used the last Reverse Bag of Wind."

"You did what?!" The one in the blazer blurted out. He stared at me, stunned.

"W-W-What's going on?" The one in the collared shirt sitting to Azmach's left asked.

"The Bag? Who is he?" The one in orange that was sitting across from Azmach questioned.

The one in a blazer turned to his left towards Azmach. "You said you used it?"

Azmach shoulders lowered as he exhaled further. Lamonte looked behind his shoulder at me, a lack of surprise on his face. He knew. Azmach must have told him. The other four at the table with Azmach exchanged looks.

"The Minotaur and the Manticore were the Monsters pulled into that bag," the one sitting behind the desk revealed.

"The what?!" The collared one nervously exclaimed. He turned to his left to look past Azmach at the person behind the desk, then at Azmach himself.

"The Minotaur and the Manticore?" The one in orange asked, her voice shifting further into disbelief.

Azmach stared forward, remaining unfazed, while the four people at his table exchanged quick looks. A hush consumed the room. The one orange was squinting as if the answers were floating in the air and would become transparent whenever he tried to read them. The rest of them kept taking glances from Azmach to me.

"Those two Monsters are some of the most powerful to have ever existed," the one sitting behind the desk slowly said. "They have been around for thousands of years. Pulling one into a Bag is already a feat. But pulling in both? And a novice at that?"

Azmach and I locked eyes for a second.

The one sitting behind the desk looked at Azmach, then me, then back at Azmach. "It was life or death," he said calmly to Azmach, his posture firm in his seat. "You did what had to be done."

"I gave him the Bag, so it's on me.," Azmach simply said, turning to his left and leaning forward, looking past the one in the collared shirt to make eye contact with the person behind the desk. "Now we're less equipped."

"You didn't tell me to use it then," I countered.

Everyone in the room looked at me.

"I did not understand the depth of the Bag's importance." I said to the entire room. "If I knew, I wouldn't have dared used it. I've put everyone here in an even graver situation. At the time, I didn't comprehend the gravity of that Bag; however, what I do comprehend is something I've been missing until this morning. It's information about Levaveus."

All eyes in the room studied me, curious as to what I was about to say. The one behind the desk didn't move a muscle, listening intently.

"When I used the Bag, Azmach had said it was like I naturally dealt with its winds. That was no coincidence. Those details. That information I'm talking about—"

Grasp it. Pull, hard.

The air whipped around as if a small wind had suddenly blown into the room. My hair and clothes flapped, and the clothes of the other people did the same. Some of the hair in the room blew. Lamonte's hair blew mainly to one side, while the one in the blazer had their afro-texture hair in twists, and they were blown behind him. The one in orange hair too was blown away from her. The ones in the denim and collared shirt had hair too short to be blown away. The person behind the desk sat unfazed. Papers waved, some gliding off the tables. The air settled down quickly, leaving the room silent outside of the few papers in the process of stopping their maneuvering.

"It's me," I said, looking at them all. "I'm Levaveus's son."

How Can One Ensure Accountability Stays Centered?

"Levaveus's son?" The person sitting at the desk asked in a questioning tone. His question was followed by a continuing silence.

Lamonte turned all the way around to face me, stunned. Azmach had the face of someone who had been solving an unassembled puzzle in their head for weeks who was now finally placing enough pieces together to see the picture. The four sitting with Azmach looked as if through the years they had become immune to lightning, but nevertheless were shocked when one bolt struck less than two feet from them.

The one sitting at the desk had a small amount of shock in his eyes, but for the most part, he didn't flinch. "How'd you know about this meeting?" His eyes locked onto me with the demeanor of someone whose mind was cycling through what should have been years of experience far beyond him. Clearly, should have isn't what is.

"I ran into Lamonte on a different day in an area nearby here. Later, I ran into Azmach around the same area. Since I ran into them both around the same vicinity, there must have been meetings around here for something. I had already figured out the Bag's importance. I put two and two together." To some extent, it was technically true. I won't say that it was Azmach who told me, nor will I say something that will push the fault onto Lamonte. Like the Wind Bags, this will be on me.

The eyes of the person behind the desk held recognition as a memory must have sparked. "You're that new person I heard about with the white hair."

White hair.

"What is your name?" He asked without breaking eye contact.

"Jason."

"Jason," he repeated. "What's your last name?"

"Side."

"Jason Side," he said, sitting tall. "I'm Tyrone Muhammad, the Head of Numetus, and the son of Lehgots. So, son of Levaveus, you want to know about this mission?"

"My point is…I'll go on this mission," I said in a tone that made the words concrete. They can't know that I know more details. I'll act as if they're missing. "Whatever's going on, me as Levaveus's son could give an advantage." I stepped forward. "It could give insurance—"

"Or is the reason for insurance." His eye contact didn't break once. "Gods can be fickle. You never know when and which ones would kill you and why."

Lamonte's eyes dropped, looking like a sudden headache of the past became present.

"What I say and what you will know will not leave this room," Tyrone said in a commanding tone so present the quietness in the room became more apparent. "Negotiations with Levaveus to acquire more Reverse Bags of Wind. That's the mission. There are times we have to leave Numetus. If there is a new Demigod that we find out about, we must bring them to safety. If we are short on our food supply, we must go out and get some. If anything is going on in the God world that gives reason to leave Numetus at times. If any of us are outside of Numetus's Barriers for any reason there is a chance that we will be attacked by Monsters. Now imagine if the Barriers were to disappear one day," Tyrone bleakly said with a blank face. "With and without the Barriers, these Bags are our last line of defense. This mission will affect Numetus's present and future."

Azmach looked at Tyrone, while Tyrone didn't break eye contact with me. The other people in the room had their eyes cast downward, already understanding the gravity of the situation but not wanting to be reminded of the depth.

"If the negotiations fail, everyone there could die." Tyrone said. He turned his attention to me. "You could be the son of some other Wind God that's not as prominent. Could be a Wind Spirit. Or, that wind you have could be a byproduct of some other powers from being the son of some other God. Are you sure that Levaveus is your father?"

"I was able to use the Wind Bag sufficiently," I instantly said. "Since the Wind Bags are Levaveus's creation, it gives some possible evidence."

"That evidence isn't evidence. As I've said, it could mean a different Wind God, a Wind Spirit, or a byproduct."

"Even if I'm the son of some other Wind God, Wind Spirit, or neither, it could still give a step towards the negotiations being successful."

"Right or wrong, that can make Levaveus target you."

"While he's targeting me, everyone else can escape," I asserted.

"What if escape isn't possible?"

"Then if feasible, I'll be a last resort for negotiations."

"Sounds like a gamble."

"I'm gambling myself." I said before he finished the last letter in gamble.

Not a single word was spoken in the room. Not one. Azmach stared at me while Lamonte's eyes shifted back and forth between me and Tyrone. The four sitting with Azmach did a combination, some staring only at me, and others whose eyes darted back and forth between me and Tyrone. Tyrone maintained eye contact, remaining silent. His breathing was not even audible and visible, his shoulders and chest not rising and falling.

"That could work," said the one in denim sitting across from Azmach's, his voice low and raspy. "As a last-ditch effort. When everything else fails, bring out the son." His right index finger tapped the table, the gears turning in his head.

"A son with no proof," the one in the blazer emphasized. "I'm just saying fraud would make any man mad. And this man is a God." He shook his head. "That's nothing to play with."

"Alright Cayden," the one in denim referred to the one in the blazer, while his finger continued tapping the table. "It. Could still work."

The one in orange turned to her towards the one in denim. "It's still dangerous."

"Hold on son," Azmach calmly jumped in. "It's not just dangerous. You are all forgetting that he's new. He just got here."

"Yeah, all of this is a bit soon for him." Lamonte agreed.

"And if Azmach's saying that…" the one in orange trailed off, allowing her point to simmer.

"We still need Wind Bags," the one in denim said, looking next to him at the one in orange, then looking across the table back and forth between Azmach, Cayden, and the one in the collared shirt.

"I see your point," Cayden continued. "Based off our information, Levaveus is a chill God when compared to others. Might be doable."

"It really could work," said the one in denim, his finger no longer tapping the table. "It would be better to have a family connection. Our only connection right now is stolen Bags." He knocked on the table once with his right knuckles. "He can't be happy about that."

Tyrone sat, considering the thoughts given. He looked at the one in the collared shirt. "Lawrence, Dread Reading."

"Uuum," the one in the collared shirt began to respond in a low reedy voice, some Aura now lightly permeating from him. He sat with his shoulders up with a small nervousness that he was clearly managing. His 4b afro-textured hair was cut low, he had hickory brown skin, and to match the long-sleeved black collared shirt, he wore navy blue trousers with casual black shoes. "I can't tell… It could be worse, but it can also be better." The feeling of his Aura disappeared.

"We're a few days away from three weeks into October," Tyrone slowly said. "It has been somewhat warm the past couple days, but we know it's going to get colder. When winter comes, we need the option of going out of Numetus for resources, food. We don't yet have the strength to take on Gods. With those Bags, we can at least compensate for Monsters." He was silent for seconds, then directed his attention to me. "We need to weigh our options. For now, you can be a part of this meeting."

Azmach's chest deflated as he silently exhaled. Lamonte looked at Azmach, then Tyrone.

"But are you sure you want to be a part of these negotiations?" Tyrone asked.

"I'm going," I quickly affirmed. Weight, my hands held it.

Azmach turned his head to look at me.

Tyrone held eye contact with me, slowly nodding his head in silence. "You already know Azmach and Lamonte. The remaining Hands, introduce yourselves."

The four people at Azmach's table looked between each other, waiting for one of them to go first.

"Uhhhhh, guess I'll start. I'm Lawrence." He sat quietly for a few seconds, then his eyes widened slightly. "Oh, I should say my last name. Reed, um, that's my last name."

"Cayden Cross," he introduced himself. He sat in a way that indicated he was tired of sitting, leaning over at an angle that so happened to show how skinny he was. He had light umber skin, and as I noticed earlier, his afro-textured hair was in twists that stopped at the bottom of his nose. He wore gray trousers to match his dark gray blazer, a black T-shirt, and somewhat formal, but still very casual, black shoes. "I'm the son of Knahxa, Goddess of balance."

"We have to do Gods too?" Lawrence asked, anxiety rising in his voice. Visually, he pushed it back down.

"Just gonna add to the memo there, Cayden?" Lamonte jokingly asked.

"I mean he added last names to the memo," Cayden grinned. "What's next, social security?"

"Um…in that case…" Lawrence raised his hand to his eye level. "I'm also the Son of Tyceium," he put his hand down, "who is the God of dread and terror before battle."

"I'm Laniah Cook, daughter of Deohla, the Goddess of force and raw power." The person in orange sitting across from Lawrence, Cayden, and Azmach said. She had sepia brown skin and wore black pants and shoes with the orange loose-fitting elegant shirt. Instead of usual braids, her hair was fashioned into multiple lines of small afro puff balls connected to each other. Each of these lines stopped halfway down her neck.

"I'm Zaid Wright," the person in denim next to Laniah said, the raspiness in his voice becoming more apparent. His lips tightened, he no longer exhibiting the patience for talking. It was obviously something he didn't like and only did if he absolutely had to due to the situation. His afro-textured hair was cut low and faded further on the sides. He had copper brown skin, and matching his gray denim jacket were black jeans, a white T-shirt, and black shoes. "I'm the son of

Briariel. The Goddess of chance and destiny."

"Good," Tyrone said. "Let's go through everything."

Everyone suddenly had a switch flipped like all concepts were mute until the intangible could be the tangible.

Lamonte went straight past me and grabbed two vacant chairs from the left side of the room, placing them on an empty side of the table. A few feet ahead of the seats sat Tyrone behind the desk, while Cayden, Azmach, and Lawrence sat to the left, and Laniah and Zaid sat to the right.

Lamonte sat down in the seat closest to Azmach.

I grabbed the seat he had placed next to his. "Thank you."

"No problem," Lamonte replied.

"Okay," Azmach started. "We'll split into two groups. Home, and the Negotiators. We have already decided on both groups, but we'll make last minute tweaks before we leave tomorrow. The Home group will consist of Laniah, Zaid, Cayden, and Lamonte. The Negotiators will need more members. At this moment, it consists of myself... and now Jason."

"And me," Lamonte interjected.

Azmach turned to him, taken aback for a second. "We need you here. If anything goes sideway, Levaveus might send Stromoios to Numetus. Or he might just send them and show up himself."

"So what if things go sideways during negotiations? A Demigod already stole some of his Bags, and we used those stolen Bags. He'll probably think we're back to steal some more, if not worse. And just you two? Yeah - nah, we're not doing that, it's too dangerous. Especially since he's untrained. Your group needs more people who know how to fight. You already know Tyrone can't go. If Levaveus feels his Aura, with the circumstances he'll see him as a threat. There won't be a chance to negotiate. He won't just think you're there to steal, he'll think you're there to attack."

Tyrone nodded, confirming what Lamonte said.

"I wasn't going to let you go alone in the first place."

Lamonte reinforced. He turned his attention to me. "And now since you're going, I can't leave either of you hangin'.'"

Azmach cracked out a small smile, letting out a puff of air from his nose. "That's a 'Lamonte move' right there."

"The Home group needs four people," Laniah pointed out. "We have to cover the north, south, east, and west quadrants of the Inner and Outer Barriers."

"He's right here," Lamonte said pointing with his thumb at Lawrence. "Person number four."

"What?!" Lawrence's neck puffed up, possibly a literal frog forming in his throat. "Uhm, I'm here to do Dread Readings. That's it."

Everyone was quiet, thinking over the change. Cayden's and Laniah's eyes were on Lawrence. Lawrence was not amused, looking between the sets of eyes as well as Lamonte.

"That's it," he repeated, stressing his words the second time.

"They are going to need more for the Negotiations group," Zaid said.

"Okay... I'll take Lamonte's spot." Lawrence eyes widened looking down. "Who's where again?"

"Cayden has the East Quadrant that's in the direction where Fabric's and Ration's Quarters, and Commune are located, Zaid has the South Quadrant between the hills and river, and Laniah's at the West Quadrant where the trees and hills are dense," Tyrone listed off. "Lawrence, you now hold the North Quadrant."

"So, um, this area, the Quadrant that the Summit House is in," Lawrence nodded, trying to push his nervousness to the side. "Okay..."

"I'll help you patrol," Tyrone assured Lawrence.

Nervousness left Lawrence's body completely, he now nodding slower. "Okay."

"I'll be patrolling all of the Inner and Outer Barrier's perimeter."

"Now that's what we're talking about," Cayden smiled.

Relief washed over Cayden, Laniah, and Zaid.

"My group needs one to two more people," Azmach interjected.

"I agree." Tyrone said. "But anymore might make Levaveus think you're there for an attack."

"That's why I'm only adding another two max."

Tyrone turned to Lawrence. "Lawrence, Dread Reading."

"Uhhh," Lawrence said, his eyes halfway shut as his mind literally processed the question to find the answer. Once again, a little bit of Aura permeated off him. "I'm feeling… it's okay. No more than that. Ummmafter that it's a big drop. "Once again, the feeling of his Aura disappeared.

"So five max in total, or Levaveus will think we're attacking," Azmach interpreted Lawrence's Dread Reading. "And that's the last thing that needs to happen."

The table grew silent, the weight of Azmach words settling in.

Weight, my hands.

"For the Home group, Stromoios or Levaveus himself might show up." Lamonte said, gently breaking the seconds of silence. "He might send a whole army of Stromoios and show up with them. Don't fight them on to the death. Just hold them back until Numetus can prepare and get everyone else down in the Railroads."

"We'll handle that," Laniah said.

"Sounds like a plan," Cayden said.

Zaid nodded in agreement.

"This officially begins tomorrow morning," Tyrone said, looking at everyone at the table. "Azmach." He turned to Azmach. "Your group will leave by five a.m."

"That was already the plan," Azmach said.

Tyrone nodded, smiling at him. His smile faded, and he addressed everyone. "Home group, get to your posts by five a.m. Does everyone understand?"

A variety of nods, "yes", and "yeah" replied to Tyrone from every person in the room except for me.

"Is there anything else?" Tyrone asked.

"My group will stay after," Azmach said. "There are a few things that we need to hash out."

"Great." Tyrone turned his head to Lawrence. "Lawrence, I'll show you your post. Wait for me outside."

Lawrence nodded.

Tyrone looked at the entire room, addressing everyone. "This will affect the future of Numetus, and all of its lives. Do not waver."

Strength mixed with a hint of fear were on the faces of Lawrence, Laniah, Zaid and Cayden, with fear being slightly more apparent in Lawrence's.

"This meeting is adjourned," Tyrone concluded.

Cayden, Zaid, Laniah, and Lawrene slowly stood up and walked out of the room. The door closed behind them, leaving Azmach, Lamonte, Tyrone, and me alone.

Tyrone turned to Azmach, nodding his head in pride. "Only in a few years, you've grown this much." Tyrone said to Azmach. "From what I see, you're just about ready."

"No," Azmach disagreed. He turned to Tyrone with a smile. "Out of all of us, you're the best one to be the Head."

"You only say that because I'm older. It's only four years."

"And you've been the Head for years since before I got here. You are what Numetus needs."

That stayed in the air.

"I'm speaking for its future." Tyrone smiled. "I need to show Lawrence his post." He stood up, walking out of the room confidently. "Azmach. Lamonte. Good luck."

"Thanks," Lamonte replied.

"We'll get it done," Azmach replied.

"Jason," Tyrone said as turned his head to look at me while grabbing the doorknob.

Tyrone opened the door and walked through the doorway

slowly. The door closed behind him.

I looked at the door, an assortment of thoughts pausing and moving paradoxically in my head.

Azmach took a deep breath then exhaled. "I understand how you feel being the one who used the last Bag," he said, grabbing my attention.

I turned to face him.

"But you're not ready for this," Azmach ascertained.

"I'm still going," I said.

"I know you are, especially with your high suspicion of being Levaveus's son. I didn't know about the Levaveus's son part, but after you left the Infirmary that night I had a feeling you might try to join this mission again." He spoke in a lower voice, processing the situation and seemingly having an inner dialogue. "I was hoping I was wrong."

"If I knew that he was trying to join the mission, I wouldn't have told him about the Summit House and led him to the meeting," Lamonte said.

"No, that's on me. I didn't think to tell you about him learning about the negotiations."

"On the way here I already told you that I was going to the meeting regardless," I reminded Lamonte while telling Azmach in conjunction. "I just so happened to run into you. I thought it would be better to have someone who knows the exact location show me instead of wasting time trying to find it."

"The problem is you still haven't finished the Adjusting Process," Azmach said. "No training."

Azmach's not incorrect in the slightest. That is without a doubt the reality of this plight.

"Use your Aura real quick," Lamonte told me. "Not the air thing, just pull some out. Let's see how far you got."

Grasp it. Pull, gently. I didn't need to grab or pull it as much. It was easier. It was becoming innate.

"Barely feel any Aura unless he does that," Lamonte leaned

back in his seat. "Feels almost like a regular mortal outside of that."

"I'd say fully Adjusted in a couple hours with the Speed Up Process..." Azmach eyes narrowed in thought. "You still might not be the son of Levaveus, but with your Aura, I'm leaning more towards it. I wasn't sure before this whole interaction; there are plenty of Wind Spirits and maybe other ways to explain a bit of wind. But, with how your Aura feels now, it can't just be a Wind Spirit..."

The room fell quiet, the situation beginning to settle in.

Azmach shifted his weight, his usual confidence coming forth. "What happened has happened." He turned to me. "Adjust on the way just like you did in the forests. You should finish before we meet Levaveus." He stopped looking at me specifically, now looking back and forth from Lamonte and I. "We have our work cut out for us. Let's get started."

"What's left to set up?" Lamonte asked.

"Levaveus's exact location is in Bake Oven Knob, Pennsylvania. It's around the top of a mountain and in a forest. If all goes well, the journey will be about two days there and one day back." Azmach had his index, middle, and ring fingers pointed up. "Three days." His hand went back down to rest on top of the table. "There's stuff we need to get done today. We need a jeep, rations, maybe clothes, and at least one more person. Y'all ready?"

"Don't forget cash," Lamonte reminded.

"Ah yeah," Azmach agreed.

"You have cash here?" I asked.

"Not much. It has to be used sparingly. There were some left here right before and after this whole war started. Some Demigods who brought money with them added it to the pool. It's for emergencies."

"Or if we have to deal with tolls," Lamonte added.

"We'll try to avoid them, but you can't forget those. Anything else?" Azmach asked.

My silence gave him my answer.

"Alright then," Azmach responded.

"Let's get it," Lamonte said.

Azmach and Lamonte stood and turned, walking out of the room with me behind them. Down the hall, stairs, and out the door, the both of them and I walked away from the Summit House and towards Fabric's Quarters.

"Let's start with the clothes," Azmach said, walking quickly. "We'll work on finding one or two people to join us after."

"You have anyone in mind?" Lamonte asked.

"Not sure. We need someone experienced, trustworthy, and able to keep a secret. No one in Numetus can know about this. It could cause panic."

"Last thing we need."

Time slipped by as the present became the recent past. It was still somewhat early in the morning and the sun sent its greetings, but not too intensely. This type of warmth was standard for October weather. Azmach, Lamonte, and I walked as people appeared on the white stone pathways, walking past and around the two of them and me. The Summit House became further in the distance, while Fabric's Quarters was just ahead.

"Azmach, I see you're better," someone excitedly greeted as they walked towards Azmach, Lamonte, and me in the opposite direction.

"Every day," Azmach smiled at the person.

The person laughed as he walked past.

As Azmach, Lamonte, and I advanced towards Fabric's Quarters, there were fewer and fewer people around. Being earlier in the morning was certainly a factor in this.

"I might get an idea who the fourth person could be for our group while in Fabric's Quarters," Azmach said.

Ahead, the pathway curved onto the crest of a large and long hill. Connected to the pathway were multiple stairs to the left that led down into a field. Fabrics Mount stood in this field. Although it's been a little less than three weeks, it feels longer since I've last been here. Last time was during the tour. Now it'll be for leaving tomorrow morning. Weight, my hands felt it.

Wait.

I stopped in my tracks, a thought occurring to me. "Why did you take the blame for using the Bag?" I asked Azmach. No, it already occurred to me, I just didn't have the chance to ask.

Azmach stopped in his tracks, causing Lamonte to do the same. He looked over to me, his face blank except for a smile. "The same reason why you didn't out me for telling you about the meeting and this mission."

He and I locked eyes. Same reason? — Don't do that. Not for me.

Not for me.

"Do my ears deceive me?" A voice rhetorically asked.

I looked straight ahead further down the pathway. Standing about ten feet away was Asher with his eyes squinted and lips perched in a joking annoyance.

"Asher." Azmach mustered out, trying to piece together what to say.

"I'm over here walking around, taking in the scenery" — he waved his hand — "about to pick up some more clothes from Fabric's Quarters — "

"Asher." Azmach mustered out.

" — when I see my broskis, my home boys, my bros, my home slices, my brothas, my homies, my brothers from another mother, my squad walkin' up. I'm like 'Those the dudes. Let me say 'What's up!'' So, I come over here, outta my way, mind you. Not yours. Mine. To give the 'hi's' and 'hellos'. Tell me why I overhear something about a 'mission'?"

"Look," Lamonte tried to explain, "here's the thing — "

"You mean to tell me! Not the"—he outstretched his left arm to the side—"random people to my left. Not the"—he put down his left arm and outstretched his right to the side—"random people to my right."—his right arm went down, then looked from side to side as if people were watching him and it wasn't vacant around. "But me? That there is a mission." He paused for dramatics. "That all of you are going on, and not a single soul! Thought! To! Let me know?! Oh, that's a rhyme. Soul thought to let me know I got bars fo sho."

Azmach chuckled. Lamonte let out a puff of air, trying to contain his laughter.

"Anyway," Asher kept going like nothing happened. "Is there a mission I don't know about?"

"Look," Azmach said, trying to regain control of the situation. "We can't—"

"Naw you good! Answer the question!"

"Okay," Azmach looked off. "Just keep it down."

"Bruh," Lamonte commented.

"Is there a mission?! Is this what's goooin' on here?! Whatcha gotta say for yourselves?"

"Asher," I spoke.

Asher's joking demeanor halfway evaporated as he started showing a fraction of how serious he actually was.

"This mission is very important," I said to him. "It affects everyone here."

"Welp, tell me on the way," Asher turned to start heading down the nearest stairs to him. "Y'all getting clothes too I'm assuming."

"Hold on," Azmach said.

"It's nothing personal," Lamonte said. "You can't come."

"Dang," Asher said, continuing down the stairs. "My ears really are deceiving me. I need my hearing checked." He waved his arm without looking behind him, gesturing for Azmach, Lamonte and me to follow. "Come on, slow pokes. Jason, last time I checked you run faster than me, you should be like down here by now." He pointed down the hill as he continued walking in that direction.

"Asher, you need to stay here," I said.

"Ah," Asher turned around, walking back up the stairs towards me. "You think I'm going to stay here?" He returned to the top, the same spot in which the entire conversation began. "Jason, all jokes aside, if it's an important mission, then it's probably dangerous, and if it's dangerous, then I got your back." All the playfulness disappeared from his voice, only to be replaced with absolute seriousness. He was unmoving. His face was blank, resting in a way to where he almost looked mad, yet he wasn't. He was as calm as he had ever shown himself to be. "How else could I ever call you my friends?" He looked at me, Azmach, and Lamonte. "How else could I call any of y'all my friend? I got all your backs. I'm ready to roll. Let's get it."

Lamonte had a small smile. Azmach couldn't help but crack one as well.

No, no no no no. Don't put yourself in danger for me. Do it for them if you want. Not me.

"See, I would," Azmach said. "But we already have one guy who lacks training. We can't cover for two."

Asher cupped his right hand, a flame engulfing the inside. Controlled, centered, it was stronger than I've ever seen his flames before.

"I've been practicing," Asher said with a smile. He closed his hand, the fire extinguishing.

Azmach was proud, smiling. Lamonte was amazed.

"I'm not gonna act like I can take on the whole world," Asher said, his smile fading. "But I can do a little somethin' somethin'."

"Alright." Lamonte said. "I can see that." He looked back and forth at Azmach and me. "You've seen what he could do on your way here." Lamonte patted the side of Azmach's shoulder with the back of his hand, then looked between me and Azmach. "I'll leave it up to you two."

Azmach stared into the distance as he considered it.

Up to me? If it were up to me, I would do this mission by myself so no one would have to go into danger; however, that would make the situation worse.

"We can do five people max…" Azmach thought out loud. "We'll just have to have five for sure. The fifth needs to have experience. No exceptions."

"You have anyone in mind?" Lamonte asked.

"I might," Azmach said, then looked at Asher. "Asher, I get that you want to go for our sakes, but this is nothing to play with. If you go, there's a good chance that you could die."

"Have you forgotten those two weeks in the forests?" Asher nonchalantly asked.

"You're not wrong at all," Azmach said, sullenness sneaking in his voice. "Dealing with death is a Demigod's path."

Lamonte stared at the ground.

"Alright," Azmach agreed, regaining himself from sullenness. "As of right now, you are a part of the mission. We'll tell you the rest as we get clothes."

"Sounds like a plan," Asher replied.

The three of them and I walked down the nearest stairs towards Fabrics Mount.

"Why do you need new clothes already?" Azmach asked.

"I burnt most of mine," Asher answered.

"You what?" Azmach queried as he tried to make sense of it, his head whipping around to look at Asher.

"Aight," Lamonte commented, looking off to the side with wide eyes. "That's enough for today."

"I told you I've been practicing." Asher said. "My practice has been burring through clothes, cause if I can burn through the clothes made specifically to take our powers, that means I'm getting stronger too fast for them to handle."

"I can get that, but most of it?" Azmach probed.

"I have the ones on my back still," Asher answered as he

pointed at his back with his thumb.

"Well then." Asher's clothes burning revelation seemed to weigh more on Azmach than the comments about death.

Fabrics Mount's oval-shaped, dark mahogany front door came into view and soon was inches away. Azmach's hand raised to the door.

Knock Knock Knock Knock.

It was opened by Mae.

"Azmach!" Her quiet voice spoke in volume that was loud coming from her. Speaking figuratively about her face lighting up upon seeing him would not describe it correctly. Simply put, it would be an understatement.

"Mae," Azmach smiled. "It's been a minute."

"How are you feeling? When did you get out of the Infirmary?"

"Yesterday. I would catch up more, but we need to get things done."

"Okay. I figured since you showed up with three other people." She backed out of the doorway to let the Azmach, Lamonte, Asher, and me inside.

"I wanted to visit you," Mae continued with Azmach as he passed through the doorway. "They had me sewing and planting more since Winter's coming."

"I'm sure you would have," Azmach believed.

Mae smiled ear to ear. She looked over at Lamonte passing through the doorway. "Hey Lamonte. How are you feeling?"

"'Winter's coming'?" Asher asked, entering the room. "Are we Starks?"

"Surviving. Day by day," Lamonte replied to Mae.

I entered last.

"It's going to get interesting." Lamonte added.

"'You know nothing, Jon Snow.'" Asher, I'm guessing, quoted, but it was done in an English accent.

English. Elizabeth.

"I can tell," Mae replied to Lamonte as she closed the door

behind me. She turned to me. "Hello, Jason."

Greeting me? I nodded my head once at her.

Mae turned to Asher, a realization hitting her. "Asher, did you burn your clothes again?"

"'Again?'" Lamonte mustered out the question, his eyes widening.

"It's not a one time thing?" Azmach asked, on the edge of being incredulous.

"You see," Asher said to everyone. "My swag burns through everything."

"Wish it could burn my ears off," Lamonte interjected. "The lies you tell."

"You're really gonna try and flame the man who can make actual flames?"

"Trying and doing are two different things."

Mae quietly snickered at the interaction.

"You tryna end up in the Infirmary?" Asher flexed his right arm, holding its shoulder, and circling it around. "Is that what you doin'? You know, now that I think about it, speaking of 'again'." Asher turned to Azmach. "Didn't you crash two cars?"

Azmach's head jerked downward.

Mae's eyes were taken aback.

"I haven't forgotten," Lamonte stared directly at Azmach.

"Oh, I know," Azmach said in a humored annoyance.

Azmach and Lamonte started chuckling.

"He didn't crash when he brought me here," Mae tried to assist Azmach.

"How was the car?" Lamonte asked, already knowing the answer. "What was its condition?"

"Ooo, I'm guessing it's the opposite of Monkey D. Luffy," Asher chimed in. "Not in One Piece."

Mae's head cast downward with a small humorous smile on her face.

"Homes and his puns," Lamonte commented about Asher.

Azmach grabbed one of Lamonte's and Asher's shoulders. "Although I would join in further, we gotta get going."

"The clothes will be ready in a few hours," Mae said at the door as Azmach, Lamonte, Asher, and I exited outside.

"We'll be back by then or later tonight," Azmach said over his shoulder.

"Good to see you all. Glad you're getting better, Azmach."

"Thank you," he said with a smile. "Good seeing you too."

She smiled while gently closing the door.

"Okay," Azmach stopped walking to address the two of them and me. "We're going to cut time down, and you both might as well get the experience of setting up for a mission" he meant that for Asher and me. "So, we'll split into two groups. You two will go to Creation's Quarters. Lamonte and I will go to Ration's Quarters to get enough food for five people for three days, and enough for two extra days in case of emergency."

"Creation's Quarters?" Asher asked, a serious intrigue filling his eyes.

"It's where stuff is made that's not clothes or food," Lamonte replied. "Tables, chairs, clocks, walls, floors, anything else, repairs on the off chance if they're needed."

"'The off chance'? Does stuff not break here?"

"Not often, unless from an attack." Azmach informed. "It's kind of like Apez Kauzus. Unless a whole battle goes down or something else crazy happens, things don't break for years and years."

"That's a strange name right there. 'Apez Kauzus'. What is that?"

"The Home of the Gods."

"Yo, like Asgard or Mount Olympus?"

"Pretty much, but on steroids."

"And 'on steroids'. That's crazy. Have you been to Apez Kauzus?"

"Nope. None of us have."

If epic music had been going through Asher's head, it must have been stopped at those words.

"The Gods are busy thinking we Demigods are trying to take control from them like they're doing to each other," Lamonte cut in, a disdain in his eye. "You think they're gonna let Demigods up there?" The disdain in his eyes disappeared, replaced with a befuddled despondency that wasn't simple to define. It disappeared soon after.

Asher clenched his teeth, looking off to the side while nodding his head.

"The reason we want you to go to Creation's Quarters is for something they don't make much of," Azmach returned the subject back to its original point. "A jeep."

"A car?" Asher asked, flabbergasted. "I thought the clothing stuff and the Barriers were on a new level but now y'all making whole cars?"

"A jeep specifically. It's the only type of car that's made the few times any car is made. It can be driven off road. How else would it be possible to get there and back in only a few days?"

Asher was nodding, his shock morphing into inquisitiveness. "Ah ha."

"Make sure they have one jeep ready by four thirty tomorrow morning at the entrance of Numetus. Four forty-five at the latest. Check out the jeep, ask questions you think are necessary. Tell them the Head asked for it, and if there are any concerns to come to me. They'll know to keep it secret. Tell them to do so anyway out of formality."

"Alright, gotcha. Where is Creation's Quarters?"

"Somewhere far ahead of Fabric's Quarters," Lamonte answered. "It's almost off to the Summit House's far right, but like I said it's down straight ahead. It's a good amount of distance, kind of towards the Entrance of Numetus. You'll see it sooner or later."

"Cool. Wait a second, I know you didn't show us everything, but if Creation's Quarters is around here though, why didn't you show us during the tour?"

"That tour was last minute and that's not a place people usually need to go to."

"Makes sense"

"We'll meet back in the front around the Summit House," Azmach said. "After that, we'll either get the clothes or find a fifth person, whatever comes first."

"You sound like you have an idea of someone," Lamonte noticed.

"Yeah, it's better now. I'm still not sure. These two are novice," he gestured to Asher and me, "you're a short-range fighter, I'm a short through long. I'm thinking we need another short through long range to cover more bases since these two aren't ready for a full-blown battle.

"There's some like that."

"I'm thinking of someone who can shoot shots, like me. We need someone who can survive outdoors and hold it down. There's only one that comes to mind with these circumstances."

"You mean her? ...Ivania, right?"

"Yeah, her."

Ivania...that person who showed me the library. Do they mean her?

"Who's that?" Asher asked.

"Mynzonus only has two kids. She's the second one."

Asher's full attention snapped into place, his eyes peering forward. "You have a sister?"

"Half siblings." Azmach answered, his eyes scrunched up as he weighed the choice. "She's close to your age...seventeen if I remember correctly. We haven't interacted much. At all, really. We've never talked. I've heard she seems nice and is a great fighter, great shot. I'm not even sure where to begin to find her..."

"No one does," Lamonte added. "She pops in when she needs to. Other than that, she's gone. She's never talked before."

Asher's head cranked to the side. "Ever?"

Lamonte shook his head. "At least since she's been here. But she's been here for years, and she hasn't spoken once. So it's safe to say she hasn't spoken ever."

With this description, she must be the one who showed me the library. The library. I am certain I passed her as I was exiting that building this morning. She might still be there right now. If that was me not wanting to interact with people, I wouldn't want someone leading people directly to me. I won't tell them.

"We'll need her for a better chance of success," Azmach determined. "I'll worry about that after the rations and jeep. Time's ticking, it's getting close to ten. We'll meet up in two hours."

I already turned partially to head towards Creation's Quarters.

In order for the mission to succeed. A better chance.

"Around the Summit House?" Asher asked for confirmation.

"Around Summit," Azmach confirmed.

The three of them broke off, Asher catching up to me walking forward as Azmach and Lamonte went in the opposite direction.

Can One Make Certain Accountability Does Not Cascade?

"Should be straight ahead," Asher thought out loud, passing the huts that reside within Fabric's Quarters and a small number of people who were also walking.

His and my shoes scuffled against the white stone pathway with the hill to the left running ahead into the distance. Periodically, stairs led down the hill and connected to a pathway in Fabric's Quarters.

"You shouldn't go Asher," I said without looking at him.

Asher stopped walking then and there. The scuffing sound was cut in half instantly.

"You could die," I underlined, still not looking back, still continuing forward.

A quickened scuffling came up behind me.

"And what about you?" Asher asked, walking beside me again, now with a somewhat scrunched up face.

"It's fine."

"I'm not leaving you by yourself, Jason. You'll get trees thrown at you," Asher smiled with a seriousness shown by his somewhat narrowed eyes.

Identity

"That was only the Minotaur."

"And?"

He shouldn't. No person should.

The huts became less frequent, disappearing altogether from sight. Fabric's Quarters was now behind. The pathway continued, now with no stairs going down the hill to the left. The walking stretched as me and Asher continued to the destination.

There's something there.

Ahead was a building that also looked like it was recently constructed. It was rectangular and assembled with light bronze stones, giving the appearance of a vibrant, restored ancient monument. Two columns on each of its ends connected to the roof. At the entrance was a doorway stretching from the bottom to the top of the structure, meeting the roof. While it wasn't the size of Commune, it was still big enough to hold hundreds, if not a few thousand, making it stand out literally and figuratively.

This must be Creation's Quarters.

I looked over the door again and again as Asher and I approached it… It wasn't the doorway that stretched from the bottom to the top to meet the roof, but rather it was the trim around it. The trim was enormous, with intricate designs carved throughout the stone. The door itself was smaller, about the size of four people for both the length and width. It was also made of stone, but instead it was smooth without a single design carved in. It was still large in its own right, but the trim was of a different extreme.

It was quiet, very quiet… was there anyone in it? Was it inhabited? There wasn't a single sound coming from it. Asher's eyebrow was raised at the door.

Was it? It had to be.

I placed my hand on the stone door. It was cool to touch. I pushed it open.

Noise hit my ears. Metal clinging, the passing of voices,

sizzling sounds. How could a door hold all this back? A mass of people was scattered around the massive room at tables working on the various projects, with and without tools, and moving when needed. Drapes were adorned high up on the walls, being the colors bronze, red, and orange, with circular and linear designs weaving throughout. It was surprisingly easy to discern most details in the dim light.

"Oh hey!" Someone cheerfully said in a light bubbly voice. She was enthusiastically walking towards me and Asher like she was a proton personified, a complete positive charge. Her eye was brown, the other was covered by hair that stopped just past her chin. Her hair was styled in thick twists, and most of the twists went down her head in normal directions unlike the front side that covered that one eye. Her purple shirt's long sleeves were rolled up, which made her copper brown skin pop out, especially when taking into account her simple navy blue pants. "Never seen you both in here."

Asher looked at me quickly, then back at the person who approached.

"Welcome to Creation's Quarters," she smiled from ear to ear. "I'm Luna. Whatcha need? Are you here for duties, or because you want to?"

Asher and I were quietly figuring out how to answer. What should I say?

"Nothing much," Asher answered. "We're here to check out a jeep. We need it by Numetus's entrance by four thirty tomorrow morning, four forty-five at the latest."

Luna's eyes widened with intrigue, her head tilting in a position to keep something secret. "Ohhh, a jeep. Is something going on?"

A hammer slammed against metal.

"Nothing crazy," Asher replied with an amused tone, trying to cover the exact details. "The Head asked for it. If you have any concerns, you can talk to Azmach."

"The Head and Azmach?" Her eyes widened.

"Make sure you keep this secret. Limit the number of people who have to know."

"No need to even say." Luna jokingly saluted. She then turned around. "Follow me." She began walking through the place.

Asher and I immediately followed.

People moved around as the two of them and I walked through the room. A table was passed where wood was being ground down.

"What's your names?" Luna asked.

"I'm Asher, the greatest man alive obviously."

Sparks flew as something was being made to the right.

"The greatest man alive?" Luna bobbed her head and turned to look at Asher as she walked. "I'd thought I'd never see the day when I would meet the greatest man alive."

"Yes yes. Bow before me peasants." Asher took steps like he was a king.

"May I have your autograph?"

"Perhaps later. There's business to attend to."

The two of them snickered.

To the left, someone picked up a large log wood and lugged it onto their right shoulder.

Luna continued to smile after her laughter subsided. She turned to look at me. "What's your name?"

"My entourage, that's all you need to know." Asher looked around as he talked. "It's hard being the most interesting man in the world."

"And the greatest. But that's a strange name." Luna turned to me. "Nice to meet you. Is it Sir Entourage, Mr. Entourage?"

"Either or." I said.

"Let's go with Sir Entourage."

Asher sounded like he was holding back a sneeze. In actuality, it was a laugh.

Blades whirled, sparks flew, hammers slammed.

"This is amazing," Asher's eyes, mouth were wide open.

"Considering that a lot of technology is built into everyday processes to construct and create. Imma take a stab at it and say that you have bypassed some of that somehow through your powers."

"Yeah, this is a world of Gods after all," Luna said. "But we also know a lot in general when it comes to this stuff."

"Now we talkin'."

Walking past people and tables, the heat could not easily be ignored. Wait. One person stuck their hand inside a fire, pulling out a piece of metal as if he were grabbing something that fell into a puddle of water.

"Yo," Asher was happily confused, also seeing what happened. "I thought I…"

"Most kids of Bracktius are fire resistant," Luna explained, bemused. "That's why most of the people in here are children of Bracktius."

"Oh, for real?"

"None of us are fully resistant. The amount varies from each of us."

"How much resistance do you have?"

"Mine's pretty strong." Luna said, swinging her arm to her chest. "Do you know your resistance level?"

"As far as I know, I have complete resistance."

"Really?" Luna turned past another table where a chair was being made. She looked at Asher with her eyebrows rising and almost separating further from each other. "I didn't hear of another Bracktius kid, and one who's completely fire resistant. None of us are completely. I feel out of the loop."

"Oh my bad, I should have said earlier. I'm not a Bracktius kid."

"You're not?"

"I'm the son of Soronos."

"Soronos!? He has a kid?"

"A very handsome one. He wouldn't know… about all this handsomeness."

414

The smell of newly sanded wood whiffed into the air as a chair was being smoothed nearby.

"Got some new people Luna?" Some person working at a table off to the side asked.

"Nuh uh," Luna answered as she kept leading the way. "Just showing them the way."

"To where?" A different person inserted their question as they hammered.

As Luna passed more people while she headed towards the back, another two more asked a question or made cheerful comments.

What is in the back?

As if to answer that question, the back came into view. There was a doorway to stairs leading down. It was down these steps that Luna led. The stairs were dimly lit by orange lamps on both sides going along the way. It looked like a sunset with decreased brightness. This decreased brightness inverted as a doorway at the bottom came into view.

Soft white light was used instead of orange for the basement. The room was incredibly large with a few tables towards the front sides of the room. One person worked at each of these tables, mostly observing what looked to be small or big clumps of natural metal. The room wasn't completely vast in space. Sitting in the middle of the room was a black jeep. It was smaller than expected, however it could still fit five people.

"Hey Keisha!" Luna greeted one person observing metal.

"Hi Luna," Keisha replied from behind the table she worked at. She was very skinny. Her 4c afro-textured hair was in two buns, looking like mouse ears, which popped out along with her light pecan brown skin. There was a deep burn from her right middle finger to the midst of her forearm that wasn't too noticeable.

Luna turned her attention back to the jeep. "So. Here it is." She made a grandiose gesture to present the jeep.

"You make these from scratch," Asher surmised, nodding his head with a wide smile. "Considering most cars have chips and software, I'm guessing you have none of that, but it can still do everything like it has that stuff."

"Mhm hm," Luna hummed, nodding her head.

"Now that's nice." Asher stepped towards the jeep, his eyes wide as he studied the machine. "What can this baby do?"

"It's tougher than most cars," Keisha said as she walked to it holding a small ball of metal. She placed her hand against the hood, looking back and forth from the metal ball and jeep. "The metal is much harder."

Asher's eyes drifted to Keisha, then the jeep. "What type of metal?" Asher asked.

"An assortment," Luna said.

"Of?"

"Whatever we need, whatever we have. We mine metal ores and make the metal stronger so it can take attacks from Gods and Monsters."

"Is that what you're doing now?" Asher asked Keisha as he turned to look at her.

Keisha nodded her head, taking her hand off the jeep. "I'm calibrating this,"—she shook her hand holding the metal ball—"to get it stronger than that." She gestured to the jeep.

"Swag, aight. Your name's Keisha, right."

"Yes, what's yours?"

"Asher."

"Nice to meet you."

"Nice to meet," Asher said quickly, his mind on other things. "How do you make the metal stronger?"

"Mainly our powers," Keisha said. "Some of us Bracktius kids can reinforce whatever we make. Some Dittial kids can make things from the earth stronger. There are other kids from other Gods who can do similar things. We assemble the cars in there." She pointed to the left of the room where there was a wall. Nothing except a wall.

416

"Not to be that guy, but there's only a wall," Asher pointed out.

"Oooo I love doing this," Luna said as she skipped to the left side of the room.

"Here we go," Keisha said while shaking her head, smiling.

Luna stopped at the wall, her right hand rising to her shoulder's height as her palm aimed towards it. "Bada bing bada—"she placed her hand against the wall.

Under her hand, the wall's surface softly illuminated in a purple glow. Suddenly, a split appeared in the wall some feet to her left. The sounds of a rockslide rumbled as an outline of a large arch appeared around the split. The left and right of the split moved to their respective sides, leaving an opening to a tunnel. The opening was a wide arch big enough for three jeeps to drive side by side, while the tunnel was long with end in sight. Soft white lights illuminated both sides of the smooth tunnel.

The purple light under Luna's hand disappeared. She looked back at Asher with a smile. "—boom."

"I gladly stand corrected," Asher smiled. "Can anyone do that?"

"No," the purple light under her hand returned, and the tunnel closed. "Some Demigods are authorized, and some of them must stay at tunnel points like this at all times."

"Da!" Asher punched the air. "So close."

Luna started walking back to where she skipped away from. "Like we were saying, there's a ginormous room down where we make and store cars. We extract metal from mines that are also in there and use them for assembly. Like Keisha and everyone else here, we start making them stronger."

"We mainly do it in the assembly room," Keisha informed. "Some of us are in here to compare some metals to the car. That car's the strongest one we've ever made. We need to see if we can replicate it and make ones that are stronger."

"Were you both a part of making this one?" Asher asked.

"Yes."

"Yep," Luna also answered.

"Well from what I can see, y'all did a great job. Seriously."

"Thank you," Luna hummed, trying to contain her smile. "Everyone did do a great job."

"Everyone did," Keisha agreed. She turned to Asher. "Thank you."

"You're welcome," Asher replied.

Keisha returned to her table as she continued to study the metal ball.

"The car's not indestructible though." Asher remarked.

"Yeah," Luna confirmed. "It's hard to make something that Gods and Monsters and, well, Demigods can't break."

"It's hard to make something that I can't break."

Luna looked down, smiling.

"Does it take gas?" Asher asked.

"Not at all," Luna replied, brushing off her smile to answer seriously. "Some Bracktius kids can make things that run from infusing some of our Aura into it."

"For real?"

"Yeah, that's how that wall works," Luna pointed to the wall. "Only difference is that the car can work for any Demigod."

"Any?"

"They take any Demigod's Aura. If that runs out, the wheels can take microparticles of whatever it's driving over and use that as energy. It doesn't sound like it but when it does do that it's actually clean energy."

"Now that's some fantasy stuff right there," Asher smiled, impressed.

"This needs to be at the entrance of Numetus by four thirty tomorrow morning, four forty-five at the latest," I said.

"We'll get it there," Luna said like she had done it plenty of times. She probably has.

"Is there another tunnel? How will it get to the surface?"

"There is. It's in the back of the room. It opens up just like the other. It only leads directly to the entrance."

I see.

"What about the VIN number and registration?" Asher asked. "License plate?"

"Fake ones," Luna answered.

"Wouldn't that be trouble? For us to keep a low profile, fake VIN numbers and registration doesn't sound like the best idea."

"We really can't register it," Luna revealed. "We'd have to connect with mortals and that could cause unwanted attention."

Asher stared at the car. "No bill of sale since it's from scratch. Registration, inspections, documents, title transfers maybe, time and money. It also depends state to state. It's too many things that could lead humans to look and find out about Demigods. It's very unlikely but could happen. Since it's a 'could'... then Gods could come to kill us."

Luna's lips perched, confirming what Asher surmised.

"Ah. Welp. That looks like everything," Asher concluded. "We have to get going." He started taking steps backwards to depart. "It was great meeting you all. Keisha, do you."

Keisha gave him a thumbs up and a smile while still looking at the metal ball.

Asher looked around the room at everyone else who was diligently working and weren't in the conversation. "Other random people who I didn't get to be introduced to, do you."

Some of the so-called random people sheepishly waved.

"Let's get it," Asher said, turning around to exit with Luna partially leading the way.

"Nice meeting you two." Luna said politely at the open doorway of the Creation's Quarter's front entrance. "The car will be ready on time."

"Fantastic," Asher said, smiling as he nodded. "Question,

can anyone go down and work on cars, even without the authorization for that tunnel that goes to the assembly room?"

"Mhm hm."

"Nice." Asher fist pumped in excitement.

"We don't do cars much. It takes a lot of metal and reinforcing. The most we have at a time is maybe six, but they still get destroyed pretty often during outings."

"In the grand scheme of things."

"Mhm hm."

Asher stroked his chin. "Still. Have a great day."

"Come in anytime! Say 'Hello.'" She waved goodbye to him- she's looking at me waving as well. I cannot be rude.

I nodded my head once as I walked away.

"That was fairly quick," Asher summarized, his shoes making scraping sounds as he went up the only stairs that led to and from Creation's Quarters. The stairs were on a hill, just like all the stairs back in Fabric's Quarters.

"Way less than two hours." Asher said as he stepped ahead of me. He was more than halfway up the steps. "Guess we'll chill in the meet up spot. Las rendezvous."

I briefly stopped walking, then continued. Wait there? I don't think I will. Wait there.

I continued up the steps, meeting Asher at the top. He walked with both his hands on top of his head, his elbows out.

"Well, we have time to kill," Asher said looking around. "Should we just wait there or?"

Should I?

Asher walked ahead of me towards the Summit House.

Should I? That person who showed me the library, I don't know her. I do not want to pull in someone else into the plight; however, if someone must join - considering the implication my actions have caused —

I stopped in my tracks. "You go ahead. There's something I should attend to."

Asher stopped walking, turning around with an amused look. "There by myself for like an hour? Naw, I'll get some food." He walked in the direction of the Main Center. "Catch ya."

I didn't move, standing there while he disappeared into the distance.

Actions on my part have deepened this plight. I must not allow this deepening to consume someone else.

I headed in the direction of the library. I know she's there. Passing the Summit House, passing time, I know she's there. My feet walking straight in the direction of tangibility and making certain there are no unjustified responsibilities pressured upon someone.

I know she is there.

The library stood in front of me.

All routine. I walked to the door, my hand hovering and pondering above the doorknob. Once I step in there, there will be something to admit and accept. Isn't that a part of the routine as well?

My hand gripped the door handle and pushed.

Crease. It was the usual sound of this older door opening. The room was dim. It wasn't enough to ruin one's eyes when reading, but it was certainly darker than it was outside. The stairs were straight ahead, long tables on both sides of the room, and there were large mahogany bookcases along the walls and surrounding the tables a few yards away from them. I usually go straight to the second floor, so with the exception of the first time I entered this place, I hadn't looked around the first floor.

In the corner near the stairs, a book rested in her delicate hands. Her dark green hood was over her head as usual.

Must someone else be pulled into this? Regardless of Asher or not, there would be the necessity of someone else. I am the reason there is a need for an experienced person. I must be the one to ask her.

Here goes.

I walked over and sat in the seat in front of her. She looked up silently from her pages. Her dark eyes looked into mine. It wasn't a lock. It was more akin to a peaceful, calm pause. Soothing.

"My apologies for interrupting and essentially coming out of nowhere," I began, noticing just how silent the room and she was in contrast to me currently. "There's something transpiring right now that's... The reason why I'm here is that your help might be necessary."

How is she taking it?

Not once did she flinch. She was as quiet and calm as ever, her eyes filled with substance looking into mine.

"I told no one that you're here, and I came alone so you wouldn't feel any pressure. There's a group of people who're about to do something that's extremely necessary for Numetus; however, it's also extremely dangerous. What they're about to do is three days in total and starts tomorrow morning. They want your help, but as I said it's extremely dangerous. You could die. I know I left a lot of information out. I can't give any more details to people who are not involved in it. You'll find out more if you decide to help. If you don't want to, it's fine. In all truth and honesty, this is something I must do. You don't have to. I will not tell anyone else you were here. You have complete authority in your decision. It is up to you."

Silence completely returned to the room.

Her eyes looked into mine, not flinching, not intimidating, just existing in pure quietness. Her book slowly closed with both of her hands. She stood up and walked to the door, pulling it open, and making sunlight pour in. She turned her head, looking at me.

Wait. The library, the day she showed me it-

"Is that a yes?" I asked for confirmation.

She daintily nodded her head.

"You truly do not have to. Are you certain?"

She nodded once again, closing her eyes this time and reopening them after. Her face was as expressionless as ever.

"Alright," I looked off to the side, processing her decision. "In that case."

I stood up, walking to the open door, and held it so she wouldn't have to. With my free hand, I gestured for her exit first. She let the door go. Her eyes seemed to study me for a second before she walked through the doorway. I walked through after and the door closed behind me.

Side by side, she and I walked. The Summit House was coming into view, the meet up location was becoming closer.

"Outside of you and me, there's three people," I told her. "You'll get more information once they show up."

Why did she decide to come?

Her face was expressionless, not smiling, not frowning, as she daintily walked.

More people. More weight. My hands feel it.

Multiple small white stones that were immovable made the smooth pathway. This was certainly the Summit House area. Now the congregation spot would be around here somewhere.

Off ahead, three people stood where the spot would be located. The three of them were talking to each other.

They're here a little bit early.

As I came closer, they started turning their heads looking, Azmach's and Lamonte's eyes widening in surprise.

"Ain't no way, boi." Lamonte shook his head.

"Who's that?" Asher asked because of Lamonte's reaction.

"That's who we were talking about finding." Azmach said. "Ivania."

"Swear?" Asher asked jokingly with emphasis.

I stopped in front of them. Ivania stopped a few inches behind me to my right.

"Hello, Ivania." Azmach said. "It's Ivania, right?"

She nodded.

"Good. You might know this, but I'm Azmach." He pointed with his thumb at Lamonte. "This is Lamonte."

Lamonte nodded, his index and middle finger extended in one hand.

"This is Asher." Azmach introduced.

"Yo!" Asher gestured making finger guns, adding a couple "pew" sounds.

Azmach turned to me. "How did you find her?"

"Walked into her," I answered. Technically true.

"Well that worked out." He turned to Ivania. "Glad for you to join us. Okay everyone, let's break it down."

Can The Degrees Of Planning Create An Optimal Solution?

"Let me get this straight. We're dealing with a God to get more of those airbag things?" Asher asked.

"Minor God," Lamonte added. "But that doesn't matter."

"Minor doesn't change anything." Azmach said, leaning over the large rectangular table in the Summit House's office from earlier. "There are some Minor Gods that probably could body a Major. Levaveus isn't on that level, but that doesn't make him any less strong. The danger is mainly the setup."

Azmach continued to lean over the table that he, Ivania, Asher, Lamonte, and I sat at. He drew a sketch of some rocky ground with half of a sphere some inches above it.

"This is Bake Oven Knob, Pennsylvania," he pointed at the rocky ground part of the sketch. "It's a forest in the Appalachian Mountains. And this is where Levaveus is at." He then pointed at the halfsphere.

"Levoao," the thought came back to me aloud.

"A floating island," Lamented summarized.

"We got a floating island now," Asher disapproved begrudgingly. In contrast, there was some excitement in his eyes. "How has no one noticed that?"

"Like the Barriers here. A couple Gods can make barriers. Levaveus's barrier is made of wind. Humans and Monsters can't see through it. Anything that flies towards it," he traced his fingers around the half sphere, "the wind currents it to the other side."

"So, how do we get in?" Asher asked.

"We can't," Azmach nonchalantly said.

"Well okay."

Ivania sat quietly next to me looking at the sketch.

"We're Demigods, he got his Bags stolen before, and we're in the middle of a war," Azmach emphasized. "You can only get in if he allows you to. There's no way Levaveus would let us into Levoao. That part's not even the issue."

"There's a cave within Bake Oven Knob that serves as a connection spot from Levoao to this world," Azmach explained further. "Only Gods and Demigods can get inside. Winds keep humans and Monsters out and from seeing what's inside. Gods and Demigods won't even be able to feel the winds. In that cave is where we'll be doing the negotiations."

"That's what you meant by 'cave'!" Asher realized. "Woah, that feels like decades ago."

"Now here's the real problem," Lamonte chimed in.

"Real problem?" Asher asked, displeasure sliding into his tone.

"There's more than Levaveus to watch out for," Azmach finished the thought.

Ivania looked up from the sketch.

"Violent Storm Spirits will be there," Azmach informed. "They're called Stromoios. They're like his guards. They got named Stromoios for being that. When I scouted the area, I didn't run into any, but we know there's a lot of them."

Asher narrowed his eyes, a thought occurring. "And the 'Stromoios', I remember now. It's all coming together." Asher's head angled upward, another thought obviously occurring. "What's a Spirit anyway? Are they ghosts or something?" Asher's hands were curved as his arms rotated over each other in front of his chest. He looked at Azmach. "Boo."

"Spirits are elements personified, mainly being wind and storms, earth, such as soil and vegetation." I answered.

"Wait, so are they Gods or Monsters?"

"Technically, they're Gods. "Lamonte answered. "They're created from God Aura. Over thousands and millions of years, certain types of God Aura related to Earth's elements collects, and a Spirit is born. The more Gods with powers related to a certain element, the more that type of Spirit pops up with that same element. That's why Wind and Earth Spirits are in high numbers. Also, they don't live forever. Most get some thousands of years, other hundreds, some millions, other eons." Lamonte shook his head. "But all Spirits die."

"They die? I thought that they were Gods?"

"They are Gods. They can have kids, fight for their own interests, everything. There are a few who can body Major Gods. Very few though. They just don't get the option to live forever like other Gods. They die naturally. This is one of the reasons why Spirits are sometimes called Lesser Gods. The main reason they're called Lesser Gods is because they're under Minor Gods in the Alkeeb hierarchy. Some are servants or followers of Minor and Major Gods, like the Stromoios."

"'Lesser God' is a bit of a derogatory term so don't use it," Azmach informed.

"He's right," Lamonte emphasized. "I'm just using it now so you understand. Reasons like that, mainly the hierarchy of the Gods, is why some Spirits have joined this war. The ones who are fighting are doing it by themselves or making allegiances with other Spirits or Gods.

"To gain power," Asher said, summarizing the point.

427

"But that's not the case for the Stromoios. Like I said, they're followers of his so they will fight to the death for him."

"Why do they follow him?" Asher asked.

"They've been doing so for eons," Azmach answered. "They are able to live in Levoao with protection and shelter, so it's a mutual exchange, respect built over time. 'Followers' might not be the right word. He probably sees them more as his people."

Asher nodded his head slowly, then abruptly stopped. "How's the cave layout?"

"No idea," Azmach said. "I was only able to scout the outside. Going in could've been suicide. There's only one small entrance to get in and out."

"But what if we have to get out?"

Lamonte shook his head.

"Swell," Asher sarcastically said. "Well nothing else can be done. So, how are we getting there?"

"Someone's ready," Lamonte commented.

"Aye, let's get straight to it."

Azmach smiled a bit before returning to seriousness. "To get Bake Oven Knob, it'll take around a fourteen hour drive. We'll leave at five a.m., so we'll get there around seven p.m., give or take. We'll then hike for four hours to a spot that's around the perimeter of the cave. We'll sleep in shifts until five a.m. Then at night, we go in."

"Why not go straight in?" Asher asked.

"Because around the time this war began, the Bags we've used were stolen from him."

"Yeah, I wanted to ask, you kind of skipped over it earlier. I didn't know they were stolen, who stole them?" Asher looked at Lamonte and Azmach.

"No one knows," Lamonte answered. "It was before our time. It was back when the older Demigods were still alive, and the one who stole it was an older Demigod to them. And it sounded like they didn't even know who he was."

"Yep," Azmach concurred. "He also dropped the Bags off at a distance so no one would see him."

"So, this 'older Demigod' just randomly dropped it off?" Asher asked.

"Exactly," Lamonte confirmed. "Well, not randomly. It was right as the war was starting, so he probably did it to keep us protected."

"So the plot thickens," Asher stroked his chin.

"The Bags being stolen is the main reason why we need to test Levaveus's attitude," Azmach returned to the main subject. "If we stay on the outskirts of his perimeter and he does nothing, it shows he's more open to our presence. If he sends Stromoios or comes to us himself, we run. Fast."

Asher stared at the sketch, continuously nodding.

"When we say stay in the perimeter, we mean the forest itself," Lamonte made clear. "We can't just stay in the car. By that point, we're not exactly testing how Levaveus feels about us being there. If we're out in the open, we'll get a better sense for what he thinks."

"That's why I needed you specifically," Azmach looked at Ivania. "I'm glad you agreed."

Ivania composure didn't change. There was nothing rude or impolite about it. She heard him simply without conveying a response in any way.

"We'll be out for three days, two days there and one day back," Azmach said. "If all goes well, we'll be leaving the same night as the negotiations."

Asher stopped nodding his head, the gravity of the situation settling in further for him.

"Five Demigods in one will likely draw out at least one Monster," Azmach said. "Us being near Levaveus's area might steer them away. God Aura sometimes does that to an extent, and the Old Domain should help a bit with keeping Monsters away, but don't count on either of these. Assume

Monsters will be after us anyway. Our formation will be very important. Lamonte and I will take the vanguard, Jason and Asher will take the main, Ivania will take the rear. You two"—he looked at me and Asher—"will always be somewhere between Ivania, and me and Lamonte. This will not change unless necessary."

Lamonte had a seriousness in his eyes, already knowing his position.

"For the negotiation itself, we'll keep the same formation," Azmach made certain that the point was clear. "I will be the only one talking. Jason."

I looked up from the sketch to Azmach, our eyes locking.

"You'll be the last resort," Azmach said deathly serious. "We won't start off with you telling him you're his son in case you're not. Or if it could make things worse."

"You're his son?" Asher quietly asked me.

"We're not completely sure," Azmach answered. "That's why it's a last resort."

"That would explain the air wind stuff you do."

"You'll tell him when we have nothing to lose," Azmach emphasized to me.

"What are we negotiating with?" I posed. Why didn't I think of this before?

"Nothing. Basically, peace and quiet. That's why I'm even considering a last resort. I hope it's not needed."

The room fell silent. The gravity of the situation pulled with such a strength that not a single person could lift their foot off the ground.

Weight. My hands were pulled down by it.

"That should be everything," Azmach concluded. "Any questions?"

The last two words floated in the air as a silence waved through the room.

"Oh yeah!" Asher realized. "You said to get the jeep to the entrance of Numetus. I didn't even know there was one."

"We'll show you right now," Azmach answered. "Any more questions before we go?"

Nothing. Silence.

"Okay. Remember, this mission must stay a secret from the rest of Numetus. War has given enough fear to everyone. We will not add anymore. Let's go," Azmach stood up and began walking out the room. Lamonte and Asher followed suit. While looking at the door, Ivania stood from her seat and slowly walked to it. That much I could see in my peripheral vision. My eyes were locked on the sketch, staring at the half sphere and rockiness inches under it.

Weight. My hands.

Azmach led down a wide, clean, white stone pathway with vegetation on both sides that didn't even reach past the toes in height. The pathway was somewhere to the right of the Summit House, beyond it. A white stone archway stood feet ahead. The pathway stopped in front of the archway, or rather that was where it began. A dirt trail continued where the stone pathway ended. Azmach, Lamonte, Asher, Ivania, and I passed through the archway and continued onward down the dirt trail. Trees were spaced and spread to the sides of a dirt path. Azmach suddenly stopped.

"The jeep will be there," Azmach pointed at a very large patch of dirt a few yards ahead.

Asher was busy looking at the arch but spun his head around to see where "there" was.

"Tomorrow morning, don't just climb in the car." Azmach said. "Wait for everyone to show up. Once we're gone, that's it. We won't be able to communicate with anyone."

"Wait, why can't we?" Asher asked. "What about phones?"

"Who's paying for it?"

"I don't have one, but there's gotta be at least a couple people who brought one with them." Asher looked behind him as if someone who would manifest with a cellular device.

"Again, who's paying for it? Even when payments are covered, the few times we tried using phones, we've found they can't connect through either Barrier. Even when we used phones outside the Barriers to call other phones outside the Barriers, we noticed that more Monsters were able to more easily home in on our location. There have been times that Gods more easily tracked us. That's why whenever someone new comes here with a phone, we explain the situation and they have to get rid of it."

"If cars that don't need gas can be made from scratch, why not make phones or other technology?"

"With the world we're in, there's not a need for a whole lot of technology," Lamonte answered. "Our powers and the stuff we do have is enough to take care of most things. When we're dealing with Gods and Monsters, what would having more technology do?"

"But what about phones though? Communication." Asher pointed with his right index finger. "Oh, and computers?"

"Where would these connect to?" Azmach rhetorically asked. "We can't really send satellites into the solar system or build towers all over the world. For computers, it's the same thing. Wi-Fi can't really be made from scratch, and it's gotta connect to the internet. We don't own the internet. We can't quite connect what we made to things that are completely independent from it. That's not how it works. Phones and computers are a bit harder to make than jeeps. We tried at one point to make them but couldn't figure it out. After all this, it could still make it easier for Monsters and Gods to track us."

"Well that's not fun," Asher said disappointedly.

"There's really not a need for us to rush and figure out a way at the moment. In the world of the Gods, there's other ways of communication."

"Ooh, now we're talking. So, what is it?"

"No point in explaining. We didn't have much, but what we did have was broken about a year ago. Even if it was working, there have been times when even the Godly forms of communication led to us being tracked more easily by Gods. Maybe if we knew how to fully use it correctly it wouldn't happen. Since it's mostly broken and the whole possibly being tracked thing, there's no point in trying it now. Perhaps later we'll use it when it's fixed, and we learn how to use it or are more equipped for the consequences."

"Gentlemen, and lady," Asher pointed right at Ivania. "It is at this moment I'm using the word 'bummer' unironically." Asher stared at Azmach. "I have never used the word 'bummer' unironically until now."

Azmach cracked a smile. "I didn't know our demographic used 'bummer' at all."

"You see I wasn't going to say it!" Lamonte laughed.

All their laughter filled the air. Ivania didn't react. As soon as it calmed, Azmach's face returned to seriousness, and he cleared his throat.

"Alright, we'll get the clothes now," Azmach said. "We won't be changing clothes during the mission. These clothes are to be put on tomorrow morning before we meet up. Ivania, do you need any clothes for the mission?"

She shook her head.

"Cool," Azmach started walking back through the archway. The other three and I followed.

"We'll all still go there in case either of you" —he looked from Ivania and I— "change your minds while we pick ours up."

Knock Knock Knock Knock.

"Back so soon," Mae said looking at Azmach as she opened Fabrics Mount's front door. A smile was filling her face.

"Felt like decades, Mae," Azmach said, walking in. "We're grabbing and goin'"

Asher and Lamonte followed behind him down the hallway they usually took.

I held the door open for Ivania to enter, then walked in after her, the door closing behind me.

Mae's eyes were wide and her mouth was a small circle as her eyes locked on Ivania. "I didn't expect you to be here?" Mae stepped forward curiously. "Do you need some clothes?"

Ivania politely shook her hand, her face expressionless as usual. She quietly eyed the designs on the walls. Her hood covering the sides and top of her head became more apparent from the small quietness of her answer.

"Okay." Mae turned to me. "Do you need clothes?"

I shook my head.

"Okay… Clothes take a few hours to make, so if you change your mind later it might be too late to get them today." Her fingers fidgeted. Her head turned to the hall Azmach, Lamonte, and Asher went through. "Do the prerequisites, so if you do change your mind, it won't be too late."

The drop of blood and Aura in soil.

Mae walked towards her room. "It doesn't take long." She looked at Ivania. "I only have one sewing machine in here, so if you want to do the prerequisites, please go down the hall to Layah where Azmach went."

Ivania looked at Mae, then at the hallway that leads to Layah's room.

Mae led me inside her room, the door closing behind her. I went straight to the back tables, pushing my Aura into the soil and letting a drop of blood fall on it, as well as the top of the wooden sewing machine.

"What if somebody else needs clothes?" I asked.

"If clothes aren't made within a time frame, the last person's blood and Aura are automatically erased," she explained. "If someone new does the prerequisites before it automatically erases, it'll overwrite the previous person."

I stared at the wooden sewing machine.

"I'm guessing you all are going on a mission?" Mae asked,

her voice fluttering as she looked down.

I didn't move. Of course, she could put the points together. Asking about said points is another thing entirely.

I stared at Mae silently, my face blank.

"You don't have to answer," she assured me. "I just...figured...since you're coming in a group...and with Azmach like this..." Her right hand gripped her left wrist, both stiffening while trying to move. "May I ask you something?" Concern slipped into her voice, her cheeks sulking inward. Her eyes shifted, looking down at the floor which was suddenly inviting to her. Her face stiffened. "You know Azmach returned less than three weeks ago. He was just released from the Infirmary yesterday. I'm pretty sure he's not fully rested..." she tightly caressed her wrist. "...and healed."

Mae looked off, her body loosening as she regained bits and pieces of her composure. Once fully regained, she brought her face back forward, looking at me intently. "Make sure he stays safe."

Safe, the opposite of this situation.

"If you could, please." She requested.

Safe. That was the point of me-

Weight. My hands.

I nodded my head once.

Relief flushed over her. Some stiffness abnormal to her drifting away.

"They might be done by now," Mae said, her head perking up. "Let's get back."

Mae and I walked out of the room and back into the entrance room. Ivania was standing in the same place looking at the staircase across from the front door. I stood nearby her, waiting for the three to return.

Footsteps.

Azmach walked back into the room with Asher and Lamonte behind him. They all carried a small fabric bag which each at the most held one shirt and one pair of pants.

435

This set of clothes was all that would be needed for the next three days.

"Layah did that fast," Asher said to Azmach.

"She usually does," Azmach replied. He stood in place and accessed the people within the room. "Everybody ready?"

"Yessir," Asher said in an exaggerated manner.

"All set," Lamonte said.

"What about you two?" Azmach asked, referring to Ivania and I.

Ivania looked over to him.

"I'll take that as a yes," Azmach said, beginning to step towards the door. "Good seeing you, Mae."

"Come back soon," she said with a smile. "And not just for clothes." Wait, she was breathing a little more visibly. The visible breathing began to simmer. She is pushing her concern down to hide it.

I pulled open the door for Azmach to walk through.

"Will do," Azmach replied to Mae with his own smile as he exited. Exiting behind him was Lamonte then Asher.

Ivania stood there and looked at me. I continued standing there holding the door. She walked through, exiting out of the Fabrics Mount.

I began walking out, stopping to turn and look at Mae.
Safe.

I turned my head back, walking through the doorway, and closing the door behind me.

Do Steps Of Concepts Towards Actuality Shift The Perception Of Them?

"Make sure you get yourselves ready in time," Azmach said. "You don't need to bring anything outside of the clothes on your back. Sleep early. We have a big day tomorrow."

The rest of the day went on. It was essentially all routine, yet it wasn't. I had a piece of whole grain bread, walked around partially for the day, and sat within the Quiet Lounge with the lights dimmed inside.

All routine, yet it wasn't.

Night fell, and upon my bed, I lay sleepless. Was I tired? Shouldn't I be? How could I not?

Eyes open. Are they really? Throughout the day as an entirety, were they open? I moved my hands from under the covers to in front of my face. Weight in them.

The room was so quiet. Four people, excluding myself, were sleeping.

...

Quiet.

Even my breathing was quiet.

Quiet. Was it calm? Peaceful? What is peaceful? Is it circumstantial, a perception of a viewpoint in a plight within specific or broad frames of time? What of this circumstance, what of this plight?

Quiet.

...Tomorrow. Tomorrow won't be quiet. The next few days will not be quiet. What after...if after-

Tomorrow.

The son of Levaveus. Is this guaranteed is this certain? Am I pushing these people towards death? Safe. My hands, weight. They must not be pushed toward death. If any person must be, then it should be me. I know what I should do, what I must do. Still, tomorrow. The silent clock ticks as sleep continues existing in a nonexistent paradoxical sense.

This I admit. This I accept. All routine.

Time to break the paradox. Eyes close, yet stay open.

Sleep.

What is that feeling when one has not even seen the time, but somehow still feels that whatever is approaching is coming soon or is already here?

It's probably thirty minutes away from five in the morning.

Slipping out of bed, I quietly and quickly dressed. Royal blue T-shirt, black joggers, dark indigo high top leather casual shoes, black hooded zipper jacket. Out of the room, I went. Down multiple stairs and out the front door, I headed towards Numetus's entrance where the jeep would be.

The surroundings were in shades of blue and black because of just how early in the morning it was. The air was slightly chilly. Numetus was silent and vacant. It wasn't even five after all.

I walked through the Main Center, feeling each step. Each

step? Feeling? Perhaps that wasn't the right word to describe what I mean. Mean. Meaning. There were more to these footsteps than what the word implied.

Step.

Meaning.

Steps.

Admittance.

Steps closer.

Acceptance.

The archway of the entrance came into view.

crackle- autumn leaves were on the ground. They didn't fill the area; however, autumn was certainly here. A few more weeks and the ground would be filled.

Past the archway and further down, the jeep sat exactly where it was supposed to be. It was black with partially tinted windows and compact in size. The inside was likely bigger than expected.

I stood next to the jeep looking off into the forest. There were leaves that were still green, but yellows and reds were becoming the more prominent colors. Some trees had enough space between them for the jeep to drive through, while other parts of the forest were not so easily passable. It would likely take some time to drive around.

A small breeze blew, and my hair waved in response. My clothes swayed from the little force it exerted. Another breeze blew, causing leaves on the ground to flutter, and my hair to wave once again. Why is it so…practically peaceful? What is peaceful in this?

Breeze, leaves fluttering, hair waving. Calm and quiet.

crackle

crackle– a person was-

shuffle- walking closer.

I turned to see Asher wide awake as if it were midday on a restful week. He was wearing some of the fresh clothes he received yesterday. Azmach and Lamonte would be doing the same. Asher wore a light brown hoodless jacket, gray jeans, black shoes, and a dark orange shirt.

"Yo," Asher said, pressing his index and middle fingers together in a greeting. He stood next to the car. "Can't believe we're doing this. You slept well?"

Sleep. What matters here is this mission, fixing what I have done, and ultimately all of this.

"I feel the same," Asher replied steadily to my silence. "I slept kind of iffy. Like 'eh.'" He placed his hand on the side of the jeep. "Pennsylvania... We got a long way to go."

crackle- one person.

shuffle

Ivania stepped forward. Her hands were softly closed and at chest level as she calmly, with her usual expressionlessness, looked at me and the jeep.

"Yo," Asher greeted with his usual expressive smile. "Looks like we're just about ready."

crackles- more than one person.

shuffles

Azmach and Lamonte were walking up. Azmach was holding a brown bag that probably held food and water.

"Right on cue," Asher commented.

"Everyone's here," Lamonte noted.

"You know what it is. Let's start driving."

"Before that," Azmach interjected with a seriousness in his tone as if he foresaw everyone's and my impending death. "I need you three to understand something." He looked back and forth between Asher, Ivania, and me. "I need to make it clear. You three don't have to do this. Especially you two," he looked at Asher and me. "What we're about to do, let's keep it a buck. Let's get real... You might not make it out. And there's a high chance of that. Let me say it straight. You could die." He stressed the word "die" more than any other word he said thus far. "If you don't want to go. Now's your last chance."

Azmach went quiet to allow his words to digest, and that quietness stayed.

"I already said I'm going regardless," I reminded with emphasis.

A breeze blew, stripping the silence that followed those words. My hair waved with my clothes acting in similar fashion. The clothes of the four people around me waved similarly as the silence gradually returned, the breeze steadily vanishing.

"So I'm going regardless," I accentuated.

"Well when you put it that way, same here," Asher agreed. "We're friends, right?"

I turned to look at Ivania. This was her chance to depart.

Ivania eyes met mine. She lightly nodded her head.

I turned back to Azmach and Lamonte.

"That settles it," Lamonte said more so to himself.

"Okay. Then, let's get started," Azmach said as he opened the trunk, the surface underneath his fingers glowing for a second before it would open. He placed the bag inside and closed the trunk. "We'll have specific seating for attack and defense. Lamonte will be in the passenger seat. Ivania, you'll sit behind the driver's seat so you can aim through all windows. I can't attack while driving, so be even more on the look out. Jason, you'll sit in the middle, and Asher, you'll sit in the seat behind Lamonte. I'll be driving mainly because I'm the only one with a license. If police pull up, we can't have them asking too many questions."

"I actually do have a license," Asher informed.

"You do?"

"Yeah."

"Why didn't you say anything back when I asked at that school?"

"You mean when the school was getting torn apart? Yeah, I wasn't thinking about driving then."

"Shoot, I can't get mad at you. You having a license gives

us more options. If anything starts bugging, you might have to drive. Be ready for that."

"Gotcha."

"Jason, while we're driving, you need to do the Speed Up Process. You should finish Adjusting sometime on the way there. I'd give it halfway. Don't push your Aura out too much. Five Demigods in a car alone is enough to have Monsters come after us."

I nodded once.

"I think we're good," Lamonte affirmed.

"Now that that's settled," Azmach said. "We're driving fourteen hours straight, if not longer. We're not stopping until we get there." He walked to the driver's door and opened it. "Let's ride."

Two more doors opened as Azmach, Lamonte, and Asher got inside the jeep.

I opened the left backseat jeep door. The inside was in fact bigger than expected. The seats were black leather and the interior was relatively warm. I slid into the middle seat.

Close-Asher's right side backseat door.

Close-Lamonte's passenger door.

Close-Azmach's driver door.

Ivania stepped into the jeep, sitting next to me. She really didn't take up much space, as she was relatively short and small. Her being slim only added more space for me and her. She gently closed the door.

Azmach placed his right hand on the dashboard, his fingers lit up in dim yellowish golden light. The dashboard where his fingertips touched also displayed that color like a heat flash, then disappearing.

Vroom-the jeep roared to life.

"Seatbelts," Azmach told the entire car as he himself clicked his into place.

Three clicks followed.

"Here we go," Azmach said, gripping the wheel. The car

drove forward, going past trees and driving over rocky and hilly terrain.

"It'll take a bit of driving through this before we're on the nearest road," Azmach informed.

Azmach would only drive faster on relatively flatter terrains. It was a jeep, still it couldn't go up ninety-degree angles. He would turn to avoid things that might have been too tight, too high, or too low. He didn't need to do this often. Some point in the past, the path must have been somewhat cleared to move through with ease.

For a second, I felt as if I had passed through a ray of light that wrapped around me then let go once I passed its threshold.

"We're now past the Inner Barrier," Azmach informed. "Watch out for any Gods."

Asher's eyes widened for a second. He instantly focused on anything outside of his window. Lamonte was already staring out his.

Azmach increased the speed. He drove further and further.

The ray of light feeling appeared then disappeared once again.

"We're now past both layers of the Barriers," Azmach informed. "Now also look out for any Monsters."

Monsters and Gods.

I turned left to look out the window and scanned the surroundings for any danger. Ivania was already looking out of it before shifting herself to look forward. She was watching where the jeep was driving.

I'll start the Speed Up Process. Grasp. Pull.

The early morning shifted as time passed, the sun becoming more prominent.

"I spy with my little eye, something green," Asher quizzed Lamonte.

"A tree," Lamonte bluntly said with no patience.

"Okay. That's the fifth time in a row, you've got to be cheating."

"That's the fifth time you chose a tree and we're surrounded by trees."

"A road's ahead," Azmach pointed out.

Sure enough, a skinny, empty road with barely room for two lanes was ahead. Both sides of it were surrounded by forest. Azmach smoothly turned onto it.

Grasp. I was pulling my Aura slowly. It was much easier than ever before. It felt natural.

"Need I remind everyone to wear seatbelts?" Azmach raised his tone a bit to make sure he was heard.

Asher and Lamonte exchanged looks, then turned to me and Ivania. Ivania glanced at me and my absently fastened seatbelt.

"Jason, remember when we were escaping the school?" Azmach asked. "Do you want to go flying like you did then?"

History need not repeat itself. I grabbed my seatbelt and slowly clicked it into place.

"There we go," Azmach said to my seatbelt clicking.

The sun was coming out further as time went on. A car passed on the left, driving in the opposite direction. The skinny road was curving right, the trees on both sides opening. Lone older houses began to appear on both sides at random. As the driving continued, the forest on both sides began to open further as more homes filled the area. The skinny road was widening. The road began intersecting with other roads. It was becoming closer to some main road, or a highway.

How many hours have passed?

Grasp.

Asher hummed to himself for a second.

Ivania had a book open in her delicate hands. She periodically looked out the window to make sure there was no danger.

Lamonte was leaning against his car door, obviously wanting to be there already.

The jeep took a turn.

Grasp. Pull. It feels almost as if I don't need to do it anymore. It's basically completely natural. I might be done Adjusting.

"Now hear me out," Asher tried to say.

"I'm not doing this," Lamonte cut through his words.

"If we give Levaveus ice cream—"

"I'm abouta slide you."

"He'll give us all the Wind Bags we want."

"I'm abouta slide you!"

"It's the food of the Gods, is it not?"

"Who allowed him in here?"

"You. Or did you forget?"

"I'm jumping out the car." Lamonte grabbed the handle and tried unlocking his door.

Azmach was trying to hold back laughter.

Ivania continued reading as if nothing except silence existed.

Periods of natural silence appeared and departed as time ticked.

"Jason, how much have you Adjusted?" Azmach asked, peering forward to see where the vehicle ahead of him would move. "Use your Aura real quick."

Grasp. I didn't even need to pull anymore. I didn't even need to grasp. A small amount of my Aura came out.

"Didn't feel anything until you did that," Azmach commented. "Feels like you're fully Adjusted." He smiled. The smile faded quickly after, his mind clearly on the Reverse Bags of Wind.

Down to the last minute. Now I don't need the Speed Up Process.

The sun was bright, yet I could still feel a slight chill emanating from the window. Warmth from the inside of the jeep counteracted this, keeping everyone and me warm.

On and off highways. The jeep bumped at a turn.

A car drove in front of the jeep as another was nearing its left. Azmach hit the turn signal, drove into the left lane, and sped up. The car that was nearing at the right, now was directly behind the jeep.

Coming from the back right was a police car.

"Police," Asher pointed out in the quiet jeep.

Lamonte straightened his back instead of leaning on his door.

Ivania looked up from her book, glancing at the police car through Asher's window, then looked straight ahead.

The police car passed, speeding up.

Lamonte went back to leaning, Azmach let go of his stiffness, and Asher hummed. Ivania returned to reading.

"How much longer?" Asher asked Azmach politely.

"Five hours."

The rocks and landscape were becoming bigger around the roads.

Azmach continued straight forward, passing through another state.

State. The state of this. The state of this plight. Weight in my hands- does one simply do an action to achieve a purposeful solution? What actions shall I take? I feel that I know;

446

however, as the minutes, seconds, time, and existences draws nearer, an elaboration upon details is seemingly necessary. Can this even be done considering the circumstances? Re-gardless. Re-gard-less. Less the excess. Less the unnecessary. Focus.

"We're here," Azmach said. He parked the jeep, turning the engine off.

"About time," Asher grunted as he stretched. "Eeaayah!"

Lamonte removed his seatbelt.

"How's everyone feeling?" Azmach asked.

"Chill," Lamonte replied.

"Fantastic," Asher replied with a hoarse voice, still stretching as he took his seatbelt off.

"Great," Azmach said, clicking his seatbelt off. "We have a four hour hike ahead of us."

"Swell," Asher sarcastically remarked.

Ivania gently took her seatbelt off.

"Let's get going," Azmach concluded, pushing his door open.

Three more car doors opened, allowing four people to exit the jeep.

I took off my seatbelt and stepped out of the vehicle. My feet met dirt and gravel. It was a parking lot where few cars were present. Perhaps there were more cars here earlier in the day; however, it was now around seven in the evening and the late night was imminently approaching.

Three doors closed.

I closed the door Ivania used to exit since I used it to exit as well.

Trees surrounded the gravel and dirt parking lot. There were trails leading past the trees and deeper into the forest.

"We'll mainly go off-trail." Azmach said. "Watch out for police. They'll be looking for illegal campsites." Azmach opened the trunk and pulled out the bag of food and water, stuffing its contents inside his quiver.

How does it hold all that?

"Most importantly," Azmach said as he was halfway done putting the food and water in his quiver. "Watch out for Monsters."

Monsters.

After putting the last apple inside the quiver, Azmach closed the trunk. He turned and began leading towards the trees. Lamonte was right behind him. Asher was behind the two of them, trying to keep pace.

"Come on everyone," Azmach said in preparation and encouragement. "Get into formation."

Azmach, Lamonte, and Asher entered the forest.

Ivania walked gracefully towards where they entered.

I stood for a second, turning to stare at the jeep. This will be...

I turned and walked forward into the forest behind the four of them, getting into formation.

How Does One Step Forward With A Concept Entering The Realm Of Physical Life?

"The moon's out, but the trees are blocking most of it," Asher pointed out. "Do you need more light?"

"No," Azmach answered. "I know the way like the back of my hand. It could be pitch black, I could still find it. Just keep your eyes out for any movement."

"Already on it."

"About two hours in," Azmach informed. "Not bad."

"Speak for yourself," Asher retorted.

"We haven't run into Monsters yet," Lamonte countered Asher.

"That's true."

Azmach and Lamonte walked in the front as the vanguard. Ivania took the rear. Asher and I were in the middle of those two positions.

crackle crackle crackle

Shuffle shuffle

crackle

"It's really dark now," Asher commented. "It's like escaping Baltimore all over again."

"Probably will be worse," Azmach said.

shuffle

shuffle

"I'm still stuck on the fact you took on the Minotaur and the Manticore," Lamonte revealed. "Didn't even know the Minotaur was still alive."

"Same here," Azmach said.

"What else could we do?" Asher asked rhetorically. "We mainly ran, though. Can't take full credit."

"Yeah that's true," Azmach concurred.

"Even then, you two survived with no training or anything," Lamonte said. He turned to Azmach. "And you were nowhere near at full strength."

"Yeah," Azmach responded.

crackle

"To be honest, I'm still not completely there," Azmach revealed.

"No cap?" Asher asked.

"Not even a little." crackle. "I'm the only one who scouted the area so I have to go on this mission. Don't get it twisted, I'll be able to hold things down. I just need a few more days of rest. But there was no more time. It's getting too close to Winter."

"Which increases the need for food and the danger of attacks," Lamonte added. "Among other things."

I looked back at Ivania for a second. She seemingly was listening to the conversation, but not reacting to its contents.

shuffle

shuffle

Snap- not from the four people and me walking.

Movement stopped immediately.

Azmach cautiously peered around his shoulders into the darkness. Lamonte did the same, his hands balled into fists. Asher looked around sporadically, trying to not miss a single detail.

I turned back to see Ivania calmly looking around, taking her time as she did so.

"Could it be the camp police or other people?" Asher asked, his flat tone conveying that he himself didn't believe the possible assertion.

"Could be." Azmach said.

Snap.

"No time like the present," Azmach said, reaching for his bow and quiver. "Do you two sense anything?" He asked Asher and me.

"Not really?" Asher said.

"Faintly," I said, feeling that there was something within the area, but not close enough for me to be certain of its existence or to realize it was simply my imagination. "Presence. Not much. May not be anything."

"There are Monsters out there," Azmach said, bringing his arm forward, deciding not to bring forth his bow. "They know we're here. They're watching us."

Asher's eyes widened slightly.

"I think they won't do anything for now," Lamonte surmised. "Let's go on."

"You're right," Azmach agreed. "Keep your guards up. We're almost there. Just a little bit more."

The two of them stepped forward, prompting, Ivania, me, and Asher to walk.

It was growing darker as the walking continued, passing trees, up and down mountainous hills, over rocks, twigs, mud, and under low hanging branches. The air cooled as the night matured, and the sky was masked by trees.

shuffle

shuffle

While walking, Azmach continuously peered around corners, his shoulders, and the darkness at the edges of where eyes adjusted to the little amount of light could see. Lamonte's hands were always at the ready, balled into fists. He was surveying around each step.

No movement so far. I looked back at Ivania to make sure nothing was behind her. All clear thus far.

shuffles

crackles

More snaps were created somewhere in the distance off to the right.

Asher looked in the direction of the snaps but continued onward towards the destination.

Up more rocks, and through more undergrowth, Azmach began to slow down.

"Here we are," Azmach said. He stopped next to a tree. "An Old Domain."

Old Domain?

I stepped up towards where he stopped. This feeling. Where have I felt it? The air, the atmosphere, all of it felt similar to something. There was something in it, like remnants of Aura. This isn't the first time I've felt it.

Where then?

"Down there, behind that big tree." Azmach pointed ahead. "That's the edge Levaveus's cave's perimeter."

Standing tens of feet ahead was a tree larger than any of its neighbors, big enough for three people to lean against its very front alone. The tree wasn't significant on its own, but circumstances are what made it so. No other trees grew to its front or on either side, but multiple trees stood behind it. It made it look as if the tree had stepped forward out of the group. Undergrowth filled the area in front of the tree, as if to compensate for the lack of other trees.

Asher stared at the area as he stood near Azmach and

Lamonte. Ivania stood slightly off to the side, looking at the large tree.

"Let's get settled." Azmach walked forward, heading for the large tree.

Lamonte and Asher walked behind him.

I know I felt this air before.

I walked towards the large tree.

shuffle- Ivania was walking somewhere behind me.

Azmach stopped a few feet from the tree and took out his quiver, pulling water bottles.

Lamonte came to a stop next to Azmach, scanning the surroundings.

"Were you attacked by Monsters when you scouted around here?" Asher asked Azmach.

"No," Azmach answered. "That's why I don't know which Monsters are in this area."

"We need to wisely choose shifts," Lamonte said as he grabbed a water bottle and continued to scan the surroundings. "I'd go with two per, one shift being solo."

"Sounds good." Azmach tossed Asher a water bottle. "Let's eat up first."

I stopped at the large tree and sat down, lying by back against its bark.

The sound of light movements came from my right, so I turned to see Ivania some feet away from me lying against the tree.

More water bottles were passed and food was taken out, the food being mainly apples and bread.

I stared at a piece of whole wheat bread, taking a bite out of it. Moist. I haven't eaten today until now. After more bites and drinking water, I laid my head back.

My legs were somewhat sore. They weren't sore strictly from walking. The soreness came from not having to walk for hours to suddenly walking for hours with no breaks. And tomorrow. Tomorrow.

"Alright everyone," Azmach called to attention.

Asher was on the ground five feet away from Azmach, and turned to look at him once he started talking. Lamonte was still standing next to Azmach as Azmach continued to dig through his quiver. Ivania stopped nibbling her bread and looked at Azmach. I turned to look at him from ten feet away.

What does he want to say?

"We're going to decide the sleeping shifts," announced Azmach. "I agree with Lamonte's idea. There's going to be two groups of two and one group of one."

"I'll be the one," Lamonte decided.

"It's fine, I got it."

"Naw. Between the two of us, I'm the only one who's running on one hundred. Plus, you're the healer—" He turned to Ivania as he cut himself off. "Can you heal too?"

Ivania daintily nodded.

"Yep," he understood. "We can't risk either of you having a shift alone. And you two"—referring to Asher and me—"aren't ready for something like that."

"As persuasive as ever," Azmach responded.

"What else do you expect?"

The two looked at each other, smiling and nodding full of respect, before returning their attention to the subject.

"Asher," Azmach turned and looked at him.

Asher listened intently.

"You and Jason will be divided up between me and Ivania," Azmach said. "You'll partner up with me since I know your powers more than her."

Asher locked eyes with me before turning back to Azmach. He gave Azmach a thumbs up. "Sounds like a plan."

I turned and made eye contact with Ivania, then turned back to Azmach, Asher, and Lamonte.

"Shifts will be in two-hour intervals. The first shift will be me and Asher."

"Of course," Asher said sarcastically.

"I'll pick up the third shift," Lamonte specified.

"So you two will be after me and Asher," Azmach figured as he referred to Ivania and me.

Second shift.

"During shifts, you won't have to worry about humans showing up in this area," Azmach said. "What we need to watch out for are Monsters, and Stromoios. You'll know Stromoios when you see them. Levaveus himself might show up. If Stromoios, Levaveus, or both come into our vicinity, we run immediately. No questions asked. Got it?"

The air was quiet, nobody breaking the silence since everyone and I understood.

"Get ready, we'll start sleeping in shifts soon." Azmach concluded.

"Before that," Asher added. "Make sure everyone sleeps kinda close to me since the temperature will drop later tonight."

"Good thinking. Let's scoot over closer to the tree."

Azmach picked up his quiver as Asher stood up. Lamonte was already walking closer to me and Ivania, stopping only a few feet to my left. Azmach and Asher casually walked over and stopped about a foot or two away from Lamonte. Asher sat down where he stood.

Azmach placed the quiver on the ground. "Since it will get colder tonight, there are extra jackets for anyone who needs them." He pushed his empty water bottle inside of the quiver. "Pass me your empty water bottles."

Asher and Lamonte did just that.

I grabbed mine off the ground and turned to Ivania. "Are you done with yours?"

She held her eyes on mine for a second, grabbing her bottle and holding it out to me.

I grabbed it and stood up, stepping over to Azmach , and held out both my and Ivania's empty bottles. Azmach grabbed—

Snap.

Pause. It wasn't loud. Doesn't mean it wasn't present.

Asher's head shifted to the trees surrounding the perimeter of the undergrowth and large tree. Azmach looked ahead, slightly crouching as his right hand crept over his shoulder, about to grab his bow. Lamonte's mouth clenched, his fists having the same disposition. Ivania was blankly looking forward at the trees.

Seconds passed. No one moved. The snapping sounds had yet to continue.

"Definitely a Monster?" Asher asked, breaking the silence.

"Yeah," Lamonte nodded his head, his eyes as narrowed as his mouth and fists were clenched.

They scanned the surrounding trees further.

"You three go to sleep," Azmach said. "Us standing around won't change what the Monsters will do."

"If you're ready," Lamonte said. He finally sat down, lying in the undergrowth. His face was aimed towards the direction where the snap came from. He was ready for a fight.

"Tomorrow will be harder," Azmach said. "Get some sleep."

I walked back to the large tree, sitting down and laying my back against its bark.

Monsters. The Stromoios. Levaveus himself.

Levaveus's Bags. Reverse Wind Bags. In two hours, a shift. In another two, sleep. Then...negotiations. With a God.

My eyes were wide open. I had to force them shut. I must rest.

Will it actually be rest?

How Can One Make Certain Each Step Takes Account Of Reality?

"Aye bro," a voice said as I was being shaken gently awake.

Asher.

I opened my eyes, seeing who I heard and was shaking me.

"It's time for your shift," Asher notified.

To my right, Ivania was already awake, sitting with her back against the large tree, but her head was forward off it. She was scanning the surrounding trees ahead.

I looked at Asher, letting him know that I was fully awake.

Was I ever completely asleep? When did I fall asleep? Suddenly, with no feeling?

"Okay," Asher said, scooting away a little from Azmach, who was already asleep in the undergrowth. "Imma catch some z's." Asher placed his head on the ground, curling up. "Don't hesitate to wake us for anything." His eyes closed, his breathing deepening. He was immediately asleep.

I looked at Ivania. She and I kept eye contact for a few seconds before turning away from each other.

The forest was quiet as the night stretched on. Oddly enough, it was peaceful. Why is this odd? The emptiness of the night? Plight, the night wasn't all that empty because of it. It was empty in the sense that did not pertain to what would transpire tomorrow. Despite its heaviness, the weight feels empty. Is there truly peace? What is peace in the grand scheme of existence? What exactly is empty here? An outside forest of openness and quietness, although considering the exact parameters of the plight's actuality, at which point describing it as a plight is certainly an epitome of an understatement, feels instead as emptiness. A bareness, a continuing increasing stress. Weight. Regardless. For days now, the increasing of the weight in my hands is like lifting a box filled with metal in which more metal is being added, and as of right now, that box is additionally being dosed in gasoline with a soon to be nearby match to set it ablaze. It's not empty. It's nowhere near empty. What is near are these Monsters. What is near is tomorrow. What is near is Levaveus.

Son of Levaveus. Am I, truly?

Gambling myself. That can be done; however, have I also gambled the people who will be affected by this? Last resort. Tomorrow. Levaveus's cave.

I must keep watch for tonight. Don't get ahead of myself.

I scanned around for a second. Nothing, no Monsters. At the very least, for the moment. Watch and keep watching.

Eyes open.

Time ticked onward. I'd say an hour passed—

Snap!-that one was louder than the other ones from earlier in the night.

I froze, only my eyes cautiously darting in the direction it came from. Somewhere, at the edge of the darkness...my head slowly leaned forward...the sound came from...some trees ahead to the left.

Smooth, slow, quiet tentative movements were to my right.

Ivania. I turned my head to her, my and her eyes locking.

Snap!-closer than the last.

I held my hand midway towards her, turning my head back to where the snap originated. Cautiously, I stood up.

There's shifting from where the snap came from…nothing breaking-minimum movements…shifting movements in the branches ahead to the left. Something is there.

I turned my head back to Ivania. Her eyes were sharp, pure concentration. My eyes returned to the direction of the shifting branches.

Whoosh-something quick, like a wind blowing. Whatever it was, it went over my and Ivania's heads.

Ivania was looking up, trying to see whatever just passed above.

It's either playing or testing the waters.

What if there's more than one?

Snap!

Probability speaking, there is more than likely more than one. Something quickly rushed above again, making the air rush with it. Either it's throwing something or trying to figure out how it will attack. Another rush. That's it moving. Or they.

Creeaaak!-a high pitch, low volume screech. It sounded like a hawk being trampled to death, mixed with the grinding of a metal grate.

I feel an Aura from one. So, it is only one.

Snap!- Further away.

It's moving fast.

Ivania's hand hovered in the air as if she was holding a crystal ball. She squatted while leaning forward towards the snap.

That fast movement in the air. No, it wasn't throwing something, nor attacking. It was flying. Scouting. What Monsters fly? An immeasurable amount.

Snap!- further away than the last one. It's retreating.

There were more shifting sounds in the branches above, but they were further away than the last snap.

The shifting sounds ceased. Nothing else was snapped. Quietness had returned. Lean forward, make certain. I did as such, trying to peer into the darkness as if I knew exactly where the Monster would manifest. My eyes altered right to left, a pendulum of cautiousness. I turned to look at Ivania, who was in the same squatting position as before. I turned back to where the last snap emanated. All of it was question-ably gone without a trace.

Seconds passed. Nothing.

Movement was behind me to my right. Ivania was sitting down once again, her back lying against the tree. If she's do-ing that, then…

The Monster did seem to be scouting. It won't do anything for now.

I stepped back to the large tree, sitting down and laying my back against its bark.

Which Monster?

My eyes stared off, focusing on the distance.

Night progressed. The air chilled, forcing me to zip up my jacket and slip my hands in my jacket pockets.

Ivania looked at the trees expressionlessly as usual.

Pure quiet.

Time. My head periodically turned left and right to make sure nothing was missed.

Something moved to my right. I turned to see Ivania lightly waving with a closed hand to get my attention. She and I made eye contact. With her closed hand, she gestured to Lamonte.

So, it's time.

I stood up and stepped over to Lamonte. "Excuse me," I said, leaning down as I lightly shook him awake.

"Mm," he groaned, waking up. He sat up, brushing off dirt from his brownish-red jacket and dark blue jeans.

"During the last shift," I began to inform him, "there was some movement from a Monster that I think can fly.

Lamonte nodded, listening and brushing off the remnants of sleep.

"It hasn't attacked." I added. "It's only appeared once".

Sleep left Lamonte completely, his mind fully awakening. "It only came by once, so it probably is weaker. If it's a weaker one, it would be too scared of the amount of Demigods here." He stretched, grunting as he did so. "Y'all get some sleep."

I stood up, took steps back to the large tree, sat down, and leaned my back against the bark. Ivania was already dozing off.

Even when I sleep, do I sleep? Could I doze off?

Whatever that Monster was…

I closed my eyes, forcing sleep to come. I'm not tired at all. I should be.

"Wake up, man," a voice said, the owner of which tapped my shoulder.

My eyes opened to see Azmach. The sky was a dimmed light blue. It was early in the morning; a cool temperature and moistness was in the air.

There was undeniably something familiar about the atmosphere here. It felt like it was rich in Aura. Where have I felt this before?

Ivania was already awake to my right.

"Like half a day?" Asher asked. The question wasn't quite audible since he sat a distance from Azmach, Ivania, and me.

"Yeah, about," Lamonte responded, his words also not quite audible.

"Gotta get up," Azmach said standing in front of me, making sure I was awake.

"I'm up," I said to Azmach.

"We have hours." Asher tried to persuade Lamonte of something I didn't hear.

"Good," Azmach said to me. "We just have to wait until nightfall."

"Of having to keep watch." Lamonte countered Asher.

Azmach stepped away.

"I never said not to do that," Asher countered Lamonte's counter. "Have to make time pass somehow, and I'm the rock paper scissors king."

Azmach sat down on a broader patch of undergrowth.

"I wouldn't wish for that. I'd rather time go by slowly." Lamonte said, a small amount of hesitancy entering his tone.

"I feel that." Asher nodded in agreement to Lamonte.

Their conversation changed and continued.

I leaned my head back against the bark. Nightfall. Hours, more than twelve if I were to estimate.

Still.

Mere.

Hours.

The sun shone brightly as the afternoon approached.

The sound of page flipping came from my right.

I looked there to see Ivania with a book in her hands around midway opened.

"Oh," I said, noticing the book. "You finished Things Fall Apart."

She locked eyes with me, nodding once while having her eyes closed, before returning to the pages.

"What book is that?" I asked.

She moved the book to reveal the cover.

Invisible Man. Ralph Ellison.

"1952," I said softly to myself. "Identity and the perception surrounding it."

She held her eyes on me for a few more seconds before she

returned to words on paper.

Identity. Self-perception versus the projection of the definition of who a person is from an environmental perspective. Is it even a versus, or is it merely an and?

Levaveus's son, am I? Last resort. That, I must be.

I leaned my head back against the tree, the atmosphere feeling…

That's it. That's where I felt it.

I stood up, the sun shining brightly on my face, and walked to where Azmach was sitting. As I was approached, he turned and looked up, noticing me.

"I have a question about this," I pointed up and gestured around …what did he call it? That's it. "An Old Domain?"

"Yeah, Old Domains," he confirmed.

I sat down exactly where I stood. "Now that I think about it, you've mentioned them a couple times. Once in the Summit House, and once last night."

"I probably did, yeah."

"What are they?"

"It's nothing crazy. Before Numetus was created, these used to be called Domains. Wherever we go as Demigods, a small amount of residual Aura is left behind. We're doing it right now."

I looked around the area as if I could visualize the residual Aura being left behind.

"The residuals dissolve overtime," Azmach explained. "But if we keep going into the same area constantly, and in numbers, it builds and builds and builds over years before it can dissolve, creating Domains."

"This sounds similar to Spirits. Why would this be created instead of a Spirit or vice versa?"

"Spirits are created from pure God Aura, and that Aura has to be specifically related to the elements. Domains are created from all types of Demigod Aura. The residual Aura within the area keeps mortals away without them even realizing it. If they're walking, driving, or anything straight into one, they'll unconsciously curve around it." Azmach abruptly looked up like a switch went off in his head. "Naw, that's not quite right. It also depends on the amount of residual Aura in the Domain. It's not a barrier, so mortals could enter if they knew and pushed themselves to do it. If there's less residual Aura in the Domain, it would be easier for them to enter. They would feel sick from the amount of concentrated Aura, though."

"That's why there was no need to watch out for people," I inferred.

"Yeah. Domains are all over and have been around for thousands of years. They're often nearby a God's location. They were where Demigods got supplies, heal, or just met up in general. Once Numetus was created, they became known as 'Old Domains'. They're a bit like a relic of the past. They're not really used anymore except for quick stops and cover."

Created.

"When was Numetus created?" I asked.

"A long time ago," Azmach looked up, waiting for the switch to go off again. "I'd say... Over four hundred years ago," he answered uncertainly. "Might be more or less."

"Why then? This war has been transpiring for seventeen years now, not even one hundred. Based on what you said, the Gods had no grievances with Demigods before this war. Outside of Monsters, there's no reason for Numetus to have been created hundreds of years ago. "

"There have been grievances in the past, small disagreements between individual Gods and Demigods. It wasn't all Gods and all Demigods like this war today."

"I don't mean disagreements when I say 'grievances'."

"Then I would say until this war began, Gods and Demigods basically had no grievances. I mean we did here and there, but not like this."

I shifted my legs to turn more towards Azmach's direction. "The Barriers don't just keep Monsters out, but they also keep out Gods. Was the Barrier that keeps Gods out added when the war first started?"

"Both Barriers have been there since Numetus was created."

I confusingly looked at Azmach. "Then why was Numetus created four hundred years ago?"

Azmach exhaled through his nose, reached between his shirt and jacket, and pulled out two dark gray, paper-thin, skinny rectangular shaped objects. He flicked them open, one becoming his quiver, the other his bow.

"Same reason why I have these," he revealed.

My confusion did not waver. In fact, it grew.

"There was a war before the one we're currently in," explained Azmach. "From it, this bow and quiver were leftovers in Numetus. They were made by my dad." He closed the bow and quiver and slipped them back in their place between his shirt and jacket. "I don't know much about that war. I heard it was much worse than the one we're currently in. Everyone was dying. Bodies were everywhere…The Gods and Demigods had to fight together."

"Against whom…or what?..." I curiously asked, flipping through mental pages to reference whoever's name he would say.

Azmach hesitated, then looked at me closely. "A God. Strong as they come. It's said his power exceeds the imagination…" He looked around the area, then turned back to me. "We don't need to get into all of that. There are Stromoios in the area. If they hear me bring him up, they might get agitated or jump to conclusions. Or both. The point is when that war began, Numetus was created to protect Demigods. Funny enough, it's still doing the same." Azmach looked off at the ground to his right.

The Barriers… their importance cannot be overstated.

Hold on-

"I just realized," I said out loud, feeling as if one thought shot through my head with such precision it pushed aside everything else in my mind. I thought about this, but not in detail. He kind of explained before, but there was not enough elaboration. "Back in Baltimore, that spot with the spiral branches you led to the day after the car crash felt like this place."

"Yes," Azmach said in a factual manner. "That was an Old Domain."

"I figured that out after you gave the definition, that's not what I'm asking. Why were you in that Old Domain in the first place?" I asked. "How did you know to go to the school at all? Not even that, how did you know to go to Baltimore? You said you were here on a scouting mission when you felt three Surges within two days, which led you to the school. Baltimore is a couple hours from here at best. I'm not sure whose Surges you felt, I don't know if they were mine or not, but there's no way you could have felt any Surge from there to here. Maybe I don't know how Surges work, but that doesn't sound right."

"No, you're right. You can only feel it if you're in the vicinity, not miles away. Those three Surges that led me to the school weren't from you or Asher."

"Then who?"

"They were from Pericly."

Pericly. It's like the world stopped and continued at the same time. Of course, it was him. I haven't heard his name in a while. Hearing that name again after so long…was it even long? It has been a little over a month since the school had been torn apart.

"I wasn't looking for you, Asher, or the school," Azmach said. "As you know, I was here scouting when I felt those Surges. The second I felt them, I knew it was Pericly's Aura. Pericly's always been a fighter, always trying to prove he's not just the bigger fish, but the biggest. He's been like that for most of the years I've known him. That's why he was at your school. He's not enrolled there. He travels around looking for fights to test his strength, to prove to himself that he's the strongest. He goes around at random without even knowing if there will be something there, but he does it on the off chance. That's why he happened to be at your school. I'm guessing once he felt your and Asher's Auras, he wanted to fight you both. He'll make a fight happen by any means. He's Surges Out on purpose to bait Monsters to fight him. He's done that with Demigods as well. Sometimes, he Surges Out to force Demigods into fights by creating the threat of incoming Monsters."

"Forcing a fight?" I asked.

"Yes," Azmach affirmed. "That's what he was doing with you and Asher. I felt three Surges near this spot" — Azmach pointed at the very ground— "within two days that came from him. I recognized his Aura immediately. It was suspicious. Then, he began Surging Out more. That's when I decided to investigate and followed the directions the Surges were leading. What I noticed was that he wasn't just Surging Out here. He was moving around this state and other states within a radius. I caught up with him at the border of this state and tried talking him out of whatever he was going to do. He brushed me off, of course, and kept doing it. Then, I noticed something else."

"Which was?" I asked.

"The Surges all led to a specific area. Baltimore. When I got there, I accidentally found that Old Domain we also used after our car crash. I used it as a makeshift home base as I continued to figure out what Pericly was up to. I tried talking him out of it again, but he just kept going. That's when I figured out that all the Surges were pointing into one direction."

"The school."

"The school." Azmach confirmed, nodding his head and

acknowledging how every event was connecting.

"About a week before I met you, I got into a small skirmish with Pericly," I explained. "Based off what you're saying, it was after this skirmish that he began intentionally Surging Out. So that would mean essentially, he was leading Monsters to the school in order to force me and Asher to not just have a bit of a skirmish, but to completely fight."

"A cage match," Azmach described. "You either fight him or the Monsters. If you don't choose in time, it'll either be both or just the Monsters, depending on how strong the Monsters are."

"So it's my responsibility for the school being torn apart."

"No. It's all Pericly's. He wanted no interference. He just didn't expect such powerful Monsters to also show up."

"Also?" I asked. My voice almost slipped into disbelief before I pushed it aside.

"There were more than just the Minotaur and the Manticore. When I first got to that Old Domain, those two Monsters hadn't appeared yet. I had to keep killing smaller Monsters that already followed Pericly. By then, I knew there was a Demigod in the school, there had to be. I had to sneak in a couple times to find who it was. It was two days after I found the school that we met. While I was leaving that day, I felt another Aura."

"Asher's."

"Yep. I knew stronger Monsters would come and there was no stopping them, so I warned you the day we met. I came back that day in the cafeteria to warn Asher. With the amount of Surges that Pericly was sending out, I thought you both were strong Demigods who just didn't finish Adjusting. You both do have strong Auras, especially you, so I can see why you two set Pericly off. I thought that you knew all your stuff, or at least some of it. That's why I didn't give you any details outside of 'They're coming' and letting my Aura out when we first met so you would know I was a Demigod like you. It wasn't until we were in the cafeteria that I learned that you and Asher knew nothing, but that wasn't going to change anything. It had been over a week of Pericly Surging Out. There was no stopping the Monsters from coming by that point. It didn't matter if it was at the school or not. Once those Monsters felt both of your Auras, they would have followed you anywhere. Either we left for Numetus or we would die. There was no time for me to tell you both things that would literally change your lives and get you to believe it. Now, add in Asher's mom. After I found out something happened to her, I got more information from Pericly when I tried stopping him again. From there, I went through news articles and asked around. Found her in a hospital."

"And healing her essentially made you human."

"Not just that. Her injuries were so bad, it took everything. I was barely able to make it back to the Old Domain. I was knocked out for days, I didn't wake up once. It was like I was in a coma. When I finally woke up, I instantly ran to the school, but as you know, the Old Domain was a couple hours' walk from where we crashed. It's also a couple hours' walk from the school. By the time I got there, it was already being torn apart."

A light breeze blew, making my hair bend in one direction while it passed.

"Hence your late entrance," I concluded.

Azmach slowly nodded once, before speaking again. "After the cafeteria conversation, I had planned to come again sooner, let you both pack and say any proper goodbyes. That whole situation forced my hand. And it got worse. Since Pericly kept sending Surge after Surge, it started grabbing the attention of more powerful Monsters, two of which being the Minotaur and the Manticore. And once the Minotaur felt your Aura"—he made an X by slicing both his hands in the air in front of his chest—"it was a wrap. Before I knew it, the Minotaur was destroying a side of the school. The Manticore might not have been attacking at that time, but it's on the same level as the Minotaur and was still in the area. At the time, I didn't see either of them, but that didn't change the threat. After that and the car crash, I knew those two powerful Monsters were following us. Even though I couldn't sense Aura as well at the time, I could sense that much. We had no choice but to get to Numetus."

A breeze blew, stronger than the last. By this point, it was just a wind that came and died. My hair whipped back, returning to its place after the wind's passing.

"I see," I said, looking off to the side as I comprehended what he said.

"I could've gotten there and found you both a lot faster if it wasn't for the school," Azmach suddenly said.

"What about the school?" I asked.

"I don't know...just...something about the school. I don't know what it was. It was like, at the school and a bit of the area surrounding it, it was...You couldn't sense anything. Not anything, but I mean any Demigod Aura, Monster Aura, if there were Gods there, you wouldn't be able to feel their Auras either. Everything felt normal. I've never seen anything like it. Like at the time, you and Asher hadn't Adjusted, so your Auras were constantly coming out and showing that you were Demigods. I couldn't sense either of you unless I was within the vicinity, and that vicinity was a lot smaller than it should have been with the amount of Aura coming off you. And this was before I healed Asher's mom."

"So you could sense fully at the time."

"I could. I don't know what it was about that school or the area, or if it's some object related to the Alkeeb Gods that I didn't see, but that's why once I found the school, it took me two days to find you. In general, the more powerful the Aura and the amount of the Aura, the more you can feel it without having to be within as close of a vicinity."

"And that wasn't the case that time."

"Not at all. Not even a little. It was like Aura sensing was being blocked. You could get the general area, but that's about it. And it got even weirder. If you think back to the day the school was attacked, you could probably feel some Monster Aura, but you probably couldn't tell exactly where. Whatever was making this Aura blocking happen was even stronger that day. It was like the interference knew what was about to happen..."

He looked off in the distance, as if what he was conversing about was manifesting a personification of itself in the air.

"That interference made the Minotaur not run straight inside," I realized. "Is that why it tore apart the school instead?"

"That's what I'm thinking. I'm thinking once it got there, it couldn't sense you as easily. It might have been able to tell the general area, but not exactly where. I'm thinking it got frustrated and decided to go wherever you felt closest to, even if it was the wrong place."

"Its patience wore out."

"That's exactly it...That school...Did you feel any of Pericly's Surges when he was doing them?"

Now that I think about it. "Not once."

"I can see you not feeling the ones away from the school and Baltimore. Plus, you were just starting to Adjust, so like most Demigods at that stage, you would have had a hard time sensing things like this unless it was a lot closer. But that school is probably why you didn't feel any at all. I don't know. Something...An Alkeeb God object that I've never heard of, that would make the most sense...I don't know...I'm just guessing...There's just something about that school."

"A something..." I trailed off...a something...like Levaveus's Wind Bags...what could...

SNAPS!-multiple branches.

SNAPS!-even more.

My head shifted right towards the trees where some of those sounds came from last night.

Asher and Lamonte stopped in the middle of what looked to be rock paper scissors.

Ivania looked up from Invisible Man, closing it gently with both hands.

A wind blew with an impact, whipping for a second before calming down.

"And I was just about to win." Asher said while looking at his fist.

"You always chose rock," Lamonte pointed out as he stood up, intently watching around the air above.

"Cause I go hard, son."

The wind blew in harder, scraping past the eardrums, before dying down.

Azmach stood straight up, looking around with a calm seriousness like the night in the forest when the Minotaur first appeared.

Ivania continued sitting, holding her book in her right hand. Her eyes were trained on the distance, waiting for a Monster to show.

SNAP!-closer and more branches.

Stand up.

I stood up, cautiously looking around-wind was blowing stronger before once again dying down.

Creeaaak!-same as last night, except louder.

Eeaaa!

"Brace yourselves!" Lamonte warned.

Snap! Snap! SNAP SNAP! —

CRack!-a large tree limb was cracked in half ahead, revealing two winged Monsters flying feet above the ground.

So, there is more than one. The pondering of possibilities from last night was correct.

Well then.

They were half the size of a person, having the body of a hawk with talons twice the size of its normal proportions. Their faces were ones of a woman contorted with a large and sharp beak and an assortment of feathers. They were colored in a mix of yellow and brown patterns. There was also something else different. A couple inches of the outline of their bodies were somewhat translucent.

Creeaaak! Their wings flapped as they looked around the Old Domain with beady eyes.

"Storm Harpies," Azmach called them by name.

Lamonte jeered. His hands turned red like metal under extreme heat in the middle of a forge.

Creeaaak!

Another gust of wind pushed past. One of the Storm Harpies swooped down in my and everyone's direction.

Dodge.

I swiftly took a step backwards to my right - a wing barely grazed by my chest.

Eeeaaak!-a scream of pain.

I looked up to see an arrow in one of the Monster's wings in front of me. Azmach bow was out, another arrow already nocked on his bow, aimed by his glowing hand.

I didn't even see the arrow fly.

Lamonte was already on top of it, his red fist crushing into its skull with his full strength. Sparks flew out from the harsh impact as if two metal pieces smashed together. His fist might as well have been metal. The Storm Harpy's body flipped through the air before slamming into a tree. It laid there motionless.

It had to be dead.

The second one was still in the air, eyeing the situation. Its wings flapped, spinning its body around, seemingly deciding if it would attack, leave, or stay and do nothing.

"These are weaker ones," Lamonte noted. "Azmach."

Azmach turned his attention to Lamonte.

"They need the training," Lamonte pointed out.

Azmach nodded. His attention returned to the last Storm Harpy. "Jason, Asher. You both will be fighting that thing."

What?

"Hold on, I know I cracked jokes sometimes, but this ain't funny," Asher protested.

The Storm Harpy dived at Ivania with its talons aimed. She ducked out of the way-the Monster stopped itself before slamming into the tree that Ivania and I used to rest against.

"I said you'd learn some things while on this mission," Azmach said.

It spun away from Ivania's proximity, afraid of retaliation.

"This is a weaker one," Lamonte said. "Don't worry, we'll be on standby."

The Monster dove at Ivania again, talons aimed at her throat - Ivania ducked, moving gracefully away from it while eyeing it closely —

Creeaaak! The Storm Harpy flew towards the way it came from, retreating.

Lamonte rushed forward, stopping in front of the direction the Storm Harpy was retreating in. The Storm Harpy tried to fly over him, but he leaped ten feet into the air, pushing it backwards with one hand. The Storm Harpy rolled in the atmosphere, trying to stop itself. When it finally halted, it eyed Lamonte and quickly turned around, finding that it was now blocked by Lamonte to its back, Ivania to its left, and me, Azmach, and Asher to its front.

The Monster looked around anxiously, shifting its head in circles. It looked skyward.

Creeaaak!

Upward it went, followed by an arrow missing it by a thread.

Azmach had narrowly missed the Monster on purpose. "I'll

keep it at ground level." He pulled another arrow further back, his eyes narrowing as the yellowish golden glow of his fingers slightly brightened. "You two go block off its right. And be ready to attack."

I hurried to the left, Asher behind me, and blocked off the Monster's right.

Now it's surrounded.

The Storm Harpy reared back, completely understanding its lack of options. Its beady eyes pulsated, looking around for a different opening it might not have seen before.

Lamonte's hands were deepening in their metal forge red color.

Ivania's right hand was chest level in the air, her fingers curled as if she were holding something.

Azmach held his arrow steady. "The first thing you do is find an opening. Next, you immobilize it."

Asher kept switching his weight from one side of his body to the next, as if he was readying himself to jump across an abyss. "You meeaan?Get its wings?" Asher asked for clarity.

"That's it," Lamonte made certain. "You go first, Asher."

"What?" Asher was bewildered—

The Storm Harpy soared at Asher with its piercing beak aimed at his chest—*Creeaaak!* Its wing was scraping past me. Asher hadn't moved out of the way yet.

I can't let that happen.

I grabbed the wing that scraped me with both hands. Pull - hard.

Its head turned, jabbing its beak at me. I arched my body around it and continued to pull its wing closer to Azmach, Lamonte, and Ivania.

Eeeaaak!

Pull - harder. With one hand still gripping the wing, I thrusted an open palm against its body, pushing it back into the center of three Demigods, Asher, and me.

"Good," Lamonte commented. "Make distance when you can't attack."

Asher rested himself, leaning forward with attention on the Storm Harpy. "Sorry about that. Don't worry though, it wouldn't have gotten me."

"It's not a worry," I said. "It just so happened."

"Speaking of 'so happened'," Asher said. His hand snapped open, a fire blazing mostly in the center but covering the entire hand. "I so happen to have this."

Asher ran up to the Storm Harpy, ducking under its wing and punching it—

Eeeaaak!

—He kept his hand on the same spot of its wing, not allowing it to slide off.

The Storm Harpy's screeches of pain echoed. With one wing severely burnt, and the severity continuing since the hand stayed in place, the Monster fell to the ground and now stood on its talons. Its head bobbed forward, aiming to pierce Asher-He moved out the way of its beak, pushing himself off its body backwards, sliding closer to where I stood.

"Hold that longer," Lamonte instructed. "You almost had 'em."

Asher exhaled heavily, grunting from his off-balanced footing from sliding backwards. He stood still to reset himself, his hand no longer on fire. "Okay," both of his hands opened, a fire igniting in and around each.

"He's coming again," Azmach brought to attention."

Scrape-Scrape-Scrape—Storm Harpy's talons dug into the ground as it ran towards Asher and me. It jabbed forward, forcing a space to open between where Asher and I were standing moments before.

An opening.

I gripped a part of its beak and slammed my fist in its left eye. It made a short screeching yelp.

Talon!

I ducked under a sharp talon that it tried to kick at me.

Eeeaaaak!

Asher gripped its beak and the burnt wing, now burning both to extreme extents. He pushed the Monster back further and further.

"Come on, now" Asher grunted, forcing the Storm Harpy lower to the ground.

"Hold it," Lamonte coached. "Push it to the ground."

"That's what I'm doing," Asher grunted.

Lamonte peered closer, his fists up to his chest level.

The Storm Harpy kicked a talon out-Asher moved, grabbing its leg—

Eeeaaaak!

—before it could pull it back. He pushed the Monster further down, grunting. His flames intensified, the Storm Harpy's leg charring.

Eeeaaaak!

Its screeches of pain grew.

The leg was unusable. Asher then placed both hands on the Storm Harpy's chest. The screeches subsided. He pushed further down to make sure. The last wisps of air rasped from its beak. Then, there was no sound. It laid motionless.

Asher took his hands off the charred chest as a diminishing amount of fire still blazed on his finger. He took deep breaths, looking at the motionless Monster.

"Not bad," Lamonte complimented.

"Eh-could be better," Asher critiqued.

"For the first one?" Lamonte examined the Monster, making sure it was dead. "Nah." He grabbed it, dragging it to the outer edge of the Old Domain.

Asher looked at his hands as if they were secretly communicating with him.

Ivania looked around expressionlessly as if the most that

had just happened was a leaf falling.

Azmach looked around the sky, his arrow still trained. Once satisfied, he loosened his pull on the bow string.

"Keep an eye out," Azmach said. "Once there's one Monster, sometimes more follow."

The back of my head felt tree bark. A mild chill was in the air. Eyes were looking around the Old Domain.

Eyes open.

Fire set ablaze in Asher's hand. Then extinguished. Ablaze. Extinguished. He examined his hands.

A page flipping sound came from my left, followed by silence for a few minutes. Another page flipping followed soon after. Silence. Flip. Silence. Flip. Repetition.

Eyes watched around. Fists were ready concurrently.

Eyes watched around. A bow and arrow were in hand concurrently.

Fire was in one of Asher's hands, this time not extinguishing. He stared at it, studying. He thrusted his hand up as if he were trying to throw a ball. The fire stayed in place.

"What are you trying to do?" Azmach asked Asher.

"IIIII think I have it figured out," Asher said, staring at the fire. "It'll just take time to do it."

Azmach nodded. "There's no written way of using powers. Whatever works and doesn't kill ya."

"That's one way to put it," Lamonte commented.

Asher failed to hold back small chuckles.

"Someone's shooting shots," Azmach smiled, turning to Lamonte.

"Aren't you the one with arrows?" Lamonte pointed out.

"Shooooot, you're not wrong," Asher added. "Speaking of shoot," Asher pointed at the bow and arrow.

Azmach's and Lamonte's eyes followed where Asher pointed. Azmach started internally chuckling, his teeth showing as he smiled in small laughter. Lamonte shook his head, cracking a grin while looking at Asher.

Page flip.

"This man here," Lamonte said towards Asher.

"It's what I do," Asher said bombastically.

Page flip.

The sky was darkening. It wasn't yet night, but it was approaching in a few short hours. It was gray with the sun peaking at certain angles. Those angles were disappearing, along with the sun, as time passed.

Page flip. Ivania was towards the end of the book.

"It's around five," Azmach said, looking at a watch he pulled out of his quiver. "I'd give it four more hours."

Admittance and acceptance.

"A few more to hold down," Lamonte said.

Before change. Before monumental decisions. Before monumental events. Before…Weight in my hands…weight in my hands. Is it only in my hands?

Aura-big-strong-coming closer-quickly

Azmach's head whipped in my direction. "Jason!"

I leaned off the large tree I had been using and started standing—*Gah!*-My body flew to the left-some force smacked the left side of my face—*Gah!*-body slammed into a tree. I feel my tongue.

"You good!?" Asher asked.

Heat was on the right side of my body, while the left side was cool.

"Don't move!" Azmach yelled, seemingly to Asher. "It'll leave you open!"

I placed a knee on the ground as I leaned onto the tree I slammed into.

What was that? Stay focused. Wasn't that the last thing Mrs. Grey said? Those two words? Now's not the time to deeply ponder.

Focus.

I looked up from my position.

"Jason?!" My name was called out. "Jason?!"

Who's talking? Lamonte. I looked in the direction his voice was coming from. I saw him in a guarded stance, eyeing the edge of the Old Domain. His hands once again were a forge metal red in color.

"Can you stand?" Lamonte asked.

I nodded, pushing myself off the tree and standing upright. What hit me? I looked around. Ivania was to my left, her and my eyes locking.

She was calm as ever, looking me over. Once satisfied, she took a guarded stance and looked off to something at the edge of the Old Domain.

What hit me—

It was taller than the last Storm Harpies. No, not just taller. It was much taller, at least seven feet in height, and each wing was at least that long. Its outline was less translucent than the other Storm Harpies, while its long and sharp talons weren't translucent at all. There were golden-yellow feathers and a splash of yellow, white, and orange colors all over its body. It was more slender than the other Storm Harpies, looking more humanlike than expected of a Monster. Its two humanlike arms had sharp claws instead of hands. It had no beak, and no nose to take its place. Outside of the lack of a nose, its face was a woman's that only had feathers bordering its oval-shaped head. These feathers were spread high and bent back far. It had human eyes, and they were full of anger and hunger.

"Storm Harpy," Azmach informed, his bow trained, the string pulled back, and his eyes narrowed. "Stronger than the last."

It stood tall, making its prominence known.

"We've noticed," Asher pointed out, his hands illuminating edgily from fire flowing underneath the skin. His body was tense as he stared the Storm Harpy down.

EEEAAAAHHHHHHHH!

-ear-splitting-

It flapped its wings, challenging those in front of it.

Breathe. Inhale, exhale.

Focus.

"Get in formation!" Azmach yelled. "Jason! Asher! You two stay behind us!"

Focus.

I quickly stepped into the open area with Azmach and Lamonte a couple of feet in front of me and Ivania a few feet behind. Asher was to my left—

The Storm Harpy soared forward. Lamonte intercepted, grabbing its wrists, trying to push it back. Neither of them were budging—It began swinging him around, using the momentum of its wings. A talon jetted from its side. Azmach slid backwards to his left, dodging.

The Storm Harpy snarled.

While being swung, Lamonte released his right hand's grip on its wrist and pulled his arm back. He let his red fist fly. The Storm Harpy moved its head-it wasn't fast enough. Sparks. Lamonte's fist scraped along the side of the Monster, he pulled back for another-the Monster yanked its arms, pulling itself free from Lamonte. Lamonte went flying—

-whoosh-

-like Azmach's arrow just did.

The Storm Harpy just barely dodged the arrow—

-whoosh-

barely

-whoosh-

barely

-whoo—

EEAAHHH!- The Storm Harpy's clawed for Azmach's face, snarling. It continued pressuring him, forcing Azmach to back up.

It was all too fast for me to see everything.

Azmach continuously stepped back, dodging the Storm Harpy's lashing claws. It just missed his head. Azmach repeatedly evaded the Storm Harpy's claws, his face strangely calm. He suddenly stopped with his legs out in a stance where his weight was balanced.

Bam! He smashed the bow against the left side of the Storm Harpy's face at full force. The Storm Harpy ferociously shrieked in pain, its body turning right where the bow's impact forced it to. That impact wasn't just for attacking, it was calculated. Lamonte was to its right, his red fist already pulled back.

Bam! Sparks, way more sparks than seen before. Lamonte pushed his fist forward, forcing the Storm Harpy's head to bend farther back than it should—

Wind burst from its wings flapping, forcing Azmach and Lamonte to slide backwards.

That's what it did to me earlier.

"This is..." Asher trailed off, his eyes studying the scene.

The Storm Harpy put its wings in front and behind it, trying to protect itself from all sides. Its arms were crossed in front with its claws out for easy movement. Its eyes sharpened, shifting between Azmach and Lamonte.

Aura. Asher's. I looked at Asher, seeing a fire in his hand bigger than any other I've seen him create before.

The Storm Harpy noticed too—I slid in front of Asher to protect him. Move!MOVE! My head barely moved in time, the claw passing near my face—MOVE! It just narrowly missed my head. It was all a rush of movement.

The Storm Harpy flapped its wings back, creating a wind that pushed away Azmach and Lamonte from coming up behind it.

It should be watching its front. There was intense heat on my left side. Asher's hand full of fire passed left of my face, slamming into the Storm Harpy's right wing-

"Ah," Asher cried out from something I didn't see—

"Gah!" I said, jolted. It's grabbing me! Wings flapping, the air rushed-no. It's flying. Grab something!

I grabbed the Storm Harpy's wrists to make sure it wouldn't puncture me with its claws. Its strength was immense, like trying to push a car backwards that was driving forward. Do it! I pulled its arms away from me. Regardless! An arrow whisked past. The grip on me lessened. Another arrow – two - four.

Now!

I pulled myself away from it, making just enough room and kicked off its torso, falling to the ground below. I was higher than I thought I was. About ten feet. I slammed onto the ground, landing on my forearms and knees.

EEAAAAKK!

I looked above to see the Storm Harpy flying higher, changing its position, about to dive bomb—arrows flew at it. Azmach shot arrow after arrow, only slowing down once the number at the top of his quiver didn't have as many available. The Storm Harpy flapped its wings hard, trying to cause a wind to push all the arrows away. Some were. Others were still hitting their targets, lodging in its wings, making the Monster gradually sink to the ground.

"Aight," Lamonte said to himself. He sprinted forward, leaping ten feet into the air and grabbing one of its talons. With his weight and momentum, he swung it downward headfirst towards the ground.

Crash! As such, its head slammed into the ground, the rest of it hitting the ground with a thud. Lamonte was quick on his feet, sliding over and smashing his red fists a multitude of times into one of its wings.

Snap! The wing broke. It won't be able to fly now. But that doesn't mean it's finished.

The Storm Harpy lashed its claws at him. Lamonte stopped his volley and rolled, keeping a safe distance away from its claws. The Storm Harpy thrusted its claws on the ground.

EEAAAAAAK!- It quickly pushed itself to stand up straight, letting out a piercing shriek.

Aura. Soothing, light, and delicate.

I looked behind me to see. Woah.

Silver light emanated from around Ivania's hand. In seconds, she was enveloped in this expanding silver light, not by a circle, but in beams and lines like the stars in a night sky in an assortment of designs. A bow and arrow were made from it; the height of the bow and the length of the arrow were both taller than her. She was already aiming the light arrow at the Storm Harpy, the light string pulled back as humanly possible as she could. No, this isn't human at all. The sound of enormous brass bells resonated with soft sounds of wind chimes.

I stood up, looking over every detail of the light surrounding her.

Ivania's eyes were concentrated purely on the Storm Harpy.

She let the arrow fly. The resounding sound of an enormous brass bell rang.

The light arrow shot out, piercing through the Storm Harpy's chest, right through its heart. It collapsed instantly, its mouth hanging open.

What the...

The light surrounding Ivania vanished, bow and all. She and I locked eyes, this contact lasting for seconds, before she returned her sights to the now motionless Storm Harpy.

Lamonte sighed and grunted as he wiped any dirt off his sleeves. "There we go."

"Any injuries?" Azmach asked.

"Think I messed up my wrist," Asher said, trying to bend

his right one without pain to no avail.

Azmach walked to Asher, assessing the injury. "Doesn't look too bad."

Ivania looked at the two of them from a few feet away, expressionless.

"Can you also create arrows like that?" Asher asked. "Ah," he lightly groaned, his wrist was touched harder than what was comfortable.

"Naw. Never saw that until today. That's probably just her thing," He looked up from the wrist at Ivania. "You waited for the best opening. They weren't kidding when they said you were a good shot." He immediately focused back on the wrist.

Ivania's head slightly tilted to her right.

Azmach's fingers glowed in a yellowish golden light as he gripped Asher's wrist. "Any more injuries?"

"I'm good," Lamonte said, brushing his jean leg on the knee area. He looked at his wrists, hands, and arms.

I felt my abdomen and sides with both hands. Nothing was out of the ordinary.

All routine.

I focused on Ivania. "Are you okay?"

She turned and made eye contact with me, nodding her head.

I broke off eye contact, looking her over. "No scratches?"

She shook her head. Truly, there wasn't a single scratch. Her eyes and mine met once more before I broke it off again.

I saw some movement where the Monster's body should have been. Taking a better look, Lamonte pulling arrows out of the Monster's body came into view.

"Asher," Azmach said as he healed his wrist. "You did great back there."

"Yeah? But I got this," Asher said, referring to his wrist, not satisfied with the outcome.

"You didn't die."

"But I was lacking bro."

"He's not wrong," Lamonte said while in the middle of pulling out an arrow. "That's literally your second Monster. I would even say first considering how weak the first one was."

"Well…" Asher looked deeply at his wrist as it was currently being healed.

Lamonte pulled out another arrow. "Monsters can get much stronger than that. You had the Minotaur and the Manticore after you. You would know." Another arrow pulled out.

"Why was this Storm Harpy stronger than the others?"

"Strengths vary per Monster," Azmach answered. "Any Monster can be strong. Like Lamonte said though, it was no Minotaur or Manticore." He let go of Asher's wrist. "It was no dragon. I'd say that's good." He said the last sentence referring to Asher's wrist.

Asher moved his wrist around, examining.

"We only have a few more hours until we go into that cave," Azmach's mouth tightened. "Sit back for now. Rest. But keep your eyes open everyone." He returned to sitting in the spot he was at before the last Monster attacked.

Lamonte carried a stack of arrows with both arms. "Here," he said to Azmach.

"Thanks man," Azmach responded with a smile, grabbing arrows and sliding them into the quiver.

My body was sore. Or was it my mind? No, it was both. My eyes were looking, but they also were not. Eyes open, mind…pressing. My head was resting against bark…time went on and the outside darkened. Weight, my hands admitted and accepted. Now to go about the routine, feeling every blood pump in my veins. Admittance and acceptance. Tomorrow is today, today is mere hours, hours is three at the maximum. Soon. Levaveus soon. My breathing was slow and deep, a heaviness in both lungs that somehow didn't hinder breathing in the slightest. No, there wasn't a heaviness. Why did I think there was?

Soon.

Ivania flipped a page, the creasing sound waving over to my right ear.

Asher was sitting quietly a couple feet away, tirelessly watching the trees at the edge of the Old Domain as night steeled in.

"How long do we have?" Lamonte asked.

"Another hour, max," Azmach answered, turning to look past the large tree past the other side of the Old Domain.

"Another hour," Lamonte repeated, stepping from Azmach and looking at the Old Domain edge like Asher.

Eyes open.

Regardless of which direction one faces, without even realizing it, each step taken will be forward or back. The reality that will or will not disprove the unelaborated of thus far with manifest. Is it the existence of time or the perception of the parameters surrounding it that changes its meaning? Isn't it both, an all the above definition in the grander sense of defining perspective of a powerfully significant aspect of reality, which can change the very foundation of what one breathes? Is it weight in those breaths, or an idealism of weight to perpetually create a mentality to be the building blocks of mindsets of reason, as to why to inhale and exhale, ultimately each breath being the logic behind taking one step after the next? Is there or isn't there a weight? Weight, my hands,

wait

Soon, Levaveus.

This is on me. I have added to this, molded this, and concluded this with a worsen plight. Soon, I will push if I must, and I will commit as such.

Admittance and acceptance.
All routine.
Levaveus's son…Soon…Soon…
Soon…

Does A Concept Brought To Actuality Decline Easily?

"Alright, it's time to go," Azmach said, making sure his voice was heard.

Time.

Lamonte was already standing next to Azmach. Asher himself was getting up, grunting a bit as he did so.

Ivania stepped forward, obviously ready to move.

I was frozen and thawed, motionless outside and completely moving inside. Soon is now. This is on me, and I will do what I must.

Stand up.

I did as such, looking at how dark the surroundings had gotten. Without a doubt, it was nighttime.

"From here on out, no one say a single word, unless I signal you to," Azmach warned. "We've been on the perimeter of Levaveus's location. We're about to go to the cave. Everyone ready?"

Seriousness and conviction made the faces of Asher and Lamonte.

"We're ready," Asher said.

"Then let's go," Azmach turned, walking around, passing

the large tree that Ivania and I had been leaning against since last night. Azmach led further through trees and across some rocky terrain. Azmach walked slowly in caution.

Over a rock, a twig snapping. The silence of the night outside of me and the four people's movements continued as the destination became only steps away. Forward with each breath.

Eyes open.

Azmach stopped next to a skinny tree, peering his head forward past its trunk and branches. "There it is."

Ahead, the area had no trees or vegetation of any kind. Small dark gray rocks were scattered across the ground, becoming bigger and more prominent as they went further out, leading towards a large rock that looked to be the side of a mountain. It had an opening the size barely enough for a single person to squeeze.

The cave.

Azmach turned to look at me and the three behind him. "We'll go out in the open—"

"You don't have a choice," an older voice said. Dark, serious, and right next to the ear.

I looked to the right, seeing someone floating in midair. No, more like hovering. It was a man who appeared somewhat transparent and blue, much like a half solid ghost. However, this was no ghost. He could be seen through if someone squinted while standing extremely close, looking for the extent of his transparency. He had dark afro-textured hair that was cut low, his short dark beard, his somehow still noticeable dark brown skin, and looked to be in his forties. He wore a long black and silver ceremonial robe that hardly covered his what looked to be black, formal, ceremonious slippers. Static lines of electricity sparked inside and outside of him at random, causing him to constantly flash. He was a storm compact in the shape of a person. It wasn't the fact that he simply wasn't completely transparent; it was because him being a literal storm prevented complete transparency.

Stromoios. Storm Spirit. Guards for Levaveus.

The Stromoios glared at Azmach, his eyes wide and mouth clenched. The storm inside him raged, causing electricity to spark out of his shoulders as the low thunder boomed from his center. His robe flapped violently as if there was a furious wind blowing.

"Glad you found us," Azmach said, regaining his words as he remained calm. "We weren't trying to sneak in."

"I remember you, son of Mynzonus," the Stromoios scowled. It wasn't his voice that was normal deep, it was the mixture of storms and thunder that made it echo and boom, while simultaneously being a regular speaking volume. He didn't blink, staring as if he wanted to summon a typhoon that could rip Azmach into shreds. "Of course we noticed you."

Azmach remained quiet for several seconds, just as he had when the Storm Spirit initially appeared, his face unmoving.

"You appeared the first time about three months ago," the Stromoios's jaw tightened, his eyes narrowing, the storms inside him swirling with thunder bursting louder and louder. "Same quiver." A line of electricity sparked off his shoulder, shooting straight backwards. "Same face. You know that we knew you were here again. You've been here since yesterday with these other Demigods." He glared at me and the rest of the group.

"We're not here to cause any problems," Azmach assured him.

"Your existence is a problem," the Stromoios's eyes were a doorway to anger. He scanned everyone, including me.

"We're here to negotiate with Levaveus."

The Stromoios paused. His clenching jaw relaxed slightly, and his narrowed eyes widened to their normal size. "Negotiate?" He drifted backwards a few inches, his demeanor calming down a mere fraction. "Leave now, or you will die."

"We won't," Azmach stood firm. "We have to negotiate."

The Stromoios once again paused. "Assistant suicide, is it?"

"It won't be." Azmach stepped forward towards him. "It's very important that we negotiate with Levaveus."

"Important?"

"*Very*," Azmach repeated.

The Stromoios went quiet in thought. Electric lines streamed inside him, one popping out of his wrist. He exhaled. "'Negotiate'…I cannot decide what is or isn't worthy of Levaveus for Levaveus…" He gradually stopped hovering, his black ceremonious slippers touching the ground. "Follow me." He walked towards the cave's narrow opening.

Azmach followed inches behind him. Lamonte, Asher, me, and Ivania followed Azmach in that order.

The rocks scratched each other as multiple shoes stepped on top of them. As the group and I approached the cave, the rocks were becoming larger. There were two other Stromoios flying that landed at the entrance feet ahead. The Stromoios leading the group and I passed them and began sliding through the cave's entrance. The two other Stromoios eyed everyone and me as each person squeezed through the opening. The entrance certainly was tight, not enough to get stuck, but enough to force someone to slow down significantly.

I pulled my foot inside, finally completely passing the entrance.

"Levaveus might be merciful," The Stromoios said to Azmach, who stood next to him. "That does not mean you won't die. Be prepared for death."

"We're also prepared for success," Azmach countered.

"Let's see if you can keep that confidence."

Ivania stepped inside, slipping her foot into the interior.

I looked up and around at the vastness of the cave. It was dim, but there was enough white lighting from the corners of the interior to see everything. There were Stromoios everywhere, with most of them being across the cave. Long, smooth rock structures with enough room to for multiple people to stand on top of ran along from the middle of the right and left walls to its corners on the opposite side of the entrance. These rock structures climbed upward, like multiple floors of a balcony without railings, and stopped at a certain height. The middle between these two ascending balcony corners had only one balcony structure higher than any other. There were no Stromoios standing there, unlike the structures along and around the corners. There were an immeasurable number of Stromoios in total standing on the rock structures at these corners. They glared down, appearing to be waiting for the signal to attack.

That's what's going on, isn't it?

"Walk forward." The Stromoios leading the way ordered.

Azmach guardedly stepped forward, walking past the Stromoios, who watched every person and me pass him.

"All the way down," The Stromoios added to the order.

The group and I walked forward on a smooth, flat, thin arch on the edge of a cliff. There were maybe four feet of space on both sides of the arch before the edge and falling into abysmal darkness. The arch continued forward and ended where Azmach stopped a few feet from the edge.

All the way down.

Azmach looked across the cave at the structures where the Stromoios stood a great distance away. In the entire cave, there was more room to fall down than to stand.

The Stromoios stared down more as the seconds ticked by. Some looked at each other, conversing, their eyes returning to fixate on the group and me, clearly more than agitated with the circumstances.

Azmach looked past his shoulders, beckoning attention without the Stromoios noticing. "A tight exit and the only way in or out," he whispered. "It'll be hard to escape. If we need to, the order will be Lamonte, Jason, Asher, Ivania, then me."

I looked back at the narrow exit. It was so far away now.

"If they start attacking before we can do that formation," Azmach added, whispering while looking around at the Stromoios and the cave itself, "keep what we have now and run as fast as we can. Everyone got that?"

Azmach stood in front, with Lamonte slightly behind him. Asher stood to my right, his mouth clenched as he seemed to be trying to swallow nothing, a part of him having anxiousness that he forced himself to press through. Ivania was behind me slightly to my left. She looked around, looking smaller than she usually was in such a vast room. Her eyes trained on each and every Stromoios.

A gust of wind burst out, blowing back my clothes and hair. The clothes flapped back for the three ahead and one behind me. Lamonte's twisted hair flipped back from the force while Asher's freeform locs blew to one side. Ivania's hood somehow didn't blow off. The gust of wind quickly vanished, but a new presence was ever more so appearing. Every person and I looked up to where it and the wind were originating from.

This feeling…

Light wind blew around, making clothes continue to flutter lightly.

Someone was coming closer. Every step could be heard. It wasn't clicks; it was more akin to quiet thuds. It was a presence that commanded attention. The room was so quiet outside of the little wind blowing around.

Thud.

Thud.

Someone was coming even closer to the edge of the middle balcony structure across the cave, high above where the group and I stood. The man stepped closer from the darkness. On that middle balcony structure were two rocks that were just below the chest level to his right and left that acted as a railing. However, there was nothing between those two rocks to block the complete view of him.

Another thud echoed past the ears, reverberating through the whole space. The earth didn't shake, but by this point what was the difference? The footsteps grew louder, until suddenly stopping. The man stood still, now completely in view of the entire cave.

The man had dark brown skin that was smooth for someone who looked to be in their fifties. Gray strands popped out from his medium-length black 4c afro-textured hair, his hair likely stopping at the bottom of his eyes when pulled down. It was tight coils going upward, so it was difficult to tell. His beard also had gray strands and it stopped halfway down his neck in length.

His ceremonial robes consisted of three layers. The bottom layer looked to be a navy blue robe, similar in style to the ones worn by the Stromoios, and stopping just high enough to hardly reveal the bottom of dull black ceremonious slippers. It was only a guess that under it were straight black pants and black socks underneath. The second layer was a black mantle which stopped just below the chest, with navy blue lines crossing each other throughout, creating a faded diamond design in the center. The top layer was a long hoodless cloak of navy blue, a few shades lighter than the navy blue from the bottom layer. It was the longest one, stopping past the ankles millimeters at the most above the ground.

The man stared down from the middle balcony rocks with wide eyes that became sharp due to the circumstances. Those eyes were fixed directly on the spot where the group of four and I were standing.

The wind blew more strongly before suddenly vanishing. The Aura emanating from the man was immense, flowing free with sharp points of poignancy.

Man? This was no man...

This was a God...

Levaveus.

"Porter?..." Levaveus's voice boomed, older, deep, and commanding the very air to silence further than it already had. "What brings this?..." He trailed off his questions, his eyes steady on the four and me.

The Stromoios who led inside the cave raised his voice to be heard from the entrance, "Lord Levaveus—"

"No 'Lord'," Levaveus waved off. "I am no X'stayn."

The Stromoios looked up from the distance. "Levaveus. They say they have something important to negotiate."

Levaveus's eyes widened, his clothes waving for a second then settling down like they should in still air. "Negotiate?..."

"Yes, 'negotiate'," Azmach spoke up, taking two steps forward, holding an open hand behind his side to signal that no one else should talk or move. He straightened his back prominently and craned his neck up to make eye contact with Levaveus's unamused dark brown eyes. "We're from Numetus. And we have a very important request to ask."

Levaveus's eyebrow rose, he looked below and across the room at Azmach. His sharpened eyes widening to their normal state further. "Which is?"

"We would like to request Reverse Bags of Wind—"

The wind spiked up, fiercely whipping.

The group and I tensed, arms raising or whatever came the most natural to instinctively protecting oneself instantly. Clothes flapped. Robes flapped. Levaveus's robes slowly flapped as if the wind hardly had any effect.

"Reverse Bags of Wind," Levaveus muttered. "You were the ones who stole my Bags, and now you want more?"

The cave became quiet again as the wind died down. Levaveus's look of wide-eyed anger did the opposite. The Stromoios looked onward with concern on their faces.

"How does a thief ask from whom they've stolen from?" Levaveus's face was stone.

"We weren't the ones who stole them," Azmach emphasized.

"I know you weren't," Levaveus said. "That man was…" He looked off to the side, seemingly reminiscing. "It doesn't matter." He brought his head forward and down again, looking at Azmach, the other three, and me. "Why didn't you return my Bags?"

Azmach's face was calm and determined, unflinching. "When we received the Bags around seventeen years ago. It was dropped off by someone who we didn't speak to or get a good look at. He left immediately. We only knew what they were and how to use them because he had attached a note."

"That doesn't answer my question."

Lamonte's eyes darted to Azmach.

"By then, the war had broken out and nothing seemed to be a safe choice except for staying out of it and away from Gods," Azmach explained.

Levaveus faced straight forward. He looked to his right and left at the Stromoios standing on the multiple rock balconies. They too were looking at their neighbors, mulling over what Azmach said.

Levaveus returned his face to staring down and across the room to Azmach. "And you need more Bags, so I will assume the ones stolen from me have all been used?"

"Yes."

"And they're a one-time use only," Levaveus reminded the cave. "You waited until after they were all used up to come here? To ask for more?"

The Stromoios looked at each other, Levaveus, and the group, including me. They whispered in hushed tones amongst themselves.

Asher's head shifted to Azmach. Lamonte's eyes went back to Levaveus.

Azmach hadn't blinked once since Levaveus's last words, unfazed. "Since the war, everything's been more unpredictable in the world of the Gods. There have been deaths. When we first received the Bags, we were unsure if coming here to return them would make it worse, so we played it safe. We only used the Bags when we absolutely had to. With all the Bags being used, the situation calls for risk."

The Stromoios whispered among themselves more, exchanging more glances, and eyeing Azmach.

Azmach's shoulders visibly went up then down as he took in a big breath.

Levaveus stood tall, his arms at his sides. Although his eyes sharpened, there was relative calmness in them. "I don't like that you used my stolen Bags."

The Stromoios ceased their whispers the second Levaveus spoke, looking at not a single thing or person except for him.

"Though using them, that I can understand. The stolen ones, I won't hold that against you." Levaveus rested his hands on the two separate rocks in front of his right and left that acted as a sort of railing. "You want more Bags. What will you give in exchange?"

"Peace," Azmach said.

Levaveus's face tightened.

The wind slowly blew, whooshing away the quietness.

Levaveus was tense, as if holding back a tornado of fury. No that's not a like. That's exactly what it was.

The wind blew to the right, gently with some pull showing it could easily be worse.

"Peace?" Levaveus repeated as a question. He removed his hands from atop the two rocks. "Is that not what we had before?"

"Yes," Azmach quickly answered, slowing down to his normal pace after saying 'Yes'. "We're saying that peace will continue." He slowed down his pace further to make his points clear without chance of a misunderstanding. "We won't steal from you or attack." His pace returned to a normal pace. "We have never done that, but since this war is still going, we wanted to tell you ourselves to assure you."

"'Assure' me? That doesn't matter." The winds rose, his

robes waving. "There would be no need to assure peace if peace would never be broken." He looked off to the side, a guarded expression on his face.

The wind blew, pushing my hair and clothes back strongly. Clothes of the people around me did the same.

Levaveus's eyes widened suddenly, a thought hitting him. "Who are you with?"

Azmach continued looking unfazed. "Numetus."

"Numetus, Alcahga, Demigod. Who? Are you with?"

Azmach's eyes narrowed. He readjusted his eyes to look normal, disregarding how he was feeling. "We're not with Alcahga. We only come from Numetus. And we're here only for Numetus."

"In this war, we're all on our own." The winds surged a bit stronger, Levaveus's robes now flapping in the lower areas instead of waving like before. "Some Gods have done their best to stay out of this power struggle. Others fight for the Empiric Throne. Some of those fighters use affiliations."

The wind blew past my ear, eating a portion of my hearing; yet I could hear Levaveus perfectly. His voice was in the very wind.

"They can be affiliated with Spirits and other Gods," Levaveus continued. "Sometimes, Gods affiliate themselves with Demigods." There was some fear in his tone during his last sentence, his head rearing back as what he seemed to fear was possibly coming true in front of his very eyes.

"If you're trying to say we're affiliated with a God, we're not," Azmach said.

"I never said these affiliations happen willingly." The wind strengthened.

"There is no affiliation."

"You can swear to the River Z'yieh for all I care!"

The wind surged even stronger, a roaring sound filling the cave. I had to squint to see as my clothes slapped me and the surrounding air. It looked to be a similar case for the four people around me. Asher had both of his hands up, trying to guard against the force. Lamonte had one arm in front of half his face, his jaw clenching. Azmach had both hands up, forcing his eyes to stay open since he was receiving most of the brunt. Ivania kept most of her body behind me, trying to shield herself while keeping a sliver of her head and body out, watching Levaveus in case there was more to come. And there certainly would be more.

Crack! The two rocks he used to rest his hands on broke in half from the force of the wind. They plummeted without a sound since their fall continued into the abyss below.

In an instant, the wind vanished, replaced by a brisk silence.

My arms steadily went down to my sides after the wind's swift disappearance. Asher's and Lamonte's arms went down as well. Azmach had his arms up for the longest, clearly thinking of what to say before letting them down gradually.

Levaveus's head was forward, while his eyes glared down. "I've made it this far by being cautious," he said, his voice echoing. "I've never intended to take the Throne. I've never wanted the Throne. I already have this," he gestured to the cave itself. "I am the King of Levoao. I have no need for anything else. As the King, I cannot allow any risks to my kingdom, the Stromoios, and myself. Which God sent you here?"

"None," Azmach said firmly.

Levaveus took a deep breath. "Block the exit."

Without hesitation, some of the Stromoios flew to the exit while the rest stayed in their same positions ready to attack. All of them became loud like the cry of war.

Lamonte's eyes flared. Asher looked around, startled. I turned my head to see Ivania looking at the exit expressionlessly. Her hand was hovering at mid chest level, readying to manifest a bow and arrow. I looked past her at where she was looking. There were at least four Stromoios on each side of the entrance with two between the very opening. And there were more coming to block it.

Levaveus's wind began blowing once again, this time at about half the strength it had when it broke the two rock railings. His robe waved and flapped as he peered down at not just Azmach, but me and the three people close by.

"Since I'm a Minor God and I keep to myself, the other Gods have not considered me much in this war." Levaveus's voice phased through the noise and wind. "Especially the Empyreans. The Wind Bags I create only affect Monsters, giving them more reasons to keep me out of their minds. All of that is gone if I do anything that other Gods could perceive as me having an affiliation."

The wind rose, becoming stronger. The Stromoios settled down in their positions, those at the door ready to guard and those in the stands ready for the order to attack.

"I need proof that you're not involved with any Gods," Levaveus said, his robe waving and flapping forward. "Even then, I'm not sure I'd be open. But if there is another God."

Was I being blown backwards? No, it just feels like it. My muscles tightened, trying to stay together. I went back to shielding myself, the group doing the same. Azmach only used one arm this time so he could concentrate on talking.

"There are no Gods with us," Azmach said, his voice somehow piercing through the wind. "We are alone. We have an answer to the affiliation problem. Say we tricked you for Bags so there's no perceived connection between us. We don't plan on coming here, unless there's a dire need like right now."

Levaveus didn't flinch at the prospects told to him. "That could work. I still need proof of there being no other Gods. Until proof is given, I'll hold everyone here."

The wind's strength decreased, along with its noise in the cave.

"For as long as it takes," Levaveus said.

My head snapped to the exit. There were more than ten Stromoios blocking the way. I more than likely couldn't take on one. Ivania looked around, most likely trying to find a different way out. I snapped my head back forward. Asher stood worriedly, shifting his weight from one foot to the next.

The Stromoios on the rock balconies swelled, their faces having no joy. They were all ready for death, and not necessarily their own.

Azmach leaned over to Lamonte. "What do you think?" He asked in a quiet tone as his hand hesitantly reached for his quiver.

"Exit's blocked. Outnumbered. More than fifty deep." Lamonte quietly summarized.

"That I can see."

"Either we take everyone on, we sit tight for Tyrone, or we push the negotiations."

"I told Tyrone not to come for us." Azmach revealed.

"You know he would anyway."

"That's true." Azmach looked back and forth from both sides of the rock balconies. "It'll be days before Tyrone realizes we're being held, and if he comes it'll be a full battle. I'm not sure he could beat Levaveus."

"And that's before getting us out." Lamonte looked at the blocked exit.

"Tyrone wouldn't come alone, so there would be more casualties," Azmach grimly said. "Even if everyone got out, he may retaliate against Numetus."

"We better choose fast. Levaveus is leaving," Lamonte pointed out.

He's what?

Levaveus looked around the cave, making sure everything was what he wanted; however, his body was angled to the side. He was turning around to leave.

No no-this

"Fighting with just ourselves isn't an option," Azmach said.

"That would be if we only had us two, three with Ivania. Sitting around isn't an option either. Which means..." He turned his head to look behind. "Jason."

I locked eyes with him immediately.

He opened his mouth. "You're up."

Last resort.

Levaveus could hardly be seen except for his back. He was on the verge of completely leaving the area.

I breathed in deeply. Say something. Stop him from leaving.

"Wait!" I called out to Levaveus. "There's something important you might need to know."

All wind died on the spot. The Stromoios silenced, looking at Levaveus. Levaveus's ears perked up, he slowly turning back and taking steps to where he was originally speaking from.

"Are you saying you have proof that you're affiliated with no Gods?" Levaveus asked, stopping where he was in full view of everyone and me.

"It's something else," I said, walking forward and stopped in front of Azmach, causing everyone to now stand behind me. "Although, it could be."

Levaveus stood patiently. His eyes locked onto mine. His face was calm, but unamused with confusion. "Which is?"

Say it. Take a breath and say it. Push and say it. Pull and say it. Inhale, say it.

"I might be your son," I said.

No noise. Nothing. The lack of wind made the silence resound. Not a pin dropped. Nothing. Not a breath or anything broke the silence, except...

Levaveus hadn't flinched at what I said. He narrowed his eyes, studying me. "Son?"

...the silence in the room stalled...

Levaveus's eyes did not break from mine. "You're not my son."

Quickly.

I pushed my Aura out, the air whipping around me and outward. Compared to Levaveus's, it was weak; however, it was still present.

"Maybe you're right. Maybe I'm not your son. Maybe I'm the son of one of the Stromoios or a Wind Spirit. Maybe I'm the child of a Wind God that follows under you or, at the very minimum, has a connection to you."

Levaveus analyzed my Aura and words, looking at me sideways in confusion. He was trying to put the pieces together when he didn't even know there was a puzzle to be solved.

"I don't have a son...my one child is gone...my son... Since the last war..." Levaveus trailed off. His eyes grew sullen, and his body slacked, especially his cheeks. "I know any Storm Spirit's, Wind Spirit's, and Wind God's Aura better than my own. You don't feel like them. There's similar. There's a wind, but its smaller than it should be for a child of a Wind God. It doesn't feel anything like the Stromoios. I feel more God in you than I should from a Demigod."

More God. What does that mean? How is being the son of at least one of them not even possible?

I looked back at Azmach. He looked at me, stuck between a rock and a hard place. He's not sure what's happening either. I turned back to Levaveus.

Levaveus stared at me inquisitively. "The God in you is more potent...you're white hair and orange eyes..."

What's he getting at?

Levaveus was looking off to the side, thinking aloud. "Why does he have so much potent God in him? And a Wind God? That couldn't have come from me or the Stromoios. No Wind Spirits. There aren't any Wind Gods similar to me left, but he could've been born before they were gone... But he doesn't feel like them... why do you have so much God—" He gasped abruptly, his head shooting up as if he saw a ghost.

"If he's not the son of me or any Wind God...and any Spir-its...the amount of God he has...and how he looks...could it be...?"

The Stromoios looked onward, concern and confusion mak-ing their faces.

Levaveus's head creaked around to look at me, his eyes bulging out, and his mouth tight. He peered at me as if he was trying to hide behind a corner without being seen or his death would be imminent.

Why is he looking at me like that? I couldn't break the eye contact that he and I now held.

Levaveus's mouth was slightly open. "They say he's gone. I don't believe it. He was supposed to be gone but came back once already. Is this him trying to return a second time!?" He breathed loudly looking nowhere else except at me. "You're his son, aren't you!?"

"What?" I immediately asked in a low voice, more out of confusion than anything else.

"I wouldn't have even expected him to have a son! Or at the very least, you're with him in some other way!" Levaveus yelled.

Wind burst against the group and me, now stronger than it ever had before. Hair blew back. Clothes blew back. Bodies almost blew back.

The robes of the Stromoios flapped and waved heavily. Some of the Stromoios looking wide-eyed at Levaveus with fear

Azmach had both of his arms shielding half of his face. Asher grunted, trying not to be flown into the abyss at his right. Lamonte skirted back some inches, his shoes scuffing the ground. Ivania crouched to the ground to have a lower center of gravity.

"Don't act like that's not what this is!?" Levaveus shouted at me. "I'm on to you!"

One of the Stromoios from a left balcony stared at

Levaveus, his eyes wide in realization. "Levaveus, are you saying—"

"That's exactly what I'm saying!" He looked at the Stromoios.

Fear struck him and the other Stromoios around who realized what Levaveus meant. They whispered amongst themselves, looking at Levaveus and eyes fixing on me.

Levaveus stood tall and firm, his robe flapping and waving. He swallowed nothing as he tried to force his eyes to stop bulging.

My arms were in front of me forming an X against the wind. "What are you talking about?"

"I knew there was more to why you came!" Levaveus's shouting voice rose further. "Coming for peace when there has been relative peace. Is that how you've been staying safe? Oh—"

"Levaveus!" Porter pleaded from across the cave. "Don't say his name!"

"Please!" Another Stromoios said.

"Lord Levaveus!" A different one.

"I am not a Lord! And I am not afraid of some name!" Levaveus snapped, wide-eyed and full of fear and anger. "He took my child! He almost did the same to me! I'll say his name! Oh—" He stopped himself, swallowing again and taking a deep breath. "Ohpreen!"

Ivania inhaled sharply after hearing the name.

Gasps rippled through the Stromoios, all of them exchanging glances of horror.

"What's your true reason for being here?!" Levaveus howled.

There were now multiple winds fiercely whipping. If the winds were any stronger, they could break bones. They were sporadic in their direction, sometimes straight back, sometimes side to side.

I forced my head up through the winds, "I'm with no—"

"Trying to get me again!? Trying to use something I have so he could fully resurrect?! Or both!?" He questioned swiftly with no pause and breath taken. "Doesn't matter!"

The winds died instantly, the roaring of them vanished. Asher stumbled forward because the force he was resisting against was now suddenly gone. I looked around. Azmach was to my right shoulder behind me by a foot. Lamonte was next to Azmach's right. Asher was behind Lamonte. Ivania was behind all of them and more so to the left of me.

I looked back up at the Wind God.

Levaveus had pulled the winds back towards him. It was rippling the air around his hands, giving the appearance of a gaseous tidal wave. It was condensing, expanding. Whatever it was, it wasn't good.

"He can't return." Levaveus's voice echoed in the silent cave. "I won't allow it. I can't allow it. He tried to end everything once as we know it. And you're here to make that happen again." The ripples swelled.

"I'm not here to make anything happen," I reasoned, "I'm not even sure what you're talking about."

"Doesn't matter, I'm not going to risk it! I'll just kill you all now!"

"Kill? Nonononono," my arms went up, stopping where my head began in a surrendering signal as I stepped forward to make sure that everyone was further behind me. "They've done nothing."

"I can't risk it."

"Then, kill me," I beseeched.

"Jason!" Asher's voice was alarmed.

"What are you—" Azmach tried to question, but he cut himself off in disbelief.

"Kill me and let them go," I contended. My arms were shaking on the inside, and it wasn't from the strain of keeping them in the same surrendering position.

"Let them go?" Levaveus loudly questioned, the ripples

building further around his hands. It looked destructive.

"Yes. Kill me and only me. This is my responsibility. And if it's my responsibility, then it's my accountability. Meaning, I must be the one, no one else. Let them go. I'll stay willingly. I won't fight back. No argument. No contention. Just as long as you kill me and only me."

Weight, my hands held it. Weight, my arms slightly shook on the outside now. I breathed deeply, waiting for his response.

Levaveus stood silently, mulling it over. His face was calm, the air around his hands being the opposite. He opened his mouth.

"I can understand where you're coming from," Levaveus said.

I lowered my arms to my sides, my breathing calming down.

The ripples around Levaveus's hands raged. Air picked up speed, becoming a wind. "I still can't risk it."

I reached out to him. "Wait!—"

Winds burst forth.

"Gah!" I grunted. I was pushed back by some inches. My head was almost being forced to recoil.

The winds were impossible to resist against. Asher slid back a little. Azmach and Lamonte hadn't been pushed back, but they couldn't move freely under all the pressure.

The air ripples around Levaveus's hands stretched out like an arch and began descending towards where the group and I were standing. Portions of it formed a denseness akin to a controlled tornado. Small thunder boomed from it. Sparks of electricity compactly appeared and disappeared.

I looked over my shoulder. The exit was still blocked. In fact, some of the Stromoios were coming closer to the ground where the group and I stood. Now there was no way backwards. Every side was blocked. There was only an abyss to the sides, Stromoios to the back, and tornadoes with lightning arching partially to the sides ahead.

"Levaveus don't!" I yelled. "Kill me!"

"I already told you, I can't risk it," Levaveus said, opening his hands and adding more power to the controlled electric tornadoes.

They were edging closer, lowering—

Electricity hit the ground, pieces of it flying up from the impacts. A line of electricity shot past Asher's head.

"No!" I yelled. "Just me!"

"It's no use!" Azmach yelled. "We have to find a way to escape!"

A lightning spark discharged, almost hitting Ivania. She tried maneuvering away from the edge to her left, but there was nowhere to go.

Lightning passed by Lamonte's shin. He noticed how narrowly it—

Asher moved his head instinctively, dodging a line of lightning coming at his face—

Lightning shot over Azmach's head—

"Let them live!" I yelled.

And closer it came—

Gah—Lightning hit my shoulder—painful but not as much as—

Lighting assaulted the ground and came closer, the edges of the ground breaking apart and flying—

"It can't be done," Levaveus replied, pushing the electric tornadoes closer.

Lightning shot—barely missing Azmach—barely missing Asher—Lamonte barely—

Almost hit me—

An inch above Ivania's head—

The ground broke further, closing in—The lightning closed in—The wind closed in—

Clothes flapped—

"You all must die," Levaveus sullenly concluded.

This needs to stop this needs to- This is all my fault my accountability I must Think focus there must be

Azmach was almost blown sideways into the abyss, he was barely standing—

Lightning shot past me and missed Ivania, hitting the ground behind her—

The tornadoes were closer, fifteen feet away at the most. I made an X with my arms, squatting to shield myself. Lightning blasted the ground, breaking a large chunk—

Lightning hit next to my feet. The ground was shrinking further, continuously being hit by lightning and broken apart by winds. There was too much—

Lightning struck Lamonte's shin. He grunted, taking a knee.

"Stop," I said.

Lightning scraped Asher's side—

"Stop!" I raised my voice.

Azmach and Asher were fighting not to fall— Lightning missed Lamonte's left side of his neck—Ivania ducked—

"STOOOOOOOOOOOOOOOOOOOOOOOOOOOOOOOP!"

My eyes were shut tight. My arms were thrust out to the side as I yelled. My entire body was straining.

Why is it so quiet? There was no sound of electricity and the wind had died down significantly. All I could hear was the heavy breathing out of my mouth.

I opened my eyes.

What is?...

The tornadoes. The tornadoes did not move forward. They were stuck in place. The lightning and other electricity coming from the tornados were also stuck in place. It was like they were frozen in time.

Are my eyes mistaken?

I was slouching over, a couple lines of sweat running down my face. My body strained further. The tornadoes were moving, just in place. The lightning and other electric lines didn't move at all. Not even a little.

Why is one moving while the other isn't?

…Why did either of them stop moving forward?

My eyes looked around for an answer in a silent cave. Az-mach had turned his head, looking at me with wide eyes in shock. No, almost every person in the room, Stromoios and all, looked at me with a similar expression. Ivania remained expressionless with her hood now blown off, yet even she was staring at me.

"You stopped it," Levaveus said, his eyes and mouth wide in shock.

I looked up at Levaveus, my arms slightly shaking from strain, my heavy breathing not yet calming down.

"You stopped the lightning…and some of the winds," he said.

Did I? What is he? What?

The lightning still wasn't moving. The tornadoes also still weren't moving besides them spinning in place. My head turned as my eyes shifted around the cave. Every eye was on me. Nowhere else.

"You're not my son…" Levaveus said, his voice trailing off a bit. His eyes and mouth widened in shock. "…You're not …Ohpreen's son…You're…the son of X'stayn."

Son of…X'stayn? I didn't hear that correctly. There's no way I heard that correctly. X'stayn?

"I didn't recognize the wind because X'stayn doesn't use it as much as lightning," Levaveus realized. "Now that I think about it, your wind is similar to his. And controlling the lightning," he stared at the lightning still frozen in midair. "That's Burnt-Face X'stayn."

X'stayn. That can't…How else can it be explained?

The tornadoes and lightning swiftly pulled back towards Levaveus's hands, vanishing as it did so. Once everything was gone, my arms collapsed to my sides. Exhausted. My breathing began to lighten.

Levaveus had calmed down completely, keeping all of his attention on me. He took a deep breath, his voice now quiet. "You must have been born right before X'stayn disappeared. If you're a son of X'stayn, if...Ohpreen was still here...he wouldn't send you out like this without you being able to get out. Meaning, I was mistaken..." Levaveus's shock quickly turned into awe and intrigue. "What is your name?"

"...Jason Side." I said, the strain on my body and the weight on my hands lessening.

"Jason Side," he ruminated over my name. "Son of X'stayn. You five will come with me."

"Come where?" Azmach asked.

Levaveus shifted his attention to Azmach. "To my floating kingdom. To Levoao. I'll give you some of my Reverse Bags of Wind."

"Are you serious?" Azmach asked, disbelieving.

Azmach, Lamonte, and Asher exchanged glances of confusion, happiness, and shock.

"You will go now," Levaveus said.

The ground lightly shook as threads of bleached yellow light beamed from the edges of the it to the ceiling. More threads appeared, adding more colors that were extremely light in tone. The ground too was covered in this light, right under the foot. They weren't simply a light; they were light-colored wind. It waved like smoke, becoming a layer on top of the ground, forming a circle where the four and I stood that followed the edge where the light threads were multiplying.

"I'll meet you up there." Levaveus said.

The light threads were connected by a waving, powerful wind. It all blasted upwards like a reverse waterfall and surrounded the group and me in a circular formation. It was moving Asher, Azmach, Lamonte, Ivania, and me somewhere high, like a tube of air and light used to travel with incredible speed.

Is Life Placed In Suddenness?

"This is crazy," Asher awed at the light colorful wind rushing upwards on all sides.

The ground was a flat wind stable enough to stand on. The top was the same as the ground, the difference being that the wind was moving upwards like the sides. It was clearly rushing towards somewhere.

"Is everybody alright?" Lamonte asked, looking at everyone and me.

"Some lightning scraped my side," Asher said, turning around to face Lamonte. "Other than that, I'm good. Are you?"

"Yeah," Lamonte said, a burn line on the left side of his neck becoming noticeable once he was brought to the forefront. "Nothing for real. What about you Azmach?"

"Surprisingly, nothing..." Azmach said, he obviously thinking of elsewhere. He turned his head to look at everyone and me. His face illustrated the look of someone whose ears were mentally ringing. "No one has more severe injuries?"

It seems that they and I haven't suffered heavily. Is it the same for my mind? It was foggy and solid.

"Jason," Asher called for my attention. "You cool?"

"Huh?" the sound slipped out of me in a question. "Yes."

"That was a lot back there," Lamonte said, some exhaustion slipping into his voice.

"What happened back there stays between us," Azmach turned, completely serious, his mind now set on one thought instead of multiple others. "Jason," he said, putting his attention on me.

I looked at him.

"Tell no one that you're the son of X'stayn," Azmach emphasized. "This could be dangerous."

"I wouldn't say 'could', Lamonte corrected. "It is. It is dangerous." His face was a stone.

"X'stayn." Asher's eyes squinted. The ramifications of what was said finally completely hit him. "That missing King of the Gods."

The son of X'stayn. It didn't feel real. In a general sense, how could any of this be real? But how is it real? How is it? How? Is? The missing King of the Gods. X'stayn. How is?

"I don't know how it's possible you're his son. And then the timing." Azmach eyes locked onto me, drops of apprehension leaking into his voice. "You were born. Then he goes missing. Then the war. Back to back to back." Azmach looked around at everyone and me, drawing in attention. "No one can know you're X'stayn's son until we have more information. Not even Numetus. This stays between us and only us. For now, we'll just say that Levaveus wasn't open at first to negotiations, but they went well. Leave out how he became open. Say 'he warmed up as the conversation went.' That's our story."

"We're on the same page," Lamonte agreed.

"Same here," Asher also agreed. He looked specifically at me. "I got your back. I won't tell anyone."

"Let's just get outta here first." Lamonte interjected.

Azmach exhaled deeply from his nostrils. He looked up at all the rushing wind and light. "There's nothing like the present."

"Like the present." Lamonte added immediately.

The wind continued to rush, the speed of transport not slowing down in the slightest. The sound of the wind curved past the ears, brushing the drums inside. It felt like standing on top of a mountain that was flying upwards into the sky.

Something dark was moving in the range of my peripheral vision. I turned to see some strands of Ivania's hair was lightly blowing backwards.

That's different. Ivania's hood was off, more than likely blown from all the chaos before.

Or was it when I stopped...did I stop?...I did...

With her hood off, her hair was shown to not be straightened at all. It looked as if someone had pulled it downward, stretching it like it was blow dried while a blow dryer wasn't even used. Her 4c afro-textured hair flowed down her head and into where the long jacket might have been zipped, meaning her hair was much longer than could be seen. The few strands that were blowing backwards weren't even completely out of the jacket. They were out just enough for the light air flowing around to maneuver those strands' placement.

Ivania always had her hood on and most likely liked it as such. "Excuse me," I quietly said to Ivania.

She turned, making eye contact with me.

"Your hood is blown off." I informed her.

Ivania hand went to her head, confirming what I pointed out. She pulled her hood back up how it usually was.

The surroundings grew brighter, becoming more and more white. The small amount of air blowing was becoming stronger, blowing my hair back.

"Looks like we're here," Asher observed the changes.

The whiteness brightened and expanded immensely. The

slides, the ceiling, and the floor faded away, and the brightness with it. What replaced all of this was a sight to behold.

The path on which the group and I stood was made of multiple dark and light gray stones. Some trees and short vegetation flourished on both sides of the path as it led forward towards open air. On the other side of the open air, there floated another air island. Multiple of these large land masses floated in midair, connected to each other by wide air spaces. Most had modernized small castles which acted as houses. One enormous castle with triangular points rose high into the air on two islands away. All the modernized castles were predominantly in dark shades of grays. Men, women, and children Stromoios were flying around, sitting, chattering, playing with one another throughout the multiple islands. Everything was active.

"Woah," Asher said in a low, impressed tone, looking around as he did so. "It's multiple islands?"

The group and I stood, taking the extraordinary view all around. The stars and moon lit everything outside of the small amount of electricity zapping through each Stromoios randomly.

"I thought it would just be one island," Asher commented.

"It is one island," a voice said from behind. Porter, the Stromoios that led into the cave, was floating a foot away to the back of me and everyone. "I'm here to escort you to the castle."

"That big one straight ahead, right?" Azmach asked.

"That is correct," Porter said, as he floated forward towards the edge of the island that he, the group, and I were currently standing on.

Azmach was a few steps behind him, only stopping at the very edge. Lamonte, Asher, Ivania, and I stopped accordingly. Porter did not. He floated past where the island ended.

I stepped forward to the tip of the edge, peering straight down. Below were nothing but clouds and vast openness, giving great potential for falling straight to death. The night concealed the distance of the fall while revealing more fear of such a feat.

"Forward," Porter said.

Azmach stared down at the potential fall, then at Porter suspiciously.

"You won't fall," Porter said.

Azmach cautiously took a step forward, his foot stepping firmly on top of the open air.

"Careful bruh," Lamonte said.

"Working on it," Azmach replied. He stopped, registering what was happening, then proceeded with his next foot, solidly stepping off the island completely. He did not plummet. It was as if he was floating like a Stromoios. Azmach turned his head to the group and me, nodding in acknowledgement to show it was safe to walk forward.

"I'll be…" Asher trailed off, glancing at the open air ahead of him. Hesitantly, he began stepping forward onto nothingness that was intriguingly the opposite of what his eyes told him.

Lamonte was already walking ahead.

I looked at the open air and took a step forward. Solid. It didn't feel like it should've been, yet it was. Another step followed. Solid. The sight below was daunting, the clouds and openness, and especially the land too far down to call a simple plunge. With it being night, the land far below was hardly visible from this height.

Focus. Forward.

I continued onward, hearing Ivania a foot behind me, and Asher ahead by a few. Lamonte and Azmach waited for Asher, Ivania, and me to catch up before they continued walking. A cloud drifted below as the group and I advanced closer to the land mass ahead.

"Walkways made of motionless winds connect each land body," Porter said, floating forward to the land mass yards ahead. "Making this all one island."

My feet stepped onto the land mass. The group and I walked forward, passing a Stromoios and her small, modernized castle of a home. They and I continued walking through the mass and stepped off, once again walking on top of open air. The main castle was straight ahead. Clouds drifted below. Soon solid land met my feet. It was the large landmass that Levaveus's castle stood upon. Up its grand, gray, stone steps, Porter held the castle's long, dark, round, metal doorknob.

"He's already inside," Porter informed, pushing the door open.

The door swung smoothly, Porter following its movement inside.

The interior was grand. The dark brown polished limestone floor had multiple geometric squares going through it. A low hanging, dark iron chandelier hung from the high, polished, dark brown ceiling. The walls were dark and medium shades of blues that matched, highlighted, and blended in with Levaveus's robes.

"There you are," Levaveus said from the center of the room. He stood tall, at least a head over me. "Come inside, quickly."

The group and I stepped further inside, looking around the huge room. Porter pushed the door closed.

"I'll bring you to the bags," Levaveus said.

That snapped the attention of every person and me away from gazing at the interior.

"Stay there, Porter," Levaveus ordered. "I'll show them the way myself."

Porter put his hand over his chest and bowed his head.

"This way," Levaveus turned on his head. There was excitement in his steps as he led down a long hallway. The polished floor reflected the people, the ceiling, and everything above it. There were no furnishings, nothing hanging on the walls, but for some reason the place didn't feel bare.

Levaveus opened a door to a room at the end of the hall and advanced inward without stopping.

The room was smaller than expected. It could fit at least twenty people; however, with the size of the castle it was expected a room would be able to fit much more. There was a long, curved, smooth, dark blue wall-like structure standing at waist level in the center with a long dark gray and black table in front of it.

"How many Bags do you need?" Levaveus enthusiastically asked, rounding past the dark blue wall-like structure. He was the only one moving while everyone else and I stood still.

"About fifty." Azmach's eyes were drawn back by the sudden question and change of mood.

"Fifty," Levaveus said as he swirled his hand and a large somewhat transparent sack appeared. He continuously swirled his right hand to create a small breeze. From the back of the room Wind Bags breezed off a shelf in sets of twos and were placed inside the sack. Once the Bags were placed inside, they could no longer be seen, which almost hurt the eyes straining to make sense of how a somewhat translucent sack contents weren't viewable. "I have that exact number."

"Then, let's go with twenty-five," Azmach compromised.

"Twenty-five?" Levaveus continued placing Bags within the sack. "You're getting fifty."

Azmach was taken aback, turning to look at Lamonte, whose face was blank, but his body language showed that he felt the same. Azmach had the same face as when he found out that Asher burned all the clothes he had except the ones on his back. Asher was also a little shocked, looking at Azmach, then Levaveus.

"You don't need to do all that," Azmach

"I can always make more," Levaveus retorted with a smile.

"That might be true, but we can't take all of yours."

"I can always make more." Levaveus had already placed at

least fifteen in the sack and the number rose steadily.

"That might be true, but why are you okay with that?"

More than twenty-two were now in the sack. "You aren't with any Gods, and you have the son of X'stayn. Anything for this son of X'stayn." He looked at me with a smile.

Son of...that's still...

Levaveus returned his attention to the Bags, now over thirty. "You also can't come here for at least two years or it'll look suspicious to any Gods who might notice. You'll have to stretch this fifty out."

Azmach's face returned from its slightly taken aback state, calming to his usual demeanor. "And we'll say we tricked you out of it."

"It happened once, and it won't be unconvincing for it to happen again." Fifty.

He swirled his hand, the sack closing tight by a somewhat transparent rope near the top. Exponentially, the sack shrunk in size until it only needed two hands to hold, being as big as half of a torso. It floated over and landed on top of the waist high wall-like structure.

"That should be it," Levaveus said. "Before I hand this off, I want to talk to you privately. Son of the King."

Son of. I looked at Levaveus, then I looked over to Asher, Azmach, Lamonte, and Ivania standing beside me. Asher nodded. Azmach's and Lamonte's faces were stern. Ivania had her expressionlessness, her eyes locking mine.

I turned away from them.

"Alright," I said. I stepped forward towards the Wind God.

Levaveus walked towards a large, rectangular oak door on the right side of the room and opened it. "This way."

I was right behind him, and the door closed behind me.

Down an empty hallway, his and my steps were heard.

Levaveus looked straight ahead as he walked. "You were born around the time this war began."

"Yes," I confirmed.

"I thought so." He let out a puff of air out from his nostrils, smiling. "Why did you think you were my son?"

My hands naturally slid into the front pockets of my pants. "The powers I had displayed up until that point, and the proximity of this location to where I come from."

"Where do you come from?"

"Maryland."

"That is nearby. I wouldn't be surprised if around there, there was another God or two."

The hallway was calmly silent outside of the sound of the footsteps.

"I do have some questions of my own," I told him.

Levaveus glanced at me. "Mhm."

"You say I'm the son of X'stayn. You yourself controlled lightning as well as winds. Why does me controlling lightning make me the son of X'stayn as opposed to being yours?"

"What I did back there was barely lightning," Levaveus said.

"You mean it doesn't constitute it?" I looked up at him.

"If you noticed, some of my lightning would be closer to being just lines of electricity. My lightning is not on the level of X'stayn's. When you controlled it, I could tell you were more akin to him. X'stayn can also control winds, but not as well as me. It's the same for you. Your Aura felt more like his than any Wind God, Wind Spirit, and Stromoios."

Son of— Calvin. I didn't push him. No. That light that flashed and he went through the wall, that was some lightning, wasn't it? The day before that, lightning had struck the utility pole that I was walking past. That wasn't a coincidence, was it?

"Thinking it over?" Levaveus asked.

"It doesn't feel…" I trailed off. Real, reality, diction of such was on the edge of my mind and the summit of my perception. "So, I'm not the son of any other Wind Gods?"

"You're the son of X'stayn," Levaveus grinned.

"If there are other Wind Gods, why aren't they here?"

Levaveus's already casual steps slowed. The hallway itself was long, and his now slowing steps made the journey longer. "When you don't count myself and Spirits, there were only four Wind Gods who had survived the Ohpreenmach. Years later, this current war began. War changes people and Gods alike. Some Gods are using this war as an excuse to assert themselves over other Gods, to gain power. When this war broke out, those four Wind Gods tried to take over Levoao. Two of the four also wanted the Empiric Throne and were going to use me as a stepping stone. Once I banished them, they began fighting amongst themselves. They are no longer with us."

"You have those Wind Bags. If you can create them to pull in Monsters, why not make them pull in Gods? Wait." I stopped walking. "If you're worried about Demigods, why didn't you make one for them too?"

"The Bags don't kill whatever's pulled inside."

"So, the Monsters are—"

"Still alive. If the Bags were to be opened or broken, whatever is inside can escape. The main issue is the process in which the Bags are made."

"In what way?"

Levaveus began walking once again. "They work by locking onto one type of Aura. I made them only able to pull inside whatever has Monster Aura. If I make it to where it can pull inside Demigods, I'd have to make it lock onto whatever has God Aura. That would mean I could get pulled inside. Once you're inside, you can't escape by yourself. I'd rather not have that. It almost happened when I tried making one Bag for God Aura a few years into this war."

Levaveus stopped at the end of the hall, which diverged to the right and left. It was the intersection of another hallway. He stood next to a small and thick oak desk that was against a wall.

"For someone so cautious, why are you helping now?" I asked.

"You're the son of X'stayn," Levaveus beamed. "Any God you were working with wouldn't toss you into that situation. It's too high of a risk of losing a child of X'stayn. That's how I know you were telling the truth about coming alone. More importantly, you were born around the time this war began. This war only began because X'stayn went missing. From what I see, your behavior is better than the other one. You could be a reason this war could end sooner rather than later. I don't want another drawn-out war, and a worse outcome than the Ohpreenmach."

Levaveus fist tightened, a flash of fear brushing his face as obvious stress etched into his eyebrows and stiffened into his face.

Ohpreenmach.

"...That's the second time you said that word," I reminded Levaveus, understanding there was more to it than what I was simply about to ask.

Levaveus body relaxed, pushing aside whatever was stressing him, as he turned to look at me.

"In the cave, there was a name you said when you thought I and the everyone else came with ill intent. A God's name. You didn't name any other God's except for him. Ohpreen."

Through Levaveus's beard, his jaw visibly tightened, becoming rigid.

"I vaguely remember reading that name before in Alkeeb stories," I processed. "Who is he?"

Levaveus looked as if he was trying to force himself to swallow despite being completely dehydrated, swallowing a mouthful of sand without water. "If only he were just stories...Ohpreen..." He was pushing back his clenched jaw through his fight to hide his obvious emotions. "Ohpreen is the God of the sky. He was a Primordial, of the earliest generation of the Gods. Ohpreen and his wife, Ay'ya, birthed the second generation, the Behiims. Ohpreen would mistreat his wife and his children. He'd toss children he deemed weak into Infern, and kept his wife under complete control, among other things. It took five of his very own children and Ay'ya to overthrow him."

"This sounds familiar," I processed.

"I need you to understand this. There was a war between the second generation and the third generation, the Behiims against the Kauzations. Zon is the strongest Behiim and led the Behiims's side in the war. X'stayn is one of the strongest of the Kauzations. It took X'stayn multiple battles to defeat Zon, and it took all his strength."

"The...Behiimmach," I recollected.

"Zon was one of the five Behiims it took to defeat Ohpreen. One of five. They were barely able to do it with five of them, six if you count Ay'ya being in the same space. But really, it took five. These five were the stronger ones of the Behiims, Zon being the strongest. X'stayn was barely able to defeat Zon alone. Zon couldn't defeat Ohpreen alone."

I looked at him, gravity briefly weighing on my face.

"We thought Ohpreen was gone, vanished...no longer with us..." Levaveus fell silent. "We were mistaken." Levaveus's eyes darted to the ground while he forced himself to keep them up. "He returned," Levaveus spoke, pushing himself through the sand that he must have still been swallowing. "It was around six hundred years ago. He returned...and he was back stronger than before."

"To what extent?"

"Much stronger," Levaveus immediately responded. "And he had Monsters following him. Gods following him. Some Spirits. There were more to it than that. He was going to wipe out the entire third generation of Gods...and he could have... It led to another war, the Ohpreenmach. I don't know how we made it out, I don't know how we survived, but. We had help from you Demigods. That still-I don't know how...I don't know how we made it out. Ohpreen was defeated. He's gone. For a few hundred years... He's gone..." He inhaled deeply through his nostrils. "At least for now."

"'For now'?"

"He disappeared once and returned... Why can't he do it again? I don't know. There's nothing that proves that he's still around. I just feel." He inhaled and exhaled deeply. "I should focus on the present. The war we're in now is what needs my attention."

"What's the war that's currently transpiring called?" I just realized. It's only been called "the war" this entire time. There were no distinctions between the past wars and the present, other than indicating which ones happened before and after or ones that were already named.

Levaveus must have realized he never called the current war by name. His body and face settled along with his disposition, the subject now verging from where it was shaking him before. "The Kauzamach."

"The Kauzamach." I repeated, the name being written over and over again within my head to make sure it was never forgotten.

"A war with no clear sides between Gods," Levaveus synopsized. "And it seems some of you Demigods are wrapped in it, for power or unwillingly."

It grew quiet for a few seconds.

"I see," I thought out loud.

"Well, son of X'stayn," Levaveus suddenly said. "Do you have any more questions? No Demigods will be allowed in here like this for at least two years. Now's your chance."

"No." My mind felt itself opening. "There's something I realized that I must attend to."

I stepped inside the room behind Levaveus, the door closing to my back, and walked straight to the people I had left inside.

"Everything cool?" Azmach asked.

I nodded.

Lamonte looked between Levaveus and me.

"What happened?" Asher asked.

"Nothing," I said.

"Demigods," Levaveus called to attention. "Here are your Bags." He handed it off to Azmach, who had to use both hands to grab and hold it.

"We'll say we tricked you into giving us the Bags if other Gods were to find out," Azmach assured Levaveus.

"That's what happened," Levaveus agreed. "What is your name? What is everyone's name here?"

"I'm Lamonte Cole, son of…Zound."

"Azmach Washington. Son of Mynzonus."

"'Mynzonus'? I wouldn't have thought he had the capacity to have a child."

"She's also a child of Mynzonus," Azmach pointed out Ivania.

"Two? What's your name?"

"Her name's Ivania," Lamonte said.

Ivania looked at Levaveus.

"Asher Craft, son of Soronos."

"Soronos's?" Levaveus was surprised. "I'm not sure he's ever had a child before." He turned to me. "And I already know you, Jason Side, son of X'stayn. If you would like, I can send you all down by winds to wherever you need to be if it's within Oven Bake Knob. After that, Gods might take notice."

"Thanks for the offer," Azmach said. "We have something here we have to take with us."

"Then I'll drop you off where it's at."

"And we'll be on our way."

Levaveus smiled. "Follow me."

Levaveus led the way out the castle's back doors to a stone path with short grass on both sides. He stepped outside of the stone path and onto the grass. Porter was behind him with two Stromoios in tow.

"Where did you leave what you left?" Levaveus asked.

"The parking lot," Azmach answered.

The moon gleamed down, illuminating Levaveus's out-stretched arm which had a wind beginning to form in front of it. Ripples became waves, expanding and fusing together. It became twenty feet in width, while also being thin like a sheet and transparent, except for its outline. The wind structure lowered to the ground until it was two inches above it.

"This will lead straight to it," Levaveus informed. "Get on."

Azmach stepped onto the calm waving wind, followed by Lamonte, Asher, Ivania, and me.

"You'd think I wouldn't be surprised," Asher commented, looking at the wind platform he was sitting on curiously, his eyebrows raised.

Ivania looked at her feet and around herself, looking at me for a second, then Levaveus.

"You need to sit down for this," Levaveus said. "As long as you're on it, the wind coming from it will conceal you from Mortals, and it'll stop you from falling."

Everyone and I sat down accordingly. Ivania sat next to me in the back behind Azmach, who was the center. In front of him were Asher and Lamonte sitting a few inches apart.

My fingers brushed the surface of the wind platform, al-most being pulled towards it like a magnet.

Levaveus's hand reached up to the sky. The two Stromoios in tow flew in the direction his hand was aimed towards. They stopped at a certain spot in the sky, looking at Levaveus.

Levaveus's fingers opened up, straining slightly as it did so.

A bit of the air between the two Stromoios cleared and darkened in comparison to everywhere else in the sky. It was like looking through light tinted lenses when suddenly the vision reverted back to its original tint.

Levaveus's hand shook in strain, yet his face didn't convey any discomfort. "I can keep that section of the barrier open long enough for you all to get through."

"Everyone ready?" Azmach asked, turning his head around to ensure he didn't miss a reply.

"Yeah," Lamonte and Asher answered.

Ivania nodded daintily, her face expressionless as usual.

"Jason?" Azmach asked.

I turned to him and nodded once.

Azmach gripped the sack tightly in his lap with one hand while having another hand tensely pressed against the wind platform's surface as if to try and keep grip. He turned to Levaveus. "We're ready."

"Then off you go," Levaveus said. His hand that wasn't outstretched waved once towards where the two Stromoios were.

The thin platform of calm waving wind moved, flying skyward. If the surface of it didn't have some of the wind pulling downward like a magnet, I might have slid right off at the speed it was going. It aimed straight for between the two Stromoios where the tint had changed.

Asher slapped both of his hands against the surface as if to grip and leaned forward. Lamonte was leaning forward, his, my, and Asher's hair all whipping back.

The wind platform flew through the tint and out the other side, and curved leftward into the night sky. To the left was the sphere of winds blowing and waving that surrounded Levoao. Some of it looked like fog and light smoke, and it was translucent to an extent. If one squinted past all of it, the castles and lands could be seen.

The platform was drifting, but its speed did not slow down.

"Woah," Asher looked around, "I can't believe it."

"We're not done yet," Lamonte said, looking ahead in the dark night.

The wind platform started angling downward, its speed increasing as it still curved around the barrier of winds. After it quickly curved around the barrier, it broke away and dove down further, continuing forward and leaving the barrier of winds behind.

Ivania leaned into the center, making sure she didn't slip off.

The platform flew calmly, feeling like it was simply drifting down breezes. As it traveled forward, it descended more and more in little to no time, drifting away from Levoao.

Trees upon trees were inches from the platform until a gap appeared, revealing a gravel and dirt parking lot with two cars in attendance. One of those cars was the black jeep. The wind platform gently descended towards the edge of the parking lot. A few inches from the ground, it began erasing away, turning into smoke and disappearing. Once it was completely gone, everyone and I softly landed on the ground.

"Oo," Asher stood up, brushing his shoulder off. "That was something."

Azmach was up and standing, brushing his navy blue bomber jacket off with one hand, while gripping the sack holding the Reverse Bags of Wind with the other. He grabbed Lamonte's hand and helped him stand up. "Let's get to the car."

Ivania was already standing. Somehow, not a speck of dirt got on her.

I stood and dusted myself off, while the rest of them walked towards the jeep.

Azmach held the trunk for some seconds, his fingers having a slight glow, then opened it as soon as the glow ended. He placed the sack inside, then rounded the vehicle, opened the driver's door, and sat inside. Lamonte stepped into the passenger's seat, with Asher sitting in the backseat behind him.

Ivania stepped towards the backseat door behind the driver's door. I grabbed the handle and pulled the door open, stepping inside and sitting down.

Ivania sat next to me and softly closed the last open door.

Azmach let out a breath, one he must have been holding in thus far. He turned around, looking at every person and me. "Is everyone alright?"

"'Alright'? Not bad," Lamonte responded.

"Not bad," Asher repeated in disbelief. "Of course you'd say 'not bad.'" Asher verbally let out a large breath out. He inhaled deeply from his mouth. "Can't believe we got out of that."

"Let's get back to Numetus before discussing anything in detail," Azmach said. He looked in the rearview mirror. To Ivania. "Ivania?"

Ivania looked up in the mirror.

"You're all good?" Azmach asked her.

She nodded.

"Cool," Azmach said. "Jason?"

I nodded once.

"Cool," Azmach said.

"Look," Asher said. "I know you said we're not going into detail before we get to Numetus, but if you could ballpark it, how crazy is this whole X'stayn thing?"

"We can't. That's why we're not going to tell anybody unless we have to. Lamonte and I will figure out what exactly it could mean. In due time, we'll tell the Head. I'm not sure about the other Hands yet."

"Let's just figure out what this could mean first," Lamonte said.

"The point is, no one in this car can tell anyone at Numetus that's he's the son of X'stayn."

Son of... X'stayn.

"We already agreed to that bro," Asher said, smiling. He turned to me. "I already said I got your back Jack."

Azmach grabbed the wheel with one hand. "That was a lot that happened and a lot to take in. But we have to get moving. We have another fourteen hours ahead of us, and we're taking no breaks. You all can sleep on the way in shifts. I'll drive the entire time."

"Bro, we'll be getting back at like seven at night tomorrow," Asher reminded. "I have my license. I can drive part of it."

"It's all good, Asher. I got this."

"If you say so, but if you need to switch, we can switch."

"I can direct the way if he needs it while driving," Lamonte said to Azmach.

"Sounds good." Azmach agreed. He turned to face forward, gripping both hands on the wheel. "Everybody ready?"

The car grew quiet, anticipating the departure.

"There needs to be a pitstop," I said.

It took a few seconds for my words to be processed.

"What? A pitstop?" Asher repeated as a question.

Azmach turned around, a slightly confused look on his face. "'Pitstop'? For what?"

"There's something I need to get," I said. "Somethings I need to confirm."

Azmach looked at Asher, then back at me. "How far?"

"Maybe three hours from here at the most," I answered.

Azmach sat silently, thinking it over.

Ivania had turned her head to look at me.

"We could find a rest stop in that area," Lamonte devised. "Sleep in shifts there. Do whatever needs to be done. Then, drive the fourteen hours, more or less, from wherever this pit stop is. Doesn't sound bad. You're going to need your sleep too, Az."

Asher smiled at the thought. "Actually, I'll be honest. Your boy wouldn't mind a pitstop."

Azmach turned his head back to the front. "Alright." He placed one hand on the dashboard with his fingers glowing and the jeep roared to life. "Pitstop it is. We should be able to find a rest stop around there. Everybody ready?"

"Yep," Lamonte said.

"You know what it is," Asher said at the same time as Lamonte's response.

"Then let's get it," Azmach smiled, shifting the automatic gear shift.

"Road trip," Asher joked.

The jeep veered forward and off the parking lot.

What Is Identity?

"Ching cling, ching cling," keys sounded, going inside a keyhole. Jimmying, they turned, and the door opened.

Click clack, footsteps came inside the room as keys continued to jangle. A door closed, followed by a continuation of the walking and jangling.

"Oh. Jason," a woman's voice said, her steps stopping immediately. The voice was and wasn't soft-spoken. It took command effortlessly without suffocating any opposition or the world around. Articulate. Calm. It filled the room with soul, culture, and knowledge. It was a voice I hadn't heard for some time.

"Ms. Grey," I replied, already sitting down in a chair that was pulled away from one of the desks in her classroom, the seat I always sat in before all that had recently transpired and will continue to transpire, the seat I used to sit in for every one of her classes in this very room.

Ms. Grey's hair was fashioned in its usual afro ponytail that had multiple cornrows leading into it. She was wearing what she wore when I finally looked at her fully for the first time.

Her black button-up shirt had tan color brown buttons and a floral design, with light brown and pink flowers that did not overpower the core blackness. She had on black pants, and black stockings, if I remember correctly what those are called, and lastly beige flats. Her hair, skin, and dark brown eyes shone.

She looked at me through her black-rimmed glasses as she held her keys. "It's been a while."

"Yes. It has."

"From the middle of September to the verge of the third week into October."

"Over a month."

"You look well. How are you feeling?"

"Fine."

She looked along the wall to her right, her face plain. "Yes, 'fine.'" She looked back at me. "It's great that you are well, but I must know. Of all the times and places, why are you here now?"

"There were some things that weren't adding up. Some things that didn't make sense. Things I didn't think nor grasp, until subjects within certain parameters within specific instances were elaborated upon. An epiphany manifested. A realization recognized. Creating room… for substantiation."

Ms. Grey stood quietly, listening intently.

"When this school was attacked, the timing was questionable," I continued.

"Life undoubtedly is coincidental," Ms. Grey slowly said, her plain expression staying the exact same.

"Without a doubt. In this case, there was more to it. There's something about this school that can block the senses, block Aura, within an unspecified radius. When the attack at this school occurred, this blocking increased significantly."

"Something about this school," she repeated.

"It's been hypothesized that maybe it's an object of some sort."

"An object?"

"Yes. An object... Supposedly."

Silence weighed in the room.

"You asked me 'Of all the times and places, why are you here now?' Couldn't I ask you the same?"

Ms. Grey stood quietly, calm as ever, looking back at me.

"This school's been closed since the attack," I pointed out. "It's only been a little more than a month since. The destruction has not been fixed to an extent that would accommodate students. The student body more than likely is virtually being taught while the construction is continuing. That being said, outside of the construction workers, there's no reason for anyone else to be here."

Ms. Grey hadn't flinched. I didn't expect her to.

"I ask you again, Ms. Grey. Why are you here?"

"Much like yourself, I am checking on particulars," Ms. Grey answered.

"There shouldn't be school supplies or teaching material. You would've gotten them by now since over a month has passed. That includes any personal items. I ask you again a third time, why are you here?"

"The reason has not changed."

"'Of all times and places, why are you here now?' Today of all days? Minutes after I entered? As if you could sense it. As if you knew." I looked at nothing except her, my full attention not deviating by even a fraction of a fraction of the slightest. "That object that blocks Aura. It's not an object. It's a God. It's you."

No words were said. Ms. Grey didn't move. Her face remained plain as seconds ticked by. Finally, she looked down and smiled, a puff of air coming from her nostrils. She then brought her head back up to me. "Seems you did figure it out. What else gave it away?"

I turned my head right, looking out the window with early morning sunlight beaming past the open blinds, which was more than enough to see everything even though it was the only light in the room. "There is an Old Domain within a couple miles from here. They're usually Gods nearby them. In addition, Levaveus said there probably could be Gods around this area."

"Levaveus," she looked off to the side, reminiscing. "It's been over five years."

"That told me there was no object, but instead a God. This school is also a public charter, which would be easier for a God to be in since they can abide by more of their own rulings than the counties of other connected schools. Why I thought you specifically were a God was because of some of the things you said."

Ms. Grey walked over to her desk, placing her keys on it, and sat down, now being only a few feet from me. "Elucidate."

"Before going to the auditorium, when the attack would begin, you told me to 'Stay Focused'. It seemed a bit out of place; however, the use of those words would be exactly where needed if you were a God warning about Monsters and said attack, including everything else after. A few days before that, you had said the air about me was different. You meant my Aura, didn't you?"

"Correct. It was coming out more than usual. You clearly hadn't started Adjusting."

"You also had an Alkeeb Gods unit in class. Within the unit, the subject matter seemed to have deeper meaning. Some Gods you talked about, in retrospect, it was as if the subject was personal to you in a literal sense. As you said, life is coincidental. However. Add in the fact that the unit even existed." I shook my head. "To have a unit exist when no one, other than a small few in a circumstantial sense, had heard of the Alkeeb Gods is astronomically adherent to the lack of coincidence. It cannot be overlooked that the Alkeeb Gods have been hidden from the world and they want to proceed as such. That unit couldn't have been a mere coincidence to such an extent."

"Possibilities are endless. But in this particular case in point, you are not wrong. I needed to teach you about the world of the Gods indirectly. You were not ready for directivity nor in the current conditions could I supply it."

"I thought this room would be your specific area, your property if you will. I thought if I, or some Demigod or God, stepped inside, you would know. You entering through that door was the final nail in the coffin."

"Your hypothesis is correct. You have figured out that I am a God," Ms. Grey said. "Do you know which?"

Which indeed?

I looked around the room. Art, writing, history, and more were on the walls and on top of bookcases. Pictures of African looking statues hung, and physical statues stood. Pictures and references to literature of all types. I already had a feeling after theorizing she was a God. Seeing the classroom once again-

I turned back to Ms. Grey. "Nayleeuh. Goddess of history."

"Right you are," a small smile grew on her face.

"Mhm." I leaned back before straightening my posture. "So, Nayleeuh. Do I call you Nayleeuh or Ms. Grey?"

"Either or," she waved her hand to the side. "I prefer Ms. Grey because you met me as such."

"Then Ms. Grey it is. Ms. Grey. How do you block Aura sensing?"

"It's one of my powers. I can nullify Aura sensing within a certain radius. The only way you'd feel another's Aura is if you're within enormously close proximity, if it's a very strong Aura, there are immense amounts of Aura coming off them, or a combination of two to all three."

"Why would you allow the attack on the school? People could have died. Did anyone die?"

"Not a single mortal died from the school and from the cars

that were also attacked. That I made sure of. I also increased my nullification to as far as I could without hindering you, because that would allow an easier escape for you and everyone else inside."

"You knew about the Monsters for a while?"

"Which is why I had to use my nullification starting a few days after the de-stress night, when I noticed some Monsters began coming closer to the area."

"Because he started Surging Out to lead Monsters here. Why didn't you stop the one who led them?"

"I don't associate with Demigods in the sense of the God world, unless I must. By the time I knew what that one Demigod was doing, and an association with him in a Godly sense became a must, it was far too late. Once that Demigod had brought those Monsters, it no longer mattered if he was here or not. What mattered were those Monsters. They could not be ignored. This was also around the time your Aura started permeating. The longer the Monsters were here, the more they could tell a Demigod was around. With my nullification, they couldn't pinpoint the exact location when you were at the school. When you went home, the Monsters were mostly near the school, so you were too far away for them to sense, especially since your Aura had just started to emanate from you. Nevertheless, that did not change the fact that it was only a matter of time, and that time was short. Since you hadn't Adjusted yet, the amount of Aura emanating from you was going to increase sooner or later. Then I noticed a different Demigod, and realized he was here to take you and a second Demigod I had felt around this school to Numetus. With your Aura already increasingly releasing the way it was, and all the other circumstances, I calculated that if an attack was going to happen, it could be the day of the assembly. As a precaution, I increased the nullification that day, but I did not realize just how powerful some of the Monsters were."

Ms. Grey, Nayleeuh, paused in thought before continuing.

"That I didn't expect. I expected the nullification to increase, the Monsters to hesitate in their search, and then you with the two other Demigods would escape to Numetus. As we both know, that is not what happened. Once this school began being torn apart, I then understood just how powerful at least two of the Monsters were. Increasing my nullification did not matter. The Monsters might have not been able to easily locate you, but one was fed up and would do whatever it took to get you and any other Demigod."

"The Minotaur," I revealed.

"The Minotaur? The Minotaur should be dead. It was killed in the Labyrinth around the fifth century, and the Labyrinth hasn't existed since around the fifteenth century. If the Minotaur had survived, it would have been killed by the Labyrinth breaking down and vanishing forever."

"I've been told."

She looked off, pondering. "Maybe it survived and escaped before the breakdown." She turned her face back to me. "What was the second powerful Monster?"

"The Manticore."

"The Manticore. That explains why the Monsters felt so powerful. Those two are ancient, one of a kind. The Minotaur. Interesting. The Minotaur couldn't tell where you Demigods were specifically located, so it ripped this school apart until you were found. By then, I had to protect the mortals while simultaneously making sure my identity and the world of the Gods were concealed. I had to trust in the Demigod that came here to lead you and the second one to safety."

"Why didn't you just stop the Monster yourself?" I questioned. "Why didn't you just tell me straight?"

"In this war? If word came out that I specifically aided Demigods, while stopping another that brought Monsters, you all might have been in worse danger from not the Monsters, but instead Gods. I would have been in danger. Even if other Gods were not a subject of worry, those two Monsters themselves were of high caliber."

"Monsters can be as strong as a God?"

"They can be stronger. It's a wonder that you and the other two Demigods survived. I am certain either of those Monsters would not be defeated without extreme effort. Think of them both at the same time, a battle of such stature could attract attention. Helping is simple, but with the situation at hand? If I were to battle those Monsters, from a God's perspective, it would be questionable. Gods would think I was helping a few Demigods far too excessively and wonder why. They would wonder if there was an alliance or a plan commencing. They would think I was trying to gain more power, to win this Kauzamach. I don't want further power. I don't want to take part in this war. I don't want to win this Kauzamach. I am content with what I have. The only reason I have survived this war thus far is my passivism. I have stayed out and away from fights, Gods, Spirits, and Demigods when necessary. I'm on thinner ice than most Gods. I am Nayleeuh, the Goddess of history. I am one of the nine Empyreans. I can possibly be perceived as creating plans that could change the very land-scape of this bloodshed. Talking to you now could be an issue if a God were to take notice, but I think this time nothing will come of it."

I nodded, leaning back.

Ms. Grey, Nayleeuh, sat quietly for a second, obviously tak-ing a pause after explaining so much. "I presume that you made it to Numetus. How were the Monsters handled?"

"Inside a Wind Bag."

"Why you had to see Levaveus."

I nodded. "There was something else that told me you were a God."

"That would be?"

"Something you didn't say."

Ms. Grey's eyes curiously quivered. "Clarify."

I shifted my legs to sit up completely straight. "In all the classes and all the days of the Alkeeb Gods unit, there was one name that was skipped again and again. One God."

Ms. Grey leaned forward anticipating with a tightness in her face, seemingly knowing what was to be said. Her elbows were on the desk with her hands holding each other.

"When you talked about him, you would essentially step around saying his name. I didn't notice until yesterday." I paused, inhaling, then opened my mouth. "Ohpreen."

Ms. Grey let her hands go, her elbows slipping off the desk, and her arms going underneath the wood as she leaned back, away from me as if the name coming out of my mouth could invoke literal wounds. And those wounds would be fatal.

"Yes..." She trailed off. "That name was skipped... Ohpreen..." She looked off.

"I heard a little bit about him and how horrific the Ohpreenmach was. How unspeakable was he to make you skip a name?"

"It's not just a name, he... He's killed many Gods."

"You can kill a God?" Now my eyes were wide, shocked. "I thought Levaveus's son and the other four Wind Gods being gone meant something else, like being trapped in Infern, or was completely metaphorical. But it was verbatim?"

"Why do you think we're so afraid of you Demigods? Unlike Spirits, we can't die from disease or age. Only injury. He's killed so many... Epkose...Periclyus... Panyown... ... Ahlayniss..."

"'Ahlayniss? Ohpreen killed her?"

"An Empyrean, Yes...." She took an almost breath that was almost soundless, then let it out. "He almost killed her brother, Mynzonus... He... He killed Ay'ya... He... He almost killed me..." She gazed deeply at the closest wall to her as if it held an illustration of her past, showing her every nanosecond of it in great detail. "He's gone now. He's dead... Gone." She turned back, but instead of looking at me, she stared downward at her desk, her mood shifting as she was gradually pushing her usual serenity to the forefront.

"Alright." If she was going to push the subject aside like that, Levaveus's reaction shouldn't be defined as simply a reaction. Saying it held merit cannot be understated and saying that Ohpreen was this merit would not be hyperbolic. Right now, I won't be able to ask any more about him from her. Additionally, there was something else on my mind.

"There's something else I want to know," I said.

Ms. Grey looked at me, energy returning to her as she was seeing the subject verge in a different direction.

"The Alkeeb Gods are older than all mythologies known," I summarized, looking down as I did the mental math. "And no stories or 'mythologies' about the Alkeeb Gods have been weaved by the major consciousness." I looked up at her.

"That is true," Ms. Grey concurred.

"There's a rule that if a Demigod commits an action that could potentially reveal the truth to the world, then they shall be killed. I'm guessing that applies to the few people who are allowed to know, those being ones in relations with Gods. Does this rule apply to Gods themselves?"

"No. There have been only a few Gods who tried to tell the world of mortals. They had trials and were promptly sentenced to fines, duties, or imprisonment. The killing of mortals and Demigods, that I do not agree with. It didn't use to be that way. They too would have a trial and be sentenced impartially. Death was the most severe punishment, but it was hardly utilized for God and Demigod. This war has changed everything. For Demigods, any infraction could be dealt with by sentencing with no trial. It always leads to death. Some Gods, who have nothing to do with this process, will kill for this supposed greater good, when in reality the Demigod they killed was one they feared and or was the child of a God they despised. An excuse obscured and used in this bloodshed."

"What about you? You taught those classes about the Alkeeb Gods. What if the other Gods were to find out?"

"They will not," Ms. Grey waved her hand at the notion. "What I did I kept at a minimum. I told only children, less than twenty in years, less believed if they were to talk. As you know, I used the class to teach you the basics indirectly. Once you were out of the class, there was no need to further those lessons. In fact, I pulled back."

"How so?" I leaned back in my seat.

"I told them what I taught was simple creative writing on my end. I used these 'made up tales to test their analytical reading and writing skills. It was moderately true; I was testing those skills. Even if the Gods were to find out and wanted to press an issue, I am an Empyrean, who thus far has not participated in the war. They would be hard-pressed to try and bring me to Apez Kauzus for trial. Advocating for my death when it is children who purportedly know the truth?" Ms. Grey shook her head, "That is not a good look. There's not enough to make a case."

"Why is there so much emphasis in this area?"

"In what sense?"

"Staying hidden. Why go to such an extent? What's the importance of the Gods being hidden?"

"The Gods want to do what they desire in their own world. We want mortals to be able to do the same. Laissez faire." Ms. Grey looked to the side. "Not quite."

"Free will."

Ms. Grey smiled, snapping her fingers and pointing at me. "Exactly that. If you know we exist, our worlds will combine. Worldviews would change. You no longer could live in the world that mortals currently have. Ruling over mortals? No. We don't want to stop the lives you Demigods and mortals want to lead. As I've said, we want our lives, we want our wills, and we want you to be free simultaneously."

I leaned forward, looking down, processing what she explained. Seconds went by, and my processing continued. I was viewing every possible angle. It did make sense.

"Have you figured out who your mother or father is?" Ms. Grey asked.

I looked up at her. "They say he's been missing for seventeen years."

Ms. Grey's eyes widened. "X'stayn?..." She asked in a whisper.

I nodded.

"No wonder Levaveus let you live." Ms. Grey's composure returned. "Bring out your Aura."

Push.

"I do feel X'stayn in there...and something more."

More?

"Something else I'm unsure if I like," Ms. Grey said. "But yes. X'stayn is in there."

"Well," I said. "Now it's more than certain."

"A child of X'stayn born right before the war began. That cannot be a coincidence. You have a difficult path ahead."

I stood up, pushing my seat back in its place.

"You're departing?" Ms. Grey asked.

I nodded.

"How long ago did you return to Baltimore?"

"Yesterday."

"How did you get here?"

"Was driven. Slept in a rest stop until the morning."

"Who drove you?"

"The Demigod who led me to Numetus. He and the other ones are in the car waiting. They don't know that you're Nayleeuh."

"'Others'? How did you get them to come here without telling them I'm a God?"

"They think that I'm here to pick up some stuff. Besides, one of them wanted to check on their mother."

"All in all, it seems everything has worked out."

"In the grand scheme of things," I understood. Has it truly worked out? In the sense she means, yes, but truly has it?

What is meaning?

"Are you close with those people?" Ms. Grey asked, a small smile on her face.

"...Close? I don't know."

"Then what would you call it?"

What would I call it? "At the most, if a title must be given, an association."

"Jason."

Close, I don't. I looked at her.

"Despite how close or far, you have time to process these lengths," Ms. Grey said. "You have time to make decisions. Use that time."

Her hand went inside a drawer of her desk, pulling out something. She stood up and walked towards me and held her hand out. In her hand was a dark silver triangle made by intricate straight lines. It was on a dark silver chain and the overall size was about the palm of my hand.

"This is how us Gods communicate," Ms. Grey said. "We each have our own. If you want to talk without traveling over here, that too is a decision you have time to make. That includes deciding whom you see as close or far."

You. Me.

"I thank you for the offer; however, I already know," I told her. "At least to the extent necessary."

"Take it anyway," Ms. Grey persuaded.

There was no counter for that. I reached forward and hesitantly grabbed the necklace, examining it, and sliding it into the right front pocket of my pants.

Close. Far. Isn't it all far? I'll exist here but am I here? Watching from the distance.

I walked towards the door, reaching and grabbing its handle.

"Last question, Jason," Ms. Grey said.

I turned to see her sitting back down in her seat.

"How did you get in?" She asked.

I looked at her questioningly. "I walked in."

"That door was locked. I had to use my keys to get in. Remember?"

...she did. "I just walked in."

"Interesting. On a side note, I put a pause to your schoolwork. If you get everything done by the end of next semester, you will graduate on time. That is it."

I stood silently, then turned my head towards the door.

"Jason Side."

Hearing my name, I turned back to her.

Ms. Grey, Nayleeuh, Goddess of history, looked at me calmly with great intent for what she was about to say. She opened her mouth. "Focus."

I held eye contact with her, then broke it off, returning to the door, turning the handle, pushing it out, stepping into the hall, and allowing it to close shut.

I stared at the door and stared and stared further. Stared and stared and stared and stared.

All of this impossibility abstractly has high probability to be the current reality, ultimately being the truth and if written to forth nonfiction. With actuality in thought, although, however, but, yet, what in an absolute sense defines perception? Where does the meaning start and end? Is there a beginning to every conclusion, or is it perpetual?

Sitting back and watching from the distance.

Meaning. Definition.

There is no absolute.

The essence of identity.

What is identity? How does one define identity? Is it the interactions one has with people, or life itself? Is it simply a definition that is given by others, their perceptions of the individual? Is it their characteristics, the mentality which forms the basis of a mindset? Is it a weight in hands if need be? Is it the title or type of being they are present? Death. Life. All. Everything and nothing influences perception, it changing one's steps forward or back, one's steps or standstills, one's existence in a fraction of the slightest.

There is silence where it all meets.

Sitting back and watching from the distance.

What is identity?

Silence.

I slid my hands into the pockets of my jacket. Slowly I turned, walking down the hall.

The essence of an identity.

This, I already know. I will continue doing what I have been. My eyes are open. Or are they closed?

Admittance.

Acceptance.

Identity.

White hair.

Orange eyes

It all ties to identity, it all connects.

Eyes open, sitting back and watching from the distance.

Who am I?

What is identity?

All connected. All routine. All admitted. All accepted.

All the above.

Made in United States
North Haven, CT
17 January 2024

47562180R00331